INTO THE CROOKED PLACE

Also by Alexandra Christo

To Kill a Kingdom

INTO THE CROOKED PLACE

ALEXANDRA CHRISTO

HOT
KEY
BOOKS

First published in Great Britain in 2019 by
HOT KEY BOOKS
80–81 Wimpole St, London W1G 9RE
www.hotkeybooks.com

Text copyright © Alexandra Christo, 2019
Illustrations copyright © Patrick Knowles, 2019

A CIP catalogue record for this book
is available from the British Library.

Paperback ISBN: 978-1-4714-0844-1
Hardback ISBN: 978-1-4714-0904-2
Also available as an ebook

1

Printed and bound by Clays Ltd, Elcograf S.p.A.

Hot Key Books is an imprint of Bonnier Books UK
www.bonnierbooks.co.uk

This is for you, whoever you are.
Because you deserve the world, but all I have is this book
and the one I imagined.

THE CITY OF
CREIJE

Consort HQ

Amity Precin[ct]

CITY OUTSKIRTS

THE STEADY MOUNTAINS

Creije Railway
Station

High Town

ONNELA
SEA

Busker Dorms

The Crook

Old Steam
Station

The Magic Markets

1

Tavia

TAVIA SYN MADE A living on magic and it was rarely the legal kind.

That sort of thing was far too weak and the only way to sell it was to give the illusion of power through sleight of hand and good old-fashioned bullshit. It had been that way ever since the war—not that Tavia had been alive to remember those days—and so most of the time she got by on the legal markets using the bare minimum of magic and the bare maximum of trickery.

Her love elixirs were usually the first to go, so Tavia made a point to line them up in front of the trick bags. It transformed her flat-pack stall into a mosaic of color, ranging from soft pink—watered down for lust—to burnt red. Which was also watered-down, because magic wasn't cheap and Tavia didn't fancy selling obsession. Besides, with a little dye in the mix, nobody was any wiser.

When it came to magic, all that really mattered was timing.

And showmanship. Perhaps a mark was a mark and money was money, but there was a difference in how you got that mark and took their money. Style was everything.

And if there was one thing Tavia had in spades, then it was style.

"Gather around," Tavia said, and then, a little louder and a lot more theatrical, "What you will see here is magic made into miracle."

The crowds swarmed by the dozen.

It was like that on market days. People came in packs with a jingle in their step and, it was worth noting, their pockets. They stopped in the middle of the cobblestones to eye the wares or play spectator to whatever the buskers were selling. That was the legal side of Tavia's work. Which her underboss—otherwise known as Wesley Thornton Walcott, otherwise known as a complete jackass—kept going because he liked to dip a toe in clean water every now and again.

If for nothing else than to wash away the blood.

"Straight from the holy realm of Wrenyal, taken from the hands of a seer." Tavia moved a fortune orb fluidly between her hands. "Ladies and gentlemen, I give you the power of foresight."

She blew discreetly on the wick of a nearby spice paste candle and a flame burst into being. It was the perfect backdrop for any stories about Wrenyal, whose magic was said to be a gift from the Indescribable God itself.

Which was utter nonsense, of course, but nonsense was Tavia's greatest commodity.

In the magic markets, the best way to find a mark was to

create one, and there was no better way to do that than to woo them with false magic.

Tavia moved the fortune orb carefully from one hand to another as though it were delicate and sacred, and not something she'd cooked up on a whim with her bastard of an underboss, under the influence of far too many reverie charms. Though, in fairness to Wesley, that was before he became the underboss and so before he actually became a bastard.

"I suppose you have proof your magic is legit?" a skeptical man in the crowd asked.

He eyed her with distrust, which was a look Tavia had not only grown used to, but almost relished in. After all, with so much trick magic mastered, sometimes her greatest challenge came from convincing the inconvincible, taking the feeble magic the law allowed and turning it into something great. Something miraculous, if the light hit her hands just right.

Perhaps Tavia wasn't a Crafter, creating new magic out of thin air, but that didn't mean she couldn't create *something*. A sense of awe and wonder for her audience.

"It'd be my pleasure to give you a demonstration," Tavia said, tipping her hat to the man.

He looked at her dubiously, his smile both a challenge and a somewhat hopeful invitation to prove him wrong.

An invitation she was more than willing to accept, because though Tavia might not have liked working for a king of criminals, she did very much like magic.

Back when she was just another street kid, trying to learn the busking ropes, Tavia didn't think she would ever get the hang of it. Magic seemed like nonsense, a fairy tale within a story she couldn't understand. But time passed—days and weeks and months—until finally Tavia realized that magic was not at all like fairy tales.

It was like math.

It was like the intricate clapping games she played with the other kids to fend off hunger. It seemed complex at first, but all it took was knowing the rhythm, understanding the formula.

After that, the rest came quick.

After that, it was kind of fun.

Now, Tavia was a natural. The best busker in all of Creije. This city was both her prison and her playground. And if it was a show this man wanted, then she was more than happy to give him one.

Her routine was flawless.

Tavia knew this because she had done it a hundred times. First, she danced her hand over the orb, using her smallest finger to flip the trick switch that made it glow just that bit brighter. Then she prepared for the levitation, readying the wind device stowed up her sleeve.

Tavia swooped her free hand up and down in dramatic movements, and then, quicker than a blink, she brought her wrists together. The wind coin propelled under the orb, nestling perfectly, unseen as the orb ascended into the air.

The crowd pointed and chuckled while Tavia motioned theatrically, letting the orb drop and rise back up. Turning it in circles and swooping it from side to side.

Mechanics, far more impressive than the weak fortune magic inside.

"Tell us our future!" someone called.

"Make a prediction!" another said.

Tavia smirked.

Whatever the customer wants, she thought, reaching into her pocket with fast fingers to grab a proficiency charm. She squeezed the small marble of not-so-legal magic artfully in her hands, careful not to be seen by the crowds or any lingering guards, and let its power soak into her skin. She rested her palms atop the orb, wiping the magic from her to the device.

It glowed bright green and the crowd jumped back, thrilled.

In Tavia's hands the orb muddled, and the intricate mechanisms she and Wesley threw together started to whistle. There were riddles hard-coded into it, and though Tavia couldn't remember how many—it seemed like a lifetime ago when she and Wesley crafted cons as a team—she knew them by heart. She would recognize them anywhere: the silly proverbs and vague predictions about the day ahead. All things that Wesley found obnoxiously funny.

Only Tavia didn't recognize the riddle this time. The words were tiny and jumbled and a sinking feeling crawled inside her when she tried to decipher them, so awful that she lost the will to speak the riddle out loud. But in moments the charm had gone from her and into the air, and the breeze blew by in a gentle hum, shaping itself into a croon.

And then, just like that, the wind began to sing.

Time will be carried in strange hands,
across the realms and through stranger lands.
What is done will be undone,
a battle lost is a battle won.

When midnight rings on a child's betrayal,
your every success is doomed to fail.

Panicked, Tavia dropped the orb and the wind shattered.

She didn't know what in the fire-gates that was, but it was definitely *not* something she and Wesley had planted. No matter how many reverie charms they'd been under, no matter how powerful and infinite they might have felt with empty vials by their hands and the glow of moonlight on their faces, even they wouldn't have concocted something so peculiar.

Riddles were like jokes, in that someone had to be in on them in order for it to be funny.

And Tavia wasn't laughing.

But the crowd was overjoyed, none the wiser to the oddity. They broke into a frenzy, pulling coin from their pockets and shoving it under Tavia's nose like they were asking her to smell their worth.

Tavia swallowed, pushing away the strange feeling in her chest that the magic had left behind. The taste in her mouth, bitter as clovers.

Whatever that riddle was didn't matter. It was all underhand nonsense anyway, and Tavia wouldn't have been surprised if Wesley had planted something into the orb without her knowing. He specialized in secrets and there was nothing Wesley liked more than going behind people's backs. All that truly mattered was that the show was a success.

Tavia checked her timepiece and sighed.

It was fast approaching the hour when the air shifted and zealots spat out onto the streets, in search of buskers with magic black enough to soot their skin.

In other words, it was time for Tavia to head to the Crook.

Time for her to really get to work.

———

THE CROOK was so named because, like most of the city, it was full of crooked things, the most crooked of which was Wesley Thornton Walcott, who was both Tavia's underboss and the closest thing Creije had to a gangster.

He'd single-handedly turned the Crook into the most profitable enterprise in the realm, both over the table and under it. Overlooking the riverbank beside the bridge that separated the two halves of the city—the tourists from the poor—the old clock tower had been converted into a fight club that served as the hub of Creije, where anyone interested in a lawless eye gathered. Thanks to Wesley, its reach was beyond compare.

Tavia eyed the tail of customers that stretched from the doors and into the folds of the city, hugging her jacket tighter as the wind grew in strength. The icy ends of her black hair sparked by the point of her chin as she looked up to the skies in wonder.

It was winter in Creije, and though that meant the days were short and the nights were long, with any darkness came the Everglow. A web of color that pulled across the sky like a curtain. Flares of pink and green lighting up the dark, so that every night for the latter half of the year, even the locals leaned out their windows to watch the sky explode. There was magic in the air, among the stars and on the fingertips of anyone who walked the streets.

Tavia approached the doors to Wesley's club.

She didn't like coming to the Crook on Sundays, because that was when Karam Talwar tended door and she was the kind of person nobody saw in broad daylight.

Karam was from Wrenyal, in the five-river city of Granka, which drew missionaries from across the realms, learning magic like it was a holy calling rather than a skill. But there was nothing holy in her. Karam's fists were perpetually sliced across the knuckles and there was a permanent bruise under her left eye.

When Karam saw Tavia she grunted, which seemed to be more of a greeting than something to be taken personally.

"Karam," Tavia said, trying to ignore the aroma of peppermint that lingered on the girl's clothes—a common salve used by fighters. "Living well, I see."

In a heavy Grankan accent, she said, "Why are you here?"

Always the charmer.

"Aren't you happy to see me?" Tavia asked.

Karam shot her a look that was a little too murderous.

She always seemed so deadly, from the stark hair long enough to slash at her elbows, to the thick eyebrows that hooded large golden irises. Her clothes were richly embroidered in a contrast of midnight and moonlight that grazed her ankles, and Tavia wasn't entirely sure how she managed to fight rowdy customers in such an outfit, but fighting was what Karam did best.

That and glaring.

Karam moved to let Tavia through. "Just so you know, you ruin your face when you talk," she said.

"Flatterer," Tavia shot back, and then winked, because Karam may have been a killer with no social skills, but she was also quite pretty.

Tavia stepped through the doors of the Crook and though she was in no mood to smell cheap tricks and even cheaper liquor, the tower was in full swing, all flashing lights and magic she could practically taste. The music moved like a virus through the air, across the fighters and into the flurry of patrons who placed their bets on a winner.

Tavia walked past the fighters and the entertainers who flung themselves across the room in aerial silk, taking care not to get kicked in the face. She pulled back a curtain at the far end and pressed her hand against the indiscreet slab of black glass, allowing her palm—her identity and her desires—to be read.

Once the glass was satisfied, a doorway slid open, and on the other side stood Tavia's underboss, a pack of four-leaf clovers in hand.

Wesley Thornton Walcott was only nineteen, but he had a name that made most people think he came out of his muma wearing a suit and suspenders. Tavia knew that wasn't true, but she did know that he wore a three-piece on every even day and a bow tie on all the odd ones.

She wasn't too sure how he worked out which days were which—the streets of Creije always seemed so odd to her—but Wesley had assigned them such attributes and got away with it, because getting away with things was what Wesley did best.

"Tavia," he said, and smiled in a way that was half dimples and all sadist. "Come on, the fight's just getting started."

He brushed past her and headed for the fighting ring.

Reluctantly, Tavia followed.

A path cleared for Wesley, as if by habit, and when he approached a small set of sofas cordoned off by gold chains, half a dozen buskers surrounded the area, keeping everyone else at a distance.

Perhaps, so they couldn't hear what Wesley would tell Tavia.

Perhaps, because they knew Wesley just didn't like people very much.

The crowd cheered, waving their betting tickets at the fighters, and Wesley watched them with a face far too youthful for someone who had killed his way to the top. His black-brown hair was immaculately styled and his skin was deep and dark. A pair of mirrored sunglasses perched on the hilltop hitch of his nose.

"Sit down," Wesley said.

Tavia didn't, but she did take a moment to relish in the joy of what an utter jackass Wesley looked in those glasses.

Unfortunately, it was short-lived, because once Wesley noticed the smug grin on her face—which he should have been used to by now, since she learned it from him—he slipped the glasses off to reveal the graveyard dirt of his eyes.

"I just came to pick up some extra magic," Tavia said. "Make it quick if you want to talk. My time is your money."

Wesley popped a four-leaf clover into his mouth, a habit he'd picked up when they were kids.

"I want to talk about the new elixir from the Kingpin," Wesley said. "You've had it for a couple of weeks now and I don't have a report of any sales."

Tavia's spine tingled at the thought of the strange magic

vials, still untouched at the very bottom of her backpack. The so-called happiness elixir twisted her gut inexplicably whenever she caught sight of it and that was saying something, considering the kind of magic she usually sold without issue. And so Tavia had simply stopped looking at it all together, leaving the elixir to the depths of her backpack, piled under so many other vials of potent magic.

"I'm working on my sales pitch," Tavia said, though she knew that didn't sound convincing.

Wesley was hard to sway at the best of times, even when Tavia attempted charm, and most definitely when she lied through her teeth.

"You know how important this is," Wesley said. "We're already the magical mecca of Uskhanya, but if we make this a success, then we can put the other realms on the ropes too. I went out on a limb giving your name as the best busker to bring it to market. Don't make me regret it. This could earn us both a lot of money."

Tavia laughed and not just because Wesley already had too much money for his own good.

Everyone in Creije wanted to get rich or kill someone trying. The more money someone had, the more money they wanted. Round and round until all that was left were guys like Wesley Thornton Walcott, standing in his three-piece suit with a briefcase full of magic.

But Tavia didn't want to get rich.

Street kids became buskers because they needed to survive and survival was what Tavia had always been most interested in. Getting rich was just one possible side effect.

"I'm flattered my face came to mind when you thought of the word *con*," Tavia said.

"I must've forgotten the part where I said it was a scam."

Tavia could barely stop herself from rolling her eyes. "I'm not a child, Wesley. I know there's no such thing as new magic. The Crafters are all gone. The War of Ages saw to that. If you're going to feed me a story, at least make it a good one."

Wesley only shrugged, which was the closest thing he ever gave to an answer. "Then let's just call it something old that's been repackaged," he said. "Either way, it's in your best interest to pass it on."

"And why's that?"

"Because it'll cut your life debt short and give you enough money to leave Creije for good."

Tavia bristled.

Like every busker in Uskhanya, she owed a life debt to the Kingpin. He saved kids from the streets and in exchange they gave him their childhood, because children made the best crooks, lulling anyone into anything.

Sweet faces with deadly magic.

It was only when a busker turned eighteen, became an adult and aged out of their childhood debt, that they were given two choices: leave and never come back, or take everything they'd learned and use it to become a career criminal, swell in coin.

Most buskers went for option two, but Tavia was counting the time until it was over.

Just seven more months to go.

She'd already spent six years under the Kingpin's thumb,

forced to do his dirty work as payment for not starving to death. Forced to jump when she was told and ruin lives on the whim of a power-crazed crook. Never free to do the magic she wanted, when she wanted. Trapped in the city her muma died in, unable to leave and explore the charms the rest of the realms surely held.

As far as Tavia was concerned, she was little more than a captive of the Kingpin's command.

"That's not funny," she said. "You don't just wipe out a life debt to Dante Ashwood."

The crowd hissed as one of the fighters fell to their knees.

"It's not a joke," Wesley said, though even he didn't sound sure. "The Kingpin's consort just told me there'd be a day less on your debt for every vial you sell. Make sure you give it to the good kind of customer though, will you? The people who can afford to keep buying when we officially bring it to market."

"So not the good kind," Tavia said. "The wealthy kind."

"Isn't that what I said?"

Tavia resisted the urge to glare.

There were plenty of wealthy folk in Creije, but these days most of them were also wide-eyed romantics, or tourists who wandered from the floating railways with thirsty hearts and idealism ripe on their tongues. Creije was a place for dreamers and Tavia stole enough from people that she thought she ought to draw the line at dreams.

Though if she were to say that to Wesley, he'd laugh and tell her that a mark was a mark and could never be something so complicated as innocent. Even so, Tavia had decided that the best way to survive after Creije—which was an important distinction to surviving *in* Creije—was to cling to any morality she could salvage.

"People have been bottling happiness for decades," Tavia said. "You haven't told me what's so great about this version."

"Don't fix what isn't broken," Wesley said.

Tavia cast a meaningful glance in his direction. "There isn't a thing in this realm that isn't broken. Including the people."

Which meant her, too, she supposed. After all, buskers weren't exactly the poster children for sunny upbringings.

For a second, Wesley paused and Tavia half-expected him to call her out for being sage in a place like the Crook, in front of a person like him while two people pummeled each other with tricks and fists in the background.

Tavia expected him to give her a look that said she was too serious sometimes and not serious enough every other time.

Instead, Wesley brought another clover to his lips and turned his attention back to the fight.

He didn't look at her again.

"If that's all," Wesley said, "you can see yourself out."

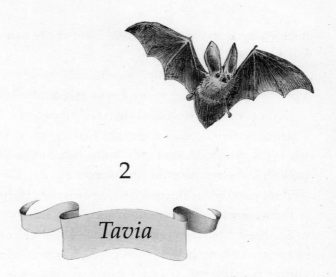

2

Tavia

"YOU'RE A CHEAT," SAXONY said, throwing a small pouch against Tavia's chest.

Tavia grinned as she caught it. The pouch was a little charred around the edges and carried the distinctly woody smell of a fire charm.

A solid win for the day.

"You're such a sore loser," Tavia said.

Saxony gave her the finger by way of reply. Her ring, emblazoned with leaves, curled over her knuckle and then circled in brightly colored vines up to her wrist. It was a fascinating piece of jewelry, equal parts delicate and deadly, just like most things in the realm.

Tavia threw her new fire charm in the air, letting the magic jingle each time it bounced back into her grasp. The two of them had been making nonsense bets for half an hour and she was up by three.

"Victory is sweet," Tavia said. "You really *can't* have too much of a good thing."

"There's nothing good in there," Saxony told her, and then, a little resentful, "That's why I'm so put out for losing it."

Saxony let out a wistful sigh and tipped her head back against the temple wall, her tight black curls splayed across the brick, threaded with gold coins, which was all the rage back in Rishiya, where Saxony was from.

Tavia smirked and leaned beside her, letting the walls of the old temple scrape across her jacket.

She liked it best when the days ended this way, with a friend by her side rather than an enemy, which was so often the case. During days like this, Creije smelled of magic and endlessness, and Tavia got a giddy feeling in her chest when she set up her stall at the magic market. When the hustle and glow of Creije streamed across her skin and she could close her eyes and hear the cogs of the city churning.

Tavia liked that it was never too quiet and never too repetitive, and there was beauty in the streams of water that curled through the city and played host to the floating railways. In the sprawling marketplaces, surrounded by pathways that served as portals from one stretch of the city to another in a glorious labyrinth, or the jugglers who performed against a backdrop of street art as bright as the buildings.

If Tavia wasn't forced to stay here, she might just find it wonderful.

"Don't make bets you can't win," Tavia said. "I think I've pretty much cleaned you out."

Saxony shoved her hands into her pockets, in what Tavia

assumed was the only way to stop from throwing her another filthy gesture.

"Another round," Saxony said. "Winner takes all."

Tavia laughed. "I'll pass."

"*Sugj*," Saxony said, which Tavia was pretty sure was Rishiyat slang for *coward*.

She elbowed her friend in the ribs. "Don't insult me in your farm lingo," Tavia said. "I'm not scared, I'm just busy."

She pointed to the sky, where the sun was low enough for night to crawl into view, and the clouds had already started to spill across rooftops, obscuring any chance of moonlight.

Creije was such a city of juxtapositions and though the day was full of wonder, when night came it welcomed the shadows with open arms, delighting in the wicked things it could hide.

"Everyone's busy," Saxony said. "Everyone always has a job to do."

"*You* have a job to do," Tavia said. "Unless you're going to march into the underboss's office, look him straight in the eye, and quit."

Saxony scoffed. "The day I look Wesley in the eye is the day I lose my mind."

"Afraid you'll fall madly in love with his baby browns?"

"I'm afraid of what I'll see in them," Saxony said. "Haven't you heard that eyes are the windows to the soul?"

Tavia pushed herself from the wall and gave Saxony a smile that was as criminal as she was. "Wesley Thornton Walcott doesn't have a soul," she said.

"Speaking of." Saxony nodded uneasily into the distance. "There's your first customer of the night."

Tavia followed her gaze to a man lingering at the edge of the temple steps. His face was obscured by a large top hat that hid everything except his mustache, but Tavia took note of his suit and how his broad chest puffed out, like just standing was something he excelled at. Tavia hated men for a lot less than standing like that.

She glanced back at Saxony, giving her a small salute.

"Duty calls," she said.

Saxony didn't offer her a smile in return.

For someone who was always so curious about magic, who seemed to love it as much as she did, Saxony never quite liked watching it being sold on the streets, given to the desperate and the dastardly.

"I need a little luck," the strange man said to Tavia, once she had approached him.

He thrust out a handful of coin.

"That's market magic." Tavia was surprised at the innocence of the request. "Come back when the sun's up."

"Not the good kind." The man looked over his shoulder, checking they were still alone in the darkness. He was clearly not used to crossing over to the wrong side of the bridge. "I know someone who needs to be taught a lesson."

Tavia's surprise faded, along with her smile.

Not so innocent after all, then.

Maybe such a thing didn't exist. Wesley told her once—told her constantly, actually—that there wasn't a person alive who couldn't be corrupted by power.

There are no good people, he said. *Just ones who haven't made bad choices yet.*

Tavia really hated it when Wesley was right.

"I've got two vials left," she said, her voice low.

Not that there was anybody around the derelict temple to hear them. Except maybe the gods.

"Everything in your hand."

The man's jaw dropped. "For two vials? Can't we slice another arrangement?"

"Sure," Tavia said, ever accommodating. "Give me half of what you've got and I'll arrange for you to have one vial."

The man sneered, but kept his hand out.

Tavia reached into her backpack, which held the mix of dark elixirs and charms never sold during the magic markets, from seeds that grew indestructible blades to voodoo dolls with a set of pins included. Some were not even magic to be used, but collected and put on shelves for people to admire alongside trophies. Magic made to collect dust, destined for a life inside finely crafted cabinets, too valuable to bother using.

In the darkness, Tavia had to rely more on the shape of the magic than what she could see: the different cuts of the vials, the smoothness of charms and how some of the loose trick dust felt like liquid in her hands, while others were as gritty as she was.

When she handed the luck to the man, he sloshed the liquid inside to check the quality. Which was a little ridiculous, because with bad luck the worse the better. That's what happened when you fermented clovers for long enough. It was kind of the point.

"Don't you worry about getting caught with all this?" he

asked. "Doyen Fenna Schulze is looking to have you lot thrown into a cell."

Tavia took in a breath. She should have known this man was the government type. Nobody outside of politics had a mustache like that.

"Our fearless leader is cracking down on the criminal element," Tavia said, all faux innocence. "I'm more than lawful."

Though Tavia spun crap better than most, even she had a hard time selling that line. Everyone knew that a busker at night was up to no good, and since her election to Realm Doyen, Fenna Schulze was on a crusade to prove it.

Tavia was kind of rooting for her. Maybe once the Doyen was through, no more kids like her would be pulled from the streets and taught to be crooks.

"Is there anything else you might be interested in?" Tavia asked.

Her hand grazed the new elixir in the corner of her backpack and an odd feeling of dread cast over her.

Happiness, Wesley had said, his promise like an echo in Tavia's mind.

One day less on her life debt for every piece she sold.

And as soon as Tavia was free, she'd leave Creije and all of this behind. It didn't matter if she had a single coin to her name; she'd travel the realms and give offerings to gods she couldn't remember the names of. Sail across the Onnela Sea, only ever laying anchor to steady her feet. She'd travel to her muma's home realm of Volo and the city of Gila she was born in, and maybe find a family or a purpose.

Tavia pulled out the vial. It felt oily and slick, like she shouldn't even be touching it.

"I have everything I want," the man said. "Unless you're offering yourself."

Tavia's jaw tightened.

Usually she could handle just about anything people threw at her, whether it was charms or punches, but the notion of being bought and sold—passing through hands like magic and whatever else the rich liked to collect—was different. It was different because Tavia didn't belong to herself yet. Not like the man in front of her, in his fine suit, with his fine, fine mustache.

He had enough money and freedom to go where he liked and treat people how he liked. He thought he was better than her. That she was just some petty criminal who'd be stuck selling charms forever.

Tavia clenched the vial.

"This elixir is the latest thing to hit the market," she said, letting her features fall into practiced complacence.

What was that line Wesley liked to feed her?

The customer is always right.

Except in this case, of course. When the customer was clearly a bastard.

She hoped the magic came with awful side effects.

"It can make all of your fantasies come true," Tavia said. "Think of it like a wish-granter. A dream-giver."

She shook the vial and the magic glowed purple. It felt lighter than any elixir she had handled before, like if she popped the cork it might just carry through the air.

The hunger in the man's eyes was fast, transforming him from trite arrogance to the kind of curious Tavia could make use of. This was what she did best. Lied and conned people. Got them hooked on dark magic and prayed to the Many Gods not to hold it against her. Prayed that her muma would forgive her for sullying her memory.

"You'd be the first person in all four realms to have it," Tavia said.

The man pulled out more coin, enthralled. "Would this cover it?"

Tavia nodded and only moments after she passed it to him did he scurry away like an insect, afraid she might change her mind. She almost sneered at his retreating shadow, hoping with all her might that the magic would give him a hangover to rival any other.

"What was *that*?" Saxony asked.

Tavia tried to avoid her gaze. She hadn't told Saxony about the bargain to ease her life debt and if she did, Saxony would surely rip her a new one for trusting Wesley.

"Some new magic from the underboss," was all Tavia said.

"*New* magic," Saxony repeated, eyebrows flaring.

"Different magic," Tavia corrected, because they both knew the former was impossible.

"You're acting weird." Saxony peeked into Tavia's backpack. "What's it really?"

"Whatever they want it to be."

Saxony gave her a look, but Tavia only shrugged.

"It's harmless. Wesley said to think of it like happiness."

Though she suspected there was more to it, Tavia tried

not to care. Caring in Creije never ended well and the more magic Tavia sold, the sooner she could escape and never have to think about it again.

Saxony held out a hand. "Give it over."

Sighing, Tavia pulled another vial from her backpack.

Saxony was always intrigued by the magic Tavia dealt, especially the kind of magic she dealt after sunset, and Tavia had gotten used to her many questions. If she was honest, sometimes she liked being seen as the library of knowledge for magic, offering her friend answers and explanations as though it wasn't just her job, but her calling.

"Did the underboss say it was new or different?" Saxony asked. "What were his exact words?"

Tavia arched an eyebrow. "Since when do you care about anything Wesley has to say?"

Saxony examined the elixir, moving it from side to side as the magic swarmed. "Did he say it was dangerous?"

"Just that it tailors to the customer. I haven't got specifics. You know how vague Wesley likes to be. He just said to sell it."

Saxony nodded, the disdain curling her top lip. "The underboss loves a good secret."

"A bad one too," Tavia said.

"New magic, though," Saxony mused. "I guess there's only one way to find out."

And then she popped the cork.

Tavia blanched.

Selling a strange elixir to a strange man was one thing, but she didn't trust the Kingpin nearly enough to give it to someone she loved.

"Saxony, don't," Tavia said, making a grab for it.

But before Tavia could get out another word, Saxony put the vial to her lips and tipped her head back.

In moments, the whole thing was drained.

Saxony blinked as the vial fell against the stone, a single spark of magic left hanging from her lips.

"Are you okay?" Tavia asked, panicked.

Saxony swallowed and her head lolled, eyes fluttering and then sharpening to near-black pits. She swayed a little, not unsteady, but like she thought the world had tilted and decided to follow suit.

"Everything is fine," Saxony said.

Her words were pronounced and purposeful, the Rishiyat inflection nearly gone from her voice.

Tavia felt cold.

There was a new emptiness around Saxony's eyes, *inside* her eyes, shooting straight through her, making every part of her still and blank. Leaving only a smile, halved and ghostly.

"Are you sure you're good?" Tavia asked.

"I feel good," Saxony said. "Don't I look good?"

Tavia wasn't sure what to say to that.

"Though now you mention it." Saxony pressed a hand to her temple. "I think there's someone . . ."

She wavered on her feet before grabbing a hand around the back of her neck.

Tavia thought instantly of a puppet on a string, trying to hold itself up.

"It's too loud!" Saxony yelled, and in the time it took for Tavia to blink, she had a charm in her hands.

Tavia didn't know anyone other than Wesley with hands that fast.

"Saxony!" Tavia looked around to make sure nobody was in sight. "If the amityguards catch us flashing dark magic around like that, then we're done for."

But Saxony wasn't listening. She brought the charm to her temple, hands shaking.

"I'm too loud," Saxony said, and then, as if correcting herself, "*She's* too loud."

She swallowed and the light from a nearby streetlamp flickered with her breath, casting a sequential torch onto the lines that made up her face. In the night, Saxony's freckles almost looked like blood splatters.

"There's someone in my head," she said, squeezing her eyes shut.

It was only when they opened again that Tavia saw the stillness. That ghost of a smile.

Her chest tugged.

There was something familiar about it—about that damned *look*—and her heart thundered.

"We need to find Wesley," Tavia said. "Whatever this is, he can fix it."

Saxony didn't answer.

There was blood curling from her nose and when she lifted a hand to wipe it away, her eyes widened.

"Tavia," she said. "Run."

But before she could even process the words, let alone think about reacting to them, Saxony thrust her arm out and Tavia flew across the ground.

She barely had time to register the pain before a beam of light shot from Saxony's palm.

Tavia rolled across the ground to avoid being hit again.

"*Djnfj,*" she swore.

She hadn't even noticed the charm up Saxony's sleeve until it was too late.

Saxony wasn't a busker and she wasn't trained in magic, so how was she suddenly so quick?

Tavia scrambled to her feet and ran behind a nearby pillar, dodging another skewer of light.

It shattered into the temple wall beside her.

Sooner or later, people were going to hear the scuffle, or see the blinding lights of magic. If the crowds swarmed, then the amityguards wouldn't be far behind.

And the last thing anyone with black magic wanted was to be caught by the amityguards.

"Many Gods damn this day," Tavia seethed, ripping her hand from her pocket and pulling out a trick bag.

Half magic, half firecracker.

Tavia threw her shoulder back and sent the explosive hurtling toward her friend. It burst at Saxony's feet with enough sparks to set her shoes on fire.

Saxony let out a furious cry, jumping backward.

"Get a grip!" Tavia yelled.

"I'm trying," Saxony said. "I don't want to hurt you. I . . ."

She trailed off and Tavia wished she could remember the name of at least one of the gods this side of the Onnela Sea, so that she could insult them personally.

With her backpack thrown across the temple steps, Tavia

fumbled in her pockets once more, searching for the few pieces of magic she had on standby for if somebody tried to kill her. Though usually those people weren't her *friends*.

Probably because she didn't have any other friends.

The moment Tavia's hand touched the invisibility charm, she felt cold. The bead was dewy between her fingers and then completely fluid as it ran up her arm, soaking her skin. It itched a little, but Tavia held back from scratching it away. Instead, she closed her eyes and let the prickling embed into her bones.

There was a rhythm to it, each sting timed to a pulse. Tavia counted in her head.

Math. She always liked the math.

Tavia squeezed her hands into fists and then dissolved before Saxony's eyes.

It wasn't a pretty sight.

Tavia had done it a dozen times and it never ceased to make her queasy. The first to go was her skin, paling to reveal the pink of her muscles, then her organs and vessels, shriveling like tree roots until all that was left was polished bone.

Saxony blinked and, in that moment, Tavia disappeared completely.

"Are you still there?" Saxony asked. "Tavia, you need to help me."

I will if you give me a damn minute, she thought.

Tavia stepped toward Saxony and reached into her pocket for the last dregs of her magic.

The trick bag wasn't elegant, but desperate times called for desperate magic. Tavia poured the contents of the drawstring into her palm and blew. The moment the sand-grain crystals whirled through the air Saxony stilled, the breeze washing each particle over her skin until there wasn't a part of her left that didn't carry a spark of starlight.

Saxony opened her mouth to speak.

And then collapsed onto the ground, her head hitting the concrete.

Tavia closed the gap between them, the temporary invisibility shattering around her. She nudged Saxony's leg with the edge of her boot to be sure the paralyzer took, and when Saxony didn't move, Tavia sucked in a grateful breath.

"What was that?" she asked, though her friend had lost consciousness.

Tavia knelt down beside her.

And then she saw it.

So small and almost hidden under the fold of Saxony's jaw, a vivid pink against the deep brown of her skin, a mark that had been seared into Tavia's mind for years.

The clearest and most awful memory she had of her muma.

Don't cry, ciolo. *It'll all be okay.*

"How did you—?"

Tavia broke off as warning buzzers shrieked through the streets.

The amityguards were coming for them.

"*Skeht*," Tavia swore.

If she and Saxony got hauled to the precinct, then Wesley was going to have to haul them back out, and with Doyen Schulze monitoring them all so closely, he wouldn't be happy to do it.

Tavia looked down at Saxony.

The paralyzer would still take another hour to wear off and it wasn't like Tavia could carry her.

The warning buzzers grew louder.

She swallowed and took in the mark on Saxony's neck once more.

And then, bleeding and cursing in equal amounts, Tavia ran, leaving her friend behind.

3

Wesley

WESLEY THORNTON WALCOTT HAD killed eleven men.

Most of them were not good men. A few of them were not altogether bad men. But all of them were men who stood in the Kingpin's way.

Of course, eleven was not a particularly large number compared to how many people everyone seemed to think Wesley had killed, and since it also included the old underboss—who was quite possibly more of a bastard than he was—Wesley thought only ten should count.

"*Skeht*," Stelios said. "Take it out."

It had been ten minutes since the knife went in and though Stelios had given up trying to pull it out, he hadn't given up on pleading for someone else to.

He was on his knees and sweating, the tongue of his tie licking up the blood that drained from his hand. Wesley was hoping it wouldn't stain. He quite liked the knife and the table and the carpet, and right now his fellow underboss was dripping blood all over them.

"I wasn't planning to make you a permanent fixture in my club," Wesley told him. He watched his carpet continue to smudge. "But we might as well finish our conversation while I've got you here."

Stelios squeezed his eyes shut and bared his teeth in a gold-rimmed sneer.

"It's only a matter of time," Ilaria said. "The Kingpin's new elixir will get to us eventually. You're just cutting the wait short by passing it on."

Wesley placed a clover on his tongue, considering.

"So you want me to do you a favor," he said.

"It's professional courtesy," Ilaria said. "We may all enjoy taking a stab at each other every now and again"—she looked at Stelios's hand, a little smug—"but when it comes down to it, we're one and the same. We're all underbosses in this realm. We're a team."

Her words made for a nice sentiment, but they were a sentiment all the same. Loyalty or betrayal. Allies or enemies. Wesley didn't think anything could be that black and white. Even this meeting, which happened each month like clockwork, had turned so quickly from touching base in the regular fashion, to a near-ambush, with Wesley's fellow underbosses clambering in a tag team, trying relentlessly to sway him into giving them magic they hadn't earned.

The elixir the Kingpin had handed exclusively, personally, to him.

"You're like hungry animals, begging for scraps," Wesley

said. "Why not just wait until Ashwood feeds you himself if you're so sure he will?"

Ilaria all but snarled. "You forget who you're dealing with."

But that wasn't true and Wesley smiled to show it.

"If there's one thing I never do," he said, "it's forget."

Because he remembered just fine how all three of these underbosses—Uskhanya's most deadly, before Wesley had arrived—thought him unworthy of their inner circle. It was almost funny to think of it now, how they'd looked down on him, as they did underbosses of the far less grand central cities, thinking he was too young, not ravaged enough by sin.

Now they grew nervous whenever he paused.

Now they saw what he could do with a city under his command.

Of course, just because the underbosses were wary, that didn't mean they weren't still dangerous. Nobody was entrusted to run the magic trade for an entire city because they were good and reasonable. Wesley knew that better than anyone.

In fact, he was acutely aware of how awful the people in front of him were.

Crooks and killers, who'd stop at nothing to rise to the top.

And Wesley was the worst of them.

Casim smirked. "Maybe we don't have your oh-so-special elixir because it's just not good enough for the rest of us."

"Or maybe," Wesley said, "I'm the Kingpin's favorite."

Ilaria sucked on her teeth and the look she gave him was tired and unflattering. "Just tell us what the magic does and what the Kingpin is planning. We outnumber you, after all."

Wesley sighed.

He really didn't like it when people implied threats instead of making them. It seemed like a waste of good conversation.

Better to kill them all and just be done with it, the voice inside him whispered.

Wesley adjusted his cuff links, and the air around him grew cold, his magic humming with the possibility of such destruction.

"It's a little rude to come into someone's house and make demands like that," he said.

Wesley slid a hand into his pocket and thumbed the tiny piece of metal he always carried with him.

Casim shifted uncomfortably.

"Someone back down," Stelios said, wincing. "I'm not having this blade in my hand all night because you lot want to prove your power."

"I don't need to prove anything," Wesley said.

Though part of him always thought he did.

Wesley leaned forward and stood the small silver bullet in the center of the table.

He inclined his head upward and it rose obediently.

"You're going to shoot us with a magic bullet?" Ilaria asked.

She stared at him, ripe with disbelief, as though she had only just remembered what a bastard Wesley was.

It wasn't her fault, of course. Wesley had two faces and he was wearing a far nicer one when the underbosses first arrived. Now the face that belonged alongside his reputation appeared, smug and a little dead around the eyes.

Tavia would have hated it.

"Do it." Stelios laughed and banged his uninjured hand against the table. "It's about time my blood had some company."

"That's a little much, even for you," Ilaria said, eyeing Wesley. "Think carefully about what you're doing."

Wesley ran a thumb over his lip and slid as far back as his chair would allow. The bullet teetered. "I am thinking," he said. "About how much of you guys I'm willing to have scrubbed off my floor."

Ilaria's laugh was brittle. "Just like Ashwood's lapdog to try to bite off more than he can chew."

Wesley exhaled and without warning, without him really meaning for it to, the bullet shot through the air, spitting through the narrow gap between Ilaria's arm and her ribs. She jumped up as it tore into the sofa behind her and continued its blazing path until the mirror at the far end of the room shattered.

"Are you out of your mind?" Ilaria roared.

It was a fair question.

"You could have killed me!"

"I'm aware of that," Wesley said. "I just wanted to make sure you were."

Ilaria only glared, which meant that Wesley had made his point.

Perhaps the underbosses were resentful that the Kingpin gave him his pick of the magic and that this new elixir, this thing Ashwood was so excited about, shrouded in awful mystery, was only Wesley's to sell. Perhaps he should have made nice and fed their egos. But the truth was, they weren't allies and they weren't on the same side.

Wesley had earned every advantage he had over them.

Creije was thriving because of him. The city was Uskhanya's magical mecca because of him. Wesley may not have been in the position for as long as the other underbosses, he may not have killed and tortured as many people as they had, ruined as many lives and burned as many bridges, but he'd done more in those short years to help his city than they could in their entire lives.

Wesley loved Creije, and these people were too awful to love anything.

He picked up the half-empty decanter of Cloverye and refilled his glass. The wind called in through the open window, mingling with every trick Wesley had in his pocket, telling him it was time to go.

"If that's all," he said, "then you'll have to excuse me. I have places to be and a city to run. I'm sure at least one of you knows what that's like."

Ilaria slammed her fists on the table.

"What happens on the day you don't have any more of the Kingpin's fancy magic to throw around?" she asked. "Because that's the day when we'll come for your city, Walcott. What are you going to do then?"

Wesley stood, straightening out his suit sleeves. "I suppose I'll just have to kill you the old-fashioned way."

"There's only one of you and three of us."

Wesley looked over to Stelios, still bleeding onto his carpet. "Two and a half," he said, and headed for the door.

The moment Wesley turned from the other underbosses, the shroud of magic he kept around himself began to hum, like it always did when his back was turned, ready to protect him in case someone decided to stick a knife in it.

Wesley crossed the Crook with its song in his ears and pushed open the door to his office.

Of all the ways for a night to end, that wasn't the worst. Nobody had tried to kill him and he'd managed to walk away making everyone think he might just kill them.

All in all, he'd call it a success.

The underbosses needed to know that he wouldn't cower to their demands, because if Wesley gave them the smallest bit of slack, they would use the rope to hang him.

They were envious and Wesley knew it, not just because Ashwood favored him, but because the other Uskhanyan cities were such a stark juxtaposition to his. Places like Ilaria's Eltriea to the east, packed with concrete buildings hidden amongst the clouds, sandwiched too close to look like anything other than a jigsaw, broken only by flashing signs that advertised food or pleasure. The southern city of Kythnu that Stelios watched over was older and brimming with a very boring kind of culture that made for pretty architecture and not much else. It was warm, always, but the glow of the sun was the only color in its stark expanse of white buildings. And then there was Rishiya, Casim's territory to the west, the most war-devastated of the realm, where farmers worked the land and buildings were covered in greenery.

They were nothing compared to Creije, where buildings were a mix of colors spread lavishly across the city, so when the sun hit them just right the windows cast paintings on the ground.

Wesley sat on the edge of his desk and reached into his pocket for another clover.

Behind him, the painting he inherited from the old underboss began to shake and Wesley eyed it with a curious smile. It depicted the four elements of the Many Gods, their symbols like watchful eyes that forever despaired over Wesley's secrets and, nestled above them, a shadow moon in the drawn sky.

In the old days, it was called the Crafter Moon and was part of some sacred ritual Wesley had read about, though he couldn't remember in which book. He did remember that the text said whenever a shadow moon appeared, magic increased tenfold. It was only a story, he supposed, and since Crafters were no longer around to ask, he couldn't be sure whether it was true. Still, Wesley always liked the idea of a magical moon imbuing people with power.

It was why he kept the painting, long after he disposed of its owner.

Wesley watched, patiently, as the image continued to shake until it finally creaked open. From the darkness behind, a face slipped through.

"Sir," Falk said, quiet and cautious. "I think I've had a breakthrough."

Though Falk was older than Wesley, it was not by much, and yet still his face was worn with magic. Stretched and then scrunched, making everything about him pointed, from his lips to his small nose.

"A breakthrough," Wesley repeated.

Falk nodded and Wesley's lips drew to a smile.

The other underbosses were so concerned with the Kingpin's

elixir, with the things that Ashwood gave to Wesley, that they never thought to worry about the things Wesley would make for himself.

The weapons and the magic, and the infinite possibility they held when paired together.

"Show me," Wesley said.

Falk pushed the door of the painting back wider, erasing the shadow moon from view.

Wesley pillowed his hands into his pockets, and with a whistle to match his magic, he stepped through.

4

Tavia

TAVIA HITCHED A HAND on her waist and looked up.

Saxony's cell was most likely on the sixth floor and Tavia hated heights. She also hated climbing and any task that required athleticism beyond street performing. She had no rope or wall-scaling materials and she certainly didn't have any acrobatic skill.

But she could fly.

Tavia had stolen the hover charms from the old underboss on her fourteenth birthday, as a present to herself because though she didn't like heights she did like the idea of being able to escape at a moment's notice.

Ironic that she was now going to use that very thing to break *into* a cell.

Tavia rubbed her hands together, letting the charm warm in her palms, and when she felt air beneath her feet, she winced. She tried her best not to look down.

"Just stare straight," she told herself, counting each of the windows that passed.

The wind swiped against her feet and Tavia jolted forward, hands slamming into the brick.

"Damn."

She dug her nails into the wall. Her feet dangled perilously.

Five. She had floated five floors up and the ledge of the sixth window, where Saxony was sure to be, hung above her like a tease. That was where they put all the magic junkies on a comedown and so it was scarcely guarded.

Tavia hitched in a breath and she could feel the hover charm faltering from under her—it was *all* she could feel under her. Any second now she was going to fall and break her neck. Or get caught by the amityguards, who'd no doubt tattle to Wesley before they told their captain.

Tavia reached for the window.

Her fingers skimmed the ledge and she gritted her teeth, digging the steel knives of her boots into the wall. Then, summoning a rarely used strength, she hoisted herself up, hands quickly curling around cell bars of the window in a vice grip.

Now she looked down.

"Oh, *skeht*," Tavia said, eyeing the black cobblestone below.

It was a lot higher looking down than it had been looking up.

Tavia shuffled closer to the bars so that she could see inside.

The holding cell was significantly larger than her bedroom, but that wasn't saying much. It was made from patchwork concrete, with large drips hanging from the ceiling like spears. To the left was a metal toilet barely off the ground, with a tap screwed to the wall beside it. Three mattresses were lined up on the floor, their sheets weathered and damp. On the one closest to the cell door was a man who was definitely not Saxony.

He was wearing the purple jumpsuit most buskers found themselves in at one point or another. Even Tavia had spent a day in the holding cells, dressed in her prison worst, while she waited for Wesley to get out of his meeting and lend her some pull. In Creije, you were guilty until someone faked enough evidence to prove otherwise.

"Hey," Tavia said.

She didn't bother whispering. She knew the guards' schedules and they wouldn't do their rounds for another eleven minutes.

The man flinched, but kept his hunched back to Tavia.

She sighed, inching closer, keeping her hold on the bars and not daring to look down again. Any minute now she was going to lose her nerve.

"*Hey*," she said again. "Has anyone else been brought into the cells tonight?"

The man's head angled in her direction. The light was steady but dim, a single bulb hanging from string that brushed the floor. When he turned, Tavia had to squint to make out his face, and it wasn't until he rose from the mattress and walked toward the window that she finally recognized him.

The man she had sold the elixir to earlier that night, before Saxony downed a vial for herself. The man with arrogant eyes and a haughty top hat and a mustache that was now thick with blood.

And what made things worse, was that Tavia somehow knew that blood wasn't his.

"Are you here to save me?" he asked, and then, far graver,

"Everyone keeps screaming." He looked down at his hands. "They say I killed someone. I've never killed someone before."

Tavia opened her mouth, but no words came.

Whatever had happened to him, the amityguards didn't even bother to clean him up before throwing him into the holding cell. They'd stripped him down, thrown on the Creijen colors, and let him stew.

"I'm looking for my friend," Tavia said, trying to pull herself together. "The amityguards picked her up outside the old temple. Have you seen them bring anyone else in?"

The man shook his head.

"What's your name?" Tavia asked.

"Deniel," he said. "Deniel Emilsson."

"What happened to you?"

Part of her hoped he wouldn't say.

The elixir. The elixir. The elixir.

"I met you earlier," Deniel said, frowning as though that was the most bizarre thing. "I wanted . . . There was magic and you said it was a dream."

He swallowed, took another step forward, so the light hit his face like a beam.

Tavia caught sight of his neck and when she did she felt like crying.

He had it too, the very thing her nightmares were made of.

The mark of the magic sickness.

The mark of her mother's doom.

It was barely the size of a finger, shaped almost like a doorway, with a line across the center that broke left and then right at the singed edges. It was a sign of the dead and the damned.

"There was a voice," Deniel said.

His hands closed over Tavia's, pinning her to the steel bars. Then his nose began to bleed and all she could do was stare.

"It whispered for me to do awful things," he said. "But when I tried not to, it stopped whispering and started screaming." He squeezed his hands tighter over Tavia's and she hissed in pain. "It told me to kill that amityguard."

Tavia pulled against his grip. "Let go," she said.

"Tell me you believe me." Deniel was crying, the blood on his cheeks rolling down with the tears. "I couldn't control myself. It was like someone was there telling me what to do and I couldn't think of anything past it. I just *had* to. You—"

Deniel stopped, hands going slack over Tavia's. For a moment, she thought maybe he was going to pass out. There was a dead look in his eyes and the corners were inked black just like Saxony's had been.

"What did you give me?" he asked, quiet and broken.

Tavia paled. She wanted to know the answer to that too, because if what this man said was true, then it damn sure wasn't happiness.

"Busker."

Tavia looked up at the man, at Deniel Emilsson, his face pale and his bloodied lips drawn to a thin line. He knew he was destined for death, or things far worse.

"What was in that magic?" he asked.

Honestly, Tavia said, "I don't know."

A tear slipped down the side of Deniel's face. His eyes searched the floor, as though written somewhere on the uneven cement there would be a spell to undo it all. Take back the day and whatever horrors he'd committed in the name of a magic Tavia conned him into taking.

Deniel's hands curled back over hers. His head shook slowly from side to side.

"You did this to me," he said. "This is all your fault."

And then he ripped Tavia's hands from the bars and pushed her from the ledge.

5

Wesley

WESLEY HAD A SECRET.

Actually, he had hundreds, but there was one in particular that nobody could ever know, and it was that Wesley was not entirely in his right mind.

People threw the word *crazy* around a lot, and Many Gods knew they all thought Wesley was criminally insane. They just didn't know how right they were. Because for years now, Wesley had voices in his head.

Specifically, one voice.

An impossible voice.

The voice of a girl he knew long ago, who even after she was dead and gone had left her voice to get stuck behind. Perhaps to remind Wesley that he didn't have a conscience and should never try to find one.

She functioned as white noise most days. Images and a sense, a knowing, that she was there, listening to his every move and he had to be on guard, constantly, to shield himself from her. But every so often, when Wesley wasn't concentrating hard enough, her voice broke through and took on a life of its own.

She scolded him when he was too good and cheered when he was very, very bad, and Wesley didn't know how to stop it. He didn't know how to stop her.

All he could do was push her down into the back of his mind, adjust his tie, fix his cuff links, and *focus*. Bury her deep until she decided to rise to the surface again.

His very own ghost.

Wesley looked at the clock and watched the seconds tick away.

The headquarters for the Kingpin's consort was a grandiose building that wisped out on one side. The sole purpose of a consort was to act as a go-between for Ashwood and the other Kingpins, shaking hands on their deals and ferrying their secrets. She was a cross between a spy and a diplomat, and rumor had it that she kept stashes of the realm's darkest magic in a host of safes. It was a busking legend all of the kids told, though Wesley had never put much stock in it.

Still, the building was grand because the consort liked to think she was. It sat brazenly on the wrong side of the bridge, each of the windows a ruffle of feathers, and to the right it bowed and dipped like the arc of a broad chest.

It was great and mighty, in an obvious way Wesley had never been fond of, but it was also sly and sneaky in a way he quite liked: to the rest of Creije and, especially to the Realm Doyen, this was nothing more than a magic factory where legal elixirs were extracted and repackaged.

The good guys just didn't know about a few hidden floors.

Across the room, a doorway bubbled and Wesley glanced up to see a thin man step out from it. Reynholt Leifsson, the secretary of the building.

He was dressed all in black, hair slicked to one side, his skin so chalky that from a distance he looked a little bit like a floating head making his way toward Wesley.

"Mr. Thornton Walcott," Leifsson said in a smooth Creijen rendition. He extended a gloved hand, which Wesley did not take, and dipped his head.

Wesley glanced down at his gloves and raised an eyebrow. "You're always wearing those."

"One finds it's always best not to leave fingerprints when dealing with dark magic."

"That's easily taken care of." Wesley closed the button of his blazer and stood. "If someone doesn't have the skill not to leave a print, you can always cut off their fingers."

The ghost in his mind applauded, as she always did when Wesley was awful.

Leifsson blinked. "Yes," he said, "that would be quite effective." He extended a hand over to the doorway he'd emerged from—"Right this way"—and turned on his polished heel, leading Wesley toward the mirror.

Wesley took in the cold gray rendition of himself—the bow tie that signaled this was going to be an odd day indeed—and reached out a hand. The mirror erupted around his touch, ripples curling from his fingertips until his face was obscured.

This was the part he could never get used to. The doorway to his office at the Crook was similar, in that it read palms like any system worth its salt, but this did more than that.

It read the person, their intentions and, most importantly, their loyalties. As far as Wesley knew, Ashwood was the only one in the realms to have developed something so sophisticated.

Wesley kept his fingers to the mirror and though it took a few moments, once the magic confirmed his allegiance, the glass stilled.

Wesley slid his hands into his pockets and stepped into his reflection.

The hall on the other side was long enough that it seemed to narrow to a point, and the walls were a solid line of mirrors, marked by silver handles at odd junctions, with no clear lines separating one doorway from the next.

Leifsson inclined his head toward the right and placed a firm grip around the first handle. "After you," he said, and the doorway dissolved before them.

The room was as much red as it was black, with walls made from the same glass Wesley had come through. The carpet was a midnight ruby and what little light there was came from charcoal-colored candles that hung from glass chains, and the subsequent reflections their dim flames cast.

In the center of the room, a dark figure reclined and the shadows around him cooed.

Leifsson backed slowly from the room.

"Wesley," the Kingpin said.

His name repeated in an echo.

Dante Ashwood was there and he was not.

He was a man and he was not.

Wesley could see the outlines of his top hat and the streamlined jacket that pinched across his body. But his face—Wesley had never seen the Kingpin's face. Nobody had. In place of skin and eyes there was darkness and smoke, only the faintest smudge of his lips was visible, and the orb of his black cane shone under his transparently pale palm.

Around him, the air flickered like flames.

Though each of the four realms had a Doyen to lead, three also had a Kingpin with a capital *K* that stood for criminal. While the Realm Doyens ran things aboveground, the Kingpins ran the black magic trade, with underbosses to manage their many cities and buskers recruited to sell their dirty magic and consorts to be their messengers. But though the other Kingpins were powerful and evil, possibly soulless, they were still undoubtedly human.

All except for Ashwood.

Not a human, but a god, his ghost said.

Wesley ignored her, as he always tried to, and bowed to the Kingpin.

Ashwood laughed at the formality. "So serious, my boy. Pour yourself something expensive and sit down."

"I'm fine, *tek*."

"Wesley." The Kingpin tapped the orb of his cane. It blinked under the touch of his long, blanched fingers. "Pour yourself a drink."

Wesley cleared his throat and headed to the bar.

The air was dense with the layers of protection they each wrapped around themselves, because you couldn't trust yourself in Creije, let alone anyone else. Though Wesley didn't kid himself, if the Kingpin wanted his magic to be silenced, then it would be.

He only liked to offer Wesley the illusion of power, never really giving him full control over anything, least of all his own life.

Wesley picked up a bottle of Cloverye, the drink of choice in Creije, and filled his glass.

"It's not often we get to see each other," Ashwood said. "You're so busy making Creije into your kingdom. Gone are the days when you relied on me for guidance."

Wesley took a swig of his drink, back still to the Kingpin.

There was a hint of nostalgia in his voice that Wesley didn't care for.

It wasn't like Ashwood had taken him on as an apprentice and they were some happy little family.

He'd found Wesley on the eve of his seventh birthday, wandering the alleys with his hands in other people's pockets, and Ashwood had been as much a shadow then as he was now, with gloved hands and a face made from chimney smoke. He'd supposed that Wesley was an orphan, surely, with no family and nowhere to go, and wouldn't he very much like both of those things?

Only Wesley did have a family and he did have somewhere to go.

The only difference was that he wished he didn't.

Wesley knew what taking the Kingpin's hand meant, but he wanted to return to the streets only after he'd grown big and strong and could prove his worth to a family that had never wanted him to begin with. But then months became years and magic became life and by the time Wesley was enough of something to show them, it was too late. Magic sickness broke out and the worst batch was in the small street on the outskirts of Creije that he'd grown up on.

His family was probably dead and even if they weren't, the boy who wanted to prove something to them was.

Wesley knew better.

He had discovered Creije now, unlocked its secrets, and he delighted in its delicate twists and rough edges. The glow of lights and stars and magic. He'd fallen under its spell and all he wanted was to keep it safe.

To protect it, the way he knew nobody else could.

"How are my other underbosses?" Ashwood asked.

Wesley took another sip of Cloverye and made his way to the sofa that sprawled parallel to the Kingpin.

"Still necessary," he said. "For now."

Ashwood laughed. "And my elixir?"

Wesley paused, unsure how to answer that.

"You look concerned," Ashwood said.

Wesley stared through his mirrored glasses, reflecting the magic of the Kingpin right back into the chasm of his face, because Dante Ashwood could see from a person's eyes and into their soul, wading through their secrets, and Wesley very much liked keeping his secrets.

Besides, he had enough people in his head.

"We haven't made much progress," Wesley admitted. "It's tough to sell something when you don't know that much about it." He tried to choose his next words carefully. "A detailed rundown of the magic could help. If you have plans, I thought I'd be the first person to know."

The Kingpin let a small crack of silence pass between them,

and then he said, "You are my right hand, Wesley, more dear to me than any other underboss. But I need a left hand too."

Wesley let the irritation simmer inside him, careful that not even a morsel slipped onto the outside.

"Is the elixir really happiness?" he asked.

"It is," Ashwood said. "And it isn't. This magic is a way to ensure I win my war."

"We're not at war."

"We will be soon."

Though Wesley couldn't see the Kingpin's face, he was sure he felt the smile crawl along it. Wesley may have liked chaos, but he had no desire for war and especially no desire for his city to be a part of it.

"I've always thought that you would make a fine second in command," Ashwood said. "You know you're like family to me, Wesley."

Which was true, Wesley supposed, because the Kingpin had raised him from the streets, crafting him into the man he was today. He'd made him special and turned him into the leader of an entire city.

Wesley owed him everything.

And he hated it.

He hated that Ashwood was family, in a way. Not the one Wesley was born with, or even the one he chose, but one that was made for him. One he was cut from. Besides, Wesley really didn't like the idea of being anyone's son. He already had a father and that man was awful enough for him to never consider having another one.

"Who do you want to go to war with?" Wesley asked. "I

thought you and the other Kingpins had an understanding."

The shadows around Ashwood slithered. "I don't care about those fools," he said. "My elixir is going to bring the Doyen to her knees."

Wesley was glad his glasses hid the growing uncertainty in his eyes.

"You're after Schulze," he said.

The Kingpin made a choked sound that straddled the line between laughter and disappointment. "I'm after a new age, my boy. Fenna Schulze thinks she can pass laws in my realm that restrain us, but I was here long before that arrogant little girl took office and I'll be here long after. Magic—black or white—keeps the realms turning. I won't let a politician ruin it all."

He said *politician* like it was the dirtiest word imaginable.

"And the elixir will help you do that," Wesley said. "Is it really that dangerous?"

He couldn't help but ask. He had given Tavia that magic and if she got hurt—

"Risks win wars," Ashwood said. "My elixir allows me to open people's minds so they can see beyond Schulze's propaganda and into my truth. When I bring them to my side, we'll take down this government with as few civilian casualties as possible."

Casualties. Not murders.

"I call it the Loj," Ashwood said proudly.

The light. Or at least the street slang for it.

The old saying used to be *lojisi uf hemga*—the light of happiness—but street kids started to see it as more than that. A peace of mind that became like a goal to attain. It was the feeling in your heart after your first warm meal in days, or when you managed to find shelter in the rain and could sleep on a firm mattress in place of street floors. It was the relief that came with knowing you could stop worrying for a while and let your bones rest.

It was the reason most street kids became buskers.

They wanted the Loj. The knowing that everything would be okay.

And Ashwood had named his magic after it.

"It's really new magic," Wesley said. "How is that possible?"

Ashwood leaned forward and the tip of his hat flickered with candlelight.

You know how, the ghost whispered.

"It's quite an easy thing to do," Ashwood said. "When you have Crafters by your side."

And there it was.

The thing Wesley hated most about Dante Ashwood.

The most awful line to cross.

The magic Wesley sold now was nothing short of mimicry, with trick dust gathered from the residue of magic, that barely hosted power past practical jokes. Or elixirs to alter the mind and body, extracted from dosed—and handsomely compensated—people in government-funded warehouses, only to then be repackaged and sold. And charms? They may have been the most powerful magic—and also entirely illegal—but with the right amount of training, buskers could wield them or use them to create cursed objects. With the right technology, they could even be duplicated.

But nothing, not a single kind of magic, could be created anew.

Unless you were a Crafter.

Before the War of Ages, Ashwood spent decades in the company of those magical captives. He'd studied them, learned their tricks, and embedded himself in their legends until their power snaked into him and became a dark, nefarious thing.

It was a story every busker in Uskhanya heard the moment they were recruited.

Ashwood was not a man and he was not a Crafter.

He was the embodiment of the in-between. A living shadow.

Powerful enough, people said, to have lived for a century.

And though the war was supposed to have put an end to the Crafter trade for good—though it was said to have put an end to the Crafters themselves, killing many and leaving the rest to flee—it seemed Ashwood wouldn't let petty things like impossibility get in his way.

He had found those rare, hidden beings and turned them into puppets.

"How many Crafters do you have?" Wesley asked.

He didn't want to know the answer.

Yes, yes you do.

"The number is of no consequence," Ashwood said. "But there will be no more hiding in the shadows once I am Doyen. We shall rise and make a brighter future, Wesley, filled with magic."

Ashwood's power coated the air like heavy rain, soaking into Wesley's breath.

Ashwood belonged in the shadows, far away from the light and those who walked in it. To have someone like that in real control would plunge the four realms into chaos and tear Wesley's city to pieces.

Besides, there wasn't a sane person in all of Uskhanya, crooked or not, who would support Ashwood as Doyen. Politicians may have been criminals, but people didn't like them being so open about it. Even if Ashwood pried the title from Schulze's cold, dead fingers, he would never be accepted. You could kill for a criminal kingdom, but not for a legitimate leadership.

Ashwood would destroy the realms trying to conquer it, because he didn't care about Uskhanya or Creije. He didn't want what was best for the city and he certainly didn't love it like Wesley did.

He would see it burn, if that's what it took.

"When your war comes, what happens to Creije?" Wesley asked.

"Nothing," Ashwood assured him. "As long as the people stand with me. Rebellions won't be tolerated, Wesley. Every player in this game must follow the rules."

"War isn't a game," Wesley said.

"Everything is a game, my boy. And by the time of the shadow moon, my Crafters will be ready to win."

The shadow moon.

Wesley thought back to the picture hanging in his office. He thought of the stories he had read about how it could amplify Crafter magic.

The Kingpin's smile snaked across to him, like he could read Wesley's mind behind the shield of his glasses. "You know as well as I do what power the shadow moon holds over magic," Ashwood said. "Our army will be a sight to behold."

He did promise to make you the world, the ghost cooed.

Wesley tried to stop himself from wiping at that damn smudge on his cuff links, or reaching up and adjusting his tie, even though his fingers shook with the urge every time the voice in his head spoke.

He squeezed his fists together instead.

There had to be a line. Somewhere in the sand, there had to be a line that even the worst people couldn't cross.

"You gave Creije to me," Wesley said. "So that I could make it great."

Ashwood tapped the orb of his cane, contemplating his words, and Wesley waited, his tie like a noose around his neck.

Hush now, it'll all be okay.

Finally, Ashwood stood, lithe and towering. The room fogged around him.

Wesley looked up at the faceless man who took him from the streets and made him into someone to be feared. The man who gave him a home and was ready to take it away with a snap of his fingers.

The man who thought of him like family.

The man he hated more than anyone.

"I don't want my city destroyed," Wesley said.

The Kingpin reached out a frostbitten hand and placed it on Wesley's shoulder, almost fatherly.

"Some things need to be destroyed," he said, "in order to be rebuilt."

6

Karam

KARAM LICKED THE BLOOD from her teeth.

Tricks and coin flew toward her, colliding with the rope that enclosed the ring. It was like an amphitheater, only instead of stone there was fancy wallpaper, and instead of warriors there was Karam.

The Crook's fighting ring was infamous for being the one place in all of Creije where it was legal to beat someone to a pulp, and it did its very best to live up to that reputation. Industrial beams thatched across the ceiling and large bulbs noosed from metal cables, with plush rows of seating that shook whenever the crowd jumped and screamed.

It felt as cold as the people who gathered there.

Though usually these fights had more magic than fists, when Karam was in the ring she put that showy nonsense to bed. Her opponents didn't rely on tricks and charms to win. There were no rules and no magic to offer protection.

It was just her and the blood waiting to be spilled.

Karam's opponent leaned against the rope and ran a thumb across his lower lip.

He was all might and no lithe, every inch of him bulky to the point of breaking. He wore no wrappings on his fists and Karam got a spray of his knuckle blood in her eye that last round.

"Little Wrenyi girl want to play?" he asked in slow Uskhanyan, like she might not understand.

Karam snarled on reflex.

She wasn't angry about the comment, or because it surprised her. It was the opposite. Karam was angry because she expected that to be the first wound her enemies tried to inflict. She seethed because she was used to it.

It had been years and she was still in a perpetual state of not-belonging. Still an outsider. Still never quite Creije enough. It wasn't that her skin was dark, but that it was a different kind of darkness. Burnished brown and decorated with the blue and gold tattoos famous among women in the Wrenyi realm. It was the ornate chains that threaded jewels across her scalp, even now, and the *setwa*—black and blue, like her face so often was—that she occasionally swept over her shoulder. It was the inflection still grasping her words, even after nearly a decade in this realm.

It was none of that and all of that.

Karam scuffed the soles of her feet against the floor and spat. "Keep smiling while you still have teeth," she said.

Her opponent laughed and threw himself toward her.

His fist struck Karam's cheek with more speed than she gave him credit for.

She crashed back to the stone.

Her palms broke her fall, which Karam realized a beat too late was not the smartest choice. Her hands were her weapons; better she let her face get broken.

The crowd booed and Karam swallowed the blood slicking her mouth.

There was no way she was going to lose to this *hijada*. This bastard. She would make him yield.

Karam pounced back to her feet and threw herself at him. Her shoulder collided with his side and Karam felt the moment the point of her bone jammed into his gut.

Her opponent let out a grunt and locked his hands around her back, squeezing.

Karam twisted her elbow between them and shoved it into his stomach. His grip on her loosened and with the distance widened she began to punch. Hard shots directly below his ribs.

One hand.

Both hands.

Until she was certain she heard some kind of crack.

He staggered back and Karam jumped, twisting her body seamlessly through the air. The knife of her foot exploded against his face.

The crowd rose.

They screamed for more.

More violence and brutality.

Anything Karam could give to feed their empty hearts.

She watched them grip desperately onto their seats, almost pitching themselves over for a better look. Rows of the poor and the slightly less poor, of the wealthy who tried their hardest to hide it and the dastardly who didn't hide it at all.

But not the one person Karam always seemed to be waiting for.

Saxony was impossible to miss, like lightning in a thunderstorm, and sometimes Karam could almost swear that she felt it when Saxony was near. That she sensed, perhaps, the almighty power that ran through that girl's veins.

Whenever Saxony came to watch her fight, she stood taller than those around her and, if they were standing side by side, which they so rarely did these days, a good six inches above Karam. And even from way in the back rows, Karam could always tell that Saxony was looking straight at her, staring with eyes the same beautiful black-brown as her skin.

Every time.

Though seeing Saxony always made Karam feel like time had stretched unfairly between them—everything they once shared, alight in magic and secrets, was fractured now—it was still better than not seeing her at all. It was a way for them to tell each other that there was still something there. That maybe there always would be.

But Saxony hadn't shown this time.

Karam cracked her fists together.

The crowd stamped their war-drum feet.

Her opponent pushed himself to stand and growled a string of curses.

Karam cocked her head to the side and took in his stance. He was running on pride and fury, and she knew how quickly that ran out.

"Wrenyi bitch," he snarled. "I'll make you pay."

Empty threats.

Karam had faced a shadow demon in this ring, on a night where the underbosses gathered and the Crook was closed to the public.

Her grandparents had fought in the War of Ages, amongst a sacred warrior sect whose duty it was to protect Crafters.

Karam was a child of the Rekhi d'Rihsni.

This man was nothing.

He lunged and Karam spun out of the way, but the hilt of his shoulder clipped her hip and the sheer force of him sent them both rolling to the floor.

Karam brought her knee up high between his legs and he roared. She gave him an almighty shove and then rolled to straddle his hips.

Once she had the upper hand, Karam punched mercilessly, until the blood coated her wrappings so much that they felt slick across her knuckles.

Her opponent spat in her face.

Then, with brutal force, he brought the heel of his palm up to her nose and Karam fell back, a blinding pain flashing across her eyes.

Her opponent threw himself clumsily on top of her, wrapping his hands around her throat and squeezing.

The blood dripped from his face onto hers.

She gasped for breath.

He didn't stop squeezing.

Karam had killed before, man and demon both, but this fight was supposed to be to the yield. Yet she could tell with one look in his eyes that her opponent wouldn't let her go.

He was going to kill her and the crowd would cheer for it.

Karam ran her hands up her leg.

It felt like with one more second he might rip her head clean from her body, but she knew better than to try to pry his hands off. That would waste time and breath, and she wasn't strong enough to loosen the hold of such a beast.

Instead, Karam pushed aside the material on her leg and clutched her hands around the hidden hilt.

A weapon, ready for an occasion like this.

In one swift movement, she brought her knife up and plunged it into his side.

Her opponent stilled.

Karam twisted the knife.

When he made an awful choking noise, she pulled out the blade and slid it into his back.

His hands finally went loose around her neck.

Heaving, Karam rolled him off her. Then she turned with her back still flat on the floor and watched him gasp.

The crowd exploded into cheers because they knew, as Karam did, that the amityguards would not come to the Crook. There would be no punishment or retribution. What did the law matter when there could be anarchy instead?

The man's blood puddled toward Karam's fingertips and she forced herself to her knees before it stained the rest of her.

She knelt over him and said a Wrenyi prayer in the back of her mind. Not for the man, but for the girl. The one she had been when she'd first come to this realm, who cowered at shadows and cried for a family she'd never see again. A girl who grew up wanting to be a warrior, vowing alongside her best friend to topple Kingpins and revive the Rekhi d'Rihsni.

A small part of Karam wished she felt guilt or shame for the way things were now, but it was too late. Too much had happened. She wasn't that girl and this wasn't Granka.

Karam pulled the knife from her opponent's back and wiped the blood onto her trousers.

This was Creije and it was kill or be killed.

KARAM STOOD with her feet shoulder width apart and took a slow sip from the dregs of her water bottle as the last hums of Creije settled into the dark.

Since her fight finished, she had been guarding the door to Wesley's office for exactly three hours and forty-eight minutes, and she was starting to get bored.

But luckily for Karam, she had enough practice killing to know how to kill time.

She pictured Saxony leaning lazily on the wall opposite, legs crossed at the ankles, hair slinking over her shoulder and a dress with geometrical holes clinched tightly over her rounded waist.

Karam sighed.

She needed to stop obsessing over the fact that Saxony hadn't shown up, and wondering what it meant. If Saxony was truly over her and if it was just Karam, still lingering behind, holding on to feelings she should have dismantled months ago.

She needed a distraction.

"Where is he?"

Tavia Syn stepped into the narrow hallway, silver dusters spread across her pale fists. Her boots were half razor blades and her short black hair shielded the top of her eyes like a cloak.

It was a shame she didn't know the first thing about how to fight, because she sure looked the part.

"The underboss is busy," Karam said.

"Busy doing what?"

Karam shrugged.

She wasn't interested in Wesley's dirty dealings. Whatever secrets he had, he could keep them to himself. He'd earned that right.

After all, it was Wesley who saw the potential in Karam when she'd first come to Creije and fought in back-alley rings. He convinced the old underboss to give her a chance tending door and when Wesley became underboss himself, he kept her on as his personal guard, bringing her with him to the top. She owed him more than she cared to admit.

Tavia snarled and crossed the hall in twelve pounding steps.

She seemed to be favoring her left leg, the ankle of her right barely touching the floor without a grimace. Her sleeves were rolled up and there were new bruises swatching up her white arms like a watercolor.

Tavia really did not know how to fight.

Karam flattened her hand against the wall. "Come back with an appointment."

Tavia glared, which Karam did not find intimidating.

The problem was, that for all of her black magic and even blacker lipstick, Tavia had the unfortunate problem of being infamously moral. And morality in Creije was not something to be frightened of.

"Move," Tavia said.

"Leave," Karam said back.

She was getting a little sick of Tavia using her easy rapport with Wesley to get her way.

She thought it made her an exception to the rules.

It did not.

So, Tavia did what anyone who made a living with sleight of hand would do, which was to shove Karam to one side and make for the door.

And Karam did what anyone who made a living punching people would do, which was to punch Tavia right in the face.

The busker spun from the blow, palms bracing against the wall for support. She heaved in a breath and tried to steady herself. Her back remained to Karam, obscuring any chance for her to survey the damage she had done.

A black eye, probably, to go with the lipstick Tavia was pulling out of her pocket.

Karam frowned as Tavia popped the cap and lifted a shaky hand to her face.

When she smacked her newly painted lips together, the sound was unreasonably loud.

"I don't have time for this," Tavia said. "You're going to regret trying to stop me."

Hei reb, she was such a makeshift warrior, with pocketknives up her sleeves and slits across her nail beds. A street kid with a chip on her shoulder, ready to take on the world.

Karam tried to hold her temper.

Saxony would be very angry if she killed her best friend.

"You cannot be threatening me," Karam said. "So I will assume I knocked the sense out of you."

There was a bruise already forming across Tavia's cheek. She lifted her lips into a callous smile and said, "When I take you down, it'll be the best night's sleep you've had in ages. You might even thank me for it."

Karam almost laughed. "And then Wesley would kill you in my place," she said. "We both know his soul is as dark as they come."

Tavia closed the gap between them. "Wesley Thornton Walcott doesn't have a soul," she said.

And then Tavia kissed her.

Karam practically threw her across the room, spitting as Tavia ricocheted off the walls.

Insane, Karam thought.

Tavia had gone insane and Karam was going to have to kill her for it.

Right after she rinsed out her mouth.

Twice.

Karam took a step forward, wiping her lips furiously on her sleeve.

Then she stumbled.

Her legs were suddenly shaky and unsteady beneath her. Too heavy to lift off the ground.

"Try not to fight it," Tavia said. "Saxony would kill me if you got hurt because of this."

Tavia looked like she was frowning, but Karam couldn't quite see. The room blurred, then focused, then spun until it distorted again.

Karam felt her pulse slow and when she tried to look at her surroundings or shake her head and piece together the multiple distortions of Tavia, her eyes started to close.

She brought a heavy hand to her mouth.

A smudge of lipstick inked across her thumb.

Gray magic. Black magic.

Opposite her, Tavia pocketed the lipstick with a wistful sigh.

"You are so dead," Karam said.

And then she was down.

7

Tavia

TAVIA WIPED THE LIPSTICK onto her sleeve and stepped over Karam's body, throwing open the curtain that hid the door to Wesley's office. She pressed her palm to it and though the black glass hesitated a little, perhaps sensing her anger, eventually it slid slowly back.

The first thing Tavia saw was Wesley perched on the edge of his desk with a collection of papers scrunched in his palm and a frown deep in his brow.

And then blood.

There was a knife on Wesley's desk and Tavia knew without a doubt that he had done something awful with it. He had that all-too-familiar look on his face, like it had been really inconvenient for him to have to stand up in order to stab someone. Or maybe it was going to be inconvenient for him to have to clean the blood off his carpet later.

Wesley adjusted the bow tie clutching his throat. He

frowned at the new bruises that snaked down Tavia's body, but when his eyes met hers, for the briefest of seconds, it was enough to let her know that he didn't appreciate how she hadn't knocked.

"I need your help," Tavia said.

Wesley sighed, but it wasn't at her. He was ignoring her completely now, and it was only when his focus shifted that Tavia noticed a second man in the room.

Falk.

Creije's resident expert on magical weaponry and a thorn in every busker's side. It was hard to know who to trust in Creije, but easier to know who not to, and Falk was a damn dirty snitch. The eyes and ears for the underboss and anyone else who would slip him a coin.

Wesley's little weasel.

Well past the point of aging out from his debt, Falk was on the right track to living his whole life in the arms of the Crook, graduating from tipster to whatever was next in a line of jobs that served as a middle ground before becoming an underboss.

Wesley's shoe shiner, perhaps.

"I need those barrels to be ready now," Wesley said.

Falk nodded. "I know what you asked, but—"

"Oh," Wesley said. Then, again, as if something had just dawned on him, "*Oh*. Well, there's our problem. You thought I was asking."

Wesley picked up a letter opener from his desk. It gleamed in his hand. "If you can't follow a simple order, Falk, then I'll find someone who can."

Tavia didn't need to see Falk's face to know that his lips were trembling.

Her hands slid to fists.

She didn't have time for this.

She pictured the mark on that man's neck again. The mark on *Saxony's* neck. The one she'd seen so often in her mind, in the dreams of her muma. Seeing it in the flesh twice in one day almost felt like a dream too, but Tavia knew better than to hope for that.

She knew Saxony was in danger and she'd be damned if she was just going to stand around and do nothing.

"*Wesley*." Tavia basically spat his name.

He turned to her as if he had forgotten she was still there at all, and Tavia spotted something cold in his eyes, right in the corner, a thing she couldn't place. But then he blinked it away and gave her his usual catlike smile.

"You look like you're having a good day," he said. "You didn't kill Karam to get in here, did you? I don't have time to find a new guard."

Tavia glared.

She was losing patience by the second.

She knew the despair was written on her face and Wesley could see it.

There was no way he couldn't see it.

"Falk," Wesley said, as if sensing her ebbing patience. "Would you excuse us?"

His weasel didn't need to be asked twice.

Falk practically jumped from the chair, nodding as he backed out of the room, keeping his eyes on Wesley and the letter opener that swirled between his fingers.

When he reached the door, he shot Tavia a look that was far too smug for someone who had nearly pissed their pants at the sight of stationery just moments before.

The door clicked shut behind him, the handle grazing Tavia's back.

She kept her eyes on Wesley.

"I need your help," she said again, stepping toward him.

"Yes," Wesley said. "I heard you."

The fire charm she'd won from Saxony burned against her ribs, and though Tavia kept it hidden in her jacket lining, Wesley's gaze flicked toward it, like he could sense the magic somehow.

"Saxony's in trouble," Tavia said. "The amityguards came for us and after the way she was acting, I don't even know if she's alive."

"Is that all?" Wesley shoved his hands into his pockets with a small sigh. "I thought something serious had happened."

Without hesitating, Tavia threw the fire charm.

Quickly, Wesley twisted and it glided past him, hitting the painting behind his desk.

He watched the embers crackle with a frown. "I liked that picture," he said.

Such a bastard.

Tavia pulled a knife from each of her boots, but Wesley only leaned back onto his desk. The painting blazed behind him.

"I'm going to go out on a limb and say you're not in the mood to talk," he said.

"Everything you say is a lie anyway."

"And I thought you wanted my help. Odd way to ask for it."

Tavia narrowed her eyes.

She twirled the knives in her hands and, angry as she was, felt a spark of relief when she didn't drop them.

She couldn't believe he was acting so indifferent when she'd just told him Saxony's life was on the line. She couldn't believe how much he'd changed from the friend she knew. It didn't seem possible for someone to turn themselves so inside out like that.

It was as though Wesley had killed the old underboss then, boom, *like magic*, the boy she knew disappeared and something else was born.

Or maybe Tavia had it wrong.

Maybe the boy was the illusion all along.

"Just so we're clear," Wesley said. "I'm not your little gofer. I'm your underboss and I have a city to run. Playing hero to your friends isn't my priority right now."

"You're right," Tavia said, knives primed. "I'm not in the mood to talk."

She surged forward, ready to take Wesley to the amity precinct by force if she had to, because there was no way she was leaving Saxony to suffer in a cell like Deniel Emilsson.

But when Wesley met her it was not with any weapons of his own.

It only took him a second to fling an arm through the air and send a wave of magic toward her.

In one fluid motion, Tavia's knifed hands were knocked back.

She stumbled, seethed, and then lurched toward him again.

Wesley snapped out his hands and Tavia couldn't move fast enough. A burst of energy grabbed hold of her, an invisible force wrapped around her arms like a clamp, squeezing down with enough force to make her want to scream.

Tavia twirled out, pulling free of the magic and throwing both of her knives before she'd completed the turn. They landed with a clatter by Wesley's feet and in the second he frowned down at them, Tavia pounced.

She threw a punch, but Wesley moved easily out of the way, grabbing her wrist and twisting until it felt like her knees might buckle.

"Stop," he said.

Tavia struggled against him. "Let go of me and I will."

"For some reason, I'm having a hard time trusting you."

Tavia sneered and threw her head back.

She felt the crack when it connected with Wesley's nose. Felt his blood spurt onto the back of her neck.

Wesley dropped her arm, pressing a hand to his face.

Tavia punched through the air, but Wesley was still too damn quick, even with blood dripping onto his lips and his eyes in a half squint as he tried to blink away the shock.

He shoved her back, hard, then advanced. Reaching out, he grabbed Tavia by the collar, and when she made to kick free, her legs froze underneath her. There was that magic again. Squeezing and crushing and pinning her in place.

It was just like when they sparred as kids, trying out new charms and new techniques.

Wesley always bested her, ready for any attack she might try, no matter how underhand. Tavia didn't know why she was surprised that things hadn't changed.

After all, Wesley taught her everything she knew.

She was only the best in the game because he stopped playing.

For what felt like minutes, Wesley's hands stayed wrapped around her collar, his face inches from hers. Until finally he let out a breath, swore, and shoved her back.

Wesley walked slowly to his desk and pulled a handkerchief out from the pocket of his suit, pressing it to his nose. The flames still crackled behind him.

He closed his eyes, breathed out a terse sigh, and then slammed his palms against the desk.

The fire spluttered and died.

"I want you to be honest with me for once," Tavia said, catching her breath.

Her voice was as low as his had been and she tried not to look at the blood on his face.

"No more lies. Just tell me straight."

Wesley slammed his hands on the desk again. When he looked up at her, his eyes were almost black. "Tell you what?"

For the first time in years, his accent lost the careful decorum he always tried so hard to maintain and a small slip of the old street kid reared its head.

Tavia ignored it. No good ever came from being sentimental.

"Saxony took that elixir you gave me," she said. "Did you know how dangerous it was?"

Wesley paused, just for a moment, before running the handkerchief under his nose.

The blood had already started to dry.

"I can't believe you came in here ready to start a war because your punk friend took something that didn't belong to her."

"You told me I was selling happiness! You lied to me."

Wesley straightened. "I've never lied to you."

When he said it, it was like he almost believed it was true. As though he thought that by ignoring the obvious, it made him less culpable. Maybe the Kingpin fed him a story, but Wesley, knowing full well that it was just that, had eaten it up. And then he'd fed the same poison to Tavia.

Telling her it wasn't a lie was a technicality at best.

"You're the Kingpin's golden boy, Wesley."

His eyes twitched to a narrow.

"He's up to something," Tavia said. "Are you really going to tell me that he didn't let you in on it?"

Wesley's lips curled. "I never told you to give that magic to your pals," he said. He folded the bloodied handkerchief back into a neat triangle and pocketed it. "You should have listened to me."

Tavia resisted the urge to throw another fire charm at his face.

"This isn't a game, Wesley. My mother—"

Tavia paused and Wesley frowned.

She hadn't spoken about her muma in years, and even then it had barely been a few words, a few tears, a few awful, gulping memories. It felt odd to talk about it now.

"Your mother what?" Wesley asked.

Tavia swallowed down the shakiness that threatened to take hold of her voice.

"It's the magic sickness," she said. "It's back."

There hadn't been a case for so long, Tavia had almost managed to forget about it.

The magic sickness had been ripe when she was a kid, with outbreaks spread across Uskhanya, back when it was practice to use magic to purify the water supply in neglected outskirts of the realm. It was a type of poisoning that tended to happen when you had too much magic in your system and the people on the wrong side of the bridge had bathed in it and used it to wash their food.

Some cases weren't so bad, a few headaches and nosebleeds if they were lucky, but once the mark appeared there was no going back. You couldn't stop a magical overdose with more magic.

There was no cure.

No way to be saved.

It shut you down, piece by piece.

That man in the cells was going to die because of something Tavia had given him and if Saxony died too, Tavia wasn't sure what she'd do.

Wesley blinked, but that was all.

Nothing flickered on his face, let alone surprise.

"What happened when Saxony took the elixir?" he asked.

"She went berserk," Tavia said. "Throwing magic like she wanted to kill me and talking about voices in her head. And there was a man I gave it to earlier, saying the same thing. He's in the cells right now with that damn mark on his neck. The elixir got in their heads and you can take a lot of things, Wesley, but not someone's mind. You can't steal that. You can't sell that."

Wesley's jaw ticked. "I told you I didn't," he said. "Are you sure that you saw the mark?"

"I'd recognize it anywhere," Tavia said. "And it only took one vial for them to be afflicted. That's how potent it is, so for all I know, Saxony is dying in a cell somewhere."

Wesley's lips parted, ever so slightly, and Tavia caught the dimple in his brow before he righted himself, smoothing his features into complacency. Then he took in a breath and made to move forward, a fraction of an inch, before he stopped that, too.

Wesley did nothing. He said nothing.

Tavia wasn't sure why she ever expected any different.

"Saxony isn't a crook," she said. "She doesn't deserve this."

Wesley's face remained blank and he stayed very, very still.

"Of course she doesn't," he said. "Bad things only happen to good people."

Tavia could almost swear she heard a sigh lingering on the words, and it made her want to hate him. Truthfully, she always wanted to hate him, but in that moment the urge felt stronger than usual. Wesley didn't have friends or family, and how stupid she was to believe that she could have been either to him.

"I have to know if Saxony is okay," Tavia said. "I need to know what happened to her and if you won't help me then I'll just do it myself. I'll burn the amity precinct to the ground to get her out."

Tavia turned, her coat swooping like wind on her back, but there was barely time to take a step forward before Wesley was pulling her back toward him, quicker than any sleight of hand.

Tavia looked down at her wrist, which was caught precariously in his fingers.

Wesley stared at her with cool, assessing eyes, and she watched him for any kind of a sign. A twitch in his jaw or the slow bob of his throat as he swallowed down the dryness she could feel tacking her own mouth.

Guilt or a sense of responsibility for what he had just learned.

As usual, there was nothing.

Wesley was the kind of book that never opened.

Once, he was just a kid, just a busker like her. They grew up on the same tricks and crafted cons together, and even when Wesley caught the eye of the old underboss and it became clear he was on the path to being a career criminal, Tavia entertained the notion that they would always be friends. Family. That there would always be some deeply hidden morality behind the coconut shell of his eyes. But then Wesley left her on his way to the top and Tavia quickly realized that his eyes weren't flecked with coconut shells at all.

It was only dirt, splattered back from the graves he dug in the Kingpin's name.

Slowly, Tavia removed Wesley's hand from her wrist.

He stared at her for a moment and then slid his hand indifferently into his pocket.

"Threats are like promises," Wesley said. "Don't make the ones you can't keep."

"I'm not going to leave Saxony to die."

Wesley sighed and his tattoo bobbed alongside his throat.

Tavia pictured the thick lines slotting down to his fingertips, leaking onto his chest and around the scars on his shoulder. The buildings and streets of Creije, covering half of his dark skin in ink. She remembered being there when he got that tattoo, both of them just kids, watching the city being built onto his back.

"Fine. Have it your way," Wesley said. "We'll go save your little friend."

Because apparently neither of them was quite ready to cut the last, fraying thread of friendship that still dangled between them.

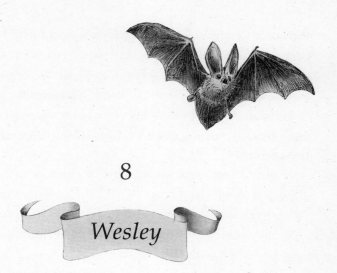

8

Wesley

WESLEY DIDN'T LIKE PEOPLE, on account of them always trying to kill him. Which made rescuing someone he knew wanted to kill him feel a little odd. Saxony may have been Tavia's friend, but she was no fan of his.

The day ebbed and night slipped across the sky in a sudden blanket. Wesley liked the city most this way: not quite bright enough to cast light on the misdeeds and miscreants. He liked that it became the perfect haven for all the wonderful and awful things to gather.

Wesley looked up at the amity precinct, which was probably one of the most depressing buildings in Creije. It was painted yellow, or had been some time ago, and now it peeled off the outer walls, cracking like wrinkles around the windowpane and toward the slow steep of the roof.

It was on the wrong side of the bridge that separated the city, where the dreamers steered clear and the sky outside was the color of an old knife wound. This was a place no tourist ever went, because the crease of dead streets on this side of the city were aglow in darkness, even when the sun tiptoed across, save for the flickers of magic and cigarette lights.

You didn't want to walk many places across the bridge after dark, but if you were going to, then it was best to stay out of the creases.

A group of amityguards hung by the entrance to the precinct, glaring at Wesley not so subtly. Their hands hovered by the sedation charms on their belts.

Wesley turned to Tavia, the walls in his mind higher than ever, guarded against his ghost.

"Keep your head down and let me do the talking," he said.

Tavia rolled her eyes and pushed past him, plowing ahead as though Wesley hadn't spoken at all.

Many Gods forbid she actually listened to him for a change.

When they entered the precinct, it was as though time stopped. Every amityguard looked up from their desks, or paused mid-walk to wherever they were headed, like they could sense the specific brand of trouble that had just walked in and were not at all welcoming of it.

"What was that you said about keeping our heads down?" Tavia asked. "Because if looks could kill . . ."

Wesley adjusted his lapels. "Nothing wrong with making an entrance."

Which was usually true, but in this case Wesley wasn't quite sure having the eyes of every amityguard in Creije focused on him was a good thing.

Still, as an underboss, it was Wesley's duty to make sure

the law and those who broke it were in harmony, and he had lined the pockets of enough amityguards in Creije to make this all go smoothly.

They may have hated him, but they were also flush because of him.

"Oh, look," a voice said. "It's the prodigal young underboss."

The man, who was far too soft-spoken to be in the dregs of the amity precinct, stepped forward and gave Wesley an uppity grin.

There were not many things that surprised Wesley—least of all people, who tended to be the easiest to predict—and Wesley's legion of spies and snitches had made it so there was rarely a secret in Creije he didn't know. So Wesley was caught a little off guard to find the Vice Doyen of the realm standing in front of him, a bodyguard in tow.

"We've been expecting you, Mr. Thornton Walcott," Vice Doyen Krause said.

"That would explain the warm welcome."

"Oh, I assure you we're all honored to finally meet the underboss of Creije."

Wesley smartened his tie. "Alleged underboss. I'm only here to pick someone up. I didn't realize I'd have such esteemed company."

Krause pushed his glasses up his nose. "If only I could say the same."

The high tilt of his chin did nothing to make Wesley fond of him.

Armin Krause was a clear politician through and through, and not just because of his woeful suit. He had a look about him, like he'd never gone through anything awful, and all the evils of the realms were things he'd witnessed secondhand, through people he'd never met and would never know, but he did offer his *dearest sympathies* to them all.

"Saxony works at the Crook," Wesley said. "She's my employee and I'd like her back."

"I thought you might," Krause said. "But she's still in the medical wing recovering from her little *spell*."

He seemed to think the pun was amusing.

"So she's going to be okay?" Tavia asked. "The magic sickness didn't—"

Krause held up a hand. "She's unconscious, but fine. The affliction was only minor and the magic sickness did not spread, despite the mark's appearance. A couple of days' rest and all will be well."

Tavia heaved a sigh of relief. "I need to see her."

"I'm afraid that's not possible. I'm under strict commands from Doyen Schulze to keep all cases of magic sickness under quarantine until symptoms subside."

"It's not contagious," Wesley said, though Krause already knew that.

"Precautions are always necessary when it comes to black magic."

Tavia stepped forward and Wesley's eyes drew to the knives he knew were hidden amongst the various pockets and slits in her clothes.

"I want to see my friend," she said. "And you don't get to stop me just because you're wearing a nice tie."

Wesley did not think it was a nice tie.

Krause's bodyguard shifted and his hand inched too close to his belt for Wesley's liking.

"Back off, busker," the guard sneered.

Tavia glared over to him and made to say something in retort, probably something that would get her thrown in a cell and put an end to this newly intriguing conversation.

Wesley stepped in front of her.

"Tell me," he said, taking in the lines of Krause's suit. "Is the Realm Doyen here too?"

Though Wesley had yet to meet Fenna Schulze in person, it wasn't for lack of wanting.

She was making quite a reputation for herself, giving speeches at rallies opposing dark magic and starting programs for addicts. There was graffiti of her throughout Uskhanya, with her hands raised devoutly and the words *Schulze for a brighter realm* underneath. She'd set up rewards for information leading to the arrests of underbosses and banks where people could hand in their dark charms, no questions asked.

Since her election, Doyen Fenna Schulze was on a mission to put an end to Wesley's business. Which made this whole situation a little interesting.

"Doyen Schulze is still in Yejlath," Krause said.

It was one of Uskhanya's smaller central cities, where the Halls of Government stood tall and laws were passed rather than broken. All of the officials worked there and most lived in the city too, making it swell in politicians and stiff upper lips.

Wesley felt a little bad for Greta, Yejlath's underboss. She must have had a hard job sticking to the shadows with such well-lit streets to find her.

"The Doyen is far too busy to waste time looking into all of your magic victims," Krause said.

"And yet you're not."

Krause's eyes narrowed ever so slightly and Wesley couldn't help but smile.

"I find it strange that she'd send her second in command here for something so trivial."

And by strange, Wesley also meant irritating. He didn't like being the last to know things. In fact, he didn't like not being the very first to know everything, especially when those things were happening in his city.

"You are not getting the girl back," Krause said. "She'll be penalized under the full extent of the law for breaking the dark magic code."

"She's hurt," Tavia said. "You can't keep her locked away."

Krause propped his chin up. "Actually, I can do whatever I want."

He shot Tavia a smug little smile that made Wesley's jaw clench, but this was not the time for anger; it was the time for opportunity.

"How about I offer you a trade?" Wesley said.

"You have nothing I want, underboss."

Wesley stepped close enough to Krause so that only a whisper could be heard between them.

"That's not entirely true," he said.

The bodyguard swallowed nervously, but he didn't make a play for his weapon, or even pretend to. Krause may have been a Vice Doyen, but Wesley was an underboss and Creije was *his* city.

"You give me what I want," Wesley said, voice low and calm. "And I'll give you Dante Ashwood on a platter."

WESLEY HAD never been in an interrogation room before and he felt a little ashamed of that. It seemed like a necessary step on the road to becoming underboss that he had skipped.

Still, part of him was also grateful, because the room was all cold grays and dirty concrete and the distinct aroma of stale coffee lingered.

"This is really the only private place we can talk?" Wesley asked. He tapped the metallic chair. "I was at least expecting cushions, considering how lucrative my offer was."

Tavia kicked her feet up onto the table. "I feel right at home," she said.

Krause took his glasses off and polished them with a crisp white handkerchief. Perhaps to try to get rid of the sight of an underboss and a busker, sitting smugly without restraints in front of him. Or maybe he just didn't want to look at the mud on Tavia's boots.

"You said you wanted no prying eyes," Krause said. "I apologize for not being able to prepare a banquet."

"Apology accepted," Wesley said.

Krause's sigh was sharp. "I'd appreciate it if you didn't insult my intelligence with this charade any longer."

"It's not a charade," Wesley said. "The Kingpin has brand-new magic. That's what made Saxony sick."

Tavia turned to Wesley with wide eyes—she looked paler then usual—but it was Krause who spoke first.

"Yes," he said. "We know. She is not the first case."

Now *that* was interesting.

"So Schulze sent you to Creije to monitor the situation," Wesley said.

Tavia stood and let out a choked laugh. "Okay, let's go back a minute. There's no such thing as new magic."

And she was right, in a way.

There was only one race of people who could alter the laws of nature and craft new magic, spinning words into spells and sun into storms.

And they were all supposed to be gone.

There hadn't been new magic, or Crafters, on the streets in over fifty years for one reason: the War of Ages. A bloody uprising that saw the only magic left behind was the same old junk that had already been made, recycling its way around the realms in different packaging.

It was why magic held such fascination and cachet, because at any moment it could all be gone.

"Be realistic," Tavia said. "You're saying that Ashwood found a Crafter hiding under a rock somewhere?"

"The realms are a big place," Wesley said. "Plenty of rocks."

Tavia's jaw dropped. "And you *knew* about this?"

Wesley could almost feel Tavia's teeth gritting together.

She doesn't understand. She could never understand.

Wesley pressed down onto his cuff links, to try and shut the voice out. His shirt looked stark against his skin.

Krause eyed him curiously.

"I knew Ashwood was up to something," Wesley said. He tried to level his voice, but it was about as smooth as the teeth of a blade. "And now I know what. He'll destroy the city with this new magic if we let him. Ashwood sees Doyen Schulze's campaigns against dark magic as an attack and he's preparing to fight."

Krause shuffled in his seat and though he was trying to hide his shock, the rigid and unblinking stare on his face told another story.

Everyone knew Ashwood was evil, but apparently the politicians of the realm didn't think he was reckless enough to directly attack a Doyen. Which meant that they didn't really know Ashwood at all.

Not like Wesley did.

"We can deal with Ashwood ourselves," Krause said, but he was blustering so obviously that Wesley let the words hang between them for a moment.

He waited, placing a clover breezily into his mouth, watching for Krause to grow more anxious.

The magic the leaf held was loose, barely there at all, and a person would be stretched to get ten minutes of luck out of it, but Wesley had always liked the taste. The tang of bitter lemon. He'd practically grown up on them. Though as he thought that he realized what a strange thing it was, to say he'd grown up on something, as if people were plants, climbing and clambering to whatever they could to survive, unable to grow without a steady constant.

Wesley never much liked constants. They didn't afford surprise or interest and they were dangerous enough to trap people inside the ordinary.

Except for Creije. That was the only constant he needed.

Krause shifted and when Wesley sensed the Vice Doyen's nerves at a peak, he finally spoke.

"Bullshit. You need me. You don't have a choice."

Krause's nostrils flared.

"The Kingpin's consort is the only one who knows where he is and I'm the only one who knows where the consort is," Wesley said. "I'm also the only one who has access to that consort. I'm the only one Ashwood trusts. And I'm clearly the only one in this room with half a brain."

"Hey," Tavia said. "Watch it."

"You've tried to take Ashwood down for years," Wesley said to Krause. "And his magic is stronger than ever. Exploiting Crafters was illegal even before the war, but all those fancy new laws the realms put in place to protect them afterward? He's ignoring those too. You don't have a choice but to work with me."

"And what would you get out of it?" Krause asked. "Why would you turn against him?"

The answer to that was simple: because Creije was Wesley's home and he had spent too long building it up just to watch it be torn down.

It was the wonder of Northern Uskhanya, with cobblestones that glistened silver with stray magic dust, and there was no feeling to match the one Wesley had when he took this place and made it his own.

The Kingpin stole so many things, mostly lives, and Wesley stood by and watched it happen. He helped it happen time and again. But this was Wesley's home and it was all he had. He traded money and magic and his damn humanity for it.

Sometimes, Wesley thought that he wasn't just born in Creije, but that he was made from it. The best and the worst parts of the city, taken shape and molded to create the man he had become.

Wesley would never let Ashwood take that from him.

He'd never let the old man's tyranny rip it apart.

"I guess I'm feeling philanthropic," Wesley said.

Krause's laugh was dry. "With Ashwood gone, there would be no need for underbosses. You would be shooting yourself in the foot."

The thought had crossed Wesley's mind.

Doyen Schulze wanted black magic out of Uskhanya and she wanted Dante Ashwood gone as much as Wesley, but there was always the chance her crusade was about more.

It was black magic now, but what if tomorrow it was all magic?

Schulze was making everyone a little paranoid, doubting what magic was right and what had the potential to be wrong. She made the streets safer and that garnered her a strange kind of devotion, which made Wesley worry if her true endgame was to turn Uskhanya into some kind of scholarly realm like Naustrio, where magic was looked down upon in favor of science and technology. He didn't think he could live in that sort of a world.

Wesley slipped his hands into his pockets. A sign that what he said next, this part of his proposal, didn't need a handshake. It was nonnegotiable. The only way to protect Creije for good and keep it as filled with wonder as it was now.

Ever my clever boy, his ghost cooed.

"I want your word," Wesley said. "That when I take down Ashwood, I get to be Kingpin."

Tavia stiffened beside him. Wesley forced himself not to look at her.

"Why would we trade one crook for another?" Krause asked.

"I'm the lesser evil," Wesley said with a shrug. "And I'm willing to negotiate terms for dark-magic-free cities. I'll lessen the hold if Schulze lessens her crusade and allows more magic to be legalized in the realm. She can play ball, just like the other Doyens do and pretend not to."

Krause sat back in his chair with a long breath.

All Wesley needed was a green light. No amityguards on his tail and no pesky legal repercussions for whatever happened once he started on this path. Just some supplies and whatever was sharpest enough to cut through red tape, before the Kingpin's elixir spread across the streets and turned them to ash.

Krause seemed to be debating it, but as far as Wesley was concerned, the officials didn't have the smarts or the connections to take Ashwood down and they weren't prepared for what evil would await them, no matter how much their bravado tried to convince them otherwise.

But Wesley was.

He knew Ashwood and what he was capable of, and that made Wesley uniquely placed to put an end to it all.

"Okay, Mr. Thornton Walcott." Krause leaned forward. He folded his hands together. "I'll speak to Doyen Schulze and see if I can get her to sign off on this little agreement, but we won't provide an underboss with an army. It would be a political nightmare, especially if we were to lose or you were to betray us and enthrall the soldiers somehow. This would be strictly under the table. Your people and your fight."

Wesley nodded. "Obviously."

"Then for all intents and purposes, I believe we have deal," Krause said. "You kill Dante Ashwood and put a stop to his new magic and we'll let you take his place."

He held out his hand and Wesley took it with a slow and wordless smile.

He felt the ghost in his mind look on, thrilled and eager.

So much blood to look forward to.

Wesley kept hold of Krause's hand and pushed her to the corner of his mind, far from this moment.

He wondered, he hoped, that if he killed the Kingpin, she might just go away for good.

9

Saxony

SAXONY AKINTOLA DIDN'T USE her real name when she worked at the Crook, which meant that the only time she ever heard it was when she spoke to her family back in Rishiya and—if it was her father—lied about how moving to Creije was the best thing she could have done, because she was earning big coin and damn if those folks at work didn't treat her good.

All other instances were either from Tavia, who said it with a busker's grin, or Karam, under the guise of sweet nothings. But Saxony winced enough times when Karam said it—because she hated how delicate her voice was then, like just being together smoothed out any rough edges Karam had, which Saxony very much liked her having, because rough edges kept people safe in Creije—that Karam stopped after a while.

Now Karam avoided calling her anything. Not even pet

names, which Saxony would have quite liked. And never her Crook name, which Saxony would have quite hated.

She avoided eye contact too, but that was another story.

So Saxony went by Brandy to everyone else, because that was what a lot of folks liked to drink and she found it a sturdy way to ensure tips, if every time someone ordered at the bar she came strolling over.

Also, because House Wine was taken.

This meant that Saxony had never heard her true name being said so many times, in such close succession, as she had on this day.

Saxony, are you okay? Can you hear me?

Saxony, let me help you.

Saxony, have some water.

Saxony, lay down and rest.

She loved Tavia, truly, and she was grateful to be out of the amity precinct and back home, but she was also more than a little glad when Tavia finally left and allowed her to get some peace.

Especially since Wesley had also been there, helping Saxony inside, then lurking in the corner as though he didn't know how to act like a human in place of an underboss.

Saxony sprawled across the sofa and rubbed her head.

She'd healed her wounds some, but there was still a pounding in the back of her skull that hadn't disappeared since she'd woken up in the amity precinct.

It was starting to grate and it was why Saxony had barely moved in the few hours since.

With a sigh, she cradled the crystal ball in her hand and from the dim glow, her grandma stared up at her.

Saxony's amja was old enough to have lived through the War of Ages, her scars mixed with the wrinkles and a smile that seemed a little sad in the light of day. Her hair was a wonderful dark steel against her skin, and her eyes were nearly the same color, polished by magic, gleaming with a thousand stories.

She was Saxony's favorite person in the world and the only piece of her mother she had left.

"There must be more," Amja said.

"There isn't." Saxony winced as the pounding in her head increased. "I'm doing all I can, Amja. I swear it."

"But it isn't enough."

Amja's voice was strained and though she didn't intend to be mean, though Saxony knew it was the fear talking, her words still cut like an allegation.

"You have been in Creije for so long," Amja said. "Sometimes I worry that you have become blinded. Sometimes it feels like we lost you when we lost Zekia."

Saxony's heart pounded at the mention of her little sister.

Zekia had disappeared three long years ago and it had been the catalyst for everything that followed. The very reason Saxony came to Creije. She had been noble then, at least somewhat, and innocent in a way the city hadn't let her be since.

Saxony had only wanted to find her lost sister and put together the broken pieces of her family, but she ended up staying for revenge and desperation.

To spy on the underboss.

To find out all she could about Dante Ashwood and his weaknesses.

To make sure the magic trade could never hurt her family again.

It was Saxony's mission to keep an ear to the ground and protect her people from afar, watching as the crooks killed and betrayed each other.

It was fine if they did, preferred even, as long as *her* people were safe.

Perhaps everyone else had forgotten and moved on after the war, going back to whatever lives they could salvage from the wreckage of battle. They rebuilt and spoke of the past only in distant memory, like it was a bad dream and something that could never happen in their reality.

But those people weren't Crafters.

They had not spent fifty years in the shadows.

The old Kins still remembered. Saxony's family still remembered, and their fight wasn't over.

"I'm sending tips to Schulze's amityguards," Saxony said. "They're pulling buskers off the streets, just like they did with me. The whole thing has Wesley's back up and if Wesley's back is up, that means the Kingpin's is too."

"You must be careful," Amja said. "If Dante Ashwood and his underboss discover who you are, then you will be in great danger."

"I'm always careful," Saxony said.

And it was true, in a way.

Saxony was careful to trust only Karam with her secret and nobody else, because Karam was a warrior whose ancient bloodline had always protected hers. And, after it became clear that Karam pulled too much of Saxony's focus on her mission, she was careful to keep her at a distance. The distance wasn't great, because Karam was still Karam and being too far from her got painful, but Saxony tried.

She was also careful to time her tips to the amityguards rigidly, making sure Tavia was never out on those nights, or that if she was, the reports were for buskers at the other end of the city.

Saxony was careful every day with everything, and everyone, but herself.

"Tell me more about the elixir," Amja said.

"It was odd," Saxony said, because she couldn't think of another way to describe it. "I can't put my finger on what was so strange, but it was different from anything I've felt before. There were voices inside my head, Amja, telling me to do awful things. I've heard rumblings that it could be new magic."

Saxony didn't dare tell her that those rumblings were from Tavia.

She had never, in the three years she had lived in Creije, mentioned her friend's name. Amja could never know that Saxony cared for someone who sold dark magic and flirted with the lines of good and not-so-good. Saxony wasn't sure what Amja would do with that information and she didn't want to find out.

Just like Saxony hadn't told Tavia that she wasn't just some girl who worked at the Crook, following Wesley's every order, but a true Crafter, hiding in plain sight and watching over the crooks of Creije, biding her time for war to come again.

Many Gods knew how Tavia would react to that.

Saxony was lying to just about everyone and it was getting her just about nowhere.

"If the elixir Ashwood has is new magic, then we are doomed," Amja said. "If he is collecting Crafters again, we will never be safe."

Saxony didn't want to think about it, but the idea that the War of Ages had been for nothing, that the suffering her amja and countless other Kins had endured was pointless, felt too awful to ignore.

It had been fifty years since the underrealm trade organized itself into an enterprise, with the most powerful crooks sectioning off pieces to command, hoarding Crafters like trophies. Since they became Kingpins that the Doyens and their laws were powerless to stop.

War was the only way.

A great battle had spread across the four realms, even the non-magical Naustrio, with Crafters rising up and declaring war on the criminals who sought to exploit them. It was a fight that drove Saxony's people to ruin.

Those of her kind who survived vowed to stay in the shadows, shielding themselves from the world, but while her people hid, the magic trade still thrived on the charms they had left behind. The old Kingpins were replaced by new, more evil versions.

Simran of Wrenyal.

Aurelia of Volo.

But not Ashwood.

Dante Ashwood of Uskhanya, somehow made immortal by his sins, kept his position and his power.

"I could be wrong," Saxony said. "Rumors are rumors, nothing more. The elixir messed with my mind a little, like poison, but that's all I can be sure of for now."

Amja nodded, her smile solemn. "Just be careful in your discoveries," she said. "I cannot lose you too."

Saxony ran a hand over the orb, over her grandma's face.

"We're not the ones who should be scared," she said. "It's them. They should fear *us*."

And she meant it.

Saxony had already lost too much. She had already watched her mother and her little brother die when she was only a child. And then Zekia had disappeared. Her family was broken, her people were in hiding, and some days the world started to close in too fast for Saxony to do anything about it.

Sometimes it felt like she had nothing to hold on to. But if she lost everything, surely all she had left to do was gain.

And there was so much Saxony wanted.

Peace. Justice. Revenge.

"Amja," Saxony began, and then someone was knocking—no, *pounding*—on her door.

Desperate and loud enough that she was sure her neighbors would not approve.

"Amja," Saxony said again, as the banging intensified. "I have to go."

Before her grandma had the time to reply, she murmured a quick spell to break the connection and reached up to hide the crystal ball behind a box of old magic tricks in her cupboard.

Saxony wasn't sure who she expected to see behind the door, but when she swung it open to find Karam standing in front of her, her heart beat just that little bit faster.

Karam was beautiful, as always, and very, very angry.

"I heard you got arrested," she said. "Who do I need to kill?"

Saxony grinned and opened the door wider to let her in.

She tried as hard as she could to push those old words out of her mind and focus on the dimple in Karam's forehead when she frowned, but still, they echoed through her like some kind of spell. Over and over until there was nothing else left.

Peace.

Justice.

Revenge.

10

Wesley

"You have utterly lost your mind," Tavia said.

Wesley stood outside her house with a breath of hesitance and eyed her splintered door, which was basically a slab of black wood bolted crookedly at all the wrong places.

It was safe to say that Tavia didn't exactly live in the nicest part of the city.

There were holes in Creije, big enough for people to fall in, and though they masqueraded as streets, the smell of magic gave them away to anyone who knew better.

Wesley knew better, so it was not at all out of place for him to say that Tavia lived in a hole.

There was a house inside the hole of course, but it was a hole nonetheless. Grouped in a small cluster of mediocre conversions by the casinos and bars that could never rival the addictive violence of the Crook. It was the dreary half of the city, across the bridge, with sandwiched shop fronts and lantern lights that carried a strange orange wash.

The busker dormitories were flush and showy, Wesley had seen to that. They had high arches and dark-beamed ceilings, while Tavia's place was less . . . well, it was just *less*. But she'd moved out of the dormitories as soon as Wesley took charge, probably because she couldn't stand owing him anything.

"You know, I think we should discuss your salary," Wesley said.

Tavia gave him a blank stare. "What's there to discuss? Raise it."

"Nice try. Are you going to invite me in?"

Tavia threw open the door the rest of the way, with enough force that Wesley had to reach out to stop it from slamming back in his face.

It wasn't exactly an invitation, but he followed her inside.

"You could at least get a doormat," he said.

"You're worried about dragging dirt into my place?"

"It's for when I leave," Wesley said. "Who knows what I'll drag out."

He meant for it to diffuse the tension, but Tavia just looked like she wanted to kill him.

More so than usual.

"Just hurry up and tell me what that thing at the amity precinct was about," she said. "Did you get hit in the head or something?"

Wesley unbuttoned his suit jacket and took a seat. "Is Saxony okay?" he asked. "Did you stay with her for long after I left?"

Tavia frowned. "Nice job pretending you care, but just get on with it."

Wesley would never stop being surprised by how simply she said things, carving out the complexity of problems she didn't like and getting right to the dirty roots. Removing the mess that came with living life, in favor of the simplicity she got from watching over it in judgment.

"You know, there's such a thing as tact," Wesley said. "Learn it, would you?"

When Tavia only stared at him, he sighed.

"I was serious about what I said to Krause. The other Doyens have shares and interests in the black magic trade of their realms, but Schulze is too clean to play ball, so Ashwood wants a fresh slate. Next month, when the shadow moon rolls around, he's going to use its power to amplify the magic of the Crafters he's found."

Tavia looked unconvinced. "Ashwood will never be able to pull that off. He'd need—"

She stopped, growing pale.

"An army," Wesley said. "Soldiers willing to die for the cause. Like you said, the magic gets inside their heads."

"And the sickness?" Tavia asked. "How can he build an army if they might die?"

Wesley knew she was not thinking about Saxony then, but about her mother.

Already gone. The dead do not matter. He will make you the world.

Wesley shifted.

He pressed his thumb against his cuff links.

Not now. He wouldn't let her in now.

"The elixir is stronger than any magic we've dealt in," Wesley said. "But I think most people can bear it. Besides, half an army is better than none at all."

"So Saxony was lucky to have survived?"

That wasn't the word Wesley would have chosen.

"I've already spoken to the other underbosses," he said. "I needed to see if Ashwood had given the elixir to them as well, so I could know how far it might spread. It seems it's just my city for now."

"And that's what you're worried about," Tavia said. "*Your* city. What happens to the rest of the realm doesn't bother you."

It wasn't a question.

You don't know what I'd do to win, Wesley had said once, before the girl in his mind became a ghost.

He'd meant it then, but these days Wesley wasn't so sure.

It was true that the idea of any one person dying didn't play on his conscience, but this was different. This was home.

"I don't think you know what bothers me anymore," Wesley said.

"I don't think I know anything about you anymore," Tavia shot back.

That was fair, but it didn't make the words sting any less. Wesley may have been terrible, but he was almost positive that he was not as terrible as Tavia thought.

"You were right to want to take Ashwood down," Tavia said. "We can't let him infect half the city with magic sickness and use those who survive as his little warrior puppets."

Poor little orphan. His ghost laughed quietly. *Ready to die for her answers.*

Wesley clenched his fists, stood, buttoned his jacket.

"You're not coming with me," he said to Tavia. "I was giving you an explanation, not a job offer."

"Wait a minute."

Tavia propelled herself up so that her chin was level with Wesley's chest. He cleared his throat and made to move past her, but Tavia sidestepped him.

"I won't stand around doing nothing while people die."

"This is Creije," Wesley said. "People die all the time."

Mostly by your hand.

Tavia sneered. "You know as well as I do what it's like to lose family to the magic sickness, and if I can help stop someone else from going through that, then I will."

Wesley sighed and ran a finger over the scar on his wrist. Just a small part of such a large souvenir, from a childhood he was glad to have forgotten.

Unlike Tavia, he wasn't sad to have lost his family.

Wesley had lived in Creije his whole life, but it was years before he saw the wonders of his city. For so long, he was hidden from its magic and cut off from its beauty, until he escaped and became a busker. He was born in Creije and then born again when he saw it for the first time as a child of magic.

New life, new freedoms, new adventure.

Wesley didn't regret who he was now. He wasn't plagued with doubt like Tavia.

When he was a child, he never felt loved or safe. Wesley's father warned him of the dangers in the realms enough times that feeling safe became a dangerous thing. His lessons were still branded into Wesley's mind, on his skin, and running into the Kingpin's clutches was a way for him to prove that he belonged somewhere, even if it wasn't in his own family.

Now there wasn't even a family to go back and bra
Tavia said, magic sickness took everything from everyone,
people like Wesley.

Though sometimes Wesley thought it was possible that
his family had survived the magic sickness and he'd passed
them on the streets a dozen times over, and they hadn't
recognized him and he hadn't bothered looking down to see
them.

Maybe they were just glad he left.

Maybe they were ashamed he'd ever been there in the first
place.

Either way, Wesley couldn't share in Tavia's pain.

"You'll get yourself killed," he said.

"This is Creije," Tavia echoed. "People die all the time."

Wesley took a step back.

She was ridiculous. He had a plan—strategies and endless
hypotheticals for how he might go about taking Ashwood
down—but though Wesley was prepared for war and all the
consequences it brought, one thing he hadn't prepared for
was Tavia being part of the battle. She'd only get herself killed
trying to be righteous and *good*. But if Wesley left her to her
own devices, she'd probably get killed that way too.

There was no winning.

With a sigh, he said, "If I let you come, then you do exactly
as I say. No running off to play the hero by yourself. And
Ashwood is mine to kill."

Careful, the ghost warned. *Rabid dogs get put down.*

Wesley loosened his tie, suddenly feeling like it was
suffocating him.

"Don't we also need an army of our own before we get carried away?" Tavia asked.

"I have some buskers in mind," Wesley said. "But we need more than people for hire. We need fighters with loyalty, integrity, and just the right amount of bloodthirsty drive."

Any hint of a grin vanished from Tavia's face as she took in the implications of Wesley's words.

A fighter, but not a busker.

A killer, but not a traitor.

Tavia grimaced. "Tell me you're not serious."

"Aren't I always?"

She ran a hand through her hair and let out a heavy sigh. "I don't see that conversation going well," she said. "Karam is a little rough around the edges."

Wesley only shrugged. "Loyalty goes a long way."

"Who says she's loyal to you?"

"I wasn't just talking about me."

Tavia studied him. "Well then," she said, no more hesitant than usual. "It looks like we've got ourselves a plan."

And just like that, they were a team again.

11

Saxony

SAXONY HITCHED FOUR WINEGLASSES between her fingers and sighed as lipstick smeared onto her thumb. If she had to spend one more night at the Crook, cleaning up after magic addicts and morons, then she was going to lose her damn mind.

She almost wished the elixir had knocked her out for a couple more days, so she could get some reprieve.

"Brandy," one of the newer waiters said. "You have guests in the VIP lounge."

"I'm unavailable," Saxony told her. "Tell them to come back when I'm not sweating through my underwear with"—she set the glasses down and sniffed her hands—"strawberry lipstick all over me."

"Yeah," the girl said, pulling her hair off her collarbone. "I'm not telling them that."

Saxony sighed and wiped her hands, bending over to untangle

the heels from her feet, hidden beneath the flowing green dress that was a favorite of hers.

She liked the way it swayed when she walked, like there was wind under her feet, carrying her through Creije. And it was green. Saxony wore green a lot, whenever she could help it. It reminded her of home, of the forest she'd grown up in and the ivy towns in Rishiya's center.

It calmed her, keeping the fire within at bay.

Saxony hooked the straps of the shoes around her finger and walked barefoot toward the VIP lounge, tired and in no mood for drunken patrons. Whatever people had the indecency to hang around after closing were going to be as unimpressed with her as she was with them.

In fact, she strode toward the lavish sofas with every intention of telling them that any drink they wanted had run out, along with her patience, and they'd better get moving unless they wanted to see how well armed Wesley liked to keep his people.

Except, when Saxony reached the lounge and saw who was actually waiting, she didn't think they would respond well to that.

"Do you guys need a referee or something?" Saxony asked.

The somber silence she was met with told her everything about the direction this conversation was going.

Karam, who had been standing with her arms crossed beside the sofa, like she'd rather be anywhere else, stepped forward.

Saxony's smile was unavoidable.

Karam was dressed in an outfit that looked like blood and water, which was not all that unusual, but she was accompanied by two very unusual people.

The first was Tavia, who wore fingerless black gloves and a pair of new boots that Saxony quickly planned to steal. Her tilted smile rippled through the room, which was probably the most *busker* of all her outfits, and she lounged across the sofa, twirling a pocketknife like a baton in her hands.

But it was the second person who struck Saxony as the most unusual, and it was not because Wesley was at the Crook after closing instead of busying himself with the ruination of someone's life. It was the dark maroon bow tie clutched around his jugular. A bow tie that meant this was an odd day.

And Wesley Thornton Walcott on an odd day was always a curious thing.

"Brandy," he said, thick Creijen accent spinning like sugar. "I'd like you to do me a favor."

It took Saxony every effort not to laugh in his face.

If there was one thing to be said for Wesley, it was that he enjoyed being polite.

Growing up in Rishiya, Amja always told Saxony there was no place she needed to go that a little courtesy couldn't get her. *Kill them with kindness*, Amja said. Saxony suspected Wesley did a lot of that. The killing alongside the kindness. Maybe he even said *please* and *do forgive me* when he carried out the Kingpin's dirty work.

"Why are you calling her *Brandy*?" Tavia asked.

"It's her Crook name," Wesley said. "Something to keep the customers out of her business. Most of my people have one. Don't you pay attention?"

Tavia whipped her head to face Saxony, mouth agape. "You never told me you had a Crook name. Or that it was Brandy."

She wrinkled her nose.

"I'm just pleased she didn't call herself Bloody Mary," Wesley said. "It would have killed business."

"How are you feeling anyway?" Tavia asked her.

She was trying very hard not to look at the mark on Saxony's neck, hidden somewhat beneath her hair, which meant that Tavia was pretty much avoiding looking at her altogether.

Saxony propped her collar up. "Why? Do I look that bad?"

"No more than usual."

"Good. I still feel like I got hit by a train though, in case you were concerned."

"Well, I still feel like I got hit by a bunch of dirty magic," Tavia countered.

She was joking, of course, but it didn't make Saxony feel any less shitty.

"Don't look so glum," Tavia said. "Since I kicked your ass and left you for the amityguards, I'd say we're even."

Saxony didn't hide her grin. "So then why are we all gathered in this weird friendship circle?"

"Wesley and I want you and Karam to help us overthrow the Kingpin," Tavia announced. "And we have a stamp of approval from Doyen Schulze to do it."

Saxony waited for the punch line, but it got quiet enough that the only sound she could hear was the fabric of Tavia's trousers squeaking against the sofa.

Overthrow Dante Ashwood?

Saxony was waiting to do just that, if by overthrow they meant bringing down in a shower of fire and unimaginable pain.

But Wesley leading the charge and allying with Schulze?

Saxony wanted to ask what kind of game he was playing and if he really expected her to be part of it, but all she said was, "Both of us?"

"You and Karam are a package deal," Tavia said. She gave Wesley a sour look. "Apparently."

Saxony let a smile spread across her lips. She liked the sound of that.

"Buy one crook and get another free?" she asked.

Karam folded her arms across her chest. "I am not a crook," she said.

"And since both of you work for me, I don't think I'm getting anything for free."

At the sound of Wesley's voice, Saxony leveled Tavia with a stare that was probably a little too judgmental for someone who had tried to kill her so recently.

"You really trust him to turn against Ashwood?"

Tavia only shrugged. "The enemy of our enemy."

"The Kingpin isn't Wesley's enemy."

"He is now that Creije is on the line," Tavia said.

Wesley cleared his throat, looking a little irritated. "You can both stop talking about me like I'm not even here."

Tavia sighed, walking toward Saxony so that she stood as a buffer between them. "He'll help us save the realms from the Kingpin."

"Don't be so dramatic," Wesley scolded, taking Tavia's seat on the sofa and kicking his legs up as she had done. "I'm saving Creije."

"What are you talking about?" Saxony asked.

"The elixir you took is new magic," Tavia explained. "Some

kind of mind-control. Ashwood plans to use it to create an army to usurp Schulze. When the shadow moon comes, he'll use its power to wage war."

Saxony stilled at the mention of the shadow moon.

The Crafter Moon.

The old legends said that the first of her kind were created under one, and though she didn't know if that was true, she did know that the power the shadow moon brought amplified Crafter magic beyond compare. On the rare instances it had occurred during her lifetime, shielding the sun from the realms and plunging them to darkness, Saxony felt eternal. Her magic, finally, after so long hiding, felt freed.

"If the Kingpin is using the shadow moon, that means he's taking Crafters again," Saxony said.

Just uttering the words made her stomach drop.

That was why the elixir felt so strange—it truly was new magic. The Kingpin was collecting what few Crafters remained, like trophies and daring to use a shadow moon, their most sacred gift, to turn them into an army.

Saxony was going to be sick.

It was like the War of Ages had never even happened. Everything her people had gone through, being stolen from their homes and left to rot by Realm Doyens who simply called it an *epidemic*. It meant nothing.

Zekia.

Her sister's face surfaced in her mind.

Zekia had been gone for years, but what if the reason Saxony hadn't been able to find her in this city, in the place she was last seen, was because Ashwood had her this whole time?

Saxony's staves thumped against her chest, the silver symbols of her specialties and achievements in the craft tattooed onto her skin in the language of magic.

They felt like war drums on her heart now.

The sweat slipped from Saxony's brow to the corner of her lip, burning like lava.

Karam started toward her, but Saxony held up a hand.

Her skin practically sizzled. If Karam were to touch her now, then Saxony's magic might just burn a hole through her.

"Are you okay?" Tavia asked.

Saxony swallowed the magic bubbling up inside of her. When she spoke, her voice burned against her tongue. "Why do you think I could help?"

Wesley stepped slowly in front of Tavia.

"The Kingpin thinks he can build himself an army from my city, and the elixir he calls the Loj is the first step," Wesley said. "I can't be fussy with my crew when the shadow moon is only weeks away, and I know that Karam won't leave you in Creije without her protection."

"I do not remember agreeing to help you," Karam said.

Though Saxony knew she would. Even if Wesley liked to front about Karam's loyalty to her, they both knew that she was just as loyal to him.

Saxony hated it.

She hated that Wesley had been the one to sharpen Karam's warrior edges. She hated that someone she disliked so strongly had helped to shape someone she cared for so deeply. Karam would fight in this battle, not just because of Saxony, but because of her family and her underboss. Because of who she was and who he had made her.

Saxony tried not to let that get to her.

She tried to home in on the sound of Karam's voice, hoping it would will the anger and flames inside her to subside so that she could concentrate, but her vision was swimming with her sister's face and the possibility of her capture, and thinking of Karam only made her think of those misplaced loyalties.

Saxony couldn't control her magic.

She wasn't Zekia.

For every second her sister was a steady river, Saxony was a volcano. It was why Zekia had been chosen to lead the Rishiyat Crafters, despite being six years younger. Her brand of tranquility and wisdom was necessary to be Liege.

Zekia was a prodigy and Saxony was a calamity, whose magic begged to be let loose on her enemies.

She had been so blind. So stupid.

All this time thinking her sister was lost, or that she had hidden herself away for some unknown reason, because she feared being Liege or hated being trapped in the forest, when really she had likely been in Dante Ashwood's clutches for years.

Saxony was sure the skin around her staves had started to melt.

Her magic boiled, embedding under her skin.

She needed to calm down and—

"Do you want Karam to splash some water on you or can we continue this discussion without you burning a hole through my sofa?" Wesley asked. "Aren't Crafters supposed to have control over magic?"

The flames inside Saxony went out like a light.

Her skin lost its red hue.

Her power dimmed, unused and bitter, and she opened her eyes to an impatient-looking underboss.

Wesley knew what she was.

"You're a *Crafter*?"

And apparently Tavia didn't.

Her friend quite literally stumbled back from the shock.

"You never told me," Tavia said.

Saxony took in a ragged breath. When she spoke, her voice was cracked, one half of her struggling to get the words out and the other fighting to keep them in.

"I didn't know I could," Saxony said. "Look at your face right now."

Tavia exhaled, trying to push away the shock, but she was doing a poor job.

"That's how you were so fast when you attacked me at the temple," she said, as though it were some sort of a comfort to know Saxony hadn't gotten the jump on her because she was sloppy. "You didn't have charms. You had true magic."

Tavia scoffed a little, like that somehow made Saxony a cheat, and turned to Wesley.

"You knew?" she asked.

"Nothing happens in Creije without me knowing," he said. "You think I agreed to get her out of the amity precinct just because she's your friend? She's a valuable resource."

"What she is, is a total idiot," Tavia said.

Saxony raised an eyebrow. "Rude."

"This city has the best black magic trade. It isn't an ideal hiding place for a Crafter," Tavia said. "You could have been caught."

Karam nodded in agreement. "That is what I told her."

Oh great. Now they were tag-teaming.

"*She* knew as well?" Tavia pointed to Karam in disbelief.

Saxony ignored her and looked back to Wesley. "You didn't give me up to your Kingpin."

"Like I told you, you're a resource. One I'm glad I kept for myself. If you help us bring down Ashwood, I'll owe you one," he said. "And a favor from an underboss is a powerful thing. You scratch my back and I'll scratch yours."

Tavia grimaced. "Nobody wants you anywhere near their back in case you stick a knife in it."

"I'll do it for Zekia," Saxony said, before she could stop herself. "I'll help if when we find Ashwood, we make her our priority."

Wesley raised an eyebrow. "Should I know who that is?"

"She's my sister and our future Liege," Saxony explained. "She disappeared three years ago and was last seen in Creije. I came here to bring her home, but no matter how hard I looked, how much magic I tried, she was just . . . gone. But after everything you've said, I think the reason I couldn't find her was because she was taken by Ashwood. Zekia has great power, so if the Kingpin is imprisoning Crafters, she's probably one of them."

Saxony expected this to strike a chord within Wesley, but all it did was make him sigh.

"Look, I sympathize," he said, though Saxony suspected he had never done such a thing. "But I'm really not interested in your family drama."

The glare Tavia gave him mirrored the anger inside Saxony perfectly.

"Besides," Wesley said, "I don't think the Crafters with Ashwood are prisoners. He seemed to think they backed the idea of his new future."

That accusation nearly set Saxony on fire all over again.

"You know nothing about my people," she said.

Wesley let out a long sigh and then clapped his hands together. "Fine," he said. "If your sister is with Ashwood, then we save her. That's two birds with one stone. So you're in?"

She was.

This was Saxony's chance to do more than just spy on the Kingpin's empire, like Amja had ordered. Her grandma and the rest of the Kin may have been scared of the kingpins and their magic, but Saxony wasn't. She could fix everything. Bring Zekia home and get revenge on the man who destroyed her family.

She could make it right.

She could save them all.

"Four crooks against a Kingpin isn't an army," Saxony said.

Karam let out an indignant huff. "Stop saying that I am a crook."

Saxony smirked. "Well, you *do* fight in the rings where they pair the matches so unfairly that the smaller man always loses."

"I never lose," Karam said.

"You're not a man."

"*Anyway,*" Wesley said. "I can gather an army of buskers, but we need to find the Kingpin if we're going to take him out."

"You don't know where he is?" Saxony was a little shocked by that. "Why can't you just arrange a meeting? Aren't you his golden boy?"

Wesley looked like he was trying very hard not to kill her.

"That's not how this works," he said. "Anytime I see the Kingpin it's on his whim, not a schedule. Sometimes I've gone months without direct contact and in case you didn't notice, we're on a bit of a deadline. The shadow moon is only weeks away. We need the consort. She's the only one in the realms who knows his location and, luckily for us, her headquarters are in Creije."

"How do we get the information from her?" Tavia palmed her pocketknife. "Ask her nicely?"

"That won't work," Wesley said.

Karam cracked her knuckles. "So let us ask her not nicely."

"I appreciate the enthusiasm, but the locations of the Kingpins are buried in the hallows of the consort's mind, guarded by magic," Wesley said. "She couldn't tell us even if she wanted to. The information is only triggered through a passphrase and once it's revealed the consort forgets."

"A combination of a memory charm and a revelation spell." Saxony wasn't sure whether to admire it or be disgusted by it, but either way she could admit that it was clever.

Twisted and convoluted and something only people with way too much money and time would bother thinking of. But clever.

"So how do we get it from the consort's mind?" Saxony asked. "We'd need—"

She stopped herself from finishing the sentence and a horrible feeling took over.

The serpent's smile on Wesley's face only made it worse.

"Pull whatever threads you can," he said. "No mercy."

Saxony blanched and the air warmed a few degrees with the heat of her magic.

"There's no way I'm doing an *extraction* on the consort," she said.

The blackest spells were the kind that invaded people's minds, just like the magic they were trying to stop the Kingpin from using. Extractions carved through memories, cutting out thought, until the agony became too much to bear. Amja always said that it was the worst kind of magic.

The kind that could curse Saxony's Kin more than they already were.

"That kind of magic is forbidden," Saxony said. "It would drive the consort insane."

Wesley merely sighed in a way that signaled his boredom with the idea of a moral debate.

"Someone can only go insane if they survive," he said. "Which I heard they rarely do. So problem solved. Besides, the Kingpin might kill your sister while we argue over this."

Saxony's eyes widened. "You manipulative son of a—"

"Careful," he said. "You're about to get personal."

"Is this really your big plan?" Saxony asked. "To make us all into murderers like you?"

"It's not murder. It's survival."

"Using black magic isn't easy. Killing someone isn't easy."

"But it can be quick," Wesley said. "And that's almost the same thing."

Saxony's jaw tensed and she wondered if she could set him ablaze just by glaring at him. It was like Wesley was *trying* to provoke her.

"So, are you ready to be part of my winning team?" Wesley

asked. "There won't be room for hesitation on the day. A couple of dozen guards patrol the consort's building and once we get what we need from her, they'll descend. Not that they'll stand a chance of catching us."

He said it without a flicker of doubt in his voice, because Wesley knew, they *all* knew, that if there was one thing he was good at, then it was winning. Whether he deserved to or not.

"Do we have a deal?"

Wesley approached Saxony slowly and deliberately, holding out his hand like it was a test. Daring her to shake it. Daring her not to.

Saxony bit down on her tongue until she felt the blood hit the back of her throat.

The ring of the underbosses was tight around Wesley's thumb. The seal of the Kingpin like a brand on his skin.

If Amja could see her now, she'd say Saxony had lost her mind.

She would think there was nothing—no excuse or reason—good enough to make a deal like this. The Kin would never team up with an underboss, even if it meant getting Zekia back, or getting their revenge for all of the wrongs done to their people.

Saxony took Wesley's hand.

"I'm in," she said.

Because she was not Amja.

She was not afraid.

Saxony would do whatever it took to find the Kingpin and put back together what little remained of her family.

And that included killing Wesley, the moment he stopped being useful.

12

Wesley

WESLEY HAD A GUN *in his hand and a man on his knees.*

"It's a gift," Ashwood said.

Only Wesley's sixteenth birthday was months before. Besides, he thought it looked more like an offering.

Take this and give me your soul, *it seemed to say.*

The man by Wesley's knees had a sack over his head, and there was a girl—the girl who was destined to haunt his thoughts—standing resolute at the Kingpin's side, smiling at Wesley like she wasn't bound in chains with blood in her teeth.

Smiling like she knew she would climb inside his mind and punish him for the choice he was about to make.

The gun in Wesley's hands was a bone gun, which was not a fancy term, but a very literal thing. The only metal was the bullets, and everything else was as gray-white as the Kingpin's fingertips, carved from person to weapon, with a grip engraved in swirls of red that Wesley thought might actually be bloodstains.

He stared from the gun to Ashwood, to the girl who was just now starting to see how awful he was.

When the sack was removed from the captive's head, Wesley was not at all surprised to see his underboss.

His face was caved in on one side from the beatings, the scar of an old knife fight now nothing more than a splinter in the hollow.

"Wesley," the underboss said, still on his knees.

He didn't look surprised either.

"Make it quick when you—"

Wesley pulled the trigger before he could finish, which was the quickest way he could think of.

The gun made no sound.

Wesley felt the kickback, saw the smoke appear at the end of the barrel, and a hole spread through the center of the underboss's forehead. But there was no noise from the gun. No gasp from the spectators.

Only the sound of the girl, whose legs collapsed beneath her.

"I liked the other future better," she said.

Wesley knelt down and ran his fingers over the underboss's eyes to close them. Then he slipped the seal from the dead man's thumb and onto his own.

That was how street kids became street kings. How buskers became underbosses.

It was the only way to survive in a realm hungry enough to swallow the weak whole.

Trust no one, betray everyone.

Kill or be killed, always.

Wesley had barely managed to sift down an entire city's worth of buskers to fifty who could probably, maybe, if he paid them enough, be trusted and who would probably, maybe, if he paid them enough, not shit their pants once they learned the mission. People who were intrigued by the shiny offers he made: freedom from their life debts, a clean slate, and an honest job, all in exchange for one tiny little coup.

They were waiting for him now, at the old railway tracks the tourists used for novelty. Having a Doyen as an ally had a few perks, including wiping the train schedule so Wesley and his buskers were free and clear to commandeer, leaving Uskhanya for the realm of Wrenyal, where they could gather supplies and allies.

It was not going to be as glamorous as the floating railways, but Wesley was used to playing whatever hand he was dealt.

He shifted.

The waiting room at the consort's headquarters was liquid black with wall-to-wall mirrors that reflected his dead eyes right back at him. Tonight was one of the few times in the month that the consort was in Creije, and with the shadow moon only weeks away, they had to act.

If not now, it was never.

"What if something goes wrong?" Tavia whispered. "I don't fancy dying today. I haven't had time to properly prepare what I want you to say at my funeral."

Karam regarded her incredulously. "This is not the time for jokes," she said.

"Lighten up," Tavia teased. "Who doesn't love a bit of breaking and entering?"

Karam glared. "This is supposed to be stealthy. We are not *breaking* anything."

"Just skulls," Tavia said, and Saxony bit back a laugh.

Wesley stretched out his arms to adjust his cuff links and then scolded himself for it, but there was a wrinkle in the wrist of his sleeve that he couldn't seem to get out.

"Nothing will go wrong," he said.

He tried not to make it sound like a prayer.

Someone cleared their throat and Wesley looked up to see the secretary standing over him.

"The consort will see you now," Leifsson said.

Wesley squeezed the shift charm in his hand, straightening his suit as a cover while the charm melted in his skin.

Magic was a language made from wishing, with glyphs in desire and consonants shaped from dreams. When the charm sank into Wesley's skin, he didn't need to think about what he wanted. He could feel it weaving through the map of his mind and finding its place in the center.

It already knew.

"This way," Leifsson said.

He clasped a gloved hand behind his back and gestured to the mirror. It surged like a vortex.

"Your hand," Leifsson said.

The charm was well into Wesley's blood now and he tried to breathe through the pain, not even letting his fingers twitch as his skin was pulled and filed away, replaced by something new.

Shift charms lasted an hour at best and were a migraine waiting to happen. They didn't just glamour someone to look a certain way, but quite literally morphed and mutated their body, burning away the old to make way for the other.

Wesley could feel his skin sizzling as Leifsson looked at him expectantly.

He could feel it reshape and remold, his head pounding as the rest of him adjusted to this new, foreign part of himself. Skin that wasn't his. A hand that wasn't his. It was the only way to stop the glass from reading Wesley's true intentions.

Clever, clever boy.

He lifted his new hand to the glass. The pain was a dull sensation now, tingling in place of searing, the pounding in his head reduced to nothing more than an echo.

Wesley's body had accepted this new part of him with ease and open arms.

Welcome, it whispered, *to the lion's den.*

The door swirled under Wesley's touch, his reflection distorting and then righting itself as it read the magic on his hands. Read secrets that weren't his and tucked them away somewhere for safekeeping.

When Wesley pulled back, the glass dissolved.

He tried not to look relieved, and turned to the others with a curt nod before they stepped through the doorway and straight into the harsh red of the consort's office.

"Walcott," came a lazy drawl.

The consort lounged on a maroon sofa, wearing a brand of arrogance that matched her suit perfectly. She took a sip of something as white as milk and winced like it burned going down.

"It's not often I get a visit from the Kingpin's most precious toy," she said, watching for a twitch in Wesley's eyes that never came. "To what do I owe the pleasure?"

Wesley pulled the bone gun from behind his back. It felt light, fitting perfectly into the grooves of his hand as he took aim.

"Pleasure's all mine," he said, and pulled the trigger.

13

Saxony

THE MOMENT THE BULLET cracked through the magical relay, it was like the fire-gates broke loose. Saxony was sure the noise from the sirens alone was going to make her head explode.

An iron wall slammed from the ceiling, blocking off the doorway they'd stepped through and the lights pulsed, blinking her from darkness and back into red.

Then another wall clamped over the window closest to Tavia.

Then behind where the consort sat with her glass smashed at her feet.

Every escape cordoned off.

They were trapped.

The wall farthest from Saxony trembled. The shelves that hosted an array of liquor quaked until the bottles crashed to the floor and glass sprinkled onto the carpet.

And then the room began to close in.

The wall shook under its weight and scraped across the floor, inching toward them. Making the room smaller and smaller by the second.

"What's going on?" Tavia yelled over the siren.

"Protocols," Wesley said. He hitched the gun back under his suit jacket.

"Did you know the walls would close in before you shot the security system?"

He gave her a look. "Obviously."

Karam ran toward the impending wall, barricading herself against it. "Then forgive me," she said, breathless in anger, "but why in spirit's name did we plan for you to fire?"

"The relay system records any magic or sound. If we kept it functional, the Kingpin would know our every move. Besides, with the room sealed, no signals can get in or out. Including warnings or distress." Wesley shot a pointed look at the consort. "Any security traps we trip in her brain will have nowhere to send their message."

Tavia threw herself beside Karam. "And what good will that be when we're dead?"

"I'll bet anything the passphrase to end the protocols is inside the consort's head," Wesley said.

The consort ran a palm over her closely shaved hair, wiping the sweat from her skin, and spat at the floor by Wesley's feet. "That passphrase is a security measure in case someone important is trapped in here," she said. "Which clearly they aren't."

Wesley touched a hand to his heart. "Ouch."

He looked to Saxony.

She knew what she had to do then and she was already picturing the consort, dead by her hand.

A life for her life. This woman, for Ashwood's location.

And the black magic, damning her family.

"I don't know what you're planning, but it won't work," the consort said. "You've killed us all, Walcott."

Wesley nodded, like that wasn't news, and suddenly Saxony wished her amja were there. Or Zekia. Her sister would know what to do. She'd know the right words and the right magic and she wouldn't panic, like Saxony was half-tempted to.

In fact, Saxony was half-tempted to just kill Wesley before she let the wall have the pleasure of crushing him.

"Whenever you're ready," Wesley said to her. "Let's get this magic show on the road."

"And fast," Karam said.

Saxony watched the sweat drip into her eyes. When Karam took a hand off the wall to wipe her brow, it advanced and Karam cursed, finding her footing and regaining her grip on the room as it crawled inward.

Saxony's hands shook.

An extraction was awful magic, outlawed by Crafters long before the war. Her amja said it was a violation of their gifts. An assault on the Many Gods and a way to ensure bad luck. If Saxony did this, her amja and their entire Kin would feel it.

Saxony felt her staves grow hot.

"It'll kill her," she said. "It will curse my Kin."

"And this room will kill us," Wesley said. "Weigh your priorities."

"Saxony." Karam's teeth were gritted to the point of buckling.

"You must do something."

"Looks like you're outvoted," Wesley said.

He gestured to the consort, who paled under the realization of what was to come.

Saxony shook her head.

Killing Ashwood was one thing—it was like wiping out a sickness—but killing the consort, who was nothing but a pawn, with black magic? It would endanger the people Saxony cared about most.

She was trying to save her family, not find new and terrible ways to destroy it.

This magic was forbidden for a reason and Saxony didn't think she could face the consequences that might come with breaking such a sacred law.

She couldn't risk it.

She just couldn't.

"Many Gods damn it!" Tavia yelled. "*Move.*"

She shoved Saxony out of the way.

"What are you doing?" Wesley asked.

"Lending a hand."

Tavia fumbled in her pockets for magic, cursing when all she came away with was some kind of reverie charm.

"If it were that simple, I would have done it myself," Wesley said. "Our charms are no good. We need a Crafter."

Tavia squeezed the charm, letting it disappear into her hands. "Just shut up and let me try."

Tavia pressed her magic-soaked hands to their new prisoner and the consort shuddered, her eyes flicking backward.

Tavia was really going to try to link her mind to the consort's with a trance charm. Saxony wasn't sure if it was genius or idiocy, but either way Tavia was willing to do what she couldn't.

"Hurry up!" Karam yelled.

She fumbled against the wall as it lurched closer, the weight of it too much for her to bear alone.

Wesley cursed, as though he'd forgotten about the room closing in. He reached into his pocket and when his hand slipped back out, it was coated in dust. He held up his palm and the wall groaned as it slowed under Karam's grip.

But it didn't stop.

Wesley swore again, then muttered something in far more revered tones.

It was magic that Saxony might not have been able to hear, but that she could almost certainly feel. It crawled over her and extinguished the fire beneath her skin, sucking the flames from her like a black hole.

Wesley clenched his fist and the wall came to a stop.

He turned to Saxony, blood trickling from his nose.

She almost gaped.

What demon bargain had he made to get power like that?

"I can't keep it at bay forever," Wesley said.

"I'm trying!" Tavia yelled.

She closed her eyes again, body rocking from side to side as the reverie charm matted between her mind and the consort's. But Saxony could feel the power, or the lack of it, barely circling the air.

The consort was dazed, but conscious, and as hard as Tavia willed the magic to work some kind of a miracle, Saxony knew it wouldn't.

You couldn't just break into someone's mind with a charm.

You couldn't just break into someone's mind without first breaking your soul.

Tavia let go of the consort and looked at Saxony with eyes halfway between pleading and apologetic. Like she was sorry she couldn't be the one to bear the burden.

"Saxony."

Saxony held up a hand. "I know," she said.

So quiet. So unlike the warrior she needed to be.

Saxony turned to the consort and her eyes flashed with fear.

"Don't," the consort said, now fully alert. "Please don't."

But Saxony couldn't be bargained with. She didn't want to do this; she *needed* to. They'd die otherwise. And if there was any chance of saving Zekia, then Saxony had to sacrifice whoever stood in her way.

She straddled the consort and raised her hands to the woman's temples.

The consort trembled beneath her.

When a tear slipped from her eyes and trailed onto Saxony's hand, she readied herself.

"Don't," the consort said again.

But Saxony did.

SAXONY'S MAGIC flooded between herself and the consort like a river, not bound by walls or banks or its own current. Their minds became estuaries, dragged and pulled into the wildness of the sea that thrashed between them. Tidal, drowning the air from their lungs.

Saxony could hear the consort's sobs inside her head, her tears on Saxony's eyes and her moans on Saxony's lips. She wanted to cry out alongside her, but her voice was dragged to the horizon, separated from her body, and whatever screams Saxony willed died quietly inside of her.

Something ragged and snakelike wrapped inside her stomach, like it was navigating a maze.

Then it began to tug.

It tugged Saxony outward and inward, and she pressed harder into the consort's mind until the tangled thing pulled with such might that Saxony broke through layers of consciousness like they were walls. One by one slamming against them until it felt like she might go on forever.

Her head split.

Saxony didn't need to see the blood to know it was there. She could feel it crawl into her mouth.

Then the pulling stopped.

When Saxony opened her eyes, reality had shifted.

The consort's mind smelled of cigars and rainwater and the air was too solid to breathe. There was nothingness, endlessness, just tiny particles of reality drifting and floating in front of Saxony, until they formed long strings that dangled by the tip of her nose.

Threads.

Wesley had told her to pull on whatever ones she could. Saxony wondered if he'd meant it to be so literal.

She reached out for one.

The darkness jarred and from the nothing, a forest sprouted. Great trees crawled from emptiness and grew fingers that turned to branches, their trunks mottled gray and their leaves slicked in deep red that wept onto the ground.

Saxony found herself on a bench, perched on the edge of a small path that whittled through the trees, like a chalk mark on the soil.

She could feel the absence of her magic instantly. There was no room for miracles inside minds, it seemed.

Beside her, the consort let out a breath.

Eirini Dimitriou.

Saxony knew her name now and, if she pressed hard enough, she sensed she could know so much more.

"This was my favorite place as a child," Eirini said.

She was younger, with hair longer and blonder—longer than Karam's, even—and the corners of her eyes not yet creased by the weariness of sin.

She leaned back and her arms eagled over the bench so that the tips of her fingers sparked against Saxony's shoulder. When Eirini met her gaze, her eyes were as red as the leaves of the forest.

"It doesn't look like a happy place," Saxony said.

"My mother died here. I suppose that sullied the memory."

Saxony swallowed. "This isn't the memory I'm looking for."

"What you're looking for isn't a memory. It's a map."

Eirini blinked and from a nearby tree a creature emerged.

It slithered from the trunk, pulling its feet from the roots and detaching like a severed limb. When it straightened to the height of a man, the forest drew in a breath and a thousand tiny monsters of light burst from the exhale and sped toward the creature in a protective shield.

It opened its arms, wide and twisted and torn, like it was half bat and half man.

The light monsters sank agreeably into its skin until the creature's arms were alive and glowing, and it jerked them in a birdlike motion, levitating a few inches off the forest floor.

Not a creature. Not just a creature.

A king of monsters and magic.

Saxony stood. "What is this?"

"You wanted to find him," Eirini said. "You wanted his map.".

Saxony eyed the creature as it curled around the forest. Its magic was strong enough to make her feel like she was drowning all over again.

Dante Ashwood.

Saxony couldn't see his face, but she once heard a group of buskers saying nobody ever had. Not even Wesley. She didn't believe it then, but seeing this incarnation of the Kingpin, it seemed possible.

It wasn't that he never showed his face, but rather he no longer had a face to show.

He was a man turned to nightmare, corrupted by the power of the Crafters he stole from their homes. Saxony's people. People like her amja and Zekia. This was what a human became when they meddled in power that was not theirs. When they bought and sold magic like a commodity.

He was magic made into madness.

"I want to know where the Kingpin is in my reality," Saxony said.

"He's here," Eirini said. "Here, there, everywhere."

Saxony glared down at her. Her magic was no use in this

place, but that didn't mean she couldn't beat Eirini to death if she didn't give her a straight answer.

Karam had really rubbed off on her.

"I don't understand what you're trying to tell me," Saxony said.

"I'm telling you to kill him."

"I will if you tell me where he is."

"No," Eirini said. "Kill him *now*."

She pointed to the ghostly incarnation of the Kingpin, who had haunted Saxony's thoughts as a faceless phantom for so long.

"Kill him if you want to find him."

Saxony didn't hesitate. She walked toward the Kingpin and reached for the knife Karam had gifted her, which was, unlike her magic, still there.

She thought about where she should strike him first. She thought about all the times she had seen Karam pummel people at the Crook. She thought about how this would be good practice for when the real day approached and she would burn through Ashwood like he was parchment paper.

She thought that would be a very good day.

Saxony didn't think about how this would be the first person she killed, because the Kingpin was not a person.

He turned to Saxony. His hood was made of wind, rusted and decayed into tangibility, as though it had tried to breeze through his invisible face and gotten stuck there.

Saxony tried to search for eyes, but the Kingpin had none. Everything from the neck up was a blur, or a memory that was being erased the moment she made it. She knew he had a face, he must have had one, but she couldn't picture it, even as she was standing before him, staring straight into the spot where his eyes should have been.

"I'm going to kill you," Saxony said. "In this reality and the next."

The Kingpin didn't speak, and though this could have been because he didn't have a mouth, Saxony suspected it was because he simply did not speak to Wesley's underlings, in any reality.

In spite of herself and the knowing that this Kingpin was not the one she searched for, nor technically the one she hated, and most definitely not the one who had taken her sister, Saxony said, "Tell me what happened to Zekia."

The Kingpin laughed, mouthless and breathless, and loud enough that the trees heard and shook their branches to join him. He was either laughing at her stupidity, for trying to bargain with a dream and a dream creature, or her audacity for trying to bargain with a kingpin. Or maybe he was laughing because that was just what evil things did.

Either way, Saxony stabbed him.

There was a blissful moment, a half of a half of a second, where the tip of Saxony's blade made contact with the place the Kingpin's heart may have been. The metal pierced the sheath covering his torso. It was glorious and wonderful and Saxony's pulse could be heard in her ears.

And then the blade stopped.

It didn't pierce through the Kingpin's skin. It didn't draw blood or gasps from his mouthless face.

It didn't kill him.

The blade stilled against his chest and then folded in on itself, crumpling to the hilt.

Saxony staggered back.

"Not with that," Eirini called. "Try something else."

"I have nothing else!" Saxony yelled. "There's no magic in your mind."

She could almost feel Eirini shrugging.

"The Kingpin seems to have some," Eirini said. "But I suppose you could also try brute force."

Saxony let out a breath. "That was what stabbing him was supposed to be."

"Maybe use your head this time," Eirini advised.

Saxony swung her fist. She aimed for the Kingpin's face and met air. He moved like the tree branches. She tried to pull her hand back, but the Kingpin caught it in his crow-like fingers and squeezed until her wrist popped like the cork of a wine bottle.

Saxony's skin turned ashen. Brown to gray and gray to nothing. Her staves stung.

Memories flashed across her mind—of her mother and brother screaming as they were engulfed in flames. Of her father and her amja. Of Zekia when she was still just a child.

Karam's face came next. Eyes like caverns and a gold chain looping from her nostril and a smile pulling her dark lips into submission.

The Kingpin's grip tightened and one by one the images dissolved inside Saxony. Karam's smile vanished and no matter how hard Saxony tried to recall it, she couldn't. She couldn't remember the way her father smelled or the prayer song Amja used to sing to get Saxony to sleep after her mother and brother died.

Saxony writhed against the Kingpin.

Even here, even now, he was taking everything from her. Not just her blood, or her magic, or even her life. He wanted her memories. He wanted her dreams.

That was when it struck her.

This thing in front of Saxony wasn't the Kingpin. He was an illusion. An imagined monster. But Saxony wasn't. She was real and that meant she wasn't bound to whatever rules Eirini's mind set.

If she needed Ashwood dead, all she had to do was want it.

Saxony closed her eyes.

Use your head, Eirini had told her.

She pictured the Kingpin's skin and the creatures that crawled beneath it. She imagined them flying from his arms, taking not only their light, but his skin, too. She thought of it peeling like a bandage, flaking from his bones and fluttering upward with the light creatures.

The image replayed over in her mind a hundred times, with the Kingpin screaming and thrashing and his facelessness morphing into a smudge of pain.

It looped so many times that it took Saxony a while to realize that the screaming had stopped being imagined.

Her eyes drifted open and the Kingpin of Uskhanya was on his knees.

His bones were black with decaying magic and his skin curled away like singed paper. Around him, the light creatures swarmed. Saxony could feel their charge electrify as they tried to launch at her, but it took hardly any focus to hold them in place. To make them watch as their Kingpin withered into the soil.

Eirini's hand slipped into Saxony's.

"Good," she said. "Now you're ready."

"Ready for what?"

Eirini's fingers pressed harder into her knuckles.

"War."

The forest bent around them, shivering until the rustling of the leaves sounded like cries. Like the Kingpin's skin, pieces from the trees began to peel away, the soil turning to pale sand. Green bloomed back and the veins of the leaves stretched to long needles.

Out of the forest, an island was born.

Saxony staggered back. Around them, the sea thrashed for miles into the air, but was stopped just short of the island by an invisible wall that turned it into a curtain of water.

"Where are we?" Saxony asked.

"The last place I will ever see. I imagine it looks something like this, though I've never been. When you leave, the map will go from my mind to yours." Eirini swallowed, the sound louder than the sea. "You can take it when you take my sanity."

"This is Ashwood's hideout," Saxony said in a gasp. "It's where he's keeping the Crafters."

Eirini cracked her knuckles rhythmically, the pops like tiny heartbeats.

"When you come to this place, your regrets will too," she said. "Don't let them trap you."

"Our regrets," Saxony repeated. "You mean we'll be tested?"

Eirini nodded and a drop of blood slipped from her eye like

a tear. "Can you take me with you when you leave?" she asked. "I don't like it here anymore."

"You know that's not how this works," Saxony said.

The change in Eirini was sudden.

She tilted her neck, assessing Saxony, and it cracked, causing her head to tremble back and forth until her ear finally rested on her shoulder. A bruise swelled up suddenly on her arm.

Two.

Three.

Four.

They were fingerprints.

Saxony was breaking her.

With every moment she was in Eirini's mind, the consort fractured.

She was the monster here, feeding on things that were not to be fed on.

"You can't leave me." Eirini popped her knuckles again and when her hand broke apart, one of her fingers snapped the wrong way.

"Give me the passphrase for the security system," Saxony said. "I don't have much time."

"Time is all you have. It's all you'll need. Carry it with you if you want your war to succeed."

Saxony gritted her teeth. "Stop talking in riddles."

Eirini smiled and a line of her teeth dropped to the floor.

Fire struck the earth between them.

Saxony jumped back. By the shore, the sea's mighty waves stretched over the invisible wall and dribbled onto the sand.

She couldn't stay. Eirini's mind was unraveling and if the

pain didn't make her body give out, then her insanity would trap Saxony here forever.

"The passphrase," Saxony demanded.

"I already told you. You have to kill for answers in this place."

Behind them, the tree trunks rocked in the soil and the crystal sky began to quake.

There wasn't time to hesitate or weigh up her conscience. Saxony knew what had to be done.

She let a hand rest on Eirini's newly skeletal shoulder, while the other reached for her blade. The one that had broken against the Kingpin's skin and was now miraculously whole again.

"The realms make monsters of us all," Eirini said.

"It's not the realms." The blade felt too light in Saxony's hands. "It's the people in them."

She gave herself a moment to breathe before she plunged the knife into Eirini's stomach.

The consort fell to the sand and the blood crawled from her like insects.

It was black under Saxony's fingernails.

"May the Many Gods guide you," she whispered.

Eirini tugged on her arm, dragging Saxony down to her knees. "Beware of your past," she said. "*Deft es gurs.*"

With a series of bangs that sounded like gunshots, the sea burst through like a broken dam.

And then the island exploded.

It splintered down the middle, dragging the trees from their roots and pulling the sand so voraciously that it whipped and cut across Saxony's face.

Then the tug came in her body again, pushing her backward

until she was stumbling and crawling toward the tear with no control.

Eirini's body lay broken on the ground, unmoving against the strong winds.

Saxony stared at the knife in her stomach and had just enough time to wish it back into her hand, clean, bloodstains long forgotten, before she fell through the crack and into reality.

14

Tavia

TAVIA KNEW WELL ENOUGH that Crafters had more power in their pinkies than she did in her whole arsenal, but seeing that power in the flesh, in Saxony's hands, was a little different.

Saxony spoke three words, just three, and the room stopped closing in.

"Deft es gurs."

The walls retreated and the iron bars that blockaded around them squealed upward.

The air thinned out.

Tavia panted on the floor, tasting the alcohol wafting over from the consort's half-empty glass. The one that was right beside her fully dead hand.

The walls trembled in fear and then slammed back on themselves, shattering a hole through the side of the building like a gaping mouth.

Saxony walked toward the edge and let out a low whistle.

"Did you mean to do that?" Tavia asked.

"At least I blasted a hole in the building and not our faces."

"Tell me you have Ashwood's location," Wesley said.

Saxony nodded. "I've got the way to his island inside my mind like a map."

"I guess I was right to put my faith in you."

Wesley took out his gun and checked the bullets. He turned to face the doorway, which solidified into a mirror that reflected back at them the horror of what they had done.

The consort's body was angled toward Tavia. Blood on her cheek, her eyes wide and accusing.

Wesley aimed the gun at the reflection and fired.

The doorway exploded at their feet.

"We need to go," he said. "Shattering it will only keep the consort's guards at bay for so long. They'll find another way in."

Tavia stood, trying not to look at the consort.

"How do we get out?" she asked. "There's no other exit."

Wesley gestured to the new hole in the building.

"You've read one too many children's tales about Crafters." Saxony peered out of the wounded building and down to the streets below. "We can't actually fly."

"Maybe *you* can't," Wesley said.

Tavia felt him looking at her and she knew he was thinking of the hover charms she'd stolen from under the nose of his predecessor. The ones she had used to break into the amity precinct.

"I've only got three left," she said.

Wesley pulled a hand through his hair, the bone gun still firm in his grip. "Many Gods, Tavia. You think I let you keep those so you could just throw them away?"

"You don't let me do anything," she said. "And they weren't yours in the first place."

"You should know better. I inherited everything when I became underboss, even the stolen things."

He adjusted his tie indignantly.

He looked ridiculously punchable.

It was typical that even when their only choices were falling to their deaths or being tortured by the consort's guards, Wesley could still make time to be a pompous ass.

Tavia folded her arms across her chest. "Three is more than enough."

"Are you volunteering to be left behind?" Wesley asked.

"I'm saying that if we hold hands, then we should be able to stretch three charms. Distribute the weight. Not to mention, Saxony is powerful enough to boost the magic."

Wesley pinched the bridge of his nose. "Fine," he said. "But if we start falling to our deaths, then it's your hand I'm letting go of."

"I'd thank you for it."

Tavia reached into her pocket to dig out the stolen hover charms and dropped them, one by one, into Wesley's outstretched palms.

The four of them gathered by the new hole in the building and looked down to the city streets that concreted miles below. Wesley palmed the stolen magic contemplatively, letting it coat his skin.

He closed his eyes and stretched out his hand for them to form a link.

Saxony's face wrinkled in disgust at the prospect and though Wesley couldn't have seen, he smirked as though he had.

Tavia eyed him, trying to remember the last time she held his hand.

It had been so long since they'd done anything but bait each other that she struggled to remember the times of tenderness and warmth. Not that a memory of his skin would matter—Tavia imagined the years of killing had probably roughened his hands quite a bit.

In fact, she hoped Wesley had a callous for every life he'd taken.

When nobody stepped forward, Karam took Wesley's hand. She waited a moment, scratched her teeth hard across her bottom lip, and then snatched Saxony's, too. Saxony rolled her shoulder as if the force had nearly loosed it from its socket.

Tavia turned to survey the mess they were going to leave. The room was in chaos, everything spilled out onto the floor and ripped from the walls and stained in glass and blood. Even the floorboards had splintered upward to knifepoints, revealing the darkness beneath.

Except, not all of it was darkness.

There was something strange about the way the floor jutted out in odd crisscrosses. Something that was glistening underneath, calling to her like a song.

"Tavia."

She looked back over her shoulder to Wesley. His eyes were still closed, right hand empty where hers should have been.

Wesley was absorbing the magic, keeping focus so that he could let the hover charm flow evenly between them all. Tavia noticed his dark skin taking on a silver sheen as he forced the charm to channel in and out of himself.

"What are you doing?" he asked.

Tavia didn't answer, but she did smile.

From her new vantage point, she could see it clearly. Hidden under the floor, with red flashing on the lock like a beacon.

A hidden safe.

Magic the consort had collected and stashed from each of her dirty deals.

There were so many rumors about those safes that it had become a bit of a busking legend, and too many times Tavia had imagined finding one of them and using the power to take her freedom by force.

She beelined for the safe just as a series of explosive pops rattled the room.

Tavia crouched to her knees and covered her head like the whole building might just come crashing down.

"It's the consort's guards," Wesley said. "They can't use magic to get in now that the doorway's smashed, so they're breaking their way through. We need to go."

"Not yet," Tavia said.

She pulled away the pieces of floor that had been loosed by the explosion. Sure enough, the safe was there. A small metallic thing built into the floor, not much wider than a briefcase.

But Tavia knew better than anyone how many charms could fit inside a briefcase.

"It's the consort's safe," she called out. "I can crack it. We need the firepower."

"I'm a Crafter," Saxony said. "I *am* your firepower."

"Everyone knows that the consort has magic not even in circulation," Tavia said. "Can you imagine what she had access to? The secrets of Wrenyal. Things nobody outside Volo has even heard of. It's a gold mine of magic."

The guards crashed against the doorway and Tavia reached into her pocket, still crouched on the floor. She pulled out a small magnet.

"You have a magical magnet?" Karam asked.

Wesley shoved a hand into his pocket. "And yet only three hover charms."

Tavia ignored him and pressed the magnet against the safe.

The doorway shook as the guards raged on, small pieces of debris crumbling to the floor. Sooner or later, they were going to rip another hole in the building.

The magnet fixed onto the lock.

Tavia closed her eyes, letting the combinations flow through her as the magic did its work. Code flashed across her mind, lines of it screaming out to her. Numbers she couldn't even count to crawled along her vision. It made her want to scratch her own eyes out.

Then a click sounded.

The first combination unlocked.

"Get a move on," Wesley said.

Tavia moved the magnet down the strip, letting the magic tap into the next combination.

In a safe like this, there couldn't be more than five.

"I've nearly got it." Tavia squeezed her eyes shut. "Just a few more minutes."

"We don't have a few minutes!" Saxony said. "Tavia, come on!"

Every word she spoke was punctured by a crescendo of bangs from the guards.

Another click. Two down.

There was no way Tavia was leaving this room without getting her hands on the consort's magic. If the Kingpin had an army of Crafters, the least they needed were a few surprises.

"Just go without me," Tavia said, waving them off.

"We're not leaving you!" Saxony said.

"You want us to let you get killed?" Wesley asked.

The banging grew louder.

Tavia gestured to the consort. "We get people killed all the time," she said. "Just give me the third hover charm and I'll catch up. Make sure the buskers are ready to go as soon as I get there."

"You're out of your mind," Wesley said.

Tavia pulled the magnet away. She was almost certain that Wesley was going to yank her to her feet and throw her out of the window before he gave in. He had that look in his eyes that he always got before tearing a busker a new one. Instead, he let out a curse—and not the magical kind—then thrust an open palm. The sheen from his hands gathered into the center and a small bead formed atop his skin.

Wesley chucked the charm at Tavia and she caught it with a lopsided grin.

He was trusting her to get the job done.

"You better get to the train tracks within an hour," Wesley said. "Or we're leaving."

He linked hands with the others and the three of them stepped backward, out into the air, floating above the city they were trying to save.

"Don't get yourself killed," Saxony said. "I'll be pissed."

"Get going before that charm wears off and you plummet to your deaths!" Tavia yelled, her hands buried in the floorboards. "I don't want to step on you on my way out."

She turned her focus back to the safe and she could just about hear the cogs churning inside, clicking with each combination. Just one more minute.

She fingered the magnet and felt the fourth combination click into place, but the rush of success was followed by a final explosive roar.

The wall that had kept them safe came crumbling down. The guards burst through the doorway, guns and magic. Charms were lassoed to their belts and pistols were primed in their hands and murder was all over their somber faces. Tavia crouched low, hidden behind the bar, while Wesley and the others floated in midair, hands still linked.

Wesley's eyes snapped to Tavia's, and in a blink his face hardened. He stepped back into the building, dragging Karam and Saxony with him, but the moment their feet touched the broken ground, the guards opened fire.

There were too many shots to count, but only one that mattered.

Karam's shoulder whipped back.

The bullet tore into her chest, blood splattering on the wall beside her. She staggered from the impact, one foot stumbling out of the building.

And then she fell.

In a blink, Karam careened out of the tower, taking Wesley and Saxony down with her.

And leaving Tavia to the guards.

15

Karam

GETTING SHOT HURT. FALLING to your death from over a thousand feet hurt a little more.

Karam's face scraped against the concrete, bones crumbling like pastries as the ground slammed into her. And that was what it felt like—not her crashing to the earth, but the earth crashing into her.

The magic slowed their fall, which was handy, since Karam didn't think dying would suit her. And if she did die, she really didn't want to do it outside of the consort's headquarters holding Wesley's hand. But, though the so-called hover charm had taken the speed off their descent and Saxony's magic had broken their fall somewhat, Karam still felt like the fall had broken her face.

"Get up," Karam said. "We have to get to the tracks."

Wesley rubbed his neck and when he pulled his hand away, it was wet with blood. "Give me a minute," he said. "It's my first time jumping from a building."

He smoothed the dust off his clothes ruefully.

"I really liked this suit."

"Karam, are you okay?" Saxony asked.

She was standing taller than them, looking mostly unharmed, except for a small scratch across her cheek, but even that had begun to heal.

Either Crafters were invincible, or Saxony had used most of her magic to keep her own collision to a minimum.

Karam stood, grabbing her shoulder where the bullet hit. She wasn't bleeding as much as she would have if it clipped an artery, and she wasn't as dead as she would have been if it clipped her heart, so she counted herself lucky.

"Let's split up," Wesley said. "Divide their attention and rendezvous with the rest of the buskers in an hour like we agreed."

"What about Tavia?" Saxony asked. "We can't just leave her."

"She told us to," Karam said. "We cannot save her. There is no way back into the building now that it is locked down."

Wesley looked up. Even from this far they could hear gunshots and see the bursts of light from the bullets scatter like dozens of tiny blinking suns.

"Tavia can take care of herself," Wesley said. "She has enough magic to protect her. She'll be okay."

"That's crap," Saxony all but spat. "You won't really leave her behind."

Karam could see something on the cusp of Wesley's face, a slight smear of humanity that was fighting to take hold. If any of them were righteous or good or even half-loyal, they would have tried, somehow, to go back up to that building and tried, even in vain, to rescue her.

Wesley readjusted his cuff links.

The humanity in him quickly faded.

"Anyone can get left behind," he said.

Because not a one of them was truly righteous or good or even half-loyal.

———

NEARLY AN hour after Karam had split from the others, she approached the old train tracks. Though she'd lost the guards in the lower towns, she'd traveled through alleys and city nooks to be sure they didn't catch her trace.

The old tracks were rugged, to say the least.

Since the expansion of the floating railways across the realms, they had become nothing more than a gimmick for tourists with little better to do. They were a museum to the past, ferreting visitors from one place to the next in guided tours that could take days.

When Karam spotted their train, she sucked in a breath and watched the black smoke bellow into the air.

It was bronzed from cold and age, with a plow attached haphazardly to the front, ready to clear snow from the lines, and large twin tracks that hid the wheels in a triangular arc. Its corroded face was like a spear, guns peeking from every window like cannons. Perhaps it was clunky, but it seemed to have enough firepower to wipe out a small city. Or a very large Kingpin.

Wesley's fifty chosen buskers meandered pitifully around the train. Some sat atop, nearly obscured by the smoke, throwing trick bags at one another and laughing loud enough that they may as well have sent up a flare for their location.

If this was the sorry state of their army, Karam was going to have to get to grips with her own mortality pretty soon. There was little chance of her doing the legend of her family and the Rekhi d'Rihsni justice with these people for soldiers.

Karam stepped onto the tracks, glancing around the other side to see if Saxony was anywhere in sight.

Nothing.

Then again, Wesley, for all his bravado about leaving anyone behind, was also nowhere to be seen.

Only one busker idled, his back to Karam, cupping a small bat in his hands. He leaned down to whisper something in the creature's ear.

It was what the Uskhanyans called a *delg* bat. The daytime messenger. Because it was not nocturnal like the rest of its species, but a creature of magic that slept only in the briefest moments of twilight.

The creature cried in acknowledgment before leaping from the busker's fingers and flying hastily out of view.

The busker turned.

Karam stared.

Falk.

The man Tavia liked to call Wesley's weasel. Up close, Karam could see why.

"What are you doing?" Karam asked him. "Wesley told you to send a bat right now?"

Who was he spiriting messages to at a time like this?

"We cannot trust anyone," Karam said. "And you will give away our location with that thing, if the rest of your comrades have not already."

Falk opened his mouth to make some sort of an excuse, but the next voice Karam heard was not his. It was a smooth Rishiyat drawl that carried the hint of a smile.

"Relax," Saxony said. "He's just doing what he's told."

Karam spun to find her leaning against the front of the train, eyes sparking almost playfully. A bead of sweat readied to drip from her collarbone, and Karam could make out a thin silver line from one of her Crafter staves peeking through her shirt.

"Nice of you to show up by the way," Saxony said. "One more minute and I could have been worried."

Karam ignored her. "We cannot be sending bats right now."

Saxony only shrugged. "You know what the underboss is like."

"So he has you following orders too?"

Saxony's smile flickered, as if the very idea were an insult. "Wesley doesn't order me to do anything," she said.

"Good for you."

Karam stepped back across the tracks, making for the front cab of the train.

Saxony meandered after her. "You know, if you need some help relaxing, then I'm happy to oblige," she said playfully.

This didn't seem like a time for jokes, but that was always when Saxony most liked to make them.

"This is not the Crook and I am not ordering a Brandy," Karam said. "Do not be sleazy."

"If that's your definition of sleazy, then stay out of the Crook," Saxony said.

Karam crossed her arms over her chest.

She may have brought it up, but the last thing she wanted to talk about with Saxony was the Crook.

Some people aren't made to be happy, Saxony had said just two months before, under the lights of the old clock tower. She hadn't been sure if Saxony was talking about Karam or herself, but either way, it hurt.

Either way, nobody deserved to be dumped under a disco ball.

"Wesley thinks that just because he is in Creije that he is untouchable," Karam said. "He needs to know that we cannot relax our guard and that we must—"

Saxony grabbed her hand.

Karam stopped walking.

Her fingers curled instinctively around Saxony's and her breath got caught somewhere in her throat.

"I told you not to worry," Saxony said.

But the truth was, Karam worried all the time.

She worried that she would never live up to her family's legacy and that Ashwood would find Saxony and see her as just another shiny new brick to build his empire.

It was in Karam's blood to make sure that didn't happen.

Back in her realm, people worshipped Crafters as holy conduits of the Indescribable God, and Karam's family had spent generations protecting them. Her grandparents were part of the Rekhi d'Rihsni. They lived as sacred warriors and died trying to save true magic.

It was why Karam had grown up wanting to be a fighter, rather than teaching at temple like her parents. They thought peace was the new way, but Karam couldn't fathom such a reality. She and her friend Arjun were just kids when they vowed to bring back the Rekhi d'Rihsni and deliver war to the Kingpins. They played warriors together, with Karam vowing to storm castles and Arjun promising to bring them down alongside her.

Karam left her realm not just because of her parents, but because she and Arjun decided that Uskhanya was where she could best learn to be a warrior worthy of the sacred cause. Protecting Saxony was literally her birthright.

Some days, it even struck Karam that part of her connection to Saxony might be because of that legacy. She worried that the thirst to be near her might be misplaced duty.

Other days, when Saxony would merely glance at her, for a second or less, and the realms felt like they might explode, Karam knew that wasn't possible.

Maybe she and Saxony were tied by destiny, but Karam was sure she had chosen that destiny. And she would again, in any other life.

"I am trying to keep us alive," Karam said now. "Worrying is what does that."

Saxony smiled. "No matter what happens, I'll protect you."

Karam almost snorted, as though she would ever be the one who needed protecting, but before she could catch her breath for long enough to come up with a reply, Wesley emerged from the train.

He stared at their entwined hands and Karam quickly pulled her grip from Saxony's. It seemed odd to be affectionate in front of her boss. In front of the person who had helped her become a warrior.

"Let's not make a habit of cutting things so tight," Wesley said.

Karam supposed that was his way of being glad she'd arrived safely.

"I did not realize Falk was one of the buskers we chose," she said.

"He's not." Wesley sat on the train steps. "He's our driver until we reach the realm of Wrenyal. Since Schulze wasn't going to provide a *civilian*, I had to go with the only guy I know who can work the old trains. Falk's obsessed with old tech. Besides, he's helping me on a little side-project. He's one of us."

Karam held back her comments on that.

If Tavia were here, she would have made them for her, saying something awful that Karam would have agreed with. Silently, of course, because Tavia's ego didn't need feeding.

"We should get going," Karam said. "Since we are all here."

"We're not all here," Saxony said.

Wesley adjusted his tie. "No, we're not."

"You both want to wait for Tavia?"

"I'm a man of my word," Wesley said. "I promised an hour, so we wait an hour. Time's not up yet."

Karam expected this from Saxony, because her odd friendship with Tavia was one of the few familiarities she had in Creije. But Wesley—*hei reb*—Wesley Thornton Walcott of all people. The man whose mere name seemed to be made of the same magic he sold, practically resolute as he checked their lives against Tavia's.

Karam often thought Wesley was as much a myth of Creije as he was the master of it, but when it came to Tavia, sometimes that myth really was nothing more than a man.

"The consort's guards could be here any minute," Karam said.

"And so could Tavia," Wesley countered.

Karam wasn't sure how he could be optimistic. "The consort's people will try and check all routes out of the city and it is only a matter of time before they think to look at this one. We cannot risk all of that on the hopes of a dead girl."

It was not kind, but it was true. The chances of Tavia having survived an assault from the consort's guards were slim. Tavia was smart, not bulletproof.

Wesley didn't flinch. "Even the dead deserve five minutes," he said.

He turned to the buskers meandering around the train and with just one look they promptly stopped throwing tricks at one another and threw their cigarettes to the ground. They were as straight as soldiers, ready to walk into battle.

"Why are you all staring at me like we're on a date?" Wesley asked. "Make yourselves useful."

"How so, sir?" one of the buskers asked.

"I don't care. Just do something. Shoot someone. Fire-gates, shoot each other for all I care."

"Or," Saxony said, "shoot them."

She pointed to the warehouse in the distance and, as if on cue, a choir of bullets exploded against the train's smoke box.

The consort's guards rushed toward them with more weaponry than Karam had ever seen. And they weren't alone.

There were two dozen buskers by their side. Ones Wesley hadn't trusted enough to invite along. They threw charms at the side of the train like they were trying to score points in a game of darts.

They weren't afraid of the amityguards seeing, or being thrown into cells. These people were out for blood.

"Disloyal bastards," Wesley said. "You kill one consort and everyone loses their minds."

He pulled his gun out and aimed a shot.

In the distance a busker fell.

Karam hated to admit how good his aim was, but *spirits damn*.

"I told you to shoot someone!" Wesley yelled. "Don't make me repeat myself!"

In an instant, the train opened fire.

Their army was only fifty strong, but each and every one of them had a gun and magic. Bullets exploded from the train windows where the buskers took aim. Those on the ground whipped rifles and pistols out from places Karam didn't even know someone could hide a gun.

And the magic.

Hei reb, there was magic everywhere.

Buskers stood on top of the train and threw back their arms in wide arches, attacking with everything from blinding trick bags to charms that seemed to melt the skin off the guards' faces.

Karam ducked and rolled under the train and to the other side, sheltering from the stream of bullets. She couldn't do much at this range. She needed something to stab or hit or kick. She'd never relied on guns to fight before.

Karam tuned to Wesley, who had joined her on the other side. His foot was nooked in the train window and he perched over the roof, firing bullets with one hand and charm after charm with his other.

It was as if he had a lever under his sleeve, shooting them

out with as much speed as the bullets. They imploded at the guards' feet, shot ice through their hearts, catapulted others what seemed like a mile back.

A bullet smashed through the window by Karam's head.

Saxony screamed her name.

And suddenly Saxony was on the roof with dozens of buskers, skin newly ablaze, turning from brown to molten yellow.

Saxony didn't just hold fire in her hands, her hands were made of fire itself. She propelled them backward and then lurched ahead like she was pushing the flame out of her soul.

It spat across the dirt and engulfed a row of the guards.

The buskers around her followed suit, throwing fire charms like cannons at their enemies. Some screamed in victory, others screamed in a cry of agony before their bodies fell to the ground like raindrops.

One. Two.

"We must get the train moving!" Karam yelled.

Wesley, suit still smooth as he aimed another shot, said, "I don't remember giving you permission to order my people around."

Karam didn't know what to make of that.

Surely he wasn't still thinking about Tavia? Even if she hadn't died back there—and that was a big *if*—there was no way she could get past their attackers to board the train. And there was no way they could afford to wait for her to try.

"She's right!" Saxony yelled above the roar of her fire. "Your arrogance will get us killed."

"Better my arrogance than your disloyalty."

Saxony heaved another ball of flame in her hands. "Tavia

wouldn't want us to die for her. And where was your loyalty when you abandoned her in the first place?"

Wesley started to pull himself up onto the roof and Karam could smell the magic on him as much as she could see it in Saxony. A constant power struggle between them. But Karam wasn't going to gamble her life on pride, no matter whose it was.

She reached out to grab Wesley.

"Sir," she said. "Anyone can get left behind."

Wesley shook his arm from hers, outraged at the move, but the sound of his own words repeated back gave Wesley pause. His eyes pulsed as he weighed any honor he might have with their chances of survival.

Another busker tumbled from the rooftop and fell to the floor beside them, spitting up dirt as he landed.

With a snarl Wesley let off a shot that took down a guard trying to board the back of the train, and said, "Someone get this pile of junk moving!"

It didn't take long for Falk to make the train jerk and rumble under their feet. Their buskers were still firing—guns and cannons and charms—as the train churned and sputtered.

Those not already on board jumped in through the doorways or clung onto the open windows. Karam could count three bodies on the ground, but she didn't have time to dwell on their losses once a few of the guards jumped on board too, trying their luck as the train broke away.

When seven filtered into the cabin Karam was in, she smiled.

Even with a bullet rammed in her shoulder, this would be a piece of cake.

She took the first three in seconds and the other four gathered around her. The buskers aboard were still firing their magic as the train sped out of the station, but this was Karam's chance to fight.

She'd stood back and watched them get attacked without being able to lift a hand.

Now she wanted retribution.

Karam seized the fingers of the guard closest to her right, bending them back until he cowered on his knees. In a swift movement, she cut her knife across his neck and leaped over his lifeless body to plunge toward the second. It only took one well-placed kick to the stomach for the guard to fall.

Never one to miss an opportunity, Karam rolled over the woman's back to crack her foot against the third's face. Then turned to slice her blade across the second's spine.

Karam cut through the guards like they were trees, feeling their blood soak her lips and edge under her fingernails.

When she was finished, she was aware of how she must have looked, painted in her kill. The buskers in the cab whispered and stepped back, Karam's heavy breathing like a roar.

Wesley clapped as he stepped over the altar of bodies.

"You never get rusty," he said. "Couldn't ask for a better bodyguard. Remind me to give you a raise."

Karam wiped the blood and sweat from her forehead and leaned out the window.

Saxony was still on the roof. Her head tipped back, gathering wind in her grasp, as Falk chugged the train from the station and propelled them onward.

It was like Saxony held the world in her hands, and when she threw her head forward, her eyes were blanketed white.

Karam's spine went rigid.

There was so much magic inside Saxony and she'd never let Karam see it clearly before now. It commanded her and suddenly Karam realized that the magic wasn't just part of Saxony, or something she used like Wesley and Tavia did.

Saxony *was* the magic.

Crafters weren't made from skin and bone like the rest of them. They were forged from spells.

A burst of light hit the old station, where guards were still attacking at long range, and Karam swiveled, spying a figure on the roof of a nearby warehouse, throwing magic like bread for birds. Flashes and flashes of light until the guards were on their knees, blinded, and some were thrown high enough into the air for Karam not to see them come back down.

The figure turned and Karam leaned farther out the window, squinting. But the train was traveling too fast and night had descended. The figure backed up a few steps, teetering on the edge of the warehouse, and then made a run for it.

"Impossible," Karam said.

The figure leaped from the building.

Karam's jaw dropped.

Rather than fall they floated, running through the air like it was road.

Karam blinked and turned to look at the others, to make sure she wasn't losing her mind. That she hadn't, perhaps, gotten blood poisoning from that bullet. But they were staring too, watching the strange figure run through the air and toward them.

It was only when they crashed onto the roof beside Saxony

with a flourish that Karam could make out their ally's smarmy face.

Tavia stood, brushed off her trousers, and peered down at the faces that gawked from the windows.

"Leaving so soon?" she asked.

16

Wesley

WESLEY HADN'T SEEN THE sun in two days.

The train was dimly lit so they could make out each other's faces during the day and not be too disturbed to sleep during the night. Or what they thought was night.

Outside the windows was nothing but darkness, peppered only by flashes of light that punctured through the gravel and concrete of the underground tunnels they were now inside, before filtering down to them. But the train passed by so quickly, the glimpses of day never offered much of a reprieve.

Wesley supposed it was not the worst thing.

He lived most of his life in the shadows, keeping company with dark magic and darker people, and the tunnels were the safest way to travel, with a clear route all the way to Wrenyal.

Falk counted the hours for them, proclaiming when it was dusk and when it was dawn like an announcer, using his wristwatch to steer Wesley and their makeshift army into sleep, or let them know it was time to wake or eat or meander.

They'd lost nearly half a dozen buskers back in Creije. The remaining walked through the days with sharp eyes and quick hands, as though another attack could come at any time.

It had been two days and they still had three to go until they reached the Wrenyi realm, which was outside Ashwood's reach and would allow them safe haven.

Three more days of waiting.

"Our biggest problem is that we do not have the element of surprise," Karam said. "The shadow moon is less than a month away and without enough time to prepare, we will fail."

"You're just a bundle of positivity, aren't you?" Tavia said. "Tell us more about how the future is dark and we're all going to get killed by the Kingpin."

"Not you," Karam said. "I am going to kill you myself."

Saxony snorted. "You two have issues."

"I will not be part of a suicide mission," Karam said.

"Would it be easier if I didn't give you a choice?" Wesley asked. "I could force you, but I think it would be easier to just pay you instead. Double your usual rate should do it."

"I was not aware I had a usual rate for getting myself killed," Karam said. "Or for saving the realms."

Wesley nearly recoiled. "We're saving a place I have great stakes in. Don't make out like I'm a good guy. It's disheartening."

"Nobody is going to mistake you for a good guy in that suit," Tavia said. "You look like a gangster threw up on you."

Wesley looked indifferent. "But a very high-end gangster."

He sat back. The four of them were gathered in the main carriage, which Wesley supposed would have been first-class once upon a time, only now the windows were shot out and the cold from the tunnels battered through.

They had been plotting for the entirety of the two days and Karam continued to discuss strategy at excruciating length.

Wesley's buskers slept and ate and used trick bags to pull pranks on each other to pass the time and ease the rigid tension impending death brought. They played cards and romanced and picked fights until something or someone ended up broken.

And all the while, Wesley did nothing but plan.

It was so incredibly tedious.

Still, he took note of what Karam and Saxony were saying, and offered solutions when he could. He glowered when they said something awful about him and smirked when they said something awful to each other. He was aware of every word they said and every move they made.

But mostly, Wesley was aware of Tavia, sitting beside him, still smelling of magic and gunpowder.

She had pouches tied to her belt, brimming with the stolen charms she hadn't let him take inventory of. To have it all so close and be unable to touch it was torture, but Wesley owed Tavia one. Or two, if they were counting her help at the train station.

Not that Wesley needed anyone's help.

Still, he liked hearing Tavia talk about fighting off the consort's guards with blinding charms and how, when she jumped from the top of the headquarters, the ground absorbed her like a sponge and then spat her back up.

How she felt like she could run through the wind and toward their train forever.

He liked how Tavia smiled when she told them that story. Wesley hadn't seen her smile like that in years.

But in the moments outside those small respites, he felt like a tiger in a cage. Like one of those zoo animals, whose claws were filed down while people stared from behind the safety of bars.

He was a predator with no prey.

Two days of only talking.

It was like his own personal fire-gate.

"We don't need surprise," Saxony said. "The Kingpin won't run from a fight."

He'll be waiting for you. And he won't be alone.

Wesley loosened his tie.

He wouldn't listen to that voice and he wouldn't think about it.

"The Kingpin will have a militia. Fifty buskers will not change things," Karam said.

Wesley set his tie on the table. "We don't even have fifty anymore."

And it still stung.

But letting people die is what you do best.

"We could have the biggest army in the realms and still lose," Wesley said. "It's not bodies we need, it's magic. The Kingpin is one of the most powerful people alive, and now that he has Crafters under his thumb we have to even the playing field."

"We're not going to Rishiya," Saxony said. "I'm not taking you to my family."

"I never mentioned your family. I told you we would go to Wrenyal and that's still the plan."

Wesley turned to Karam, who stiffened as though she knew what he was going to say.

"We're heading to the five-river city," he said. "Granka."

Karam blinked.

Wesley knew how long it had been since she'd left Granka and exactly how long it had been since she'd decided never to go back. The two were coincidentally the same.

There was no life for Karam there. She was rough and deadly and belonged in Creije more than she could ever belong in the holy realm. Wesley could barely imagine her as a dutiful daughter, praying to her Indescribable God and preaching peace. She was a weapon and he'd spent years making sure she was pleased about it. The last thing he wanted was to undo all of that hard work by making her nostalgic.

"You want me to arrange a meeting with the Crafters in Granka," Karam said. Her voice was more gravel-toned than usual. "You assume I would be able to do such a thing."

"Let's not pretend we don't know our history," Wesley said. "Wrenyal worships Crafters and your grandparents led insurgent groups to protect them during the War of Ages. You're a child of the Rekhi d'Rihsni."

Karam's hands twitched by her sides.

"I've known it for a while," Wesley said. "Just like I knew what Saxony was."

"So you're exploiting all of our pasts, one by one," Saxony said. "And not even giving us the chance to say no."

Wesley almost laughed at the idea.

If Saxony thought he hadn't given her chances, then she was delusional.

He could have turned her in to the Kingpin when he first discovered what she was, or bribed her to help build his city into greatness, but he didn't. He didn't force her to create magical weaponry or put her life in danger at any turn.

Wesley hadn't so much as looked at her wrong.

He had left Saxony to live her secret life in Creije, undisturbed.

Despite what they all thought of him, how evil they liked to preach that he was, Wesley was not Dante Ashwood, stealing Crafters from the streets and harnessing their magic with no regard.

He had a line. He had sins to atone for.

"The reason I've survived this long is because I know my assets and keep them close," Wesley said.

Karam was too well trained to look hurt by the notion that Wesley might have used her, but years in the trenches meant he knew her well enough to read the signs.

And he was a little sorry for it.

"You really are unbelievable," Tavia said.

It wasn't exactly a compliment, but Wesley shrugged it off.

"Even if Karam doesn't know where any Crafters are, her family does," he said. "That kind of loyalty lives through generations. The only way we stand a chance against Ashwood is with Crafters of our own."

"I do not know where you heard those stories about my family," Karam said. "But nothing was proven."

"Right. The old Kingpins executed them due to reasonable suspicion."

"There is nothing reasonable about execution."

Wesley didn't agree.

After all, he'd executed his old underboss and that was most definitely reasonable.

Or was it only execution when those in power did it? Everyone else just got saddled with plain old murder.

"If we do this, then any Crafters who join our side are under my command," Saxony said. "Not yours."

Wesley laughed. "You went from not wanting to give me Crafters to asking to be their leader?"

"I won't have you deciding the fates of my people."

"They're Karam's people."

Karam folded her arms across her chest defiantly. "And I will not take you to them unless she is the one to lead."

And that was precisely why Wesley hated working with a crew. He sighed.

Wesley always preferred to get things done alone, or order someone else to carry out the task, because teams were messy and encouraged sentimentality alongside camaraderie.

They made everyone so damn sensitive of each other's feelings.

"I've been training with my amja since I was a child," Saxony said. "I'm skilled in both magical and hand-to-hand combat. I was made to lead."

Wesley remained unimpressed. "Aren't we all."

"And my specialty is in Energy," Saxony said. "Which is going to be a great help in the battle."

"And here I thought your specialty was being a magical snob," Tavia said.

Her tone was teasing and Saxony let out a sarcastic "har har."

But Wesley's curiosity was piqued.

Crafter magic was split into three specialties: Intuition, Energy, and Spirit. Though any Crafter could cast spells and master all kinds of magic, they were only gifted with one specialty.

Wesley had spent his childhood alongside Tavia, memorizing all there was to know about Crafters and their powers. There were records, endless archives, of every trick and charm and elixir, every spell and curse, every piece of magic that had come before, written into word and filed away for history.

Energycrafters, with control over the element they were most akin to, able to create protection and invisibility fields.

Spiritcrafters, who could commune with the dead and control nature's spirit of the weather.

And Intuitcrafters, the most dangerous of all, who could spawn illusions and work their way into people's minds and futures.

Wesley and Tavia had spent so much time in the libraries, studying those tales, flooding their childhoods with them, imagining what a place with such free magic might have looked like. They got lost together, in stories and memories of the past.

"So we agree to officially split the leadership," Tavia said. "Wesley handles the buskers and Saxony handles the Crafters. What about the journey?"

Wesley stared at the route Saxony had drawn from her mind.

Their journey to the Kingpin's isle was traced over a map of the four realms, culminating in their arrival at a point of the Onnela Sea, a place commonly referred to as Ejm Voten. Which translated to *lonely water*, because it was miles away from civilization and deadly enough that nobody dared cross. Plagued by tumultuous storms and hard-to-navigate rock formations, Ejm Voten offered no through-route to any city or realm.

At least, no safe route.

It had been the subject of sailors' stories for years. Travelers said there was a sunken city beneath it and that cries from the ghosts of all who drowned in its depths could be heard in the wind, readying to pull boats under. Compasses spun madly because the sea devils patrolling the waters had so much iron in their blood. The list went on.

The more Wesley thought about it, the more it made sense that the Kingpin would make his home in those waters. Where better to hide than a place nobody dared go?

"If there are Spiritcrafters in Granka, it will come in handy when we cross Ejm Voten," he said. "Maybe all of the legends are actually part of the Kingpin's trials Eirini mentioned."

"Well, that's just great," Tavia said. "Leave it to the would-be dictator to make us face our regrets. Who is he to pass judgment on us?"

"It's not about judgment," Wesley said. "It's about strength."

"If you're going to say *strength of character*, then I'm going to throw up."

"My guess is the trials will be about defeating our own weakness," Wesley said. "Proving that we're capable of being more than human."

"Gods do not have regrets," Karam said sagely.

Tavia turned to Wesley. "You're half set. Nobody would ever accuse you of being human."

"Are you saying I'm godly?"

Tavia snorted and something in Wesley's chest jolted too suddenly for his liking.

"Eirini also said something about time," Saxony said. "She told me we should carry it with us. I don't know what she meant."

Wesley withheld his frown alongside his surprise.

"I know," he said. "It's one of the reasons why I brought Falk along with us. He's not just here to drive the train."

Tavia groaned inwardly. "Please tell me that you two haven't been working on a way to magically blow everyone to pieces."

Apparently, Falk's reputation as a magical weapons expert preceded him.

"They're time barrels," Wesley explained. "They're yet to be perfected, but I've had Falk helping me work on them for a while. A time charm can freeze someone in a second, but I've been trying for nearly a year to find a way to engineer it so the magic isn't focused on just one person. The plan is for the barrels to go off with a bang and freeze any enemies in our path."

Wesley sighed, a little put out.

"I thought I'd be presenting it to the Kingpin rather than using it against him," he said. "Life's funny that way."

"A time bomb." Saxony shook her head, like she was caught halfway between outrage and appreciation. "What's to stop it from freezing us too?"

"That's the *yet to be perfected* part."

"Maybe the consort knew about the weapon," Saxony said. "It would explain what she meant. And if she knew, then maybe Ashwood does too."

"We can't be sure that Eirini was talking about the time bombs," Wesley said.

"I still can't believe that you *have* time bombs," Tavia said, incredulous.

Wesley almost grinned. "Brilliant, aren't I? When they're finished, they'll incapacitate anyone with nonlethal force. We get the bang, but not the destruction."

"And you are sure you can finish?" Karam asked. "I do not want to carry around unperfected ticking time bombs."

"We're nearly there," Wesley said. "The timeline isn't ideal, but I'll crack the fine-tuning with Falk."

"On the subject of time," Tavia said. "Back when I was performing at the magic markets, I tried to hock a fortune orb to the crowds." Tavia looked at Wesley by way of inclining her head and not meeting his eyes. "You know the one."

He did.

They'd worked it together, drunk on magic, the stars sprinkled above them and a wild, wild feeling in Wesley's chest whenever their hands entangled.

It was full of junk riddles and mostly mechanics in place of magic, but somewhere deep inside, Wesley felt like he'd placed a piece of himself in that orb, buried amongst the trickery and illusion. A sliver of magic that felt very much like part of his soul.

Though perhaps that had been the reverie charm talking, or the feeling of Tavia so very close and the grin that slid onto her lips when she held up the finished orb.

That grin was a drug in itself. Magic, in itself.

When you get a girlfriend, Tavia had said, eyes dancing, *I hope she's awful at this.*

It was as much a curse as anything she carried around in her pocket.

Wesley bristled, pulling himself a little straighter. "I know the one," he said.

Tavia nodded, then, to Karam and Saxony, she said, "It was mostly a trick orb, not much real magic inside. Something for the tourists. Only, the crowd was kind of restless, so I used a proficiency charm to bump up the show and give them something to fawn over."

The frown across her brows was delicate.

"The orb made a prediction I'd never heard, something Wesley and I didn't put inside. It mentioned time undoing battles. I thought maybe it malfunctioned, because trick magic is so damn testy. But now it seems like too big of a coincidence."

Wesley knew coincidences and that wasn't one.

"It seems the realms are trying to tell us something," Karam said.

"I think *magic* is trying to tell us something," Saxony said.

Karam nodded. "The Indescribable God speaks in many voices."

Wesley resisted the urge to roll his eyes. "Whatever the reason, I'll make sure to perfect the time barrels. But if we're going to get to the Kingpin in time for the shadow moon, then we have to steal a ship once we reach Granka."

"Why not just steal a train?" Tavia asked.

"The floating railways will be too hard to commandeer and there are no magic tracks anywhere near Ejm Voten. It's a no-go zone. A ship is our only choice."

"Ships belong in museums," Tavia said. "And the lines for

the floating railways are just fancy magic dust. Can't we use Saxony's powers to create our own lines and keep a train afloat on whatever course we plot? Falk could drive and she could be the compass."

Wesley turned to Saxony. "I supposed that's a question for you. Do you think you could work on a spell?"

Saxony straightened. "If you think my powers can be conquered by a train line, then I'm not sure why I'm even here."

Wesley smirked.

If that was the case, they could plow the train straight into the sand and any Energycrafters they found in Granka could shield their army from view. They could walk right up to the gates without even being seen.

It was all coming together, the plan he had hurriedly tried to jigsaw.

And even if Ashwood did spot Wesley with Crafters and his best busker at his side, he would still be too curious not to hear him out. Too arrogant to think that letting Wesley in could ever lead to his own destruction.

It would be the Kingpin's downfall.

You'd do anything to win, the voice said, and for once Wesley agreed.

He was coming for Ashwood and when he found him, he would have no mercy.

17

Tavia

HER MUMA'S EYES WERE black and her smile was wide, and these were the days Tavia hated more than anything.

The days she held on tightly to her muma's hand as she was pulled across the room, tugged one way and then the next, while her muma gazed into odd, vacant spaces like someone very important was standing in them.

"There," she said, pointing at her shadow. "Can you see them now? My ghosts."

Tavia shook her head.

She wanted to see. Very desperately she wanted to see the thing that haunted her muma's eyes, but when Tavia looked all she could find was her shadow, still and waiting patiently for her to move.

She thought maybe it was because she wasn't old enough. There were some things only grown-ups knew, and Tavia often found herself struggling to decipher the many things that came easy to the people older than her. She wondered if she tried just *a bit harder, putting all of her might into it, whether she might be able to see what was hidden in the shadows. The things her muma saw that scared her so much.*

But it never worked, even if she tried her very hardest.

Tavia nuzzled into her muma's embrace, cheek pressed against her stomach, and considered lying, if for nothing else than to stop her tears.

"Right there," her muma always said. "Can't you hear them whispering?"

———

TAVIA WOKE to an empty carriage and little light, save for a flickering lantern overhead.

Outside the windows, darkness still echoed. They had left the tunnels and would arrive in Wrenyal in a matter of days, or even hours—Tavia had lost track—but for now the world was still a stranger, blanketed in night, with barely a trace of stars for company.

Tavia stifled a yawn.

She hadn't slept properly in days and the one thing she could not wait for was a real, honest to the gods, bed. Thick blankets and pillows and a space of her own that wasn't invaded by a horde of snoring buskers. As it was, though there were beds in the far carriage, Tavia couldn't relax enough to take up residence in one of them. Her nights were too filled with the awful echoes of the past.

Before the elixir, Tavia kept the memories of her childhood sacred, printed in various pictures inside her mind. She shuffled through them sometimes, conjuring whichever ones she needed when she felt herself sinking too deep into the grips of the criminal underrealm. There was one Tavia used more often than the rest and it had become worn and ragged inside her memory, fading over time so that Tavia had to squeeze her eyes shut in order to see the finer details.

The way her muma's face curved and her eyes wrinkled when she smiled. How her arms wrapped around Tavia's waist so tightly, they almost became one person. How her voice sounded so gentle when she said Tavia's name, like it was a secret between them.

It was a beautiful thing to be loved that much, but now Tavia was ruining those memories by conjuring the ones that lurked behind.

Ones of her muma very, very cold.

Of her eyes black and a mark printed on her neck like a child's drawing.

She tried to push away those thoughts and let her memories be overtaken with incomprehensible niceties about a woman who called her *ciolo* like it was a term of endearment, and being young and small in Creije was closer to good fortune than a calamity.

But it was getting so much harder.

Tavia was too on edge and every night when she closed her eyes all she saw was her muma's face staring back. And that man, Deniel Emilsson, trapped in a Creijen cell, perhaps dead because of her.

It was not exactly a motivation for a peaceful night's sleep.

Besides, there were only a few dozen beds on offer, so Tavia thought it best to let the other buskers fight it out among themselves. Wesley, of course, had his own private carriage with his own private bunk, for no other reason than because he was Wesley.

Tavia bet that he slept like a baby, even if he always had one eye open.

She pulled the silken black hood over her eyes as the cold from the window, broken by the attack on the station, settled in. Her bones ached with the bite of it, but they all needed the fresh air. It was getting a little cramped and Tavia was pleasantly surprised they hadn't all killed each other yet.

She headed to the next carriage, where she could hear Saxony's voice carrying through.

When Tavia slid open the door, Saxony was lying across two chairs, her head dangling over the edge, wild curls sprawling to the floor, a piece of bread in her hand. Karam sat opposite, sharpening her blade with quirked lips.

Tavia liked seeing the two of them together like that. It reminded her of the old days, when she and Wesley were still friends, laughing over nothing and everything.

If in the old days she and Wesley had a history of kissing.

Which they most certainly did not.

"I'm starving," Saxony said.

She threw the bread down onto the platter between them, as though it didn't count as food.

"I can barely sleep with this train making so much noise and every time I want to pee there's a queue the size of a small city. I think *this* might be the Kingpin's first test. I can't imagine him coming up with anything worse."

Karam smirked.

"You mean you're not enjoying all the team bonding?" Tavia asked, stepping into view.

Saxony sat up with a grin. "Nice of you to join the living," she said. "Good nap?"

"Oh, the best." Tavia slumped into the seat beside her. "I had a full twenty minutes."

"Utter luxury," Saxony said.

"And not to make you jealous, but an hour ago the bathroom was free and I managed to pee without a single person knocking on the door. There was even toilet paper on the roll."

"You're killing me," Saxony said. "How did people live before the floating railways? I can't believe I took those trains for granted and talked about them being too big. Too luxurious. Who complains about something being *too luxurious*? I was such a fool."

She looked out the window wistfully, hand on her heart, and the moment she turned, Tavia's eyes drew to the mark on her neck.

She couldn't help it.

It was pinked like a new burn, or at least it had been, though now it was blending back into Saxony's dark skin like an old wound. Every time Tavia caught sight of it, her mind filled with dread.

All the bad nights of her childhood she'd tried so hard to forget bubbled to the surface.

Don't cry, ciolo.

The mark of the magic sickness was so clear when Tavia had seen it on her muma, even long after her body had gone stiff and her hand grew cold in Tavia's tiny fingers. And yet it was disappearing from Saxony like it didn't want to be seen. Maybe it only left its stain on the dead, like a brand.

She wondered if Deniel Emilsson was dead yet.

Tavia cleared her throat.

She was going to drive herself crazy thinking about it.

Saxony leaned her head against the window. "I bet your underboss is loving being so cooped up like this."

Her underboss. As though Wesley belonged only to Tavia.

"Now, now," Tavia said. "Didn't anyone ever teach you not to speak ill of the great Wesley Thornton Walcott?"

"He needs three names for all of his personalities," Saxony said.

Tavia smirked and picked up a piece of bread from the platter. "Who was in charge of bringing the food supplies?"

"I think it's best we don't ask," Saxony said. "I won't be able to control my rage when I find out."

"Good point." Tavia took a bite of the dry bread. "Don't disturb the peace. I haven't been attacked by anyone in days. I'm getting used to the lack of bruises."

"Easy for you to say," Karam said. "You did not get shot."

Tavia gave her a consolatory smile, though in fairness she had been shot *at*, and it was very nearly the same thing. It wasn't Tavia's fault that Karam needed to be a little quicker on her feet. Besides, Saxony had healed the wound in a pinch and Karam seemed like she was back to normal. Glares and all.

"If it still hurts, I can give you something for the pain," Tavia said. "I have a relief charm that could knock you into next week."

"I have no pain," Karam said.

"Oh." Tavia smiled. "So you just wanted an excuse to moan, then?"

Karam's eyes narrowed in a look that told Tavia she didn't appreciate her humor as much as she should have.

Saxony's laugh was like a loud boom in the night. "I really love how you two get along so well." She slung an arm over Tavia's shoulder. "My two best girls, being the best of friends."

Tavia raised an eyebrow, but the grin on Saxony's face was infectious and she couldn't stop herself from laughing alongside her.

It was a nice respite from the war that loomed ahead.

Tavia nudged away Saxony's arm, and through the open buttons of her shirt a small silver mark, right near the cusp of her heart, peeked through.

"I didn't know you had a tattoo," Tavia said.

Saxony rolled her eyes and stroked Tavia's hair. "Poor, little busker," she said, pretending not to see her glare. "It's one of my staves. Every Crafter has them to signal our specialty and magical triumphs. This one's my Energycrafter sign."

Of course it was.

Of course Saxony had one.

Because Saxony was a Crafter.

Tavia didn't know if she'd ever get used to that.

She didn't want to be angry about it, because that seemed really selfish and it made complete sense that Saxony hadn't revealed she was hiding from the very people they both worked for. It was a secret that could cost her life.

But the fact that Saxony didn't trust her, however justified, wasn't easy to swallow.

"They're like those runes the tourists draw on themselves," Tavia said.

Saxony visibly tensed, wrinkling her nose like she'd smelled something awful. "*Suvi.*"

Scumbags.

Apparently, she didn't appreciate her traditions reduced to a costume for Creije's sightseers.

"Are you nervous about meeting with the Crafters?" Tavia asked Karam. "Will they trust you after all this time?"

"I am more nervous about meeting with my father," Karam said, continuing to sharpen her blade. "It has been years since we last spoke and we did not part on good terms. He never approved of who I wanted to be."

Tavia kept quiet, because that seemed like the thing to do when someone looked this vulnerable.

"My entire family, my friends, and all the promises I made them were abandoned," Karam said. "I chose my life in Creije over everything and now I am going back, not to make amends, but to ask them to put their lives on the line for me. Put a trust in me that I broke."

Karam sucked in a breath and Saxony squeezed her knee, like she knew Karam needed comfort but wasn't quite sure how to give it.

Tavia stayed still. She'd never disappointed her father, because he wasn't around to disappoint. Tavia knew nothing about him, not the look he got when he was mad or if they shared the same colored eyes or even his name. And her memories were so full of her muma, each one precious and overused, that dreams of her father had become a rarity.

Her muma had never spoken of him and so Tavia's imagination was all she had. She thought of him in two ways: a dreamer who loved her muma dearly and had died tragically, causing her muma to flee from Volo in a wave of despair and travel to Uskhanya. She settled in Creije, which was his home city, hoping to be close to his spirit. And in the winters, when Creije grew cold and her muma missed the balmy nights of Gila, she'd look out her window and spot the Everglow, and a feeling of calm would wash over her. She'd feel the magic and the presence of her lost love in those lights and be satiated.

The other thought Tavia had was that her father was just a huge bastard.

But she tried not to focus too much on that one.

"I feel the same about my amja," Saxony said. "I don't know what she'll do when she finds out I've teamed up with Wesley to take down the Kingpin. She was alive for the War of Ages and saw firsthand what the dark magic trade did to our people. She hates everything they stand for."

"You mean not everyone thinks Wesley Thornton Walcott is the greatest thing ever?" Tavia asked.

"Strangely, no," Saxony said. "And Many Gods know how my father is going to react when he realizes I went to Creije to find Zekia and stayed to spy on the underboss. When he finds out all I've done, he—"

She cut herself off, growing quiet, her smile barely there and grim.

Tavia hated not knowing what that smile meant. She hated not being able to read the people closest to her.

Tavia would know if it was Wesley. With just one tug of his tie, or a touch of his cuff links at the wrong time, Tavia would know in half a second what Wesley was thinking.

Liars were the easiest to catch.

"So it's angry families all round?" Tavia said. "That'll be fun."

"I think my father will be more scared than angry," Saxony said. "He used to want to fight to take back our place in the world, but after losing my mother and Malik, and then Zekia, I think he's just afraid of outliving everyone."

"Malik?" Tavia repeated.

"My brother," Saxony said. "He died in a fire with my mother when I was a child."

Though she said it so easily, like it was just another fact about her life that she hadn't mentioned, the air grew thick and Tavia felt like the worst friend in the realms.

She didn't even know Saxony had a brother.

What kind of friend didn't ask those questions?

"Malik was only five, but he was the biggest troublemaker you could imagine," Saxony said. "He always needed things to go his way and because he didn't look much like me, or Zekia, I used to tease him that we'd found him in the woods and he was a child of trickster spirits. For some reason, he thought that was a good thing."

Saxony laughed and though it was sad, she also looked a little happy, like she was glad to be able to say her brother's name and tell his stories.

"I'm sorry," Tavia said, which was probably the worst thing to say, because it solved nothing and definitely did not bring Saxony's family back.

Saxony poked her in the ribs. "Don't look so glum," she said. "It was a long time ago and all that matters now is finding Zekia."

"We'll find her," Tavia said. "No matter what. We'll get your sister back."

Saxony linked her arm through Tavia's. "Creije's best busker, making me a promise," she said. "Now that's a sight for sore eyes."

"You can count on me to get the job done," Tavia said. "Self-doubt isn't a good trait to have in our profession."

"In your profession you are not supposed to have good traits," Karam said.

She was joking, in that deadly serious way that only Karam did, but Tavia couldn't bring herself to disagree.

All she ever dreamed of was leaving Creije and traveling to her mother's home realm of Volo, because she thought it would give her some kind of clean slate and erase all the bad she had done. She'd built it up in her head so wonderfully, reading books upon books, until it almost seemed like a fantasy.

The Volens believed in the Lonely Goddess and the Betrayer, who she had created to live out her immortal life with, only he grew bitter at her power and sent sin down to the realms, so she was forced to kill him as punishment. Each year the Volens had celebration in thanks for the Lonely Goddess's sacrifice. In the capital of Gila, where Tavia's muma was from, the city she was born in, they filled the streets with paper lanterns and cast magic to the sky so the stars beamed down in an array of colors. It was said to be one of the most beautiful festivals in the four realms.

If Tavia found her way there, she always thought she could live the life she was meant to. Be the type of person who wouldn't curse or throw charms if someone pissed her off, but grimace and say *Betrayer set sin on you* in a haughty voice.

Instead, Tavia sold dangerous charms and elixirs to people, pretending it didn't matter and convincing herself they might deserve it, even if she knew that was a lie. Tavia's mother had died from the magic sickness and for all she knew, Tavia might have given that sickness to someone else.

She'd nearly given it to Saxony that day by the temple.

Tavia didn't know how many lives she'd ruined under the guise of keeping her head down and doing what she was told. She wasn't sure what was left in her after so many years on the streets—or what would be left after this was all over—but Tavia hoped desperately it was something close to goodness.

She owed her muma that much.

18

Karam

KARAM WAS BORN ON the holy banks of Granka, with her mother's feet doused in the biggest of its five rivers.

They spread like arteries from the heart of the city and when Karam's mother realized that her first daughter was arriving, she journeyed one mile on foot to the waterfall at Cipa—the river of grace, because that was what she hoped her daughter would be. Graceful and devoted to their ancient ways. Only Karam was not graceful, and these days the one thing she seemed to be able to devote herself to was chaos.

It had been many years since Karam had seen her once-home and her once-family, and those years didn't dull her bitterness toward them, or her love. Time didn't heal wounds like the stories said, but only made it harder to look at them, and the longer Karam left those wounds, the deeper they ran, until they had buried themselves so far that they became easier to ignore altogether.

To find the Grankan Crafters, she would need to face her parents. And they would know Karam had aligned herself with violence and they wouldn't care if she still prayed to the Indescribable God, because what use was prayer when all she did was ask for forgiveness?

And Arjun. The old friend she had left behind with promises to return as a warrior. Karam only hoped he still had that same fighting spirit she remembered from their childhood and that he wouldn't hate her for teaming up with the very people she promised to bring down in a blaze of glory by his side.

"I've never been outside of Uskhanya," Tavia said. "This is beautiful."

The Grankan sky beamed down, its white-gold rays like arms enveloping them. Karam forgot how clear and bright the city was, as though the heavens were open to them so the Indescribable God could watch over its devoted children.

In Uskhanya, their so-called Many Gods would rather not see what was going on, which explained people like Wesley.

Karam took in a breath. The streets she had grown up on still smelled like peppercorns, and a little way from where she had played warriors with Arjun there was scripture on the cobblestones, preaching selfless servitude, peace among all, and the aberration of sin.

"It's not that Granka's beautiful." Saxony clapped an arm over Tavia's shoulder. "It's just that you haven't seen the sun in a week."

"Well, it was winter when we left," Tavia said. "Remind me to never spend so long on a train. I can't wait to see the stars."

"You won't." Wesley pulled off his blazer and folded it neatly over his arm. His shirt clung to him amid the heat. "This is a simple in-and-out mission. We're not here to sightsee."

"Stars are not sights," Karam said.

"All the same, we won't be wandering the streets."

"You live in Creije and you are worried about the streets here?" Karam asked.

"I'm worried about the people," Wesley said. "Crafter worshippers aren't fond of those who buy and sell magic. We need to keep a low profile."

Karam didn't hide her smirk. "We arrived with an army of crooks on a stolen steam train."

"Starting from now," Wesley said. He loosened a button on his collar as the heat took hold. "We keep a low profile starting from now."

Saxony settled herself beside Karam, looking a little out of place. Karam always thought that she was easier to spot than a forest fire, but in Granka, Saxony should have fit in. After all, she was a Crafter in a realm that saw her kind as the spirit of a god.

Even so, Saxony seemed to stand out most of all, and not because she towered above most men or carried herself with an effortless confidence, or the way her clothes hugged her a little tighter than was commonplace. It was the way she looked at Karam and lit the air between them on fire with just one smile.

Saxony touched the knife at her side and Karam swallowed, remembering the day she had given it to her. The day Saxony revealed her powers and trusted Karam for the first time.

The knife was Karam's way of saying she trusted her too. It was her best one, after all, and she had to get Wesley to front her the coin for a replacement.

"Do you want me to come?" Saxony asked.

Karam cleared her throat. "No."

Saxony nudged her. "I'm great with parents. My wiles are irresistible to all. I've got an ageless charm."

"No," Karam said again.

Saxony's smile dimmed. "Why not?"

Karam hesitated.

As much as Creije had taught her not to give a spirit's damn about what people thought, she wouldn't be able to stand it if her parents looked at Saxony with the same disappointment they usually reserved for her. They hated the thought of Karam fighting for peace, so what would they think of a *Crafter* standing beside the likes of an underboss?

Karam hated to think about them making Saxony feel like a traitor too.

"Three's a crowd," Wesley said. "Karam and I will go. We don't need a babysitter."

If Karam didn't know any better, she might think Wesley had just helped her out.

"What are we supposed to do then?" Saxony asked.

"Not sightsee, apparently," Tavia said.

She gave Wesley a dry look and his lips edged up in a half smile. He smiled too much when she was around.

"You'll need to grease a few palms," Wesley said. "Before we left Creije, our friendly Vice Doyen gave me some contacts to ensure we have a smooth stay, for a price."

He pulled a slip of paper out from his coat, with a list of half a dozen names, and handed it to Tavia.

"So these contacts are legit?" she asked. "We don't need to threaten them?"

"You don't need to threaten the people you pay," Wesley said. "They'll provide us with the ammunition we lost at the station, load the buskers up on any extra charms, provide safe room and board where we won't get robbed or killed. I can write you a list, but it'll be easier if you just pay them and don't ask questions. Tell them the Uskhanyan Doyen sent you and they'll know what to do."

"And if they don't?" Tavia asked.

Wesley smirked. "Then you can threaten them."

KARAM LED Wesley through the labyrinth of her city.

It was a maze entirely different to that of Creije's winding alleys and sharp, hidden corners. Granka was a lush expanse of open space and bulging streets, with thick cobbles big enough to host prayers. The houses were small and dotted in clusters arranged to mirror the holy symbol.

It was a city of wisdom and pilgrimage at its heart, with the bones of the first Crafters perched atop the temple, and there were days, even weeks, in the year still devoted to their worship. Here, magic was not a thing to be traded and fought over. It was a calling and, before the war, when Crafters passed on their tutelage and taught the faithful how to handle charms, they were teaching them how to be in harmony with the Indescribable God.

It was peaceful in Granka and even with the constant thrum of people, a calm coated the streets like hot wax, sealing everyone inside. There was nothing wild or untamed about the five rivers. There was no danger in the sky or in the eyes of the crowd.

Karam hated herself for hating that.

They followed the path of Tebhi, the river of destruction, which was fitting to the havoc Karam was about to wreak. Each of the five rivers represented a facet of the Indescribable God— Cipa for grace, Tebhi for destruction, Suhke for protection, Bihi for wisdom, and the river Sirta for creation. People spent days on the banks of their chosen river, praying and drinking from the water as if it would bless them.

Karam's old home had not changed in all the years she was gone. It was small, but ornate, with black iron fencing and sand-colored walls. The windows jutted out like blocks from the face, each with a small balcony that was barely the width of Karam's arm. When she was a child she would squash herself into those balconies, back pressed tightly to one wall and the soles of her feet to the other, and read books on the *hei rekhi* science of self-defense.

When her father left home to teach at temple and her mother brought food to the poor, Karam and Arjun would practice in the garden with her grandfather's old fighting stick. It was one of the few things her pehti jal left for her.

She wanted to be a warrior like him. Her parents wanted her to be as far from that as she could.

Wesley lingered behind Karam, letting her take the lead. His shirtsleeves were rolled up and he had pocketed his cuff links. Karam sighed at his tattoos, which were now in full view up his arms.

Her parents were going to have the time of their lives when they saw those.

"Are you readying for a fight?" she asked, gesturing to his rolled sleeves.

"Do I need to be?"

Karam shrugged. "That would depend on whether you are planning to admit to my pehta who you are."

"I have a feeling he'll know."

"You are infamous."

"These days, so are you."

Karam liked the sound of that more than she cared to admit.

There was something about earning her place in Creije, rather than being handed it on a platter, that made her proud. She had fought her way to her position and hadn't needed prayer or magic to do it. Just her fists and her smarts and the knowledge that she could.

It was Karam's mother who opened the door once they knocked, wearing a four-piece orange *setwa* and not a hint of surprise. She cast a look at the bruises that took up permanent residence on her daughter's face, then to the dirt that clung to the edges of her clothing.

She did not look at Wesley.

"Mete," Karam said. "I need your help."

They were the first words she had spoken to her mother in five years and Karam felt the shame of that fact.

Five years since her father had told her to go and find a war if she wanted one so badly.

Five years since Karam had run like there were demons chasing her.

She wanted to return one day, with her head held as steady as her breath, knowing she had done the right thing by leaving, and proving that her decision to study the fighting arts was the right one.

In all that time her mother's face had remained like a painting, preserved forever. Karam could still smell spices from the kitchen and see the flour under her fingernails. When she saw her father, no doubt he would be as stalwart and stubborn as ever, with kind eyes and hands that always reached to clutch the pendant on his neck.

Five years and nothing had changed but Karam.

"Help."

Her mother repeated the word in Uskhanyan and Karam immediately scolded herself at having forgotten to speak in the holy language.

It had been so long since she'd had someone to speak it to.

"My help is always here, *dila*," her mother said.

It had been forever since anyone had called Karam *darling*.

"But I will not help him."

Her mother looked at Wesley for the first time and her eyes hardened.

"So you've heard of me," Wesley said.

"No."

Wesley's smile fell. He wasn't used to anonymity.

"But I know you are an underboss," her mother said. "I would recognize one anywhere."

She looked to Karam with a face full of accusation.

"You should not have brought him here."

Wesley straightened his collar. "I get that a lot."

"Perhaps you should listen," her mother said. "Men like you should be imprisoned."

"There aren't many men like me."

"Yes. There are."

Karam cleared her throat. "Where is Pehta?" she asked. "I thought he would be back from temple by now."

"Your pehta is not at temple." Her mother wiped the flour from her hands and onto the bright orange cloth of her legs. "He is with the Indescribable God."

Karam's legs nearly gave way.

Surely she hadn't heard right. He couldn't be—

"It has been many months."

Karam put her hand on the wall to steady herself.

Her father could not be dead without her knowing.

Men like him didn't die quietly. They perished in front of crowds, preaching peace. They were killed on days when the heavens wept and time stood still among the thunder of the Indescribable God's anger.

He could not just be gone and she could not just have spent months without knowing.

"You did not tell me," Karam said.

"You were not here to tell."

Her mother walked back inside the house, leaving the door open for them to enter.

Karam followed her into the kitchen, incensed. "You did not even send word."

Her mother continued cooking. "How would I know where to send it?"

"*You* told me to leave."

"You and Arjun had that plan yourselves."

"You said to go," Karam repeated.

Her mother rested her hands on the counter and sighed. "Sometimes, words spoken in anger are not words spoken in truth, *dila*."

"I do not need your proverbs."

"Just my help."

"Mete, *please*," Karam said, with a shaking voice.

It was so far from her own in that moment, in that single word, that Karam almost felt like a girl again. Like all those years she'd spent on the streets of Creije, cutting through the city, leaving the past like it was dust and ash, and building herself anew from it, hadn't happened at all.

She was here, home, just like before, coming undone in front of her family.

Her father was dead. She would never get to see him or make amends. She'd never get to feel his arms around her and have him say he was proud of who she'd become, even if it was different from who he wanted.

He was just gone.

Karam had set the flames to her old life and Creije had helped burn it away. There was no chance to piece it back together now, because all the parts were cinder.

Karam fell to the floor.

When the tears came, they were silent and hot. Her chest

ached, the room fogged, and Karam felt like maybe she was the one who was really dying.

And then her mother knelt down on the floor beside her and placed a steadying hand on Karam's shoulder. From somewhere, she found the strength to look into her mother's eyes and she saw tears there, too.

"*Dila,*" her mother said. "You wanted to be a warrior. Warriors do not cry."

And then she hugged her.

For the first time in five years, Karam hugged her mother and felt safe.

And then someone cleared their throat.

Wesley had followed them into the house, as silent as death. He looked ridiculously uncomfortable at the sight of Karam, crying in front of him. She considered if it was a mistake being vulnerable with Wesley there, but as awful as people thought he was, Karam knew there were few things Wesley saw as sacred, and one was family. Loyalty.

Perhaps not his own, but he at least respected those traits in others.

"I can wait outside," Wesley said.

He was trying to look anywhere other than at Karam.

"You live such secrets now," her mother said, wiping away Karam's tears. "With so many demons around you."

Wesley's face didn't change.

If anything, Karam guessed he took it as a compliment. She supposed it was better than being called the Kingpin's lapdog all the time.

"Mete," Karam said.

Her voice was finding its footing, still too breathy, but it was there and it was hers.

"The work we are doing is important."

"Violence is never important, *dila*."

Karam threw her hands up. She had forgotten that her stubbornness was hereditary. It was practically the only thing she was passed down from her parents.

"Are you doing the Indescribable God's work?" her mother asked.

Karam nodded. She got to her feet and her mother did the same.

"Do you really believe that to be true?" her mother asked.

Karam nodded again. "The Kingpin of Uskhanya is planning something awful and he is using magic to do it," she explained. "Their realm is in danger."

Her mother shook her head. "Those criminals are not kings and the sooner our Doyens put them in prison, the better."

Wesley took a seat at the small wooden table in the corner of the room and rolled his shirtsleeves back down. "The Kingpins have lined too many pockets for that to be possible."

Karam's mother stalked over to him and swatted his legs, to indicate he should stand up. Karam blanched.

"Mete," she warned, but Wesley stood without fuss.

"The will of your people to corrupt is endless."

"So is the desire of your Doyens to be corrupted," Wesley countered.

"The Kingpin of Uskhanya has Crafters," Karam said. "He is using them to create awful magic and wage war."

"The holy conduits are not to be used."

"Which is why we want to stop him," Wesley said. "To save the holy conduits. And all we need is to meet with the Grankan Kin."

Though it was Wesley who had spoken, it was Karam her mother hit across the back. "You dare request such a thing? You would endanger innocents for him? Innocents like Arjun, who you grew up with!"

Karam's heart lifted at the mention of her old friend. At least he was safe, then.

"Arjun would not be the only Crafter on our side," Karam said. "We already have someone."

Her mother paused. "You have a Crafter with you?"

"Her name is Saxony," Karam said. "And she wants to help put a stop to all of the madness. You should see the power she has, Mete. It is like nothing I have ever known. She is glorious."

Her mother smiled knowingly. "There is a light in your eyes I have never seen, *dila*. Your father would be proud of it."

Karam swallowed.

"Saxony will make sure any Crafters who join us are protected," Karam said. "You and Pehta taught me that Crafters should be protected at all costs. Pehti Jal and Meta Jil were killed trying to do just that. By stopping the Kingpin, I am honoring our family. I am finishing their work."

Karam's mother placed her hands flat on each of Karam's shoulders and let out a long sigh.

"Even if I help you," she said, "there is no guarantee they will. Perhaps Arjun will choose to trust you and convince the Liege to do the same, but if he does, it will put Crafter lives in your hands. If you cause them harm, fleeing to another realm will not save you from the Indescribable God. I will not be able to protect you from its wrath, *dila*."

Karam placed a hand on top of her mother's. She wished she could hold her father's hand too.

"I promise you, I will win this battle and finish the work our ancestors started," Karam said. "I have never needed your protection, Mete. Only your trust."

19

Saxony

KINS WERE LIKE GANGS.

There was one in every city in every realm and their Lieges were a little like underbosses, except without the murder. Usually.

Ever since the war, Kins didn't talk to other Crafters outside of their own. It just wasn't safe. Nobody could be trusted, risks were always too great, and so they kept to themselves, never swapping secrets or trading spells. Each Kin had their own traditions and not a one of them wanted to share.

Yet here Saxony was, about to meet the Grankan Kin and see other Crafters outside of her own for the first time.

The forest surrounding the holy temple was a little over three hundred acres and birthed trees the color of kiwi, right down to their trunks. They had leaves of clovers and roots that lay above ground like strands of seaweed. The soil was magic dust and covered the dirt until the brown beneath was barely visible, and the magic atop looked like wet sand in the afternoon sun.

When they walked, it lit beneath their feet, leaving footprints for them to find their way back.

Saxony couldn't help but think that if this were Creije, the buskers would have had it collected and sold in half a second.

The Kin was not inside the holy temple, but beneath it, and Karam's mother was very specific about them not approaching the steps of the ancient monument unless they wanted to meet their doom. Which they decided quickly not to.

Instead, they were to approach a secret entrance under its roots that allowed safe passage to allies.

The four of them scoured the forest, with Falk by Wesley's side, ready to pretend he would be any use in a fight.

It was sudden when Karam stopped walking and drew an X in the dust with her foot, lighting up the ground to mark their position.

Her father's old necklace was in her hand, given by her mother to act as a beacon, though Karam gripped it more like it was life support.

"It's here," she said.

The necklace glowed brightly.

Karam crouched low.

"All I see is sand," Wesley said.

"Of course." Karam studied the spot, waving her hand over the ground. "The likes of you are not meant to notice such things. It would not be a secret passage if you did."

"The likes of me," Wesley repeated.

Saxony crouched beside Karam, close enough that their knees were touching.

The warmth of her being this near was mind-numbing.

"I can sense the magic," Saxony said.

Karam took her hand and placed it on the ground in the center of the X she'd drawn. There was heat. Fire the same as that which Saxony conjured from within herself. It pulsed, and as Saxony's palm began to sweat, specks of the magic dust glued across her lifeline.

When Saxony withdrew, Karam allowed her own hand to hover over the magic for a few seconds before clenching it into a fist. The dust floated up to meet her in a rope and when Karam stood, pulling the new thread with her, a sheath rose like a doorway, revealing a staircase.

"You go first," Karam said to Saxony. "It is best they see a friendly face."

"I'm not a friendly face."

"It is best they sense you are like them."

"I'm not like them," Saxony said.

Karam sighed in that no-nonsense way that only she could ever seem to make equal parts threatening and seductive. Or maybe the seductive part was just Saxony, because Tavia only looked bemused and Wesley just looked like an asshole.

"I will throw you down there in a minute if you are not careful," Karam said.

"Any excuse to touch me."

Saxony winked and stepped down into the passageway.

The gunshots were sudden.

The sound rang in Saxony's ears and she was flung quickly

backward, out of the safety of the Grankan passage and back through the forest, rolling and turning like tumbleweed.

Saxony caught only the blurs of their strange new attackers, before she was thrown against a tree by their magic.

Saxony counted the gunshots, felt the scraping of blades in the distance, but she couldn't stand.

The Kingpin couldn't have known to follow them to the holy land and no Crafter would draw blood in this sacred forest, especially from those entering as allies.

Saxony tried to make sense of it, putting her hand on the ground to steady both her body and her mind.

Her palm fell through the earth.

The forest began to fade.

Saxony blinked and she could barely make out the foggy sight of Karam running toward her, screaming, before everything went dark.

The world shifted.

Great towers rose in the distance, dripping with vines and flowers. The ground was suddenly grass, ready to be plowed, and in the quiet beyond she could smell the orange tree farms.

Saxony wasn't in Granka anymore.

She was in Rishiya.

It was like a dream, only she was aware and wondering how in the fire-gates to wake up.

Tears rolled from her cheeks and onto the collar of her shirt so that Saxony's neck felt damp. She didn't know why she was crying, or why she felt a sudden pull of emotions, as though there was a great energy tugging at her senses. But it didn't make sense for her skin to be wet, because Saxony's staves

~ 212 ~

were burning. Inside, her fire tore through bone and sinew.

Her magic felt so staggeringly awake.

And then, as if from the wind itself, came her grandma's voice.

"You are safe."

Amja's dark metallic hair was braided down the length of her spine, and though her smile was soft, her silver eyes were hard and gleaming. She wore a white dress that moved with the wind and her voice sounded like it was made from liquid or magic or both.

The entire Rishiyat Kin stood with her.

A family.

An army.

It occurred to Saxony then that her grandma looked like a warrior. That she looked like a Liege, even though she wasn't.

"Is this a dream?" Saxony asked. "How am I here?"

"We were worried for you," Amja said. "We felt it when you used the dark magics and risked cursing us all. The heavens cried that day and our power felt like lead in our veins."

Saxony tried not to bow her head in shame. She knew invading Eirini's mind was a risk, but she had stupidly hoped that the Many Gods would spare her Kin any more pain.

"Amja, it was the only way. You don't understand—"

"We understand you are with an underboss," she said. "He has you in his clutches."

She reached out and took Saxony's hand.

"You have strayed, just like I feared, and you have put us all in danger."

Saxony drew in a breath.

"I'm doing this for us, Amja," she said. "For Zekia. That elixir I told you about *is* new magic and Dante Ashwood has Crafters imprisoned. I think Zekia is one of them. Wesley and the others are going to help me find her."

"Impossible!" her amja shouted.

Behind her, the Kin stirred.

Saxony felt the might of them.

Their hurt and their anger. They mourned Zekia as much as she did. Kins were bound by something deeper than blood and the Liege was the string that connected the force inside them all. With Zekia gone, it was like they had lost part of themselves.

They wanted her back, the same as Saxony. They just didn't trust that it was possible.

"It's true," Saxony said. "Wesley and the others will help me save her."

"Filthy lies to trap you like they once tried to trap us all in the war," Amja spat. "They can never be trusted. All they want is to take our magic and use our powers for their gain."

"You're wrong," Saxony said. "You don't know everything, Amja."

You don't know Karam, she wanted to say. The fact that her beautiful warrior had a sacred duty to protect Crafters. Or that even if she didn't, she'd still go to the ends of the realms to protect Saxony.

Amja didn't know that good people could exist in Creije, or anywhere outside of their Kin. The war had left so many scars on her. She didn't know that not everyone could be more than simply good or evil. That there were people like Tavia, who was

Wesley's best busker and yet the best friend she'd ever had.

"I promise that I can bring Zekia back," Saxony said. "I can fix our family. We have an army of buskers and right now we're on our way to gather the Grankan Kin to help fight Ashwood. When we reach his fortress, I'll put an end to him and rescue Zekia."

"You will get yourself killed trying," Amja said. "His power is too great. You forget that I have seen his past. I was there when the war broke out."

Saxony hadn't forgotten. She never could.

"Even if your power could match his, those buskers cannot be trusted. The underboss of Creije cannot be trusted," Amja urged. "You should kill him before he kills you. He is a snake, waiting for the right moment to strike. Eliminating him is the only victory we can hope for."

An awful feeling lodged in the pit of Saxony's stomach.

It wasn't like she truly intended to be Wesley's ally, or let him take the Kingpin's place at the helm of the Uskhanyan magic trade. But to kill him now?

To murder him in front of everyone?

In front of Tavia?

There were dozens of buskers aboard the train and they would turn on her in an instant, with her closest friend spearheading their rage. And Many Gods knew how Karam would act if Saxony murdered someone in the holy land. If she killed someone who was helping them, just because she could.

Just because her grandma told her to.

"Wesley is on my side," Saxony said. "If the time comes when that changes, I'll deal with him. But until then, I need his help."

"He must *die*," Amja said again. "Before he can betray you. Do not let him enchant you. That boy will bring war and death. It is his destiny. One look at his face and you must see that."

Saxony dropped her grandma's hands.

She was willing to kill for survival, when it was necessary, but taking Wesley's life right now was neither of those things. And it was certainly not destiny.

Besides, Saxony didn't trust people on their faces, because faces lied and were rarely laid bare, always coated in a thin layer of bullshit. Instead, Saxony knew people by their sense. The feel of them. How her insides twisted and settled in their presence.

Like how she knew Karam because of the way her organs jolted suddenly whenever they touched. Which told her that Karam was for sure a good person beneath the black eyes. Or, at least, too good for her.

And Saxony knew Wesley by the way her fingers went cold at the tips and she got a mighty bad case of heartburn that could never settle without a cup of ginger root. Which told her that he was probably half as good as he was bad. That he probably hadn't decided which one was more profitable yet.

"You need to let me go," Saxony said. "I have to get back. I think we were being attacked."

Amja's silver eyes sparked with something Saxony hadn't seen before. An anger, perhaps at her defiance, because Saxony had never gone against her grandma's wishes or even spoken out of turn.

"Saxony," her amja said. Her voice was soft and calm. Too level to mean it. "I will not lose a third grandchild and I will not let you risk your life for a fool's errand. With Zekia gone, our Kin's safety falls to me. I will protect you at any cost."

"Enough, Amja!" Saxony shouted. "Let me out of here right now. I need to help my friends."

The desperate urge to leave rose up in Saxony's stomach like a sickness. She heard those gunshots echoing in her mind again and pictured Karam running toward her. Being in this dream place was wrong and if Saxony didn't go soon, then she knew something awful would happen. Or perhaps something awful already had.

"Kill the underboss and return to us," Amja pleaded.

"I'm not a murderer," Saxony said, looking up to the skies in the hopes that the enchantment would hear and break her grandma's spell. Pull her out of this replica world.

She closed her eyes, willing the forest to come back and for her to be in Granka, with Karam.

"Saxony."

Amja's voice was distant.

No longer the wind, but an echo of it. A fading hand stretching out to Saxony, only she was suddenly too far.

The sky groaned and Saxony reached up to touch the back of her head. It came away wet. Blood pooled into the lines of her hands. The distance was no longer peaceful; the quiet lull of Rishiya and its farms were filled with screaming.

Saxony couldn't smell the orange trees anymore, but she could smell gunpowder.

She could smell smoke and the earthy dirt of trees.

Eyes closed, Saxony screamed into the darkness. "I'm not a murderer!"

"Now that's a crying shame," someone said.

Not her grandma or a member of the Kin, but a voice she recognized nonetheless. A gravelly Creijen tilt. A not-so-thinly-veiled arrogance.

Wesley.

Saxony opened her eyes and found herself back inside the forest of Granka. She felt the leaves and soil beneath her palms and smelled spice in the air.

The underboss stood in front of her, scowling.

His suit was marred by blood and earth, and beside him a breathless Tavia pocketed knife after knife inside the slits of her clothes and shoes, and then bent down to crouch beside Saxony.

"Are you okay?" she asked.

Saxony nodded, but she wasn't sure it was true.

The Grankan Crafters surrounded them like warriors.

They were dressed in brightly colored garments that hung breezily from their bodies. Some wore shirts, others did not, and their staves reflected gold in the sunlight over their brown skin. The men wore vibrant colors around their heads and the women had the kind of ornate jewelry Saxony had only ever seen on Karam.

Being around them, Saxony felt an immediate sense of peace and kinship. She could almost imagine a time before the War of Ages had sent them all into hiding. A time when they weren't used as currency, before Kingpins and crooks, where magic roamed free and Crafters were seen as holy across the realms.

Where none of them had to be scared or watch the people they loved die.

The Grankan Crafters looked fearless and deadly, not in the least because they were surrounded by bodies.

On the floor around them were a dozen dead. Not the Crafters, but strange enemies that had descended at the exact moment Saxony's grandma trapped her in that memory.

Saxony bit her lip.

"Where is—"

"I am here," Karam said, as though reading Saxony's mind.

Saxony followed her voice and a few Crafters parted way to reveal Karam sitting on the ground, slouched against a tree in a near mirror of Saxony.

Her face was as bruised as usual, though a little muddier. But it was her arm, slung over her waist and wet with blood that made Saxony's jaw tense.

Karam was either stabbed or shot, and all the while Saxony was useless to help. She was getting really sick of that feeling.

Tavia placed a hand on Saxony's shoulder to pull her to her feet and with a grimace Saxony stood.

"What happened?" she asked.

"You decided to take a nap and we got ambushed," Wesley said.

"I wasn't napping, I was—"

Saxony broke off. She wasn't quite sure what to say.

I was transported to a memory by my grandma, where she tried to convince me to kill you and run back home to Rishiya didn't quite have a ring of sanity to it.

"I think the Kingpin was trying to get in my head," she lied.

Wesley narrowed his eyes and she could see the suspicion, the distrust so open on his face. "How so?"

Saxony swallowed. "I don't remember much," she said. "Just the feeling of dark magic."

Tavia raised her eyebrows. "Are you sure you weren't dreaming?"

"Or sleeping," Wesley said.

"She hit her head hard when she flew against that tree," Tavia agreed.

Saxony wished she had the strength to throw a fireball at them.

"It was mind games," she said, which wasn't technically a lie. "The Kingpin was trying to get me over to his side. Making false promises for if I turned against you."

"That would explain the attack," Wesley said. "Divide and conquer. The Kingpin sends people in to distract us and then goes after our resident Crafter."

Saxony gestured to the fallen enemies around them. "They were with the Kingpin?"

Tavia nodded. "Seems so. But he only sent twelve, so they didn't stand a chance against us all. Thankfully Ashwood doesn't have many people in Granka, but the bastard still knew where we were."

"Maybe he guessed because of Karam's family," Falk said. "There ain't a way he could know our route otherwise."

"No," Wesley said, turning to him with a thinly veiled scowl. "I suppose there isn't."

"Either way, it is a good thing we were here to save you," one of the Crafters said.

He was younger than Saxony, but broadly built with wide shoulders and a hard edge to his boyish face, as though it had been beaten into strength. His knuckles were bloody and fisted around a sword with four hooked blades that looked like it had seen its share of battle.

Wesley rolled his eyes and hitched his gun back into his belt. "I didn't need saving," he said.

The Crafter rolled his eyes right back. "The Uskhanyan have an odd way of saying thank you. I expect you to pay this life debt. If I am ever at the wrong end of a gun, you can take the bullet in my place."

Wesley looked affronted. "I'd rather pull the trigger."

"Arjun," Karam said, addressing the Crafter.

He turned to her and his lips twitched like he was trying to swallow something bitter. A hard silence passed between them.

"We are grateful," Karam said.

"You are slow," he said back.

He had the same severe gravel to his voice that Karam did, like they were two sides of a single coin.

This was the childhood friend she had left behind; someone who knew parts of her that Saxony hadn't yet uncovered. And he didn't seem too pleased about those parts.

"It looks as though Creije is not the best place to study combat after all," he said.

There was nothing lighthearted about the dig, but Karam smirked, biting down on the unpleasant retort Saxony could see threatening to spill out.

"If you like, I will come over there and show you just what I learned on the streets of Creije," Karam said.

She tried to stand and then sucked in a breath, clutching her side tighter.

Saxony winced.

"They did not teach you how to stand in Creije then," Arjun said. He turned to Saxony. "You should heal her. We cannot spill blood near the holy temple and our Liege is waiting."

"Your concern warms my heart," Karam said.

Saxony walked toward her.

She tried her hardest not to look at the dead, but her eyes were drawn to their faces. To the shock and surprise painted on each of them, as though victory had been the only outcome they had considered.

They were dressed in dark blue, arms exposed at the shoulders, hands outstretched and clinging to swords or guns or trick bags. They all bore a symbol on their wrists, rigid lines connecting to make an odd, disjointed kind of circle, cut through the center so that it almost looked like an eye.

Saxony stopped, heart pounding fiercely.

It was a symbol she knew all too well.

"They were Crafters?" she asked, turning back to Wesley.

She knew the answer before he said it.

"No." He shook his head. "But they had some pretty strong charms. Ashwood arms his people well."

I will not lose a third grandchild. I will protect you at any cost.

Is this what Amja had meant by those words? Had the dream-world been a distraction?

No. Saxony wouldn't believe it. Amja was not capable of such things.

Saxony pushed down the pang in her heart, the familiarity of that symbol, and stepped over the fallen bodies.

She hurried toward Karam.

"Is she going to be okay?" Tavia asked.

Saxony crouched beside Karam and nodded, though she wasn't sure if she even had the strength to heal, with her head still dancing circles from being thrown clear across the forest.

"She'll be fine," Saxony said. "It's just a flesh wound."

"It is actually quite bad," Karam said, arching her head to look at Tavia. "I think it is deep."

Tavia grimaced, which Saxony suspected was Karam's intention. She'd probably been injured saving Tavia, jumping in front of a knife or a charm like the hero she was. It was the only way someone as fast as Karam could be bleeding while Tavia remained unscathed. And Karam wouldn't let her forget it. Still, the guilt faded from Tavia's face quick enough and she simply shrugged.

"I guess this makes us even," Tavia said.

Karam's mouth was agape. "When did you get stabbed for me?"

Saxony inched Karam's shirt upward. Blood crawled under her ribs and down to her waist. The wound was large, but not deep. It wasn't the worst Saxony had seen and certainly not the worst Karam had ever gotten.

"I basically saved you at the train station," Tavia said. "Ergo, we're even."

Wesley sighed. "For the last time, I didn't need saving. I never need saving."

They ignored him.

"I got shot waiting for you to rob a safe," Karam said. "*Ergo*, you already owed me."

Tavia paused. And then, "You know, we really shouldn't keep

score. What's a bullet or two between friends?"

"We are not—"

Saxony pressed a hand against Karam's wound.

"*Hei reb,*" Karam said. "Just heal it already."

Her brown skin was dulled, lips blanched, and when Saxony touched her Karam shivered like the cold was too much to bear.

"I'm concentrating," Saxony said. "Healing requires focus and my head is still pounding. I don't want to sever you in half."

Karam blinked. "Is that a risk?" She looked over to Arjun. "You did not say that was a risk."

Saxony wiped some of Karam's blood away with her sleeve to get a better look at the wound.

"You are a sadist," Karam said.

Saxony tried not to smile. She liked Karam most when she was angry. Though since Karam was always angry, that meant Saxony pretty much liked her all of the time.

It made kissing her real hard to resist.

"Here goes," Saxony said.

She held her hands out above Karam's wound and took in a breath.

When Zekia healed, she closed her eyes, feeling the energy ripple through her as she stitched skin to skin and made blood fade like water marks, but Saxony liked to see her magic in action, watching as her power erased all that had come before.

Gold light sprinkled from Saxony's palms and sank into the hole that sliced through Karam's side. Her skin began to bubble.

Saxony watched, tight-lipped, as she writhed in agony. It almost seemed like she was creating new wounds, instead of fixing the old.

Gold veins spread like roots across Karam's stomach, up to her chest, leeching onto her neck as Saxony's power crawled into every inch of her, pumping through her body beside her blood.

And then Karam's skin began to melt together.

It darkened, pink blurring back to brown before her eyes, blood hissing and evaporating into the air. Karam's breathing slowed and the damp film that clung to her cheeks dissipated. Her lips turned rosy, the sweat on her brow now more like a glow.

Tavia whistled a breath.

"That was so unbelievably cool," she said. "Does it work on any kind of injury? Because one of Ashwood's guys knocked me straight on my ass and I just know I'll be feeling it tomorrow."

Saxony didn't answer. She turned back to stare at the bodies still strewn across the forest and wiped her palms across her skirt.

The healing magic glimmered over the fabric for a moment and then faded to nothing.

20

Deniel

THE WORLD WAS FALLING APART and it was Deniel's job to fix it.

There were awful things hidden in the winding arteries of Creije, where magic was dealt like the hands of a card game, ready to be sold to the desperate and the lonely who wanted to escape whatever reality they had been born into, for one they could create themselves. Magic, not sacred and revered, but worshipped in a different kind of way, as the source that could give people temporary relief from their lives.

A way to satiate the hunger to change themselves.

The world inside that place was falling apart and Deniel Emilsson was at its center.

Ready.

Just as hungry as they were.

His black eyes took in the blood that hardened under his fingernails. It had rusted to brown against his graying skin.

Dirty blood. Traitor blood.

The amityguards lay in a pile around his cell, hands still on their guns, on their sedation charms. Eyes open, mouths open, as though they had died in the time it took to breathe or blink.

It had been longer, but only slightly.

They couldn't see the truth of the world and Deniel couldn't let them live in the lie.

They'd spread it like a plague.

Deniel knew what the world had to be now.

He knew what had to be done and where to find the thing to do it.

He touched the mark on his neck.

The voices hissed.

"Yes," he told them. "I know."

Deniel picked up the knife from the floor and headed into the night.

21

Wesley

THEY WEREN'T PERMITTED ENTRY inside the temple, but that was fine with Wesley. He never much liked holy places and they never much liked him back.

They were, however, allowed into a secret room beneath it, where nearly a hundred hooded figures sat cross-legged. It took Wesley a moment to realize they were arranged into the shape of the holy Wrenyi symbol.

Nobody had spoken a word since their arrival. Not even the Crafter with the four-bladed sword. Arjun.

He hadn't taken his eyes off Wesley since they'd entered the room, his golden irises following his every move. He also didn't seem to want to drop that damn sword while Wesley was around. Which was smart, if not a little irritating.

"Saxony Akintola," a woman said.

She stood in the center of the Kin and though she wasn't

particularly tall or particularly large, her presence was beyond compare.

Her eyes were dark and glittering, her black hair swept to the side in a thick braid and her arms were so covered in staves that it was almost hard to make out her skin beneath it all.

When she spoke every Crafter in the room looked at her.

"My name is Asees, protector of the five-river city and Liege of the Grankan Crafters." Her voice was soft and mighty. "I see you have already met my second in command, Arjun."

Wesley held back his surprise.

No wonder Arjun stood so close to her, like a bodyguard.

That cocky son of a bitch was a second.

"If not for his loyalty to you, Karam, you would not be permitted anywhere near my temple," Asees said. "You should count yourself fortunate for that."

Karam looked chided, which was not something Wesley had seen before.

Asees turned to Saxony. "As you are next in line to be Liege of the Rishiyat Crafters—"

"We don't need a new Liege," Saxony interrupted. "That position is filled. We'll find my sister so she can ascend to her rightful place."

Wesley sighed.

They weren't going to rally any troops with Saxony's winning personality at the helm.

"I know of your sister," Asees said. "I heard she was kind and wise."

"*Is*," Saxony corrected, though she seemed more sad than

angry to have to spell out the difference. "You must be kind too, to grant us a meeting."

"I must be a lot of things for you to ask for my help with an underboss by your side."

"So you've heard of me," Wesley said.

"No."

His smile tensed.

Apparently, Wesley's reputation was good for nothing outside of his own realm.

"I already know of your problems," Asees said. "Arjun has explained your plight, but this is something for your realm to deal with, not ours."

It was a slight if Wesley had ever heard one, because though Karam lived in Uskhanya, that didn't mean Wrenyal wasn't still her home too.

"This fight goes beyond realms," Wesley said. "It's about your people."

"Our people are right here." Asees shot a pointed look at Karam. "*I* would never forget that."

"Ashwood won't be satisfied taking one realm when he can have three," Wesley said. "Trust me."

"Trust is earned."

"Or taken."

Asees did not seem impressed by the notion.

"We need you," Saxony said.

When she spoke, even Wesley could feel the room tense. They looked at her as though she could not be trusted, and her strange Uskhanyan magic as suspicious as his borrowed and stolen charms.

"From one Crafter to another, don't leave us in this fight alone," Saxony said. "My sister could die in the Kingpin's hold. Ashwood will keep taking Crafters and everything our Kins sacrificed in the War of Ages will have been for nothing."

Her voice nearly broke and she swallowed. Tears, perhaps, or anger.

Wesley wasn't sure, but he felt like he couldn't look her in the eye.

If he had just told the Kingpin no, let the underboss live and—

Then you would not be so mighty, with worlds at your feet.

"They are right," Arjun said. "Dante Ashwood will not stop and that means he may come for us, too. We must avenge those of us who fell in the war and honor their memory by making sure no more have to die."

Spoken like a true believer of the Rekhi d'Rihsni.

When Wesley had read about them, he'd memorized their rallying cries: *We fight so we may live in peace. We fall so those after us will not have to.* Arjun was basically a walking textbook for the past.

Asees considered his words for the briefest of moments, and when she looked to Arjun she let out a long breath, as though she were more troubled by the thought of upsetting his ego, than the thought of hanging Wesley out to dry.

"What magic will best help?" Arjun asked.

It took Wesley a moment to realize Arjun was looking at him.

Wesley adjusted his tie. "The more the merrier," he said. "I'll take whatever volunteers I can get. Though a Spiritcrafter would be useful to control the seas of Ejm Voten."

"That would be my specialty."

"*Arjun*," Asees warned. "Enough."

She looked to Wesley with fiery eyes. "We will offer you safe refuge," she said. "But that is all we can give."

"I understand you may want time to deliberate," Wesley said, slowly, because he wasn't quite sure he'd heard her right. "But we're on a deadline. The shadow moon is—"

Asees held up a hand to stop him.

"I know when our Crafter Moon will rise. I do not need an underboss to tell me," Asees said. "My answer is no."

She stared at him with hard eyes and when Wesley took a step toward her, Asees held her chin high and gave him a look to freeze fire.

"The Grankan Kin cannot help you. I know how painful it is to lose family, which is exactly why I will not risk mine for someone else's war."

"My *sister* is with Ashwood!" Saxony said, practically seething.

"And I appreciate your plight," Asees said, though her voice remained even. "But I must think of my people."

"*Asees*." Arjun's voice was gruff and confused. "We cannot turn our backs on them."

"Your judgment is clouded," Asees said. "By Karam and your childhood ties. This is not your decision to make."

"But—"

Asees shook her head and that alone was enough to silence her second.

Such power a Liege held.

"The time for the Rekhi d'Rihsni is over," Asees said. "The time for war and violence is over. That is my final word."

Arjun swallowed, jaw tense, and in that moment he looked every bit the scolded warrior. "Then we can help them in another way," he said.

Asees snapped her head to him. "I told you that I will not put our people at risk."

"I know that," he said, but his teeth were gritted. "Though if we will not give them Crafters, then we can still give them some kind of magic."

Wesley wasn't sure what Arjun meant, but Karam stepped forward with no sign of the same bewilderment in her hooded eyes.

"You cannot give us Crafters," she said. "But you can make us one."

Wesley paused.

The way Saxony shuffled, hand twitching as though she wanted to reach out and shake some sense into Karam, made him feel like the only one not in on a very big secret.

"Hold your tongue," Asees said.

But Karam was never the type to heed warnings.

"I remember our teachings just as well as you do," Karam said. "According to the holy book, the Indescribable God imbued worthy Grankans with its spirit, creating the first Crafters and giving them the power to do so in return. This is the only Kin in the four realms who can give someone Crafter powers."

Wesley stilled.

That was a myth.

Some playground story that children passed around so they could make believe one day they might be able to hold true magic and escape their crappy lives.

It was a street-kid fantasy. Nothing more.

"Crafters can create other Crafters?" Tavia asked.

"They are called vessels," Arjun said.

Saxony took in a breath, as though she didn't want to speak of this next part, but her intrigue was too much to bear.

"We have a ritual in my own Kin that can determine whether someone has Crafter potential," she said. "It's how we pick our allies and see whether any non-magical companions are trustworthy. If any of our Crafters fall in love or create friendships outside the Kin, we don't keep those bonds if they fail the test. The Intuitcrafters say that if a person passes, they were a Crafter in another life and can be trusted with our secrets in this one. We mark them with a stave as proof. But I've never heard of awakening that potential and turning them into one of us."

"It is unique to our Kin," Arjun said.

"And it is not as simple as that," Asees said. "The spell is temporary and if we put forward an unworthy vessel, it could anger the Indescribable God's wrath."

"Is this how someone like Dante Ashwood got to be so almighty?" Wesley asked.

Something shifted in Arjun's face and when he spoke, his words were like a matchstick. "The Kingpins traded between the realms back then," he said. "Ashwood had a taste for our people and forced dozens of Grankan Crafters to imbue him with their gift, over and over until the magic froze in his blood and could not be separated. He became half man and half abomination. He is not one of us."

"But he's not one of us, either."

~ 234 ~

Arjun tilted his head to the side, appraising Wesley. "You do not seem to think anyone is like you."

"We can only create a single vessel each orbit," Asees said. "So even if I did agree, we will not be able to imbue all of your crooks."

"One a year?" Wesley asked, disappointed.

"It is a sacred magic."

"And it's not going to help a whole lot."

Asees smiled. Wesley glared.

"We will need blood," Arjun said. "To see if the Indescribable God deems you worthy."

He gestured to Wesley with his four-pointed sword.

It was a no-brainer. The potential to have Crafter powers when Wesley took on the Kingpin was too good to pass up. Wesley took a step toward Arjun and then felt himself being tugged back.

For a moment, he wondered who would be so stupid as to try to stop him from doing something he'd set his mind to. But the touch carried a familiar warmth against Wesley's skin and when he looked down, it was Tavia's hand that wrapped around his wrist.

Her fingers covered part of Wesley's scars and for a moment he imagined never having them at all. He imagined a childhood where he clung to his memories and felt sad about those he forgot.

Tavia's fingers tightened, keeping him in place. She so rarely reached out for him that Wesley almost didn't ask her why she had.

"You're being an idiot," Tavia said.

That broke the spell rather quickly.

Wesley shook from her hold. "Charming as ever."

"Many Gods, Wesley, you can't trust the first person with a sword who demands your blood for some ritual."

"If this is you being worried, I'm touched. But I'm a big boy and I make my own decisions."

"That's what worries me. You make the *worst* decisions." Tavia sidestepped him. "I'll do it," she said to Arjun. "In case your plan is to poison our fearless leader. If he dies, he'll never let me hear the end of it."

But her voice wavered so obviously that Wesley almost laughed.

Tavia didn't want to be a Crafter, not even a pretend one and not even for a little while. Not because she didn't like magic or want more of it, but because she didn't want to be in anyone's debt. She didn't want to risk having something to lose.

That was the thing with Tavia. She wanted to earn all that she had so it could never be taken away, while Wesley was content to just grab hold of things tightly enough that nobody dared try.

He pushed past her. "If you die, you'll haunt me for an eternity," Wesley said. "Besides, I didn't get to be underboss by running away from risk."

And he was damned if he was going to let Tavia take that risk for him.

Before she could protest, Wesley squeezed his hand over the serrated edge of Arjun's blade.

It was just another scar to add to the collection, after all.

Arjun passed the blade to his Liege.

"It will change color if you have potential to be a vessel," Asees explained.

Wesley nodded.

Asees let his blood run off the blade and into a small canister.

From the sidelines, Saxony watched in silence, a pained look on her face that told Wesley she didn't approve of someone like him becoming someone like her.

That he wasn't quite good enough to have true power.

The Grankan Kin hummed in chorus around the canister with Wesley's blood. Their bodies swayed back and forth as their magic turned like a spindle in the air, threading its way through the room.

The air grew hot and Wesley's skin felt sticky with it. He took in a long breath, trying to keep his mind focused on the room and the people inside and not on how he felt like he was being strategically dipped in scalding water.

Instinctively, Wesley ran a hand over the scars on his wrist. They ran hotter than the rest of him. It was like he could smell them burning all over again.

Closer, the ghost inside his mind cooed. *Come closer.*

Asees spoke words in Wrenyi that Wesley couldn't understand and picked trick dust from the floor to sprinkle into the canister.

Wesley's blood rippled.

If this worked, he'd be a Crafter.

If Wesley cared about the family he'd left behind, this would prove to them that he was worth something.

Wesley wasn't just some street kid people crossed the road

to avoid and he wasn't some irredeemable underboss people left Creije to escape.

He was something else entirely.

He mattered.

Asees picked up the canister and whispered to it. Her words carried in the wind and tickled at Wesley's hair.

Wesley lifted a hand to swat them away and when they began to prick at his neck, he cursed silently under his breath.

Apparently, blood magic was a nuisance.

The room was tense while they waited for Wesley's fate and he knew instantly what everyone was thinking: *The last thing the underboss of Creije needs is his ego pumped.* Or *Dante Ashwood is proof of what happens when men like Wesley discover their potential.*

Something gnawed at Wesley then. Not only the petty judgment from those in the room, but a very real and tangible thing. He could hear a voice and it wasn't Asees and it wasn't the one he so often tried to hide from. It was lighter and jumbled and seemed to travel straight from Wesley's mind and into the world.

The wind was calling out to him, first a whistle and then a melody Wesley could feel in his bones.

Time will be carried in strange hands
across the realms and through stranger lands.
What is done will be undone,
a battle lost is a battle won.
When midnight rings on a child's betrayal,
your every success is doomed to fail.

Wesley closed his eyes and images shot against the back of his lids like a flip book. The hands of a clock spinning madly until they shattered. Wind that moved like ghosts and a thin black line across the center of the realms, like a rip in time.

Shaken, he turned to Tavia, but she showed no sign of hearing it. None of them did. But it was so loud and clear and it kept repeating over and over like a dream.

This was the prediction Tavia had heard from the fortune orb. It had to be. And now it had found Wesley, too.

The realms really were trying to tell them something.

Wesley took in a breath and he could smell that damn burning again. His head ached with it. He closed his eyes to try to stamp out whatever it was, but there wasn't any peace. Inside his mind, visions flooded like a great wave and he couldn't make sense of them or discern one properly from the other. They moved so fast across that it was almost blinding.

Wesley caught sight of the moon careening through the sky. Saw flames in a forest, stealing something important. And Tavia, grabbing his hand and telling Wesley to run, her face not quite right, her voice not quite hers.

You're so, so close.

Wesley jumped back and reality punctured through.

"Are you okay?" Tavia asked, reaching for him.

There was silence again.

There was stillness.

Wesley looked at her with a smile all teeth and pretense. Whatever that was, he would forget it. He wouldn't let it ruin this.

"I'm always okay," Wesley said. "Didn't you know?"

He turned to Asees, resisting the urge to straighten out his tie or adjust his cuff links. Tavia would notice if he did. She'd know something was wrong.

"Well?" Wesley asked. "What's the verdict?"

Asees frowned and handed him the canister.

Wesley's blood was black.

Arjun stepped to her side and eyed it with equal confusion. They didn't seem angry, which was something, but Wesley didn't care for the uncertain looks on their faces.

"It is strange," Asees said, and Arjun nodded.

"What's strange?" Wesley asked.

"Nothing," Arjun said. "I suppose your blood really does represent your soul."

Asees smiled at that.

"Does this mean I passed?" Wesley asked.

"Congratulations," Asees said, though she didn't sound like she meant it.

Wesley stood and dipped a finger in his blood.

"Shouldn't it be—" Saxony broke off and then shook her head, like the thought was too ridiculous to finish.

Wesley didn't bother to ask what she was thinking. He didn't care about any of their ridiculous uncertainties.

He was going to be a Crafter.

It was odd. Not just the color of his blood, but the sensation in his heart when he touched it. The realms swayed and Wesley squinted to keep the room straight.

There was a faint echo in the back of his mind, like a song he couldn't quite remember the tune to. The words were there, but they were muddled and out of sync, and there were pictures in his blood. Or perhaps not in the blood, but in Wesley's eyes.

He could still smell that burning, only now he could also see a woman crying. Wesley's scars crackled like embers, and something deep inside him, a wicked, caged thing, begged to be released.

A memory rising from the ashes.

Look harder. See what's in there.

Wesley pushed it all the way down, the ghost and the memory, into the very pits of his mind, where it was darkest and most awful.

He didn't want to know.

He didn't want to remember.

He didn't care.

Wesley dipped another finger in his blood and let the black slip down to his knuckles.

"Pay up," he said to Asees. "You promised me a power boost."

22

Karam

GRANKA HAD AN INNOCENCE and a purity that Karam was so
unfamiliar with now.

Outside the temple window, her mother sat cross-legged on
the soil, a few of the children gathered around her, listening in
reverence as she taught them prayer songs and equations in a
single breath. Across the way, another group of children circled
Wesley in fascination. They ran, playing and throwing mud, and
whenever they tugged on his shirtsleeves to try to convince
him to join in on their game, he frowned and crossed the camp.

At which point, they followed.

They were all so free, unafraid of their magic or people
who might try to take it from them. They didn't know war
and couldn't fathom the prospect of it.

"Fancy meeting you here."

Karam turned as Saxony entered the temple, walking like
she was made of the wind and the stories it told.

"Did you follow me?" Karam asked. "Because stalking people is not attractive."

Saxony's grin lit up her face. "I was summoned, actually. Your old pal Arjun said to meet him. But look at you trying to pretend you don't think all my qualities are attractive."

Karam shot her a withering look.

Arjun was nowhere to be seen and so they stood in the center of the wide prayer room, looking and feeling a little lost.

Karam didn't want to move or touch anything, for fear she might sully it. The floors were such a pristine mix of white and not-so-white, with walls and ceilings that were carved in impossibly intricate patterns of gold and red. The ceiling draped over them like a painting, and beside her there was a circular window that stretched up to the nosebleed heights of the roof and offered a view of the endless forest outside.

Karam could see the Crafter children now hurling mud onto Wesley's suit.

He gasped and then began to chase them around a tree.

"I love this place," Saxony said. "It feels a little like home."

Karam loved it too, even if she didn't agree with that last part.

"I saw a couple of the other Crafters giving you the eye before," Saxony said with a sly smile. "They were real pretty. Did you talk to any of them?"

Karam rolled her eyes. "No," she said. "And before you say anything else about it, I am not territory to be marked, so you do not need to pee on me."

Saxony gaped, her laugh short and surprised. "*Pee on you?*" she said. "You've been spending way too much time with Tavia."

Someone cleared their throat and when Karam turned, Asees and Arjun were watching them.

Karam wasn't sure when they'd arrived, but their footsteps were as silent as death and she felt a twitch of irritation at being snuck up on. That sort of thing got you killed in Creije.

Arjun stared from Karam to Saxony, shaking his head a little admonishingly. "This is a holy place," he said. "Nobody pees on anybody."

"I'll hold myself back," Saxony said.

"Did you bring it?" Arjun asked.

"It would be a waste of our time if she did not," Asees said.

Karam stared at them all blankly. "What was I supposed to bring?"

"Not you." Saxony wagged a vial in her hands. "Delivered, as promised. Courtesy of my favorite busker."

The Loj elixir. Though Karam had not seen it before, there was no mistaking what it was. The magic echoed from the vial like the remnants of a cry.

Karam bristled. "Tavia brought that with us?"

"Actually, Wesley brought it," Saxony said. "But I wasn't about to ask him. So I asked Tavia and she asked him instead."

"Very efficient."

Asees forced a thin smile. "So this is the thing the underboss wants us to protect him from."

She took it from Saxony's open hand, turning it over, watching the purple liquid crawl from one end of the vial to the next like a timer.

When she popped the cork, Saxony took a step back.

"Be careful with that," she said. She brought a hand up,

a little absentmindedly, to touch the now almost-invisible mark on her neck.

"I am not going to drink it," Asees said. "That would be very stupid."

Saxony turned to Karam and arched an eyebrow. *Stupid*, she mouthed. As if to say, *Thank goodness I have been educated on such a thing.*

Karam bit down on a smile. "What do you want with the elixir?" she asked.

"It is true this is not our battle," Asees said. "But that does not mean we want to be unprepared for the day it might be."

Arjun's eyes wouldn't quite meet Karam's. It told her a lot about how little he agreed with Asees's decision. Arjun was a warrior, he had been since they were kids, and so Karam knew that he thought running from a fight and choosing not to fight at all were one in the same.

Asees passed the elixir to him and Arjun brought it close to his nose.

Karam shifted.

There was laughter outside the window, where Wesley was now chasing the children with his hands full of mud, uncharacteristic disregard for his suit. Then Tavia tapped him on the shoulder, he nodded, and they disappeared quickly somewhere together.

Karam hoped they wouldn't cause too much trouble.

She also hoped they wouldn't be gone long. They should have been here, in the temple. It felt wrong to even look at the elixir without the two people who surely knew the most about how to handle it.

"How does it work?" Arjun asked.

"You drink it and the whole world stops making sense," Saxony said, as simply as if she were giving directions. "It felt like black was white and wrong was right and all of my friends were my enemies. It turned things upside down. And there was this whispering, telling me all the awful things I should do and how they were actually wonderful."

Saxony looked a little stricken by the memory and so Karam moved closer to her.

"A kind of mind control," Arjun said, more interested than afraid. "And it must be ingested?"

Saxony shrugged. "Far as I know."

Arjun dipped a finger inside the open vial, touching just the smallest drop, and then rubbed it against his thumb.

The change in him was instant.

Though it was not something Karam could properly place, because he still looked very much like Arjun, for all intents and purposes, but this Arjun was stiff and purposeful, with a tilt to his movements and a hauntingly slow smile.

When he spoke, his voice was almost empty.

"I can smell the traitor on you," he said.

He was looking at Karam, and only at Karam, and when he frowned at her, it was then that she noticed his eyes. The smallest splatters of black crisscrossed against the white, like paint stains.

Karam tensed.

"Arjun," she said. "Sit down for a moment."

He did not seem interested in that idea. "You have betrayed the magic," he said to her.

Looking into his eyes, Karam felt a chill she had never felt before, not even on the streets of Creije, or in the fighting rings with a shadow demon ready to tear the life from her.

There was a ghostliness in her old friend's face and in his voice, which spoke words like curses.

"Traitors cannot be redeemed," Arjun said. "We must rise from the shadows and cut down all who seek to hide us there."

"Arjun, enough," Asees said, taking his hand in hers. "What is wrong with you?"

Karam saw the moment a shimmer crossed his pupils, like a swipe of silver passing through his eyes, erasing the black for a second.

There and then gone.

A shooting star of recognition and familiarity, before his stare glazed back over.

"She is not one of us," he said. "Not a Crafter. Not an ally. She does not seek the truth. She does not seek to let the magic rise."

His arm lashed out, catching Karam's wrist. The world around him was alight with magic, so much so that it shimmered. Karam could see the air moving and swaying in a dull glimmer beside him.

She could smell it, even. Like decay.

"I am going to make you scream," he said.

He squeezed tighter on her wrist.

Karam swallowed.

"I do not want to hurt you, Arjun," she said.

Her old friend smiled.

"*Scream*," he commanded.

And then his grip hardened and Karam felt her bones snap.

The pain was astounding and she could only be grateful it had been her right hand and not her left. She didn't need both to fight.

"Arjun!" Asees yelled, and she was pulling and tugging at him to release his grip.

But Arjun barely moved.

Karam was aware of Saxony doing the same, pulling and tugging from the other side, yelling about the elixir and how she thought Asees and Arjun weren't supposed to be *stupid*. She was aware of them both screaming.

But Karam did not scream.

Her knees quaked and she thought for a second she might collapse, but she had never fallen to an enemy before and she was not about to start now, in this holy place.

Karam clenched her left fist and punched.

She punched Arjun too many times to count and she wasn't sure how long it took, but eventually he stumbled backward.

"*Traitor*," he spat. "You will never be like us. You are the shackles that hold us down. You are the curse of the mundane that would destroy us."

"Spirits damn," Karam cursed, readying for the fight she knew was coming. "This is not you, Arjun."

His eyes darkened. "You may think we were friends, but that is nothing. You left once, betrayed me once, because that is all your kind do."

Her kind.

People who were not made of magic and fire.

"I am going to give you three seconds," Karam said.

"Three seconds to get your sanity back before I show you all that Creije has made of me."

But Arjun did not wait.

A burst of wind crashed from the window and into the room, lifting Karam into the air by her neck.

Her legs dangled below and when she tried uselessly to tear the wind from her throat, Arjun growled. Karam reached for the knife beneath her clothing, but before she could send it catapulting toward her friend, Arjun's magic twisted and Karam was slammed into one of the temple columns.

She slid to the floor, wincing in pain as the blood trickled down her neck and onto her spine. She didn't know where it had come from, but she was already dizzy with it.

Saxony lunged for Arjun and Karam could see the fire soaking her skin.

So much magic.

So much destruction.

In this holy place, of all places.

Arjun snapped his gaze to Saxony and she shot across the room like a bullet, like she was part of the wind, no longer made from fire, but from nothing at all. Weightless and entirely inconsequential.

Saxony careened across the floor, pounding into the wall with such force that Karam gasped.

She lifted her aching body from the floor and ran for Saxony, but then Arjun was somehow standing in her path.

"You will scream," Arjun said again, like a promise. "And the magic will rise."

Asees grabbed at his arm and Karam knew she would not

use magic to stop him, or to help her. A Liege would never attack a member of her own Kin and it was unspeakable to even consider it.

"*Arjun*," Asees urged. "Stop this, please."

He did not stop.

He did not look at her.

He waved a hand, almost lazily, and Asees froze in place. Black smoke, black magic, curling around her wrists like chains.

He focused his attention back to Karam.

When he came for her, it was not with the wind, or with the heavy sword strapped to his back. It was with the fire of the Indescribable God.

Overhead, the sky roared and crackled.

Karam looked out of the smashed window, into her mother's face, frozen in horror.

The children were not playing now; they were staring. Not at Karam, but at the sky. At the light that fractured across it like scars.

Spiritcrafter, Karam thought.

She swallowed.

The sky screamed in place of her.

And then from the clouds, a burst of lightning shot through the temple and headed straight for her.

23

Saxony

EVERYTHING WAS TOO FAST.

One moment the sky rumbled and the next Karam was diving from the path of a lightning bolt.

It missed her by no space at all and when she threw herself out of the way, her head hit the floor so hard that Saxony felt it in her bones.

Karam was bleeding.

Karam was not conscious.

And Saxony was on fire.

She let it rise up inside her. Magic blazing deep in her chest, burning until it felt like a thousand blisters on her staves. On her heart.

It branched off and buried deep within her, ancient and powerful, until Saxony's veins became tree roots and she felt the steady pulse of earth and fire and destruction.

The magic grew in her hands.

She set her sights on Arjun and readied to send it his way.

"No!" Asees yelled, surging forward.

She slammed into Saxony, hard, and they both fell to the floor in a twist of limbs and desperation.

"Get off me, you moron," Saxony said.

"Do not hurt him," Asees pleaded. "He cannot control himself."

Saxony struggled against her, kicking to get free.

Across the room Karam had, by some miracle, gotten up and was running toward Arjun with a knife in her left hand, her right hanging uselessly by her side. Arjun pulled his sword from the strap and grinned. They grappled, weapons and fists, and while Karam was quite clearly trying to hold herself back, Arjun was out for blood.

At any minute he could summon another bolt of lightning, using his Spiritcrafter powers to command nature in a thousand ways.

Saxony brought her elbow up and jerked it into Asees's nose. She fell on the floor.

Asees may have been a Liege, but that meant she relied on her magic a little too much, and if there was one thing Karam had taught Saxony, then it was how to survive in a fight without magic.

It was how to throw one heck of a punch.

"Saxony!" yelled Karam, and she spun, taking in the sight.

Karam had wrestled Arjun to the floor and a burst of lightning struck the place by her feet, missing her by barely an inch.

Karam punched him.

"Help me get him to the column!" she said.

Saxony grabbed one of the nearby curtains and pulled the tie loose. It would do for a rope.

She ran to Karam, grabbing one of Arjun's arms, trying to use her own energy to subdue him. She could feel him fighting against it. His magic battling hers for control, wrestling against her protection shields.

Fire versus spirit.

They shoved Arjun against the column and used the curtain rope to hold him down.

His eyes grew darker and more muddled.

Saxony hoped she hadn't looked that awful when the Loj had struck her.

"Asees," Arjun breathed. The darkness in his eyes shifted. Blinked. "Where is she?"

He swallowed, then turned back to Karam.

"Filthy . . . traitor," he panted.

But Saxony could see the black in his eyes dulling.

"You are a dirty—"

Karam punched him again.

Saxony was a little sad that she'd beaten her to it.

Arjun shuffled, squinted, cleared his throat. "What are you . . . ?"

He trailed off and then his eyes rolled, black disappearing to white.

He blinked and when his stare returned, he looked as though he couldn't quite work out what had happened or was happening or would happen.

"What is this?" he asked, pulling at the ropes.

"Did you just literally knock sense into him?" Saxony asked.

Karam shrugged. "He barely touched the magic," she said. "Perhaps it is wearing off already?"

"Out of my way," Asees said.

She pushed Saxony to the side and knelt hurriedly over Arjun, stroking his bleeding forehead and squinting to see what other injuries he may have had.

"Are you okay?" she asked. "Did they hurt you?"

"Did *we* hurt *him*?" Saxony was aghast.

"Asees." Arjun's eyes sparked. Back to brown, a less murderous and more contrite stare. "Are you okay?"

"She is not the one you tried to kill," Karam said.

She slumped back onto the floor beside Arjun, exhaling in relief. The blood on her neck was thick.

"Speaking of getting killed," Saxony said to her. "Can you stop getting attacked? I'm going to drain myself trying to heal you all the time. This is strike three."

Karam laughed and the sound was more of a comfort to Saxony than anything in the realms.

"Can you untie me now?" Arjun asked.

"No," Karam said. She patted him on the knee, like a consolation. "You threw a lightning bolt and knocked me out."

"You punched me," Arjun said. "A lot."

"But not hard enough to knock you out."

Arjun rolled his eyes, but didn't argue. He rested his head against the column and breathed in a deep, calming sigh.

"Can we all make a deal to stop drinking, touching, or even looking at that elixir?" Saxony asked. "Because we have enough people trying to kill us without us trying to kill each other, too."

"You should never have brought it here," Asees said.

Saxony's mouth very nearly dropped open.

"You *asked* me to!" she snapped defensively.

But Asees wouldn't meet her gaze. She was still looking at Arjun with such guilt and sorrow, such true and unyielding fear. It was a sight Saxony had never seen in her sister, the destined Liege of her own Kin, and one she had never seen in her grandma, the temporary replacement they had chosen.

It was one she did not think a Liege was supposed to have in the face of danger and death. They were meant to be stronger and more steadfast than that.

"We must help them fight it," Arjun said. He swallowed with a wince, like he thought there might still be some magic left in his words, and wanted desperately for it to be gone. "This would destroy us all. We cannot stand by and watch."

Asees nodded. "I know," she said. "That is why we will not watch. That is why we will hide."

She looked to Karam. To Saxony.

"Take that evil and go fight your war," she said. "Never bring it to my people again."

24

Tavia

"Are we really going to do this?" Tavia asked.

She stood side by side with Wesley, surveying the train station.

Though it was not so much a train station as it was a hut on the riverbank of Sirta, with tree trunks holding up the wooden roof and casting a line of shade. There were benches made from vines and iron, sprinkled with pink blossoms from nearby trees.

Floating railway stations were usually large and lavish, with sweeping theaters and ceilings high enough to house clouds. The trains were sleek swords that swept through enchanted waters, with windows tall and large so no part of the journey was missed. They were beautiful and grandiose and a tribute to the architecture of the city.

At least, they were in Creije.

But the Grankan station was not at all like that. Instead, it was beautiful for its simplicity. Tavia suspected that in Deshri or

Maynit, the two larger Wrenyi cities, the stations had more in common with those she was used to. But Granka was the holy land and this was its five-river city, and there was something wonderful and serene in its modesty. Something that made it seem far more magical.

"Don't tell me you're having second thoughts," Wesley said. "We need a floating train to get across the Onnela Sea in time to find the Kingpin. You said that a ship wouldn't do and we can't use the old steam train we rode in on since that uses *actual tracks*. This was your idea. If I knew you were going to flake out, I would've brought Falk or one of the other buskers."

Tavia knew that wasn't true.

Sure, Wesley could have brought any number of people, but he never would have.

He brought her, because they both knew that was all he needed. Not just because this station was small and barely guarded, but because together they were a force to be reckoned with.

Together, they didn't need anyone else.

Wesley gestured to the many pouches Tavia had stolen from the consort. "Magic at the ready," he said.

Tavia's face scrunched. "We won't need it. I think I could steal this train alone, blindfolded, with one hand behind my back."

"Don't get cocky," Wesley scolded. "They could press an alarm and have guards here in minutes."

"Or," Tavia said, strolling forward without him, "they could piss their pants at the sight of me."

The train station had four ticket booths, three of which were empty. In the only open one a young man, a few years older than Tavia, leaned on his elbows, poking his head through the window to catch the passing breeze.

He wore glasses—which were rare in Creije, where vision-correction charms were all the rage among the swells and tourists—and on the table beside him was a neat row of items, beginning with various colored charms and ending with a dagger.

A line of protection, the preciseness of which told Tavia that he never had much use for it.

The man asked them a question in Wrenyi and when Tavia and Wesley only blinked, he paused to take in their outfits. Tavia's steel-tipped boots and Wesley's fine-pressed suit.

"Uskhanyan?" he asked.

They nodded.

"Creijen," he said with enthusiasm.

They nodded again.

"How can I help you?" he asked in an excited rendition of their language.

He did not suspect them to be anything more than tourists. Wesley smiled, all lazy charm and handsome edges.

And yes, Tavia could admit that his edges were handsome.

"We just have a quick question, if that's okay?"

Wesley's voice was like pure honey and Tavia was surprised enough by it that she chided herself.

She'd forgotten that outside the shroud of Creije, to perfect strangers who knew no better, Wesley could seem innocent and approachable. That at any given moment he could give the illusion of being any given thing and he did not need tricks and magic to do it. All he needed was a suit and a smile, and whatever masqueraded as charm among the rich.

"I can help you," the man said. "What question?"

Wesley pulled out his gun and set it on the counter. "Are you alone?"

The man's face dropped and he darted for his long, neat line of protection.

They disappeared before his eyes.

Before the man had a chance to be confused, Tavia held out her hand. The marbles of his magic were in her palms.

They were almost too easy to lift.

"Stealing is a lot simpler when you have the consort's dirty magic," Tavia said. "If I had a trick that let me summon an item from someone's pocket back in Creije, I would have had so much fun."

"It's clearly wasted on helping us save the realm," Wesley said.

"Exactly." Tavia gestured to the new dagger tucked into her waist, which she'd also taken from the man. "Thanks for the extra weapon," she said. "I've always said that you can never have too much of a good thing."

Sometimes she really couldn't help herself and the look on the man's face only egged her on.

Wesley grinned, real and wide.

It made Tavia nostalgic for the days when they had crafted cons as a team. When they were kids and Wesley was just an orphan like her, only a little older and lot smugger.

Back then, the other buskers were more focused on sabotaging each other than learning the trade, but Wesley was talented enough that he didn't need to bother being cruel, which meant Tavia didn't need to bother hating him.

Wesley was the one who made her practice magic, even when she got the flu or a dodgy stomach from the rations. Days and weeks and months and all Tavia did was practice, read the books he brought her, and memorize the natural way Wesley wielded charms, until finally they could busk the center of the market square together. And then, once they were older, create fortune orbs in the still of night.

Tavia didn't realize how much she'd missed it until now.

How much she'd missed *him*. Not Wesley Thornton Walcott, the underboss of Creije and a complete bastard, but *her* Wesley. Her friend. And the girl Tavia had been when she was with him, as wide-eyed as those people who came to Creije looking for a dream.

"I don't think you want me to ask whether you're alone again," Wesley said. "It won't be pretty."

The man slumped back into his chair. "I am alone, but soon three more come."

"The other ticket booths won't be closed for long then," Tavia said.

She took some joy in knowing she was right. They really could have taken this place blindfolded.

Tavia palmed her newly stolen charms, reading each one before she added them to her pouch.

"Hopefully there's some kind of binding magic here," she said. "Because we're definitely going to need him and his colleagues tied up and out of commission. Maybe a silencing charm too, so they don't run their mouths and scream for help."

Wesley leaned over the counter, his smile wicked as the young man regarded him with a mix of fear and resignation.

"You'd think with all those charms she has, some would've rubbed off on her," Wesley said in a mock whisper. He tapped his gun on the counter. "Now, there's just one more thing we need from you."

He turned to Tavia and for the first time in years, she felt like they were a real team again.

Tavia leaned beside him and eyed the booth worker.

With a grin to echo Wesley's she said, "I don't suppose you know when the next supply train is coming through?"

25

Wesley

WESLEY LOOKED ENTIRELY THE same.

He thought becoming a vessel for Crafter magic would mean shooting ice from his eyes or the ability to kill someone with a click of his fingers.

Sadly, it did not.

Instead, Wesley felt charged. Not different, but elevated. Like he'd spent his entire life with only half of his energy and now, finally, he had been given the missing part. He was awake for what felt like the first time.

Whatever lived inside of Wesley, it was born for magic.

After only a day, he figured out how to conjure good luck—not much, but enough to win a few card games against Tavia—and an invisibility charm that made his scars disappear for an entire hour.

He had not conjured the plague, like everyone clearly expected, and once he reached the Kingpin, he was going to use this new power to fix a very old mistake.

If only it were that easy.

Wesley let the warm breeze sweep across his neck.

His feet dangled over the edge of the train roof, which sat in wait on the Sirta River, the winding stretch of water serving as a track.

Wesley still kind of wanted a ship, similar to those he'd read about. He imagined setting sail on an old pirate cruiser with black sails, but this was not going to be at all like that.

They had a supply train used in trade shipments and there was not a sail or a cannon in sight, and since everything was automated by magic, there also wasn't a wheel or a conductor's seat Wesley could stand by and pretend he knew a thing about navigation.

Everything was mechanics and magic, and Wesley felt a little disappointed by the whole thing. It was hardly a vessel for war.

Still, he supposed it was better than swimming to the Kingpin's island.

The station's ticket booths were closed, courtesy of Wesley and Tavia—who used a few binding charms to keep the ticket officers tied up in the back—and the next passenger train was not due for a while, so passersby were few and far between.

Wesley exhaled.

They had been waiting thirty minutes for Karam to say goodbye to her mother and to her friends, which Wesley thought was a little long, considering that Arjun had tried to kill her.

Elixir or not, Wesley didn't think that warranted a pleasant farewell.

He stood and stretched out his arms, feeling the drag of

impatience cramp his bones as he walked the length of the train roof in a pace.

The buskers toward the back were laughing and throwing trick bags while cigarettes hung from their lips. They cast routine glares to those at the front, the deadlier career criminals who waited in silence, barely blinking as they twirled knives in their hands or stroked voodoo dolls with eerie smirks.

And then there was Falk, nearly obscured, keeping away from them all as he whispered to a *delg* bat nestled in the crook of his arm.

Everything about him set Wesley on edge.

Being a snitch was one thing, but being entirely without loyalty was another. Any man who could be bought for such a small amount of coin was one to be watched closely.

"I'll give you a fire charm for a spell that makes someone incapable of being an idiot," Tavia said.

Wesley turned to see her climbing up the ladder to join him on the train top. When he sat down, she sat beside him, her hair cutting a sharp line across her chin.

She flashed the charm pouches looped to her belt. "Name anything," she said.

"The other buskers giving you a hard time?" Wesley asked.

"They won't stop asking me questions and following me around like little puppies. It's like when you're not there, they assume I have all the answers."

"You are my best busker," Wesley said. "They look up to you. It's a compliment, so try to pretend like you don't hate them."

"Yeah, yeah." Tavia pulled out her knife and stabbed it into the space between them. "But if I throw one or two off the train once we get going, that won't hurt our chances against the Kingpin, will it?"

Wesley smiled, even though he knew Tavia wasn't serious. She had a habit of talking gray and then getting all moral on him.

"Grit your teeth," Wesley said. "After we dethrone Ashwood and return to the newly saved Creije, you can go back to never speaking to any of them again."

"Surely defeating the man who owns my debt makes it void," Tavia said. "When this is all over, it's goodbye Creije and hello somewhere far, far away."

There was a note of sadness in her voice that gave Wesley pause.

Usually talk of leaving made Tavia far too excited. Second to debt, the last thing she wanted to be tied down by was people, and Wesley wasn't sure when, but somehow he knew he had become an anchor to her.

"Was Creije ever home to you?" he asked before he could think not to. "Or was it always your dream to leave?"

Tavia scraped her teeth across her bottom lip, which she always did when she thought long and hard about something, as though the steady pain and rhythm of the action would give her an answer. Like how Wesley always touched the scars that crawled across half of his body, confident the sting of the past would propel him to focus on the present.

"I don't know," she said. Honest, almost grave.

"You don't know?"

Tavia spoke in a shrug. "That's the thing about dreams. They happen overnight."

"And then fade away," Wesley said.

Tavia shot him an odd look. "My muma said that you should always listen to the kind that stick around, demanding you follow them."

"That's really corny."

"It's supposed to be comforting," she said. "That's what parents do, Wesley. They make up pretty words and stories so you don't have to. That way you get to believe them. You get to feel better."

Wesley shifted and turned away from her.

He was glad Tavia had memories like that. Platitudes and proverbs to comfort her when things got too dark. He was glad she remembered the sound of her mother's voice so fondly and that she tried to cling to those memories.

But Wesley could never do the same.

The only adages his father taught him were about learning to never create more than one enemy, because then he'd have to turn his back on one to keep an eye on the other.

In truth, Wesley remembered little of his father—his old life never felt enough like his own to bother keeping—but what he did remember were warnings like that. If there was one thing Wesley's father loved, and that thing was most certainly not Wesley, then it was warnings.

Wesley tried to shake off the moment, but Tavia kept her eyes on him, pressing harder into it, as she always did, pushing Wesley to the limits of nostalgia. She sat in an almost determined silence beside him, like she'd asked a question and knew he wouldn't answer, but wanted to be there just in case.

He picked Tavia's knife from the train and handed it back to her with a sigh. "Volo won't know what hit it," he said.

"What makes you think I'd go there when I leave Creije?"

"It's all you talked about when we were kids."

Tavia's smile was wistful. "You remember."

Truthfully, Wesley remembered everything anyone ever said to him, but he especially remembered everything to do with Tavia. Once someone was under your skin, there was no getting them out.

He knew he should move past it, but Wesley had pushed aside every part of his old self and he wanted to keep just this one thing. When Tavia left Creije, that would be the end of it. He'd never see her again and sooner or later—sooner for her, probably, and later for him—they would forget each other.

Wesley would be a Kingpin and Tavia would be a nomad and, just like his family, maybe one day they'd pass each other in the street and she wouldn't recognize him and he wouldn't let himself recognize her.

He knew they weren't destined to be anything other than temporary allies, existing alongside each other until the world gave her the means to do otherwise.

But for now, while he could, Wesley wanted to remember everything.

"Do you ever think about that time, a few years back, when we were running from the amityguards?" he asked. "We got trapped in that dead-end alley by the bridge."

Tavia snorted. "No blades. Not even defense magic or something to make them lose sight of us for a minute."

"Nothing but a shoddy transmutation charm."

"Many Gods," Tavia said, her eyes newly alight with mischief. "We used it to walk through the first wall we saw."

"And straight into a brothel," Wesley said.

Tavia burst into a wide grin. "The looks on our faces must have been priceless." She was barely able to contain her laughter. "I've never seen so many naked people."

"I like to think we carried the shock well," Wesley said. "Besides, it was better than being sent to the cells. The old underboss would've beaten us to a pulp if we got snapped by the amityguards."

"Especially if it was because we were stupid enough to run out of magic," Tavia said. "I suppose that isn't something you have to worry about anymore." She looked to Wesley, the smile still fresh on her lips. "Do you feel different having Crafter powers?"

Wesley lifted his chin so that she could appraise him. "Do I look different?"

"You don't want me to tell you what you look like."

"Guess I'm pretty enough to render you speechless," he said.

Tavia pulled a face. "You're definitely carrying Crafter power. The ego is a prerequisite. I swear, it explains so much about Saxony."

"You'll miss it when you're in Volo," Wesley said. "Just like you'll miss having so much magic. I bet the busking scene over there is lousy."

"I'll have to find another profession."

Tavia bit her lip, like she was putting a lot of thought into what that could be. Neither of them had been in any business outside of magic.

"Maybe I could do something that doesn't require me almost getting killed five days out of the week," she said.

"Sounds boring."

"I was shooting for normal."

Wesley shrugged. "That's what I said. Either way, you'll have more free time if you're not busy patching up your battle wounds."

"Doesn't mean much if the old ones have already scarred."

"Scars fade," Wesley said.

Tavia's smile wavered. "Not all of them."

Though Wesley knew she wasn't just talking about physical scars, he couldn't help but look down at her hand. True enough, there were knife marks across her knuckles, some stretching to her wrists in defensive crisscrosses.

His throat tightened.

Wesley thought back to the nights they had busked together, trading charms and staying up until morning. They had combined technology with magic and created something from nothing as though they were Crafters. Then he remembered all the times he hadn't been there, too busy climbing the ranks and earning the underboss's trust.

Wesley wondered how many of Tavia's scars he could have stopped if he stayed on the streets by her side.

Tavia didn't need saving. He knew that. She wasn't his best busker because she got scared easily, but if Wesley had stuck by her, then maybe Tavia would have changed her mind about wanting to leave.

It was a selfish thing to think, but Wesley was always selfish when it came to Tavia.

That was how he knew he was a bastard.

Not because he headed up Creije's branch of the black

magic market and not because of all the things he had done to get blood on his hands, but because of Tavia. Because he cared about her and let her care about him back.

That was what made Wesley the biggest bastard of all.

He placed his hand on top of Tavia's, hiding the cuts and scrapes as though that would fix anything.

She stiffened but Wesley stayed still, staring at his hand on hers, wondering who would walk away first.

One of them always walked away.

"For the underboss of Creije, you really are not that scary," a voice said.

Tavia's hand shot into her pocket and Wesley's stomach tightened.

He leaned over the train's edge to face the new arrival.

Arjun looked more like an asshole than Wesley ever had, from the sheathed four-bladed sword, down to the smirk that made up his face. Behind him, Karam stood with a smile and at least a few dozen of the Grankan Crafters.

"I suppose your reputation is all talk?" Arjun said, staring up at him.

Wesley jumped down onto the riverbank, landing with catlike grace. "You go your whole life without seeing a Crafter and suddenly there's a horde of them at your feet," he said.

Tavia landed beside him and propped up her hood. "Infestations usually work that way."

"As opposed to plagues," Arjun said.

Wesley tensed. He was getting a little tired of people comparing his business to a disease.

"Everyone but Doyen Schulze deals in the underrealm,"

he said. "Even your holier-than-thou Grankans. I'm not some illusive devil who has the corner on magic markets."

"I am not debating morals with a murderer," Arjun said.

"Just semantics, then."

Arjun sneered. "You're a con artist."

"But an artist all the same."

"You make a living on other people's backs," Arjun said.

Wesley smiled. "I mostly make a killing. What are you all doing here anyway?"

Arjun practically puffed out his chest. "We are coming with you," he said.

Wesley tried to keep his face even. "I thought your Liege wasn't going to give us any help. Especially after the Loj made you go all murder-hungry on one of my people."

Arjun cleared his throat, looking like he was trying to hide how uncomfortable he felt with the idea that Karam was one of Wesley's people. And doing a damn awful job at it.

"Asees is wise and her decision to stay is understandable," Arjun said. "But there are those of us who do not agree it is the only path to take."

It was a very diplomatic way of saying that he was ignoring orders.

"So she's just going to let you leave with us?" Wesley asked. "Taking half of her Kin with you?"

"We have made our own decision," Arjun said. "We will not let more Crafters fall prey to Kingpins and their dark magic."

"So you snuck out with your fellow rebels to come see the big bad underboss." Wesley was almost impressed. "I guess you being a traitor works out great for me."

Arjun practically snarled.

He clearly did not appreciate that last part.

"You listen to me, underboss," he said, stepping forward menacingly. "Just because we are agreeing to fight in this war, it does not mean we are allegiant to you. We are here because our people are in danger and once we help free every Crafter your Kingpin has, we will leave you in the dust."

Wesley smirked.

Two minutes and he already had Arjun sussed out.

Stubbornly righteous, loyal to a fault—because loyalty was always a fault—and carrying a weight his shoulders were too inexperienced to bear.

"And maybe it won't just be us," Arjun said. "Maybe all of your precious buskers will abandon you. Without a real threat like Ashwood, there is no need for them to stay."

He glanced over to Tavia and something inside Wesley simmered.

"Criminals are not known for their loyalty," Arjun said.

Wesley didn't kid himself into thinking he had many virtues, but if there was one he always thought he possessed without a doubt, then it was patience.

But that had just about worn.

"Once Ashwood is gone, I'll be the new Kingpin," Wesley said. "So who's to say I won't just pick up where he left off? Crafters and all."

Arjun's hand shot out faster than predicted.

A burst of white, which Wesley soon realized was lightning, hurtled for him. He dropped his shoulder and the beam crashed into the water.

If Wesley turned out to have Spiritcrafter powers, he'd make a mental note to learn that one.

Arjun raised his blade and Wesley quickly lifted his hand. He clenched it to a fist and his new magic dragged Arjun toward him. The Crafter froze inches from Wesley's face, struggling against the vice that held him there.

Wesley stretched out his other hand and the magic propelled Tavia's knife from her pocket and into his palm.

He pressed it against Arjun's throat.

"Let him go!" Saxony said, running out from one of the carriages.

Karam was beside her and Wesley could see her hands dangerously close to her own knife.

"He is the second in command for his Kin," Karam said. "Who are all surrounding you."

True enough, out of the corner of Wesley's eye, the Grankans gathered.

They sneered at Wesley and he felt their magic burning through him, but his buskers were there too and they were always spoiling for a fight.

"I'll let him go as soon as we come to an understanding."

"You will do it now," Arjun said.

Wesley inclined his head to the side, watching Arjun's face change, taking in the different shades of defiance, like it was a work of art.

"Wesley." Tavia was by his side, her voice a warning bell. "Don't do something that will screw over the huge opportunity we just got."

Wesley took his eyes off Arjun to look at her, but it was a

stupid move. The lull in his attention gave his magic pause and Arjun took the opportunity to bring his head forward and crack it awkwardly against Wesley's lip.

Wesley tasted blood in his mouth.

He seized Arjun's collar. "Now can I kill him?" Wesley asked.

But Arjun was already swinging his fist, catching Wesley in the jaw.

Wesley winced and brought his elbow down hard on Arjun's nose. The Crafter stumbled back, blinking away the dizziness, and then collapsed onto the riverbank.

He may have been a Crafter, but he was no underboss.

Arjun shook his head and made to push himself up.

Damn, Wesley thought. *He's got guts.*

He kicked Arjun's hands out from under him.

"Enough," Karam said. She knelt by Arjun's side.

Tavia pushed herself in front of Wesley before he could strike again. "Quit being such an idiot."

Her hand pressed against Wesley's chest and he wondered if she could feel his heartbeat. He wondered if he still had one.

"If you're not careful, you're going to start a war with the wrong people before we even reach Ashwood," Tavia hissed. "Arjun's on our side now."

Wesley shrugged. "He also started it. It was a fair fight."

Many Gods he sounded like a child.

From across the way, Saxony glared at him. "You've never fought fair in your life. All you do is take what isn't yours."

Wesley's clenched his jaw.

And all Saxony ever did was speak to him like he was something she'd scraped off the bottom of her shoe. For what?

He'd been nothing but an ally to her. To all of them.

"You think that just because we're not in Creije there isn't a pecking order," Wesley said, loud enough for everyone to hear, Crafters and buskers alike. "But I only have limited goodwill and it's wearing thin. The next time anyone comes at me, whether it's with magic or a side-eye, then I'm going to start living up to my reputation. *Skjla?*"

The Grankans scoffed indignantly but said nothing. Even Saxony, whose lips shook as she tried to hold in whatever spell or curse she wanted to throw at him.

Wesley waited a few seconds to see if she would anyway, but Saxony stayed silent, her eyes burning. She needed him if she was going to get to the Kingpin and Wesley knew it. If any of them were going to get what they wanted, they had to work together.

They had to be a team.

"I'm glad we understand each other," he said.

Saxony shook her head. "I'll never understand you."

But Wesley could live with that.

Everyone else might have been in this for a noble cause, but Wesley was in it for an empire. To protect the one he'd created and forge an even greater one in its place. Maybe sentimentality crept up on him sometimes, the urge to keep Tavia safe like an old habit, but that didn't change anything.

They may have been about to save the realm, but there was no saving him.

And now that Wesley had true magic, there was no stopping him either.

26

Karam

KARAM SPENT MOST OF HER time training the crew on how not to die.

They had spent a week on the train, crossing endless waters to reach Ejm Voten, following the map Saxony traced from her mind. Their army was split, with the buskers they had gathered from Creije on one side and the Grankan Kin on the other.

The buskers were versed in violence and the Crafters were versed in all manner of magic they had never seen, and so their army, haphazardly flung together, mortal enemies in another life—and in this one too—became mentors for each other.

On the days Karam headed things up, the Crafters were split into groups and assigned a busker to school them in hand-to-hand combat. On the days in between, Saxony and Arjun took the lead, and the Crafters played teacher to the chosen crooks of Creije, giving them access to new magic and showing the best way to use it as a weapon.

It was a hard thing to do cramped within the confines of a train, but the supply carriages were large enough to provide a worthy enough arena.

"Was this what you had in mind when you wanted to be a protector?" Arjun asked.

Karam heard the carriage door close behind him.

She continued wrapping her fists, preparing for the day of training ahead. When she finally turned to him, she saw that he was shirtless, too many staves to count inked on his skin. All the magic he had conquered and created, bound to him forever.

She understood taking pride in his accomplishments, but she wished he could do it with his clothes on.

"I'm saving the realms, aren't I?" Karam said. It felt good to speak in the holy language again. "I'd say I'm fulfilling the duties of the Rekhi d'Rihsni pretty well."

Arjun looked at her in the same way that a disappointed older brother might. He still hadn't forgiven her for leaving Granka and while Karam understood that, acting as though she had failed her childhood self was something she couldn't quite get behind. Maybe this wasn't the future she had anticipated, but taking down a Kingpin and rescuing Crafters wasn't a bad course to be on.

It was still honoring the ways of the Rekhi d'Rihsni.

"You wanted to save the realms from people like Wesley. Not work alongside him," Arjun said.

Karam raised an eyebrow. "Look who's talking."

At this, Arjun smiled, though it wasn't the wide grin Karam remembered. It was stiff and a little resentful.

"I felt betrayed when you didn't come back," he said. "When you left me to pursue our dream on your own."

"I didn't have a choice," Karam said. "Mete and Pehta—"

"I know what your parents are like. You forget, I've known them longer than you."

Karam tensed with the truth of it.

All the years she was gone, Arjun had remained. He saw her mete buy fruit from the markets and had, perhaps, been witness when her father spoke his last words.

Arjun was part of the family Karam had left behind and it hurt her to realize they had gone on being a family in her absence.

"I cursed your name to the spirits every night," Arjun said. "I told myself you could've taken me with you if you planned to stay away. That we could've run and been warriors together. We could've been brother and sister against the realms."

He looked back at Karam and she noticed how the *teera* wrapped around his head had the same golden hue as his eyes. It made the color look sad.

"I know that's not true," Arjun said. "I'm glad you left me behind."

Karam shook her head. "I didn't see it that way. Only that I wouldn't be able to breathe if I stayed and that all I'd become would've been unmade if I returned."

"And I would've died if I left," Arjun said. "The realms are dangerous for Crafters, and for the reckless boy I was, it would have been deadly. When you left, it taught me to trust nobody and never let my guard down. Crafters can only rely on ourselves."

Karam didn't think that sounded like a good thing.

"I'm not saying this to hurt you," Arjun said. "I don't resent you. After all these years, I'm happy to see you, Karam."

"It doesn't sound like it."

Arjun placed a heavy hand on her shoulder. This close, she could see the echo of the elixir's mark on his neck.

"I am glad," he said. "But it would be foolish to leave words unsaid between us while we have the chance to make things right."

Karam took Arjun's hand in hers. "If we're being honest," she said, "then I should tell you how embarrassing it was to watch you get beaten by an underboss with novice Crafter magic."

Arjun laughed. Glorious and loud and Karam's heart swelled with the sound. She saw the boy of her childhood again. Her brother. Her friend.

They had both changed so much from the children who dreamed of being heroes, to the killers they had become. But something about Arjun was so severe in certain moments, that when his guard did slip and his eyes creased with happiness, Karam felt like she was looking at the person he could have been if the realms weren't so awful.

"Perhaps I let Wesley win," Arjun said.

Karam scoffed. "Asees must have her plate full with you as her second."

"Asees can handle herself."

Karam didn't fail to notice his smile. "You should see your face when you say her name. It's a little sickening."

Arjun's grin didn't subside. "She really is wonderful, Karam. She brought life back to our Kin. The children roam free in Granka, unafraid, because she's there to take care of them.

The people of the city don't fear us, the buskers don't come near, and though we might not be what we once were, we're not hiding, either. It is a sanctuary. Asees built us a home."

"I'm not denying any of that," Karam said. "But even after she saw what the elixir did to you, she still refused to fight."

Arjun leaned backward. "I know you think she was being stern, or even afraid, but she cares for her people. Staying behind to protect them is her way of fighting too."

Karam wrinkled her nose. "Are you speaking as her second, or as her lover?"

Arjun raised an eyebrow. "You are not allowed to say the word *lover*," he said.

"Then you're not allowed to talk about your Liege like a lovesick child," she countered, trying to resist sticking her tongue out as Tavia would have done.

Arjun ruffled her hair and Karam scowled.

"Do you want me to kill you?" she asked, flattening it back down.

Arjun kept his grin and Karam wished that such happiness would never leave his face again.

"One day," he said, eyes twinkling. "That fight will come. And you should hope Saxony isn't there to see you eat your words."

Karam gestured for the Crafters on her training team to make their move. They were in the largest of the storage containers with the doors thrown wide to allow the light in. The ocean was calm and endless on the other side.

A dozen Crafters surrounded her like starved vultures,

hungry to prove they had learned well from their training sessions and desperate to rip Karam apart to do it.

The first Crafter barreled toward her like the train hurtling through the ocean. His shoulder angled for Karam's chest, but he was slow and clumsy and she glided out of his path quick enough to send him straight into the Crafter who tried to attack her from behind.

They both crashed to the floor. An uncoordinated mess.

Karam threw her fist out and the punch sent her third attacker looping.

She grabbed his shoulders, flinging him the rest of the way, and then brought her elbow down hard on his neck and thrust her foot into his spine.

Another came from behind and Karam threw her head back, hearing the crunch.

She propelled her foot forward when the fifth lunged, then drove her boot into the woman's chest, sending her gasping onto her back.

Two more to go.

Karam charged for another and he jabbed out defensively.

His fist caught Karam's eye, but there wasn't enough power in the punch to make her dizzy.

She blinked away the hit, feeling blood dampen her brow as the Crafter's ring cut through her skin.

He went to punch again, but he was too slow, and all Karam had to do was drop her shoulder and slip to the left before she landed a hook straight across his cheek.

She grabbed his shoulders, pulling him low enough to ram a knee into his stomach.

The Crafter pitched over and Karam leaped onto him, her feet springing off his shoulders so she could propel herself into the Crafter behind.

Her legs wrapped around the girl's neck and twisted, flinging her backward and slamming them both onto the ground.

In the ring, this would be the part where Karam squeezed until she heard the snap.

But this wasn't the ring.

Karam released her hold, catapulting herself back to her feet.

"And you are dead," she said, sighing.

From the side of the carriage, leaning against the open doors, Saxony slow-clapped.

Her hair was tangled into a bun, curls flying every which way in the wind, as wild as she was. Beside her, Tavia sat on the floor, one arm leaning out to sporadically touch the ocean below. A trademark busker smirk on her painted lips.

"Can anyone tell me what they did wrong?" Karam asked.

"Aside from pissing you off?" Tavia said. "Remind me not do that, by the way."

Karam blew the hair from her face. "Too late," she said, and turned back to the Crafters. "Every one of you signaled your moves. When you wanted to punch, you glanced to your fist. When you wanted to kick, you stepped forward. Not to mention how loud you were attacking from behind. Your breathing was like a hurricane."

Saxony and Tavia laughed.

Karam did not.

Dying wasn't something to take lightly.

"You have to be shadows," she said. "The worst thing about

death is that you rarely see it coming. It sneaks up on you and snatches your life away in an instant. That is what you all need to become."

"You want them to become death?" Tavia asked.

Karam exhaled. "I want them to survive. The shadow moon is approaching and we will be at war with the Kingpin soon." She cranked her neck, hearing it click as she worked out the kinks. "That is enough for today."

Most of the Crafters left the carriage quick enough that Karam suspected they were worried she might change her mind and demand to beat them senseless again. But there were a few still bleeding by her feet, gulping down air like it was water, until eventually Tavia gave them a hand and led them to another carriage, where Karam assumed a healer waited.

"You're a tough teacher," Saxony said, once everyone dispersed.

"As though the Kingpin will take it easy on them."

"There might not be anyone left to fight him if you keep this up."

Karam shrugged. "A few less loose cannons."

She collapsed to the floor and reclined back on her palms. The ocean air smelled like sweat and salt water, but it was cool against her damp neck.

"How are you holding up?" Saxony asked.

"If you think the likes of them can hurt me, I am taking offense."

Saxony slumped down beside Karam. "I meant what happened with your father. We didn't speak about it in Granka."

Karam tried not to think about that.

No good came of wallowing or resentment, which she knew because she had spent the last few years in Creije doing both of those things. She'd lost her father a long time ago and she'd mourned for him then. It felt odd to do it again now.

Still, she hated that everything was so final. There was no going back. No jumping on a train home to say her apologies and beg for forgiveness. Everything had truly gone to the spirits and she was going to put off thinking about it for as long as she could.

Karam swiped a hand across her face.

"Are you crying?" Saxony asked in alarm.

Karam gave her a sullen look. "I have blood in my eye."

She gestured to the cut on her brow and Saxony's laugh echoed like a music box. "Anything to change the subject."

"There is nothing to say on that subject," Karam said.

She heard cheering filter down from the other carriages and checked her wristwatch. It was about time for dinner. They really were like vultures.

"What about you?" Karam asked. "The Kingpin tried to get inside your mind."

Saxony kept her eyes trained on the ocean, away from Karam's. "I live to tell the tale," she said. "We should be more worried about whatever regrets the Kingpin will make us face. I bet they will be doozies."

"A doozy sounds terrifying," Karam said.

Saxony placed a hand on her knee.

Karam tried to stop her whole body from tensing.

"The offer to talk still holds," Saxony said. "If you decide to stop repressing every single thing you feel."

"And you are always so open about everything," Karam shot back.

When Saxony sighed, it was like the light around them dimmed. She took her hand off Karam's knee and the absence of it gave the night air a bite.

"What happened between us wasn't about you," Saxony said.

Karam didn't think that made it any better.

In fact, it made it a little worse.

"Then who was it about?"

"My sister was gone and every time I spoke to my grandma I was reminded about how I had failed to find Zekia and heal our family. I wanted to do something, to do just *one* thing right, even if it was only spying on Wesley. I could still make a difference. And what was between us risked distracting me from that mission."

"You dumped me under a disco ball," Karam said.

She was never getting past that.

Saxony made a noise halfway between a whine and a grunt and threw her head back onto the floor.

Slowly, Karam lay down beside her.

She didn't realize how much her body ached until she let her head touch the ground. The days had been too long and the nights were stretching even further.

"Would you have preferred for me to end things under the fluorescent lights of the changing rooms?" Saxony asked.

Karam turned so her cheek was pressed against the cold cement of the carriage. Saxony's eyes looked far too brown from this angle, and her lips were damp and Karam could see freckles splashed across her forehead.

Do not think about it, she told herself.

But she could never stop thinking or overthinking when it came to Saxony. No other girl had done that to her. Not because they weren't special or smart or pretty enough for Karam to lose her breath. They just weren't Saxony, and that seemed to be the only thing that mattered.

"You know, my father always wanted me to live a normal life," Saxony said. "To abandon Kin traditions and stay true to our family's fifty-year legacy of hiding. He's never been the same since the fire took Malik and my mother. He'd probably have a heart attack if he saw me now."

"You rarely talk about your father," Karam said.

"You never talk about yours," Saxony countered. "You didn't tell me much about Arjun, either."

Karam did not want to think about Arjun right now.

"I suppose both of us have complicated families."

Saxony nodded. "Nothing's ever simple when it comes to a pretty girl."

Karam gave her a look she usually reserved for the likes of Tavia.

"What?" Saxony asked, the picture of innocence. There was an awful thumping inside Karam's chest. "I think you're real pretty."

Karam looked to see if anyone was listening. "Stop," she said, embarrassed.

"It's just a different kind of pretty is all," Saxony said, as though she hadn't heard her.

Karam glared, trying to dull the sound of her heartbeat. "Just how many kinds are there?"

Saxony pretended to count on her fingers and when Karam's scowl grew, she shot her a smile as fierce as her eyes.

"You're not the polished kind," Saxony said. "But polishing is a waste of time. Gold is still gold, no matter how shiny it is."

Karam swallowed and when Saxony pushed a clump of hair from her sweat-licked brow, she didn't shift away. At which point Karam forgot how to blink—and also how to breathe—and Saxony did nothing but smile.

Karam was tired of the endlessness that wouldn't stop stretching between them.

She wanted to rest, finally. She wanted everything to undo itself and then fix back the easy way.

There was a moment when Saxony paused, like she was waiting for Karam to back out, but when she didn't, Saxony ran a tongue across her bottom lip.

Karam's feet curled in anticipation.

Saxony sucked in a breath and just that nearly sent Karam over the edge. She was waiting, her eyes wandering to Saxony's lips, her fists clenching by her sides as neither of them moved.

Karam knew this game well.

Saxony liked to test the waters and watch the ripples form, but she was so rarely brave enough to dive in.

It was Karam who broke the silence.

"Now who is repressing," she said.

Saxony grinned, licked her bottom lip once more, and then she kissed her.

It was both everything Karam remembered and nothing like she had ever imagined.

Saxony's mouth was soft and warm, tracing Karam's lips

delicately enough to make her groan. But there was nothing about this moment that Karam wanted to be delicate.

She pushed herself forward, grabbing Saxony's collar with one hand and sliding the other to her waist. The fabric was rough beneath her hands and Saxony curved into her touch, pressing harder against her.

Her lips and her body and Karam felt too dizzy to focus on anything else but the heat between them.

The moment Saxony's tongue grazed hers, the realms burst into fire and ash.

Her hand was in Saxony's hair and Saxony's hand was clutched around Karam's jaw and they were tangled, inseparable, unable to unravel themselves from each other even if they wanted to.

There was no beginning or end.

Just the fire and the realms that Karam would happily let burn around them.

She thought they could stay like that forever, but the Indescribable God had other plans.

Above them, a bat screeched, shrill enough for Karam to pull back from Saxony.

They looked up to the sky. The creature screamed down at them, circling the train over and over with bloody cries.

"Somebody put that thing out of its misery," Wesley said, walking into the carriage.

He looked out of the open doors with a disgruntled sneer.

Tavia and Arjun were beside him. The creature's cries had apparently pierced the dinner carriage and interrupted their sacred mealtime.

"It is a messenger bat," Karam said. She got to her feet and held out a hand to hoist Saxony up.

When they stood, Saxony didn't let go.

"Well, we've gotten the message loud and clear!" Wesley yelled, raising his voice over the bat's shrieks, as though it were a competition.

Tavia smirked. "Now you know what you sound like when you bark orders at us."

Wesley shot her a rude gesture. Outside, the creature continued its cries.

"We need to beckon it down," Arjun said. "At this rate, even your Kingpin will hear it."

"Is anyone expecting a bat?" Tavia asked. "It won't land without its code word."

"Zekia," Saxony said, which Karam assumed was the code she used with her Kin.

When the bat didn't land at her sister's name, Saxony shrugged.

Wesley sighed and, under his breath, muttered the Uskhanyan word for *almighty*, at which point Tavia shot him a filthy look.

Karam wasn't sure why. It seemed like a very Wesley code to have.

They turned to her next and Karam rolled her eyes. "Everyone I know except for my mete is on this ship," she said.

Arjun stepped forward, resigned, and took in a deep breath. *"Hei ithna,"* he said.

The bat shrieked in recognition and barreled down to them like a lightning bolt.

Arjun lifted his arm in the air and the creature swooped

into the carriage, latching onto him. He ran a hand along its stomach, stroking the tired beast. It cooed with his touch.

"What does *hei ithna* mean?" Tavia asked.

"Land," Karam said dryly, even though the translation was closer to *come to me*.

Tavia snorted. "Your Kin's code word is *land*?"

"Highly secure," Wesley agreed.

Arjun ignored them. "Speak, my friend," he whispered in Wrenyi.

The bat shook, its head turning in circles like the hands of a clock.

When the creature opened its mouth again, its eyes glazed to mirrors and the voice that echoed from it was no longer animal.

"Arjun."

Asees's voice was low and throaty, but Karam recognized it.

"The Kin has fallen," Asees said in Uskhanyan. "The holy temple was attacked. We were outnumbered. I tried to—" She broke off. The bat screeched. "I tried, Arjun. But any minute now the enemy's forces will break through to this room and take what survives of us."

Karam's heart pounded.

"Granka is unprotected," Asees said. "We are destroyed."

It couldn't be.

The Kin protected Granka and in return Karam's family protected the Kin.

If they were gone, it meant she had failed in her sacred duty, both that of the Rekhi d'Rihsni and of her father's peaceful guardianship.

The weight of that pressed against her heart.

Arjun stared at the floor. His fists shook by his sides and if he had his dagger, Karam thought he might just tear through the realms with it.

She should never have fled Granka when she was a child. She should never have dragged Arjun into this war. This wouldn't have happened if it weren't for her actions. Without the Kin, Granka was vulnerable against the Kingpins of the realms.

Destroyed.

All those people. Asees. The children who had thrown mud at Wesley.

They had taken more than half of the Kin for their mission and Ashwood seized the opportunity to decimate those who had stayed behind.

Karam's breath got stuck halfway down her throat, so she had to swallow it the rest of the way.

Saxony squeezed her hand.

Karam didn't realize she had been shaking.

"Arjun," Asees said.

Her voice faded to a whisper.

She's dying, Karam thought.

And then she realized that wasn't true at all, because Asees was already dead.

The message had probably taken the week to reach them. Asees was long gone. The rest of the Grankan Crafters were long gone.

It was all too late.

"You were right to want to fight," Asees said. "Rescue the others. Avenge this madness. Create the future our ancestors fought to give us."

Her voice sounded like the wind.

That's all there is, Karam thought.

The legacy of an entire Kin packed into a messenger bat and then gone, just like that.

Karam looked to Arjun.

He did not blink.

He did not speak and he did not cry.

He looked like Karam felt. As though the realms had ended in the time it took for him to breathe. All this time and they hadn't even known.

Arjun's people, Karam's people, Saxony's people.

"Ashwood killed them all," Tavia said.

Her voice was softer than Karam had ever heard. Delicate, even. She swiped a tear from her cheek.

"Because of us," Tavia said. "Punishment for helping us."

Something like guilt flashed across Wesley's stoic face. He adjusted his cuff links, like there was nothing else to do but that.

Karam wanted to cry. Her father's pendant sat on her heart like a weight. *Hei reb*, if he were alive to see this, it would have broken him. To know that their family had failed their duties because there was nobody left to carry them out.

Karam's selfishness had damned them.

"I am going to find Dante Ashwood," Arjun said. "And I am going to make him pay."

"You won't be alone," Wesley said. "We're in this fight together."

Arjun looked up at him and something new passed between them. An unspoken truce to put away their differences. To forge a true alliance, even if it was temporary.

Arjun had lost part of his family, and Wesley Thornton Walcott, underboss of all of Creije, would fight to avenge them.

If there was one thing a man like Wesley understood, then it was vengeance.

Karam clutched her father's pendant. "Whatever it takes," she said. "If it is blood the Kingpin wants, then we will spill his next."

27

Krause

VICE DOYEN ARMIN KRAUSE was not impressed with the underboss of Creije. The only problem was, he had no way of telling him.

Wesley *damn* Thornton Walcott still had not checked in. He had not made contact through crystal ball or *delg* bat, and at this moment, Krause would have settled for a flare so he could at the very least know where the underboss was heading next. What was he planning? And were those plans going to betray the ones they had agreed on?

The magic markets carried on, buskers selling their cheap tricks and gullible little magic-lovers lapping it all up. Krause cleaned his glasses just to take a break from looking at them.

He needed to get out of this city and away from its charms. Better Fenna Schulze get rid of it all and throw anyone who dared use magic in a cell. Better, when once Wesley—*if* Wesley—managed to kill Ashwood, they burn it all to the ground. Better they burn the underbosses with it. If only Fenna had the backbone to do so.

The mess Wesley and his band of crooks had caused at the train station was a political nightmare, which was the most dreadful kind of nightmare. Shooting up factory buildings and public property with dark magic, in full view. Destroying tourist monuments with that same kind of *paraphernalia*.

Krause sighed.

Nearby, a group of buskers was putting on an excessive performance, throwing tricks into the air like fireworks, juggling with balls of light and speaking in riddles to the patrons. Pretending like nothing was happening, had happened, or was going to happen very soon. Though they must have known, because all buskers were crooks and had their ears to the awful deeds of past and future. Krause didn't doubt they knew of the elixir and had, perhaps, even sold it themselves.

Without their underboss, they were going quite rogue.

As much as Krause hated to admit it, the streets of Creije were restless without Wesley, and the magic sickness was creeping slowly into the quiet of the night. There had been five cases just this week alone and Fenna was powerless to stop it. They all were. The only man who knew where Ashwood was and had the same darkness in his heart, the same awful magic and crooked crew, had disappeared into the ether. Krause had no way of informing the underboss that his city was reaching its limits.

Then again, perhaps Wesley was dead.

Perhaps they were all doomed.

"Do you believe in magic?" a man asked in his ear.

Krause took a disgusted step back.

Despite the stretching sun, the man was hidden by the shadows of a building, his voice as quiet as a whisper.

"Get away from me," Krause said.

He had no patience for buskers trying to peddle their filth.

"We must protect the magic," the man said.

His voice was not quite right.

He held out a pale hand, fingers short and bony. In the center of his palm was a vial and inside that vial was a magic more beautiful than Krause had ever seen. It glowed purple in the day, tiny orbs of sunlight running through it like blood.

Krause couldn't look away.

In the distance, someone screamed.

There were panicked footsteps, a crash. Someone swore. And Krause knew, he could sense it, perhaps even see out of the corner of his eye, that people were running. But Krause couldn't stop looking at that vial. It was so beautiful and so bright, and against the stark white of the man's hands it looked almost like a chasm. A pathway into another world.

Krause reached out for it, but just as he was moments from taking the strange vial, one of the running people clipped his shoulder and his concentration broke.

Krause swiveled around to confront the clumsy fool and saw chaos.

The stalls of the magic markets, broken by bodies. People were fleeing in panic, their screams so loud that Krause wasn't sure how they hadn't pierced through to him sooner.

There was blood everywhere, alongside magic and knives,

and Krause couldn't work out who was doing the killing and who was doing the defending.

A boy lay on the ground, begging and bleeding. A woman poured something into his mouth.

Magic. Purple. Like the one in the man's hand that was so, so beautiful.

The boy sat up, smiled at the woman, and ran into the crowd.

"Would you like to help us?" the man asked.

Krause looked back to him and the moment he stepped out from the shadows Krause's breath stopped. His heart felt like it stopped. The man's eyes were as black as rotten trick dust, and there was blood across his face like vessels rising to the surface.

"You filthy little addicts," Krause spat. "What is this madness?"

"It is not madness," the man said. "It is magic. It is truth."

And then from nowhere, Krause felt the slice of a blade. Through his heart, across his spine. He felt the ungodly pain as it pierced through skin and bone, and heard the noise, over the man's laughter, when he slid it back out. A wretched, damp swish.

Krause fell to his knees.

The man looked down on him.

Krause grabbed at his ankles to stay upright.

"We must protect the magic," the man said.

Krause staggered for breath and looked up and into the black, black holes of the man's eyes, which held the end of everything.

And then the world faded away, until only screams remained.

28

Wesley

THOUGH WESLEY HAD BEEN working on a way to turn time into a weapon for a while, the shadow moon's fast-approaching deadline was doing nothing to make the process any easier.

They had just over a week to reach the Kingpin before he harnessed the power of the shadow moon to amplify his Crafters into unstoppable killers. Before he used the Loj to make Creije into an army.

Unfortunately, Falk, for all his blustering and experience, was a nervous worker. With the threat of war—and the threat of Wesley—his hands turned clumsy and his excuses became repeats of the day before.

Wesley didn't tolerate failure on a good day, but now war was on the horizon and Creije was in the firing line. He could only hope that Krause was watching over his city while he was away.

"The problem is the binder," Falk said.

He wiped the sweat from his brow, but the beads trickled down the tattoo on his neck, giving tears to the bat above his collar.

"I don't have a binder," Wesley said.

"Exactly."

Arjun peered into the barrel.

It was brimming with time charms the Crafters had collectively spent days manufacturing. Wesley had even conjured a few himself, and though they didn't shine quite as brightly as the others, he bet they still packed a mean punch.

The barrel was a mix of magic and wires, with Wesley's tech and explosives precariously entwined. The plan was simple: use the charges to freeze time and give them the upper hand they would surely need against the Kingpin.

Thanks to Arjun—not that Wesley ever would thank him—they'd finally figured out a way to make the charges go off safely, which was the most important part. But they hadn't found a way to exclude themselves from the blasts, which was definitely the next most important part.

Still, Arjun was a welcome respite from Falk. He had a knack for understanding the wrinkles of it all and helping to iron them out. They made a good temporary team. Falk linked the charms to the explosives, but Arjun linked the charms to a spell. Or, more precisely, a passphrase that would set them off. And Wesley had discovered a way to thread multiple barrels together so they would all respond to the phrase at the same moment.

There was just that small matter of not getting time all over themselves.

"What is a binder?" Arjun asked.

"It's like immunity," Wesley said. "We bind ourselves to the charms, so when they go off, they know to skip over us."

"We need part of everyone," Falk said. "We've got to figure out a way of gettin' the entire army to bind to it."

"We could use a psychic link," Wesley said.

"Too much risk," Arjun said. "If we all link to the charms, then we will all be linking to each other. We will be able to see into each other's souls and hear each other's thoughts. It would be enough to make anyone lose their minds."

And what a shame that would be.

Wesley's fingers twitched by his side.

He didn't like that idea at all. Especially the part where their army saw into his thoughts. He hadn't built his career on secrets just to have his every whim exposed.

Besides, one intruder in his mind was more than enough.

"We could use blood magic," Arjun said. "It is the most powerful kind."

It was not the worst idea Wesley had heard. In fact, it seemed like a pretty good idea. He was bothered to not have thought of it first.

Falk shook his head. "We'd drain this whole vessel just tryin' to fill barrels," he said. "We'll have to think of somethin' else. What if we just used one barrel? It'd still pack a punch and—"

"We would not need to fill every barrel if they are all linked," Arjun said. "Just one drop of blood from each person would be enough." He frowned at Falk. "Do buskers know nothing of magic?"

Wesley put a hand on Falk's shoulder. "He's more bang than brains."

"But you agree it could work?" Arjun asked.

"Maybe." Falk swallowed, running his hands across the wires. "If the link is steady, I guess the blood could piggyback off it."

Wesley resisted the urge to clap Arjun on the back. He didn't want them to do something as perilous as bonding.

"We have a plan, then," Wesley said.

"Actually, I had the plan," Arjun said.

"If you live into next week, remind me to express my gratitude."

Wesley rolled his shirtsleeves up to the elbow. The oil from the explosives seeped through the material and smudged across his tattoo. Across his scars. If any of them lived into next week, Wesley would need a lot of new suits. And if they won this battle, he planned to return to Creije and never leave again.

The realms outside of his were unpredictable and alien. They held no spark of home, and the adventures they offered were the wrong kind of hazardous. Wesley liked his risk measured and calculated. He liked knowing what was around the corner so he could figure out exactly how to beat it.

He liked having a clean suit.

When the battle was over, he'd go back to the home he'd built and make it even stronger. He'd make the entirety of Uskhanya a fortress from the Dante Ashwoods of the realms. He'd unite the cities like they had never been before.

When Wesley was Kingpin, he'd build a family to go alongside his home.

"Make it happen," he said to Falk. "I'll let the others know we'll be spilling blood a little early."

Wesley exited the hold, leaving Falk to work. Arjun was hot on his tail, jogging to catch up with his brisk pace as Wesley moved through the carriages.

"Did you get those marks in battle?" Arjun asked. "Or defense?"

It was a good question and Wesley shifted. Nobody had asked him about his scars before. Probably because he rarely had them on show underneath his suits and even if he did, the tattoos did their job of hiding quite a lot. But Wesley also suspected that people didn't want to know the answer or how he would react to the question.

Arjun being so brazen caught him off guard.

"I don't know," Wesley said, keeping stride. "Scars are the past and I'm more focused on the future."

"You never asked your family?"

"I don't have a family," Wesley said.

Lies. You always were such a liar.

"Everybody has a family."

Wesley stopped walking and fixed Arjun with a tired look. "Maybe in Granka, but Creije was built on the backs of orphans. Buskers are the kids the realms forgot. *Skjla?*"

Arjun gave a solemn nod, showing that he did indeed understand.

"I did not mean to offend you," he said. "I only ask to know more about the man I have aligned myself with."

"Well, now you know. Do you have any more irritating questions?"

Wesley walked ahead, a little faster than before, but Arjun kept pace easily beside him.

"Do you think you are powerful enough to stop your Kingpin with just these charges and some borrowed magic?" Arjun asked, as though he were genuinely curious as to whether Wesley's confidence was a charade, or if they actually had a chance of winning.

Wesley slipped his hands into his pockets. "Are you underestimating me?"

"Enough of my people were slaughtered through the ages," Arjun said. "With your Kingpin stealing us from the streets again, it is only right that I am wary."

"Wary? Or scared?"

"Vigilant."

Wesley shrugged. "Fortune favors the brave."

"And only a fool does not heed the warnings of cautious men," Arjun said.

Wesley arched an eyebrow at him. "You just made that up."

"After what happened in Granka, I need to be a protector for my people," Arjun said. "With Asees . . . gone."

He did not seem to be able to say the word *dead*, like refusing to speak it somehow made it not true.

"I must become Liege now and I must protect what is left of us. I cannot fail them the way I failed Asees."

Arjun's eyes held a look of pain so raw that Wesley had to fight not to look away. He tried to imagine if it were his family—if it were Tavia. If the Kingpin took her from him. Wesley tried to imagine a life where she wasn't safe. Where she wasn't by his side, not because she was roaming the realms, free, finally, but because she would never be free again.

It felt like something inside him was cracking.

Your weakness is in sight.

Careful, careful, who you show those cracks to.

Wesley took his hands out of his pockets and then shoved them back in, the absence of his cuff links throwing him off balance.

"We both worry for our people. I suppose we are alike in that way," Arjun said.

Wesley put a hand to his heart, swallowing the weight of the conversation. He hated the exposed feeling rising in his chest.

"I'm offended," he said, and Arjun laughed.

That was better. Comfortable. It was far easier to tease Arjun than to think about all they both had to lose in this war and the common ground they shared. Truthfully, Wesley saw a lot of himself in Arjun. Not physically, of course, because where Wesley was lithe and agile, Arjun was thick-shouldered and intensely muscular. But in other, more unnerving ways, like the stubbornness and the confidence. The thirst to prove himself to his people and the way Arjun's eyes shimmered with magic, like it wasn't just a skill, but a part of him he could never be separated from.

There were even the gold staves tattooed down the length of Arjun's arms, so similar to the map of Creije on Wesley's own body. A map that covered the scars of his past with a new future. It was a reminder that the only home that mattered was the one Wesley had built for himself. It seemed to Wesley they both carried what mattered most on their skin like a sacred brand that could never be taken.

Arjun was a little of who Wesley was and a little of who he could have been. Someone righteous and stalwart, who fought for honor rather than power. The man Wesley set out to become when he'd taken the Kingpin's hand all those years ago.

The man he knew it was too late to be now.

"You promised me that you would help save my people, or get vengeance," Arjun said.

"I know what I promised."

"Was it all just words?" he asked. "Because, by the spirits, if it was a way to look good in front of your buskers, then—"

"I don't make promises easily," Wesley said. "And I never break them."

Maybe for the first time, Wesley wasn't thinking about being a Kingpin or finally feeling like he was worth a damn. His mind was filled with Arjun and Saxony and Karam and the people they'd lost. Their family. In a lot of ways, Wesley was responsible for that.

He thought about everything he had done to become underboss. All of his dirty secrets buried so, so deep, and the dead girl's voice that still crept into his mind. It struck Wesley that maybe, just maybe, this promise might be a way to make amends for it all.

"If you really were telling the truth, then we are going to need to teach you how to handle your magic properly," Arjun said.

Wesley raised his eyebrows. "I'm a natural. Not much left to master."

For the first time since Wesley had met him, Arjun's lips curved up into a sly smile. "I will be the judge of that," he said.

29

Wesley

WESLEY PINCHED THE BRIDGE of his nose with a sigh.

"You're not punching right. How have you survived this long? Be honest, you bribed your way to second, didn't you?"

Arjun mumbled something foul under his breath in Wrenyi. "Let us not forget that *I* am supposed to be training *you*," he said, a little breathless from sparring.

Wesley shrugged. "I figured we could do an exchange. You teach me how to handle my magic, I teach you how to hit with your knuckles rather than your damn fingers. And you need to keep your wrist straight and throw your hips into it. Your whole body, really," Wesley said.

He acted out the movement slowly, as though Arjun were someone who had never even seen a fight before.

Arjun only blinked. "Are you done?" he asked.

Wesley suspected that if he had his shiny little sword, Arjun might very well have used it to try to carve him to pieces.

"Give-and-take is the key to success," Wesley said.

"And listening to a powerful Crafter of an ancient Kin is the key to learning how to use your magic properly."

Wesley couldn't argue there.

Or, he *could* but he decided not to.

"Take it away, o mighty teacher," Wesley said, arms spread wide.

Arjun's sigh was unreasonably loud and Wesley felt a small moment of glee. For some reason, he couldn't help but want to annoy him. Kind of like Tavia, only without the added want of it to be more, more, *more*.

Besides, sparring was letting off some much-needed steam. Being confined to a train for so long did not suit Wesley, but at the very least this would satisfy his penchant for trouble and violence.

"Are you sure you are ready?" Arjun asked.

"Give me a minute," Wesley said. "I need to catch my breath from barely having to move to avoid your—"

Arjun conjured a ball of lightning and flung it at Wesley.

Wesley twisted on his heel and threw himself onto the floor.

The supply carriage was large and empty, and the floors were cold and coated in small sparks of scrap metal and wood dust. When Wesley's elbow hit the ground, it took all the arrogance he had not to let the wince show.

Arjun raised his hand again, but Wesley was already on his feet, eyes narrowed and smirk widening.

It had been a while since he'd been in a fair fight.

The lightning sailed past Wesley's head and cracked against the train walls.

Wesley threw himself forward, kicking his leg out and swiping Arjun's ankles from under him.

Arjun fell to the floor and Wesley didn't hesitate at the advantage. His hand shot out and Arjun lifted into the air, held up by the collar, Wesley's magic pinning him in place.

Arjun's ankles dangled perilously as he clutched at his throat.

He wasn't choking. Wesley wouldn't press the magic that hard, but he could see Arjun's breath catching, feel his powers begging him for more carnage. A greater victory.

Wesley pushed his palm farther upward and Arjun slammed into the small glass window of the train.

It shattered against his back.

Wesley felt hungry with the noise.

Again. Again. There you are, my underboss.

For the first time, Wesley didn't swat the ghostly voice away. He let it linger in his mind, the pride in her imagined glee, all of his insanity bubbling to the surface. He relished in her praise and how mighty she thought him now that he had such power.

Perhaps being driven mad by guilt wasn't so bad when you had this much magic to console you.

The wind rolled in from the broken window and Arjun snarled.

Around him the air grew heavy and hot with Arjun's magic. Wesley could feel it whirling over to him, constricting his own breath, clogging in the back of his throat. Trying to tangle in his lungs.

Wesley took a step forward and his magic followed, pushing Arjun farther out of the window in an attempt to quell his magic.

The sea raged like a furious enemy below, water spitting up to dampen Arjun's hair as the wind howled in his ears.

But he didn't falter.

Arjun kept pushing back and Wesley's own throat seized with his power. The air was burning in his mouth, too thick to swallow. Black splintered over Wesley's eyes as he began choking on his own breath.

They were going to strangle each other before either of them gave in.

He started to feel half-bad for mocking Arjun so ferociously. He truly did hold great power.

But Wesley felt greater.

Finish him, the ghost urged. *It's in you to finish him.*

And Wesley could feel that it was.

His magic clawed inside him.

Wesley could thin the air out if he wanted. He could turn the night to day and throw Arjun out of the train and into the seas and swallow the realms whole. His magic was a hungry beast demanding to be fed.

Give in to it. Give in to it like I did.

Wesley released Arjun, took a somewhat breathless step back, remembered himself.

Arjun coughed in a breath and the air returned to normal as his magic ceased its own attack. In turn, Wesley swallowed his ravenous power and that awful voice that always brought out the worst in him.

This new magic he had, the wickedness of it combined with Wesley's growing insanity, was truly worthy of Ashwood. It was, perhaps, what the Kingpin had wanted for him all along—his right hand, doused in black magic, sitting beside him as the realms burned. Which meant that when Wesley next saw him, he could use the very thing the Kingpin had always hoped for to bring him to his knees.

Wesley patted Arjun on the back, just as the door to the carriage slid open. It was sudden enough that Wesley tensed.

A rush of new air rolled in when Saxony entered, her hair wild and her eyes wide, with a look that told Wesley she hated few people more than him.

Beside her was Tavia, dressed in blacks and grays, with a smile to cut through steel.

Everything about Tavia was always so monochrome. From the raven hair cut to a point along the angle of her chin, to the color of her eyes, which resembled a watered-down swatch of her stark black lipstick. Even her clothes: leather trousers, steel-tipped boots, and a sweater the same shade as her irises, that stood bold against her moonlight skin.

The realms may not have been black and white, but Tavia was, and every time Wesley caught sight of her, he almost forgot himself.

It was odd how someone could do that, even after so many years. Sometimes, Wesley thought that it was her greatest trick, to catch him so off guard, so often.

"Were you trying to kill each other?" Saxony asked, taking in the broken glass and the sight of Wesley and Arjun, equally breathless.

It was a pretty stupid question, because if Wesley wanted to kill Arjun, then Arjun wouldn't be alive.

Wesley didn't *try* to do anything. He just did.

"We're training," Wesley said. "A bit of practice with my new powers."

"You're practicing trying to throw Arjun off the train?" Tavia asked.

The way the light cut through the broken window and caught her smile made Wesley's throat go dry.

"Everything an underboss does involves trying to hurt someone," Saxony said.

It wasn't technically a lie, but it soured Wesley's mood nonetheless.

Saxony was good at a great many things, but it seemed what she liked best was making Wesley feel like he would never be anything more than a petty crook. Considering her choice of girlfriend, Wesley thought Saxony would be a bit less judgmental about people letting off steam with harmless violence. But it seemed that when it came to anything she thought Wesley might like, Saxony truly was a killjoy.

"Shouldn't you be helping Tavia?" he asked.

"Helping her with what?"

Saxony's hand was on her hip, eyebrows raised, like she relished being older than an underboss and thought it offered her some authority.

Wesley looked at Tavia, almost pleading. He was trying, if not just for their army's sake, then for Tavia's—because she truly had the worst taste in friends—to rein himself in.

"You have the magic from the consort that you haven't finished reading yet," Wesley said. "Saxony could help you with that."

"Did we interrupt your boys' club?" Saxony asked.

"No," Wesley said, feeling petty. "Just all the fun."

"Trust you to think beating people up is fun."

"It can be," Arjun said with a shrug.

The remark was enough of a surprise that Wesley laughed. He was starting to like Arjun more and more.

Wesley gestured to him with a satisfied flick of the head. "See? You're outvoted."

Tavia rolled her eyes, sensing the growing hostility. "Settle down, kids. No need for a pissing contest. We're all friends here."

Wesley liked the way she said that she was his friend, as though it wasn't something to be ashamed of.

Tavia nudged Saxony and gestured toward the door. "Let's leave them to kill each other," she said. "Many Gods know that it would give us all some peace and quiet."

She did a half smile that made Wesley want to tell her that he'd changed his mind and they could most definitely stay.

But he didn't.

Never did, never would.

Even though the mere thought of it made him grin: sparring with Tavia's new magic versus his Crafter powers, both of them primed with their street smarts and a shared history of each other's worst weaknesses. It would make for a damn good fight.

Wesley stayed silent.

Tavia's quip seemed to satisfy Saxony enough and she smirked at Tavia, then glared at Wesley—because that was all she ever did when it came to him—before making for the door.

As soon as it clicked shut, Arjun rounded, his fist hurtling for Wesley's nose without warning. It was good, just like Wesley had shown him.

Straight wrist, primed knuckles, and his entire body thrown in.

But Wesley still saw it coming.

There wasn't much that surprised him these days, save for tricks and charms. Magic kept him guessing in a way few people ever managed to.

Wesley caught Arjun's fist in his hand, a few inches from his nose, and smirked.

"Good use of surprise," Wesley said. "Though some might say that was nearing a sucker punch."

"You are fast," Arjun said.

Yes, Wesley was fast.

He prided himself on that. On many things, really, but that especially.

Magic had always been kind to him and it whispered sometimes, in the very back of his mind, whenever it was near.

A sense, Wesley always thought.

But now it was different.

Now the magic *screamed*.

I'M HERE, it said. *DANGER. RUN, ATTACK, GO.*

And so Wesley listened.

Moments before Arjun threw yet another burst of lightning, perhaps before he even thought to, Wesley moved. He spun on his heel, curved a little to the left, and then thrust his own hand out.

It was different to before.

It was energy. A spirit. A piece of Wesley's heart, pushed into the air and hurtling at Arjun faster and brighter than any bolt of lightning could be.

All of his excitement and anger and hope and frustration.

All of his worst fears and forgotten memories.

And the magic, Wesley's old friend, twisting into something he could use.

It struck Arjun in the center of his chest and he careened through the air, spinning until the glass door of the carriage was perilously close.

Wesley held out a hand, stopping Arjun in his tracks, inches from the door, his head so, so close to cracking. Shattered glass, spilt blood. Usually those were the things that would give Wesley cause to smile, but Arjun wasn't his enemy and this wasn't a fight to the death.

Wesley dropped him to the floor.

For a few moments, Arjun didn't move, so Wesley sauntered over, feeling kind of pleased with himself. Taking down a Crafter was a pretty big deal and he'd done it twice. Three, if they counted Granka. It was a shame Wesley couldn't brag about it to the Kingpin, since he was too busy plotting realm domination and being a complete bastard.

Ashwood would have been proud of him.

Wesley hated that a part of him still craved that.

"Knocked the wind out of you, did I?" he asked.

Wesley held out a hand and Arjun took it, pulling himself to his feet.

"What did you just do?" Arjun asked.

Wesley shrugged. "Energy sphere?" he offered. "Light circle? Great big ball of doom? I haven't thought of a name for it yet. Maybe Wesley's Crafter Slayer."

Arjun didn't laugh.

"It was a joke," Wesley said. "I do that sometimes."

"This is not about your sense of humor," Arjun said. "I saw things in that light, underboss, and I was paralyzed by them."

That was daunting and not in the fun way Wesley was used to. "Like illusions?"

Arjun shook his head. "Those were no illusions. They were . . ." He stumbled on his words, sighed, and then seemed to abandon them altogether.

Wesley did not care for the tense silence that followed.

It seemed everyone wanted to rain on his new Crafter parade and it was doing nothing for his mood. First he wasn't worthy enough for the magic and now it was somehow faulty?

"Does this mean the student has become the master?" Wesley asked, his grin positively shit-eating.

Arjun's blank, unimpressed stare returned. "Hail the crooked king, master of defective magic," he deadpanned.

"At least I'm being hailed," Wesley said. "I can live with that."

Arjun rolled his eyes, but there was a smile in the corner of his lips that Wesley was rather proud of.

"We go again," Arjun said. "And this time, I will not let you win."

Wesley opened his arms in welcome.

If preparing for the upcoming war against Ashwood involved kicking Arjun's ass repeatedly, for *training*, then he was not about to complain.

30

Tavia

THE STORM WAS UNRELENTING.

Tavia wiped the rain from her face, clutching onto the ladder between train carriages to keep from falling overboard.

She screamed up at Saxony to veer the train left and avoid a rock formation the size of a small city that had sprouted from nowhere.

Lightning cracked the sky, rain falling like glass on Tavia's skin. Hours passed and there was no sign of the storm letting up. The farther they traveled, the faster it chased them.

Arjun knelt on top of the train beside Saxony, one hand clasped to a small holder to steady his footing, and the other pressed up to the sky in an attempt to tame it. The wind battered his face, throwing his soaked hair every which way.

"Come on!" Tavia snarled, climbing up a few steps. "Earn your keep!"

Arjun broke his concentration to glare and the momentary

loss of focus caused the train to lurch right. Waves swarmed higher, their foamed edges like teeth, hurtling down toward their makeshift army.

Tavia braced herself, but the water hit like a fist. She slipped on the ladder but managed to keep her hold as the wave collided. Her legs flung out from under her and though her grip was sound, her head cracked against the side of the train.

For a second, her vision was black.

In the moment's darkness, she heard the screams of the crew being flung across the carriages.

Ejm Voten truly lived up to its name.

Nobody but an idiot with a death wish would cross these waters. Saxony's map was one step away from getting them killed.

Tavia cursed and climbed down from the ladder. She ran through the carriages, pushing past buskers and Crafters, until she reached the front cab. Its large door was slid open and Wesley leaned out.

"Keep your focus!" he yelled up to Arjun.

Tavia clung to a metal loop dangling from the ceiling to keep her balance. She heard Arjun shout spells into the wind in response to Wesley, but it was little use. Every anomaly he stopped spawned another. If Arjun ceased the rain, lightning blew a hole through the train. If he dismantled a cyclone, tidal waves sprouted like weeds along the sea's surface.

Saxony was beside him, whispering magic so fast that Tavia could barely see her lips move when she caught sight of her.

She tried to steer the train while the other Energycrafters worked to gather a force field of protection, but every time the vessel lurched from the storm, Saxony fell to the floor and her concentration broke.

Karam was by her side, always, pulling her back to standing. But even she couldn't hold her footing long enough to keep them both steady.

"We're going to die before we can even get to the Kingpin," Tavia said.

She was practically screaming to be heard over the winds.

"I'm not dying in the middle of nowhere," Wesley said. "When I go out, it'll be in a blaze of glory, with all four of the Many Gods staring down in wonder."

If Tavia could let go of the loop for long enough to stay upright, then she would've punched him.

"Be sure to tell the storm that," she said.

Wesley clutched a good luck charm in his hand, freshly conjured.

He threw it out into the sea.

Then another.

Wesley fired them into the center of the growing maelstroms in quick succession, closing them instantly.

The train shook again and Tavia turned to Arjun. Among the chaos of Crafters trying madly to keep afloat, Arjun looked close to being swallowed by the storm he was protecting them from.

Another great wave rose, double the size of the train.

Arjun lurched forward as if to grab it, and the wave stuttered and stilled in its path.

He brought his arm down and the water lowered like an

obedient servant, but when the train seesawed furiously again, Arjun grabbed at the holder to keep his footing.

And the wave exploded against the train.

Tavia heard the sounds of someone screaming as they fell into the raging waters.

Her legs buckled and Wesley's arm shot to her waist, stopping her from tumbling along with them. She grabbed onto his shoulder for balance and he squeezed tightly, pressing her against him so close that Tavia could smell the magic on Wesley's skin.

Her heartbeat quickened, faster than in any battle. Tavia could see the rain on his eyelashes and the way his graveyard eyes sparkled with the storm.

"Some girls are so easily swept off their feet," Wesley said.

Well, *that* was one way to knock her back to sanity.

Tavia punched him in the arm, hard enough that Wesley's hand shot from her waist.

"Next time, let me fall," she said.

Rain painted the smile on Wesley's lips and Tavia took in a breath that was far too deep. In this night light, in this endless storm with magic set to save them at his fingertips, Wesley looked so wild with possibility. He looked like he could make the realms a little better instead of a lot worse.

"Sir, over there!" Falk yelled, bursting through the carriage.

Tavia and Wesley broke their gaze, following the weasel's pointed finger. In the near distance, a waterspout fell from the clouds and twisted into the ocean. It spun madly, sucking clouds into its wake, dragging their train toward it, readying to swallow them whole.

The sea began to rumble.

And then, from the growing storm, the monsters came.

Ghostly beings drenched in moonlight slipped from the vortex of water, hands straight to their sides, lower bodies dispersing to wind. They were made from a dull blue-green light, like murky seawater, and their faces melted into skinless bodies.

They had the look of humans and the look of demons.

Rising from the sea in dozens, the creatures shuddered through the train, in and out of the carriage windows and through the walls, howling down at them. Their cries turned the air to fog.

Tavia stumbled back in sync with Wesley.

"*Djnfj*," he swore, and then reached for the radio at the front of the train. "Calling all Crafters and killers to center supply carriage now!"

He grabbed Tavia's hand and ran, dragging her through four carriages before they practically fell into the correct one.

Some of their army had filtered there too, with Saxony, Karam, and Arjun at the forefront, staring through the open door as the dead weaved in and out. They moved in screams.

Wesley darted for the other side of the carriage and heaved open the opposite access point.

The light spilled in.

The ghosts spilled in.

"Keep together," he said, backing away.

Tavia followed his lead, until half of them had formed a makeshift circle, backs to each other, watching the realms lose their minds.

The train steadied, stopping moments from the waterspout, and every one of them whipped out their weapons: magic and knives and guns. They scouted their new enemies, and not a one of them dared blink.

Wesley's hand dangled beside Tavia's, close enough that her focus drifted.

"When the time comes," he said, "put every last one of those stolen charms to use."

Tavia could only nod and then watch as the dead crept aboard their train.

"Lie and tell me those aren't ghosts," she said.

She was shoulder to shoulder with Karam, both of them with knives at the ready. Neither of them sure what use such weapons would be.

"They're not ghosts," Saxony said.

The rain slowed to spittle, but the wind still howled loud enough that she had to yell.

"I'm no expert," Wesley said, "but they sure look dead to me."

"They're phantoms," Saxony corrected. "Memories of the dead conjured into form."

Tavia winced. "That doesn't make me feel any better."

Saxony shuffled, like she was steadying herself for bravery. "They're harmless." Though she didn't even sound like she was convincing herself. "They're simply controlled by the spell that cast them."

Tavia nodded, and then—

"Wait. Like if the spell told them to kill us?"

Saxony didn't have an answer and Tavia suddenly wished that she hadn't asked.

"This might be a good time to use that spirit magic," Wesley said to Arjun. "Connecting with the dead sounds like a great idea right about now."

"That's not what it means," Arjun practically growled over the wind. "I can only conjure spirits into willing vessels and deliver messages to and from the other side."

Wesley clutched his gun. "Then deliver them a message to get off my train."

"It doesn't work that way," Arjun said. "And they're *not* ghosts."

The phantoms drifted closer.

"The rest of us will be if you don't do something," Tavia said.

But there was nothing to be done.

Just as Arjun's powers hadn't been a match for the storm, there was no way they would be a match for whatever these creatures were.

The Kingpin charmed this sea and all that wreaked havoc on it. They had to go through things his way, or not at all. Tavia only hoped that the Kingpin's way didn't involve them dying.

One of the phantoms drifted closer, its bottomless shape oozing onto the floor. It dragged itself toward them with white eyes, and it was only when it inclined its head that Tavia knew it was looking at each of them in turn.

Its mouth stretched open. "Your worth is a trial," it croaked. "Through regrets wicked and vile."

Its lips didn't move, its mouth a still picture pulled down the length of its neck, as though it were only a vessel for the words. Like a *delg* bat straight from the fire-gates.

"Oh great," Tavia said with a shiver. "It *rhymes*. That's not creepy at all."

Wesley turned to Saxony. "Are these the trials Eirini was talking about?"

"She never mentioned ghosts."

"I thought they were *phantoms*," Tavia said.

Saxony shot her a look.

Tavia racked her mind trying to think which part of her past she regretted most. There were too many things to count. When she was younger, the buskers had sung about the dangers of living in the past and how deadly it could be—they had a song for just about everything, especially remembering—but Tavia couldn't recall a word of it now.

"The leaders among you must relieve your pasts, looking to where you rest your hearts." The phantom cracked its head to face Wesley. "But though regrets are prone to repeat, if you wish, then the world shifts under your feet."

"We can change the past?" Wesley asked.

"*No.*" Arjun turned to him. "You cannot alter your lives like that. Time windows are dark magic that prey on desire for change, but it is all an illusion. If you try, it will leave you in an endless loop. An alternate life you would never realize is a dream. It is why the magic is forbidden."

"He's right," Saxony said. "Changing the past is impossible. I've told you how dangerous magic is when it invades people's minds. It's a one-way trip to insanity."

"Right," Tavia said. "No changing the past. Check. How do we pick our leaders?"

The moment she said it, five phantoms shot their arms out,

fingers pointed straight at them.

Tavia. Wesley. Saxony. Karam. Arjun.

"You are the leaders," they said in unison. And then, again, "You are the leaders."

"Okay," Tavia said. "It's getting creepier."

And suddenly she remembered the busker's song.

In the face of regret, get down on your knees;
death may be swayed by your final pleas.

Just thinking about it made her skin itch.

"Any idea on what your regret is?" Saxony asked her.

"Being perpetually annoying," Karam replied in Tavia's place.

Tavia felt inclined to poke out her tongue, but she was too busy fearing for her life. She was also not happy about the prospect of dying while being judged by the Kingpin.

"Are you ready to face what must be faced, your every regret and wicked disgrace?" the phantom asked.

Wesley folded his collar and gave a curt nod.

The phantom raised a fragmented hand in the air and Tavia's breath fogged. A beam of light pulled itself from its fingers, stretching and shaping into a doorway.

It turned black as soon as it took form, veins rippling down and spreading until it became an endless vortex of darkness.

"Whatever you see in there, don't let it get the better of you," Wesley said. "Don't try to change a thing."

He turned to Tavia and she held a hand up to stop him.

"I don't need a lecture," she said, but his gaze held such

fierceness that she suddenly felt at a loss for words.

Her stupid heart banged madly in her chest.

"What happens if we fail?" she asked.

Karam sheathed her knife. "We die, probably."

Tavia took that in with a nod. "Good to know."

The doorway was like a slit in the fabric of the realms. Tavia turned her focus to Wesley, needing to see the look of fearlessness on his face before she could school one onto her own. But Wesley didn't look fearless. He looked like he was about to throw up.

"What's with your face?" Tavia asked.

He raised an eyebrow. "This is how my face looks. I've never had any complaints before."

But the easy smirk on his lips did nothing to fool her. Tavia could see the uncertainty. She knew his many faces well enough to tell them apart.

"What is it?" she asked.

She didn't think he would answer: Wesley never liked answering questions if he didn't have a knife to his throat, or an agenda up his sleeve.

"I know what my regret will be," he said.

Tavia opened her mouth to ask what it was, but Wesley was already stepping into the darkness. Tavia reached out a hand for him, but he was gone in a blink and all she could do was watch.

Karam, Saxony, and Arjun stood close enough that their shoulders brushed. Warriors prepared to take on whatever the Kingpin threw at them, in order to avenge their people.

Tavia didn't know what regret Wesley thought he was going

to come across and she certainly didn't know what her own would be, but she decided that it didn't matter. Whatever was waiting on the other side wasn't important, because Wesley would be waiting too.

They would face it together, all of them, enemies and allies. And they would make damn sure to win.

31

Wesley

WESLEY REMEMBERED THE DAY he truly became a bastard.

He was sixteen and had just met with the Kingpin. He did it often, so the meeting itself was not the special thing. After all, Ashwood enjoyed talking with Wesley, guiding him through the perils of Creije like he was a worthy apprentice.

The special thing was that this time the Kingpin had given Wesley a direct order.

It was not words whispered through the old underboss, or the usual sage advice Ashwood often gave him, and only him, because Wesley had somehow become his favorite among a swell of orphans.

It was a true order, from Ashwood's shadow lips to Wesley's ears. It felt a bit like a promotion, if promotions involved killing people. Which they often did in Creije.

Wesley crawled into bed that night, trying very hard to think about what it meant for his career and not what it meant for the man he was supposed to kill.

Hello.

It came as a whisper, like the wind was talking to him. Wesley knew enough to figure that was possible, but he'd had a long enough day that he was willing to shake it off.

He settled back into bed, but when it came again, the voice was a sudden girlish yelp.

Please don't sleep with me in here!

Wesley reached for the gun under his pillow. His eyes searched the room, but there was nobody.

He reached for the light.

Nothing.

Wesley checked under the bed, feeling like a child.

I really am sorry, the voice said.

It was a girl, he knew that much. Young and with an accent that was mostly definitely not Creijen.

"Where are you?" Wesley asked.

In your head.

Wesley nearly dropped the candle. "That's a brave place to be."

There was a pause, and then—*It is pretty dark in here.*

Wesley laughed.

It was absurd. A girl inside his mind? He walked over to the mirror and looked very hard at his reflection, but there was just him, standing with a candle, sneering at himself like an utter moron.

He shook his head and made to check under the bed again.

I don't think you can see me, the girl said.

Wesley jumped at the sudden closeness of her voice.

He looked at himself in the mirror and said, "Get out."

I don't know how I got in. I'm lost.

Wesley was losing patience. Whatever trick this was, he didn't find it funny anymore.

"Are you using some kind of charm?" he asked. "Did Tavia put you up to this? Because if she's still bitter that I wouldn't put her boring little proverbs inside that fortune orb, then—"

I don't know who Tavia is, the girl said. *I was just practicing my specialty and the next thing I knew I was here.*

Wesley turned from the mirror in case the girl saw his surprise. A specialty. He'd studied enough history books to know what that meant. Had he really just found what the Kingpin was looking for, in his head?

And so it began. A real live Crafter. A girl who refused to tell him her name.

A girl who, every now and again, lived inside Wesley's mind.

He wanted so badly to tell Tavia, but she would just think he was losing it or get that odd look on her face she tended to have whenever Wesley did something she didn't like. Which seemed to be most of the time. And so instead, Wesley's memories and thoughts became stories to this strange girl. She remembered them and thought them too. Everything that made Wesley feel like he was nobody and everything he believed he needed in order to become somebody.

You need to find someone like me, the girl said one day, months later.

Wesley nodded. "If I hand the Kingpin a Crafter, I'll become underboss in a second." He sighed, almost wistfully. "But I buy and sell magic, not people."

The girl went quiet, considering her next words carefully. Wesley could sense her hesitance. He was getting good at knowing her emotions as if they were his own.

If I go to him, such big things will happen.

"Are you predicting the future?"

Predictions are unreliable. There are far too many futures to know which will happen. I see them all and that's not much use. Time is as indecisive as those who live in it.

Wesley chuckled. "Lighten up, kid."

He felt the girl frown. *You should stop calling me a kid. I'm destined to do great things.*

"You're also eleven," he said. "Enjoy the compliment. The last thing anyone wants is to be a grown-up."

I don't think either of us will get that chance, she said. *There are so many awful futures of you and me and even Tavia.*

At that, Wesley stilled.

"Tavia will be golden," he said, because the thought of anything else was not something he would consider. "She'll travel the realms and be whatever she wants to be. There's nothing awful in her future."

In some of them there is, the girl said. *In some she betrays you. In some you kill her to save the lives of so many Crafters.*

Wesley sat up, rigid, anger crawling on his skin and biting down like an insect. "I'd sooner kill you and every Crafter alive than turn my back on Tavia," he said.

And he meant it too. Maybe Wesley wasn't a saint, but he wasn't a disloyal prick. There were many lines he would never cross and all of them were to do with Tavia.

"You don't know what it's like to create a family from

nothing," Wesley said. "Not out of blood, but sweat and graft. To *earn* those closest to you."

Is that not what we are? the girl asked. *Are we not family too?*

"You're a Crafter."

Wesley said it as though it were the worst kind of accusation. Worse than her accusing him of betraying his best friend.

"You and I are not family," Wesley said. "You should be grateful I haven't handed you over to the Kingpin."

They were awful, untrue words, and the moment Wesley spoke them they tasted like poison—like a reverie charm gone bad—and though he wanted to take them back, he couldn't.

He was too angry to be kind.

You wouldn't betray me, the girl said. *I know you.*

And that, right there, was the problem.

Wesley letting people know him was his greatest weakness and one he wanted desperately to keep to himself.

"No," Wesley said. "You don't know what I'd do to win."

It was just three days later when Wesley saw the girl at the consort's headquarters, standing beside the Kingpin.

She was bound and bleeding.

Wesley knew her without hearing her speak.

He recognized her face, even if he had only ever seen it in his mind.

"She came to find you," the Kingpin said. "Crossed the realm and went straight to the underboss to see where you might be."

She thought Wesley would save her, proving that he was better than the Kingpin, that he was good and she was his friend as much as Tavia. Or that he'd spare his underboss when the bone gun was in his hands. Or that if Wesley came to power, he'd do something good.

Perhaps she thought a lot of things, as children often did, but Wesley only proved her wrong. He hadn't saved her, or spared his old underboss.

He hadn't done anything close to good.

"This is the start of a new era," the Kingpin had said. "Once I absorb her powers, I can begin to create a better realm, with you by my side."

"I'd be honored," Wesley said, slipping the seal of the old underboss from the dead man's hand and onto his own.

He felt numb.

He felt dread.

"You don't mean it," the girl said. "It's not a choice between me and her."

Wesley saw the moment the Kingpin shifted, interest piqued, wondering just who else Wesley might be loyal to aside from him.

When Ashwood spoke, Wesley felt the words grate across his bones.

"Her, who?"

Tavia.

Always, Tavia.

His closest friend. His partner. His family.

Wesley didn't want the Kingpin knowing her name.

Maybe one day, when he was a powerful underboss and could protect her and make her the greatest busker in Creije. But not yet. Not like this, in a way that told Ashwood she could be an obstacle, rather than an asset. Not in a way that told the most dangerous person in the realms exactly what Wesley's weakness was.

"It's a choice between you and my Kingpin," Wesley said to the girl. "And I will always choose him."

Maybe he was too stubborn to admit he cared.

Maybe he hated the possibility of the girl's predictions being true, and so hated her for seeing a future where Tavia wasn't by his side.

Maybe Wesley really was just a bastard.

Whatever the reason, he signed that girl's death warrant, and the Kingpin's laughter turned the air to bristles and the blackness around him danced.

"Oh, my boy," he said. "I will make us the world."

Everything that happened since was Wesley's fault. Everything the Kingpin had done was Wesley's fault. He had rekindled the Kingpin's madness. He was responsible for anyone who died because of it.

Some blood never washed away, and after all Wesley had done, he deserved to be haunted. So when he stepped into the conjured doorway aboard the train, Wesley knew with absolute certainty what regret would greet him.

The word doubled over in his mind, loud and accusing.

Coward.

32

Tavia

TAVIA WENT THROUGH A rip in the realms and came out walking on water.

It looked as though she was still in Ejm Voten—the sea was the color of old bathwater—but there was nothing else. No rock formations or waterspouts. No train with their so-called army, and definitely no phantoms circling them like prey.

There was just a body of water that stretched for miles and Wesley, standing in its center.

Tavia's footprints cast ripples in the water. She held out her arms to steady herself, as though it might stop her from tumbling through and drowning.

"Where are the others?" she called out.

She took a while to get to Wesley and he looked far too entertained by the way she wobbled uncertainly along the water.

"Maybe it split us into groups," he said.

Tavia wrinkled her nose. "How come I got stuck with you?"

she asked, and then, before Wesley had a chance to retort, she said, "I don't see any regrets lying around."

Tavia looked up to the cloudless sky. It was like a blank canvas, with no stars or moon to speak of. Just the eerie half dark of dusk.

"Come with me, or starve," a low voice said.

Tavia's face went dark.

Those words were all too familiar. Ones she couldn't forget even if she wanted to, that haunted her for years, spilling into nightmares, deciding her fate. Her breath shuddered inward and she turned, praying to whatever of the Many Gods were listening that she was hearing things.

The old underboss of Creije was like a giant, his hand held out as he offered Tavia a lifeline and a death sentence. He floated on the water with the Kingpin's seal, something Wesley now wore, around his thumb. He had an easy, warm smile that promised lies of a life better lived.

Suddenly Tavia was a child again.

The underboss towered over her and the endless water rippled into the streets of Creije. Tavia shivered, goose bumps trailing up her arms as the cold bit like a bug and the city of her childhood emerged.

Her stomach growled, the hungry monster she remembered. But what she hadn't remembered was the pain of it and how it felt like it was eating her from the inside out.

"I can save you," the underboss said. "Join my buskers and you'll be fed and clothed and warm. You'll have a family again."

It was a lie, of course, but pretty enough for a child to believe. Tavia was so young, her muma's death still fresh in her tears, and the hunger was so strong that it turned to nausea at night. Being alone in Creije was different from being alone anywhere else; dreams turned to nightmares and the beauty of the stars was nothing compared to the depths of the shadows. Tavia found the days ended too quickly and when the night stretched into eternity, she heard whispers of her muma's voice.

Don't cry, ciolo.

Tavia didn't want to be alone and the underboss had such sweet promises for children's ears. She was too scared not to believe.

But she wouldn't make that mistake again.

Tavia took a step back.

"I can give you everything you ever wanted," the underboss said.

Tavia turned from him, only to find Wesley towering over her.

"Take his hand, Tavia."

She hadn't realized he was still there. He looked so tall compared to her now. Like a real grown-up.

"I don't have to go with him again," Tavia said.

"Yes, you do."

Tavia shook her head furiously.

She just wanted to run, quick as anything. Quick as her tiny, frail legs could carry her.

Quick, quick, before the old underboss pulled her in again and made her into the type of person who ruined lives.

Tavia's stomach growled with the hunger.

"You can't judge me for wanting to change it."

Wesley's smile was a soft, delicate thing, the likes of which she rarely saw. "I'm not judging you, Tavia."

His hand twitched by his side, as though he might reach out and wipe away the tear that lagged on her jaw. He didn't and Tavia was glad of it. If Wesley touched her, she might just crumble.

"This is the game," Wesley said. "You heard what Arjun and Saxony told us. It preys on your need to fix your mistakes."

Wesley looked to the old underboss, the man he'd killed and replaced, and his eyes narrowed, as though he wanted to be wrong. As though Wesley wanted Tavia to run.

"If you don't take his hand, you could be stuck living in some kind of dream-world forever."

Tavia licked her chapped lips. She tasted the blood and it only made her hunger grow.

She didn't think living in a dream was such a bad thing. Tavia wanted to erase all the awful deeds she had done, every vial of magic she had sold, never thinking of the consequences or pain it could cause. And maybe, just maybe, in a world of dreams, her muma could be alive. Tavia could see her face again.

"I know you want to go back, but life doesn't work that way," Wesley said. "I get having blood on your hands and wanting so badly to wash it off."

Tavia's heart pounded. She'd never heard Wesley talk about responsibility, much less regret.

"Nobody is going to call me a good person," Wesley said. "But I don't run from my mistakes. If you regret something, then make it right. You don't just get to erase it, Tavia."

"Yes, I do," she said. "I can run to Volo and find my muma's family and I—"

Wesley gripped her shoulders. "Many Gods, Tavia, aren't

I your family too? Isn't Creije your home? You have people there who care about you."

There was something like hurt in his eyes.

"Sometimes you get to choose," he said. "Me, Saxony, Karam. The only reason we're in this fight together is because of you. You're the glue, Tavia. Without you, we all fall apart."

The glue.

A family.

A home.

Things she'd spent so long searching for that she never realized they might already be there.

"Don't lose sight of that." Wesley paused and then, so much quieter, he said, "Don't make me lose you."

Something pulled inside Tavia's stomach, stronger than the hunger.

For so long she convinced herself that running from Creije could erase the person she'd become. Tavia thought she could just start anew, with the life she was supposed to have and be the person she was supposed to be.

Because *this* was who Tavia was.

A crook who sold magic she knew could hurt people.

A girl who wanted to save the world.

Maybe Tavia could run from a city, but she couldn't run from herself anymore.

"If you do this, you erase me, too," Wesley said.

Tavia thought back to all those times they traded charms and tricks, how growing up on the streets had shaped them so similarly. Tavia thought about the way Wesley used to smile when he nailed a charm and how she smiled just watching him. He made sure she never felt scared or alone.

She thought about a place where none of that was real. A realm, an entire life, where they hadn't grown up together. Where she didn't know him at all.

Tavia looked back to the old underboss.

His hand still lingered, reaching out to her.

She stepped forward.

Once.

Twice.

Until she was close enough to smell the magic on him.

Then she reached out and took the underboss's hand, sealing her fate like she'd done all those years ago. His grip tightened around hers and then, just like that, he dissolved into the air.

Tavia's hand hovered in place. She felt herself come back to the present and the hunger faded, old scars appearing across her usual body. Wesley took her hand from the air and laced it through his, their pulses pressing together. He leaned his forehead to hers and when he breathed out, she breathed him in.

Tavia put a hand to Wesley's chest. The rhythm of him was the only thing keeping her from falling to her knees. The familiar warmth and cold of him. His heartbeat under her hands.

Wesley swallowed, licked his lips, didn't move.

They stood like that for minutes, until the memory of Creije followed the old underboss and faded to nothingness.

"My boy."

They whirled at the sound of that voice, Tavia's heart almost stopping.

Dante Ashwood stood in front of them and, *damn*, these

regrets were coming thick and fast. Wesley's grip on her hand tightened. He was shaking, staring straight ahead.

Tavia took in the scene.

Ashwood was a shadow of a man, sitting on a throne of magic and gold, with barely an outline of him visible. His voice was like a crow song, floating across the water, casting furrows into the sea.

To his side was a girl, her wrists and ankles in chains. Blood coated her smiling lips. Her hair was long and black, a mixture of braids and twists catching along the gold bangles she wore on her wrists. Her dress was white and it soaked into the sea like it, too, was made from water.

Wesley looked at the girl and did not blink.

Tavia didn't know what to make of that. She thought she knew everyone Wesley did and the ones she didn't know were the ones even Wesley found too murderous and immoral to let out of the shadows, but this girl didn't look like one of those. She was young and her face was soft, and though she was clearly a prisoner, she didn't look scared.

She looked at Wesley like he would keep her safe.

"It's not a choice between me and her," the girl said.

Wesley's hand shook in Tavia's. "Don't watch this," he told her.

And then he dropped her hand.

A new cold settled into Tavia's fingers as Wesley stepped into his regret.

He approached a man on his knees who Tavia hadn't noticed until right then, and pulled the sack from his head.

Tavia's mouth hung open.

The underboss. The one whose hand she had just taken, only he was a little older and a lot more bloody. From his waistband, Wesley pulled out his gun and pressed it to the man's temple.

"Wesley," the underboss said.

"Don't watch," Wesley said again.

Tavia had no desire to see the underboss die and she certainly had no desire to see Wesley kill him, but she couldn't turn away. As though he could sense this, Wesley looked over his shoulder and his expression tightened.

"Tavia," he said. His voice was raspy. "Please."

She shut her eyes.

The gun fired.

The underboss's body sank into the sea and Wesley dropped to his knees.

The girl cried.

The Kingpin clapped.

"Oh, my boy," Ashwood said. "I will make us the world. My gift to you, in exchange for your gift to me."

He gestured to the girl, who collapsed onto the sea's surface alongside Wesley. Her face was no longer soft and kind. She looked broken.

"What is he talking about?" Tavia asked. "Why is she your gift to him?"

Wesley brushed the water from his knees.

He did not look at her.

"She's a Crafter," he said. "She was inside my mind when I was younger, talking to me like a phantom. I'm not sure how or why. I almost thought I was going crazy until I finally saw her here. Ironic that I lost my mind straight after."

Wesley laughed to himself, but it was sad and angry.

"She's gone and I can still hear her," he said. "A ghost in my mind, punishing me for this day. Making sure I never forget how awful I am."

"Wesley."

Tavia wasn't sure what else to say apart from his name. Every word and feeling stopped inside her. This girl had been in his mind and Tavia had never known. She'd *haunted* him.

How had Tavia never known?

"If I do nothing and let the Kingpin take her, then he'll give me my future," Wesley said. "I'll be an underboss."

"I liked the other future better," the girl said.

Wesley gripped his gun.

Tavia had always seen him as an unstoppable force, fearless and reckless enough to succeed in whatever he wanted. Knowing he had been weak, even once, and scared, even just for a moment, made her ache.

"It's already done," Tavia said. "You can't change the past, remember?"

Wesley shoved a hand through his hair. "You don't hear her voice every day, whispering at me to be an awful person because that's what I'm best at."

Wesley's eyes burned into Tavia.

"She trusted me and I left her to rot," he said. "She was the first Crafter the Kingpin saw after the War of Ages and she walked right into his hands because she was looking for *me*. This is what inspired all of his madness. Everyone he's taken since, even Saxony's sister, is because of me, Tavia. Arjun's Kin might still be alive if—"

"Stop."

She wouldn't let Wesley do this to himself. Whatever he had done didn't make him responsible for every bad thing in the realms.

"We're not here to change the past," Tavia said. "We're here to change the future." She looked to Ashwood. "We were both as bad as the Kingpin, but you're the one who told me we can make amends for that."

Wesley shook his head. "You were never as bad as him."

"Parts of me were."

Wesley looked more tired than Tavia had ever seen. "I think those were the parts I made."

"Don't take credit for my choices, Wesley."

Tavia held out her hand. She would help him through this just as he had helped her.

Together, they could make it right.

Wesley glanced back at the girl and Tavia saw something in him waver. He inched toward her, just a little, and sighed.

When he took Tavia's hand, she could sense the regret.

She gripped Wesley's fingers tightly in hers, feeling his calluses against her scars. Ahead, the doorway opened. The great black chasm ripping back into the realm, providing a way for Wesley to complete his regret with finality.

All they had to do was walk through and they would pass the Kingpin's sadistic test, leaving this girl, whoever she was, to the life she had already lived.

Tavia led Wesley to the door, and with each step they took, his hand squeezed hers. Like he was holding himself from going back.

But he wouldn't need to do so for long.

When this was all over, they would come for the girl Wesley left and for Saxony's sister and for everyone else they'd let suffer in their past.

They would find a way to come back and save them all.

33

Saxony

IN ALL THE DARKNESS, there was Karam.

She lit the void of the world in a way Saxony could not.

Everything else was muted and gray, as though they were floating through the very essence of the world, misplaced and untethered.

When Saxony took a step forward, it felt a little like flying and a little like falling.

"Do you think we're in the fire-gates?" she asked.

"The fire-gates are not real," Karam said. "And if they were, Wesley would be in here with us."

Saxony couldn't argue with that.

She took Karam's hand. It felt so good to be able to do that again. For the first time in so long there were no walls between them.

Maybe this was a nightmare world, but Saxony wanted to cling to it—cling to Karam—before they were spat back into the realms, where vulnerabilities got people killed.

"I can't see anything sin-like," Saxony said.

She tried to blink away the darkness, but that was all there was. Until, in the distance, with a sudden ferocity, as though the gray world heard her complaint and was dissatisfied, the particles that made up the dark started to swirl. Small pieces broke off and circled their entwined hands, blowing whispers onto the back of Saxony's neck.

She could feel the magic of this place fighting to take shape.

Saxony wasn't sure why every world she got sucked into had to be so eerie. The consort's mind, Amja's spell, and now this. She wondered if Tavia and the others were having such a hard time.

She wondered how their worlds—their nightmares—took shape.

It started as a smudge on the air, like a piece of the world was damaged, moved irreparably into the wrong place, but then it severed completely and floated toward them. The closer it got, the more it twisted into something else. An outline that stretched to Karam's height, and then sprouted arms and broke apart into legs and focused into a face.

It stopped floating and started walking, coming to a halt a few meters beyond them.

Saxony blinked and the conjured man blinked in return.

His eyes were the color of tree bark and when his skin turned from gray to deep brown, Saxony had the sense that she'd seen him somewhere before.

When he finally spoke, she realized why.

"Karam," the man said.

And Saxony knew that the place she had seen him was in

Karam's eyes. In her face. Her straight mouth and her strong jaw.

This was Karam's father.

Karam closed the gap between them.

Hardev Talwar was small and thin, with muted clothing adorned with beads and gray gems. He wore the holy Wrenyi symbol around his neck that Karam now had mirrored around her own, and when he looked at his daughter, he thumbed it pensively.

There was no fighter in him. He wasn't a warrior and when Saxony met his gaze, she could only think about how at peace he seemed, believing that whatever was not good could be made so with time.

Around him Granka took shape.

It spilled into the world like paint, coloring the space above them to sky and brightening the ground to sand and cobblestone. The air was warm, and if Saxony listened, not even very hard, she could hear the temple bells chiming in rhythm with the warm breeze.

Saxony savored it. The peace before the inevitable pain.

"You cannot take this path," Hardev said.

Karam sniffed.

From where Saxony stood, it sounded a lot like she was trying not to cry, which struck Saxony as the strangest thing, because if there was one thing Karam did well, aside from killing, then it was being very good at not crying. Only when Saxony looked closer, she realized that it was not so strange after all, because the person in front her wasn't the Karam she knew. It was not her beautiful warrior, but a small girl she barely recognized.

A fourteen-year-old Karam, even shorter, if that was possible, stared into her father's eyes with an equal mix of fear, which Saxony had never seen, and stubbornness, which she had seen more times than she could count.

"Pehta," Karam pleaded. "I want to be a warrior like Pehti Jal and Meta Jil. They fought to save the Crafters. I want to fight and protect Arjun."

"That was a time of war, *dila*. We are beyond that now."

Karam turned back to Saxony and she could see the conflict in her eyes. The childlike desire to please her father coupled with the adult knowledge that he was gone and this would be the last time she saw him again.

Karam would have to use this second chance to break his heart all over, because the alternative would be to abandon this war and live forever in a dream. And if Karam stayed, Saxony wasn't sure she'd have the courage to leave without her.

"It's okay," Saxony said. "I'm here now. We're in this together, right? Always."

Karam squared her jaw, newly resolute, and took in a breath before she returned to her father's gaze.

"We will always be at war," Karam said. "No matter what you and Mete say, the fighting is not over and the Crafters will always need the Rekhi d'Rihsni to protect them."

Hardev bowed his head in disappointment. "If you choose to go against peace, then you should leave and never look back. Flee Wrenyal. Go to the likes of Uskhanya or some other awful realm."

"Pehta," Karam pleaded.

But she knew what was coming. Even Saxony knew.

This was the moment Karam left her old life and ran to Creije to meet Wesley and climb the ranks of the underrealm. To meet Saxony and light a spark inside of her like she'd never known before.

How awful that the worst moment of Karam's life was somehow the best of Saxony's.

She felt like a terrible person for even thinking it, especially knowing what had become of Karam's father, but Saxony couldn't imagine going through this war, this life, without Karam by her side.

"*Hei prytehn,*" Karam said.

Saxony knew enough of Wrenyi, of Karam, to know what that meant.

I love you.

Hardev shook his head, thumbs still pinched against his necklace. "Do not do this," he said. "No daughter of mine will live as a war bringer."

Karam's hands shook to fists and Saxony could see everything unspoken forming on her lips. The regrets and apologies threatened to spill out and for a moment, when Karam's mouth parted, Saxony thought for sure that she was going to fold into her father's arms, relenting, sobbing as she promised to stay by his side and protect Arjun's Kin the way she couldn't in the real world.

Instead, Karam looked to the ground and said, "I suppose I am no longer a daughter of yours."

And then she ran, fast and straight into Saxony's arms, knocking her back a few steps.

Saxony squeezed Karam tight against her, letting her warrior finally do the very thing she had spent years trying not to.

Karam cried until the world shifted, creating itself anew, returning her as she was. But Saxony didn't let go. Even as the skies darkened and the air grew cold and she felt the sand turn to soil beneath her feet.

Saxony didn't open her eyes.

She didn't want to see the regret that waited for her.

She didn't want to stop touching Karam.

"Who is that?"

Karam's voice was muffled on her shoulder.

Reluctantly, Saxony pulled away and took in the world with an aching breath.

They were surrounded by a forest that wound into clouds, with arms of vines and purple holly hugging together at the sky to create a makeshift roof.

This was home.

Saxony was finally home.

Not that awful place in her grandma's vision, but her true home. The place she had grown up learning to craft and where her Kin found shelter from the world.

In Rishiya, the buildings were as grand and tall as these trees, stretching in beautiful curves that were amassed with greenery. After the war, the city was nearly destroyed and nature sought to take it back. Now it was a striking coil of once-grand manmade architecture and the forestation that encompassed it, too beautiful for even Schulze to try to change. The rivers that ran through the city were narrow and filled with sleek trains, hordes of people on the street banks who were waiting to be spirited away.

It held a certain kind of charm. But it was not the forest.

The forest held magic.

In this place, in Saxony's home village, the waterways were wide and surrounded by high arches of trees. The streams acted as pathways and the rocks that enclosed them glistened with magic that sprinkled into the water, propelling the lantern-lit boats forward. It was an oasis, and the quiet absence of the world soothed the forest into hums, its branches swaying in song and the wind calling to the Kin, delivering messages from one Crafter to another.

The spirit of this forest protected them, protected the land, protected the wondrous magic within.

They'd built a home here. An entire village in and among the trees, from the mossy trunks to the tallest branches. Saxony spent her childhood running along the collective arms, from one part of the forest to another, each of her steps rich in moonlight.

She'd forgotten how many good memories were hidden behind all the awful ones.

"Saxony," Karam said. "Look."

She held out a finger to the distance and Saxony followed her stare with a racing heart.

She knew who she was about to see.

She'd spent fourteen years praying for this day.

Vea Akintola was beautiful.

Her arms were a maze of staves, and her closely cropped hair drew attention to the severe edge of her jaw and the sprinkle of freckles across her forehead that were the same copper as her eyes. She looked ethereal and strong, with a purple dress that moved like the wind against her dark skin.

Seeing Vea was like looking into a mirror. There was so much of Saxony in her mother's smile and her small freckles, which Karam had always loved. Even the way Vea walked, strong and ready to face whatever the world threw at her.

She carried little Malik in her arms and Saxony couldn't hold back the tears.

Her brother. Alive and smiling as Saxony's mother hugged him tight, like she couldn't bear to put him down. He looked so tiny that Saxony was struck once more with the grief of losing them both.

This was the worst day of her life.

They'd just finished celebrating Malik's fifth birthday and though Saxony was only a year older, Amja let her make him a charm for his stave bracelet. It was a custom until Crafters came into their powers, though Malik could already conjure small hallucinations.

He was already so good at getting inside people's heads.

"This is your family," Karam said.

She laced her fingers through Saxony's and they watched from a distance as Malik conjured a ball of light in his tiny hands over and over, while Amja approached and whispered something in Vea's ear.

"She looks like a warrior," Karam said, regarding Saxony's mother. It was the nicest thing she could have said. "And Malik looks like trouble."

She laughed and Saxony did too.

Her brother was too big for his tiny boots, even at just five, and with large brown eyes that could charm anyone into doing anything. Saxony had no doubt he would've grown up to be the most annoying younger brother ever and that she would have loved him for it.

She would have loved him regardless of what he became.

She imagined Malik teasing her mercilessly whenever he mastered a spell before her and how she would have scolded him, while trying to hide a proud smile. Zekia would've played peacekeeper between them, with their mother looking on.

So many memories they missed making.

So much time, stolen from them.

"Malik was born with the *ensi* stave on his heart," Saxony explained. "He was the first Crafter in our Kin to have powers from birth. It's why he was destined to become Liege. Amja said he'd command with wisdom, but I always thought he'd run riot once he took charge."

But they never got to see which would be true.

It took everything Saxony had in her, every ounce of strength and magic, not to surge forward and scream for her mother and Malik to go, run from the danger and escape this day before it was too late.

But she couldn't. Saxony knew she couldn't.

If she did, she'd be stuck in this place forever, repeating the day over and over, and Zekia would die knowing that her sister had abandoned her for a dream.

Saxony would not let Zekia down again.

"I thought your sister was your Liege," Karam said.

Saxony swallowed. She had to keep talking. If she didn't, her grief was going to drown her.

"Malik was chosen first," Saxony said. "The day he was born, everyone in our Kin wept. He was so strong. It wasn't until years after he died that Zekia was chosen to take his place."

"You never told me that."

Nobody outside their Kin spoke of it. It was the worst thing to ever happen. Worse, Saxony sometimes thought, than the war. Because at least her Kin had survived that, whereas Malik's death had nearly destroyed them all.

"In Rishiya, the first baby born after the death of a Liege is meant to take their place. While they age, the old Liege's adviser temporarily takes charge, intuiting their wisdom and training them to be a worthy leader. Malik's death changed that. After the fire took him, there were no newborns in our Kin," Saxony said. "Not a one of our Crafters could conceive. It took seven dark years until we realized that it was a sign. Our new Liege was already here and the Many Gods wouldn't let another child come until she was chosen and had fulfilled her destiny."

Saxony pushed away a tear.

Malik let out a laugh as a ball of conjured light bounced from his hand and onto the ground.

Keep talking, she told herself. *Don't move. Don't go to them.*

"Zekia was born a few months before Malik died," Saxony said. "The last child of the Rishiyat Kin. Nobody believes there will be another until her death. It's how I know she's still alive, somewhere."

"That is a lot for Zekia to bear," Karam said.

Saxony nodded. "Lieges have their entire lives to come to terms with their destiny. They're trained and taught from birth, but Zekia had someone else's fate thrust upon her when she was seven. The Kin think Malik's essence was transferred into her when he died because they share the same blood and the same gift."

"Malik is an Intuitcrafter?"

Saxony paused on the word.

Is.

It was such a small thing, but for fourteen years she'd only ever known *was*. But here, right now, in this place, her brother was alive. Her mother was alive. Her family was whole. They weren't memories or ghosts, but real and smiling and so, so alive.

In the distance, Saxony's mother gave Amja a solemn nod and they headed into the spell shed together.

Malik was still clutched in her arms.

And suddenly Saxony was running.

It was like she didn't have control of her body. It propelled her forward so quickly that she barely felt the ground beneath her feet.

Karam called out her name, but Saxony ignored it.

She ran until her fingers slammed into the glass of the shed window and it splintered into her skin. She pressed herself against it, watching desperately as her grandma lit candles in a circle around her mother and Malik.

Some kind of protection charm, she'd always thought. But seeing it now, through grown-up eyes, Saxony wasn't sure what it looked like. She wasn't sure what Amja was doing and she'd never thought to ask.

"Saxony." Karam was breathless as she caught up with her. "You cannot go in there. Whatever happened needs to—"

"I know," Saxony said.

Her cheeks stung with tears.

Was she really going to have to watch this?

It didn't feel possible for Saxony to be in this much pain and still be alive, breathing and standing while she broke into pieces.

She wanted to look away, at least, but she could barely blink.

Saxony waited for the blinding flash of light that would propel her backward through the forest. For the smell of burning and screams of cinder. She waited for this spell, whatever it was, to go wrong and swallow her family.

"You are not your past self," Karam said. "I thought we had to relive our regrets as we were."

Saxony turned from the window and when she looked at Karam, she realized it was true.

Saxony was not a child, watching with curious eyes, desperate to know what spell her mother and grandmother were doing, and jealous that Malik was at its center rather than her. Malik was always at the center of things.

Instead, Saxony was tall and grief-stricken and she felt the weight of her Kin as heavy as ever. She hadn't been made into a child again, like Karam.

Saxony looked back to the window, ready to steal one last glance at her family, but she barely had time to take in their faces—to try to make sense of why they were all suddenly crying, as if they somehow knew what was coming—before the world ruptured.

The entire forest was blinding white.

The force of the explosion threw Saxony and Karam back until they crashed onto the soil and splintered the roots of a tree. The pain was new and fresh and much worse than Saxony remembered. But the blaze was smaller.

It didn't engulf the forest like her memories told her. It was just that shed, brandished in black flame that looked like shadows clawing and scratching, smashing the windows and crumbling walls to ash.

It didn't move from the building or touch the surrounding trees.

It didn't tarnish the grass or the soil.

It didn't crackle and spit.

But Many Gods did it burn.

Saxony felt the heat of it in the air, like the very fire that tore through her veins.

The Kin screamed.

Saxony screamed.

The forest wailed in grief.

Karam clutched on to her tightly, anchoring Saxony to the ground.

And then she recoiled, shouting in pain.

"Spirits."

Karam crawled back a couple of steps, nursing her new burns.

Saxony's skin was on fire, but she couldn't even look at Karam or blink as her eyes pierced the black flames, watching them engulf her family.

Saxony shook with magic and anger and resentment and thirst.

It erupted within her.

This was it. The first time the Kingpin destroyed her family.

It was Ashwood's fault they were here, shielding their magic and themselves from the world. If it weren't for him and the war he helped create, Saxony's mother and brother would be alive. Her grandma wouldn't have needed to help them cast some kind of protection spell. They could have been living in Rishiya, free and revered.

Malik could have been Liege. Saxony's mother could have watched her grow up and when she met Karam—which Saxony knew, in any life, she would—her mother would have led the ritual to welcome her as an official ally of the Kin.

Instead, Amja lay singed on the ground, watching in silent horror as the Crafters gathered and threw magic on the flames.

The world was ending all over.

Saxony's skin hissed and she knew then, with such sudden clarity, that her regret wasn't what she had done.

It was what she *hadn't* done.

Avenge her family.

It had all started here, in the fire, and when Saxony found Ashwood, she'd make sure to end it there.

She'd set the world aflame, one enemy at a time.

34

Wesley

WESLEY WAS SPAT BACK into the realms with Tavia in his arms.

Or rather, her head cracked against his arm and the rest of her sprawled on top of him in a way that made it hard to breathe.

He groaned and when she rolled off him, reality hit Wesley like a brick to the head. Some of the buskers called to him, murmuring loud enough to give him a migraine.

When Wesley opened his eyes to try to steady himself, he saw that the phantoms hovered around him and Tavia in a makeshift blockade that the few buskers in the carriage were too scared to break.

Only Falk approached.

Such a loyal army.

Wesley pressed the heel of his hand to his brow, trying to stamp out the pain, but blood trickled from his nose and down to his lips.

Jumping through reality took its toll.

Tavia rolled her neck to get the stiffness out and Wesley watched her movements, a little hypnotized. He felt undeniably groggy and the realms hadn't quite righted, but while most things blurred and pounded in his vision, Tavia was clear and sharp-edged. She stayed in focus while the rest of the realms spun.

He thought back to her hand against his chest, her fingers clutched around his, her breath mingling with his own.

"Are you okay, sir?" Falk asked.

"No," Tavia answered for him. "Someone pinch me so I know we're not still dreaming."

Wesley leaned forward with a wry smile. "I could kiss you instead."

Tavia froze.

Wesley was close enough to smell the seawater on her skin and see the flicker of light bounce from the knife at her hip. He was joking, kind of, but it felt like his chest might explode.

There were inches between them.

And then Tavia's blade was on his neck.

"You haven't nearly died enough times already?" she asked.

"I was only being thorough."

Wesley let an easy smile slide onto his face, though his palms were somewhat sweaty. There wasn't much else to do with the likes of their army and half the dead in the sea watching. This back-and-forth between them was getting more dangerous the longer they were together. It brought out a side to Wesley he thought he'd buried.

Tavia had seen the worst thing he had ever done—she'd seen how he became underboss—and didn't look at him like he was a monster.

But that is what you are. My beautiful monster.

Wesley cleared his throat and Tavia swiped her lips furiously with the back of her hand, as though he really had kissed her.

"You should kiss every person on this train, then," she said. "To be *thorough*."

"Even Karam?" Wesley painted a cartoon look of horror on his face.

Tavia lowered her knife. "Is she not pretty enough for you?"

When she smirked, Wesley almost sighed in relief. "It's not that," Wesley said, because he supposed Karam was pretty in the same rough and tarnished way that an uncut diamond might be.

Wesley just never much liked diamonds.

"Then what?"

Wesley wanted to tell Tavia that it was because he only really felt like kissing her at that specific moment in time and, if he was honest, most moments in time. But he quickly decided against honesty.

It had never suited him in the past.

"I don't think I'm her type," Wesley said.

"I don't think you're anybody's type."

"Say that to the tingling feeling in your stomach."

Tavia pocketed her knife. "It's called nausea."

"I prefer to think of it as lovesickness."

Falk held out a hand to pull Wesley up, leaving Tavia to stumble to her feet unaided.

She craned her neck to search the carriage. "Where are Saxony and the others?"

The tear in the realm remained open but dormant and there was no sign of Karam or Saxony. And no sign of Arjun, either.

Not that Wesley cared.

"Maybe our team won," he said.

Tavia shot him a look. "They were *on* our team."

Wesley shrugged. "Winning's winning."

As though the doorway was listening and displeased by the thought of Wesley winning anything, it began to shudder. He took a step back alongside Tavia, and just as they moved from the path of the tear, Karam was flung from the darkness and into the carriage.

Then Saxony.

And then Arjun, at which point Wesley sighed.

They landed in a pile on top of each other, groaning and trying to roll out of the trajectory of the doorway before anything else was spat out.

They looked about as shitty as Wesley felt.

Tavia stared down at the haphazard bundle with a grin. "You guys took your time."

Karam wiped the blood from her nose with her shirtsleeve and Arjun rubbed his eyes.

"Are you hurt?" Tavia asked.

Karam looked offended at the thought.

"Name and shame then," Tavia said. "I want to know everyone's regrets so I feel less like crap."

Karam cleared her throat. "My father," she said, in a tone that told them she wouldn't elaborate any more than that.

From the floor, Arjun pushed a busker off his leg. "My pride."

"Your regret was being a jackass?" Tavia asked.

"And he seemed so down-to-earth when he said he was better than me," Wesley said.

Arjun stood, his balance unsteady. "Be happy my sin wasn't death. You wouldn't be unscathed."

Wesley gave him a half smile. "I love it when you get all manly with me."

"And you?" Tavia asked Saxony. "What was your regret?"

Saxony took in a breath big enough to make it seem like she was preparing herself for a great battle. Wesley didn't know what to make of that, since he thought they'd just won one.

"My regret was my family," Saxony said. "I walked through the door and had to watch—"

She paused and closed her eyes, holding in something too terrible for words. Karam stood close to her.

"I had to relive the day my mother and brother died," Saxony said. "My regret was not being able to stop it from happening."

Wesley begged to differ.

Saxony was talking far too quickly and the way she shuffled her feet gave him pause.

Tavia pulled her into a tight hug, murmuring words Wesley couldn't quite make out, but though Saxony returned the gesture, her eyes shifted. To the ground, to the phantoms, and then to Wesley, before she quickly looked away.

He brought his hands to his cuff links to stop them from going to his gun.

Wesley did not like whatever unspoken thing sat in the air and he especially did not like that nobody else seemed to notice.

"So what's next?" Tavia asked, pulling away from Saxony. "We've completed all of our regrets."

Karam settled against the train wall. "Maybe they kill us?"

Tavia groaned. "As if there aren't already enough ghosts on this train."

"Phantoms," Saxony corrected, and even Karam rolled her eyes at that.

One of the creatures stepped from the blockade and Wesley reached for his gun on instinct, only to chide himself.

"The ultimate sacrifice will need to be made if you want to finish this crusade. Death waits for you together; embrace it or risk losing the battle forever."

It was more person-like than the other phantoms, with a small cap shielding its smudged forehead and the barely there face of a child. When the boy's mouth pulled open and a voice that couldn't have been his croaked out their orders, Wesley grimaced.

"The ultimate sacrifice," Tavia repeated. "So one of us has to die?"

"Not a problem," Wesley said.

He pulled out his gun and most of the buskers took a quick step back.

Arjun scowled. "Trust you to be so ready to kill."

"I'm happy to sit this one out," Tavia said.

Wesley cocked his gun. "Suits me." He checked the sight. "I already have a sacrifice in mind."

His eyes didn't bother to search their army.

Wesley knew which of them needed to die. He rolled his shoulder, then his neck, just to make sure his vision had settled.

If he missed, then that would be really embarrassing.

He pointed his gun at Saxony and she sneered.

"Yeah," she said. "Sure you will."

Wesley smirked. He didn't trust her as far as he could throw her, but Tavia did and that meant something.

He moved the gun to Arjun.

"Close your eyes," Wesley said.

Karam surged forward. "Wait—"

Wesley pulled the trigger.

Behind Arjun, Falk slumped to the floor.

The bullet took root in his brow.

A bull's-eye shot.

Arjun jumped out of the gun's trajectory and swore profusely in Wrenyi. He pressed a hand to his ear to check if the bullet had nicked him. It hadn't, though Wesley was tempted.

"What was that?" Tavia yelled.

"*Pelg hijada,*" Arjun spat.

Wesley didn't think that sounded like a compliment on his shooting skills, which was a pity because that was a shot to be applauded.

"You're completely insane!" Saxony said. "You just murdered an innocent man."

Wesley put the gun back into his belt. "No such creature. That bastard's been sending *delg* bats to the Kingpin since Creije."

Wesley may not have trusted Falk, but he knew better than to be blinded by his dislike for someone. He knew how to be impartial. Wesley dealt in facts and the fact was that Falk hadn't been keeping tabs for him; he'd been keeping tabs *on* him.

"You think he was spying for Ashwood?" Saxony asked.

"Yes."

"But you can't be sure."

"It's my business to be sure. If I wasn't, half the people on this train would be dead."

Even Karam looked doubtful. "If you have no proof—"

"It started in Creije," Wesley said, impatient. "First at the train station, where the consort's men just happened to know we would be commandeering the old train tracks. He sent a *delg* bat."

"I thought that was on your orders," Karam said.

"It wasn't. And then we're attacked in Granka? Not to mention I saw him with a bat before we set off on these waters."

Arjun blanched. "He sent a messenger after you met with my Kin?"

Wesley nodded. He knew the difference between coincidence and sloppy spying, and though Falk may have been decent company in small doses, he was not a decent man in any dose. He was not to be trusted. Sending those bats to Ashwood had not only meant doom for Arjun's Kin, but it risked everything Wesley was working to achieve. It had put Tavia and their entire army in danger.

"You think he was responsible for the attack in Granka," Saxony said. She stared down at Falk's body with a look of horror.

Arjun's jaw locked and when he took in Falk's lifeless corpse, it was with the kind of hatred Wesley thought only he was capable of.

"Why keep him around?" Tavia asked.

"I needed him to help complete the time charges," Wesley said. "The bastard was slow-walking the whole thing, but once

Arjun came on board, Falk had no choice but to finish. I killed him as soon as it was possible."

Tavia was still.

She had always been wary of Falk, even going so far as to nickname him Wesley's weasel, which Wesley took as much as an insult to him. Still, he seemed to be making a habit of killing people in front of her, even dream people, and Wesley hated that.

Tavia took in a deep breath and then uttered three words Wesley hadn't heard from her since they were children.

"I trust you," she said.

Karam nodded. "I will too."

Arjun practically snarled at Falk's lifeless body. "Good riddance."

But it was Saxony who surprised Wesley most. "You did what was necessary," she said. "It's all any of us can do."

Wesley cleared his throat.

Nobody had trusted him in a long time. Even as a child, his family quietened whenever he walked into a room and never let him out of their sight. Like he needed to be watched and judged. Like they knew he was destined for awful things.

Wesley wasn't sure that trusting him was a good thing to do, nobody else had ever thought so, but these people did and that stirred something in him.

"Are we done?" Wesley asked the phantoms. "We passed, right?"

The ghostly figures smiled and in perfect unison, they said, "Keep steady on your course, underboss. Your king is waiting."

35

Deniel

THE STARS LOOKED UPON Deniel and quivered.

One by one they blinked from the sky, hiding behind clouds and rain and dark.

Deniel set himself onto the pavement and watched the hungry take Creije. The magic, the *truth*, roaming the city and stealing what needed to be stolen.

Around him footsteps thundered.

The amityguards were like hunters, circling him, and when they saw Deniel was covered in blood and his eyes were black, a succession of contradictory shouts roared through the night.

Step back.

Don't move.

Hands up.

Throw us your weapons and your magic.

They did not see that the dark was starting to fade. That there was color and light, that there was *Deniel*, buried underneath it all, trying to claw his way back.

Deniel Emilsson. Son to Margaret and Emil. He had a husband, too, he thought. And possibly a son, or a daughter. He couldn't remember exactly, but he was sure they were there, in the shiny places of his mind that now cowered and hid, for fear they would be erased.

Deniel fingered his knife, used it to pick the dirt and blood from under his nails.

"We're warning you," an amityguard said. "Surrender or die."

Deniel was already dead and so he did not surrender.

Not because he didn't want to, but because he really couldn't. The voices were listening and watching, if voices could do such things, and if Deniel were to breathe without their command, he would feel the pain of it. Their screams would bleed from his ears and he would forget wrong from right again.

Better he be still.

"Listen," Deniel said. "Can you hear them? Are they still inside?"

Silence.

The amityguards kept their weapons primed, stances firm and angled, and the mirrored visors that obscured half their faces kept Deniel from seeing any sign of deliberation or mercy in their eyes.

There was nothing but quiet and a gun's length between him and the law of Creije.

Deniel laughed.

He ran a thumb across the corner of his lip, picking at a scab of blood.

That was all there was to do.

"Run," Deniel told them. Not a threat, but a plea. "Run from the mad king and his mad truths."

Deniel felt the butt of a gun jam into his stomach and he keeled forward.

A second hit pounded into his back, knocking him to his knees. He went down hard, palms smacking the cobblestone. Deniel gasped in air like it was Cloverye.

It hurt. Not more than the whispers, nothing else ever had, but it hurt worse than most things.

The cold metal of a gun pressed to Deniel's temple and he braced himself.

"Wait."

An amityguard placed her hand over the gun of her comrade. "The Doyen will want to see him. She'll want to study whatever this is."

The one with the gun to Deniel's head sighed. "Let her study another," he said. "They're all over the city. I doubt she'll miss just one."

Deniel blinked up at them. The amityguard's gun was crooked into his armpit, a visor shielding his face so that he could barely be told apart from his comrades. But the scruff on his chin and pitched inclination of his vowels told Deniel that they were not far apart in age.

"Do you want to die?" the amityguard asked him.

Deniel looked up to the hiding stars, then back down to his hands, thinking that it didn't matter what he wanted. The blood was already drying on his knuckles. The stains were there. He knew there was no chance they'd come out.

Deniel hadn't known himself for a while now, but he did know this: the ashen king was coming, and he would bring death and magic and new worlds.

"You are traitors," Deniel said.

He was too.

They all were, and traitors needed to die.

Everyone needed to die and it was best they did so before the new world came.

The amityguard pressed his gun back to Deniel's temple.

Deniel closed his eyes and besides that, he didn't move, or think to run.

He wasn't afraid anymore.

He welcomed the darkness and the final peace it would bring.

36

Tavia

CLOVERYE WAS WHAT ALL the swells in Creije drank and Wesley had enough bottles to kill a small army. Tavia wondered whether they might actually be able to use it against the Kingpin.

She wasn't sure why he prioritized packing so many bottles, and who he'd tasked with bringing them aboard. Looking around at the collection Wesley had amassed, she half-suspected he planned on opening a new Crook aboard the train.

"Is this an underboss thing?" Tavia asked, with raised eyebrows. "Collect a bottle of Cloverye for every dead body?"

Wesley's laugh was monotone. "I see Saxony has been teaching you how to make jokes."

Tavia withheld a snort.

He and Saxony were caught halfway between mortal enemies and petty rivalry, and as entertaining as it was to watch, it wasn't going to help them win this war.

Wesley made to hand Tavia a glass and she shook her head,

snatching the bottle instead. "If we're about to die, you can be a little less tight with the drinks."

She swallowed a bitter mouthful and then quickly remembered why she rarely drank. Specifically, why she rarely drank Cloverye. The rich and the ruthless may have loved the prestige, but that shit was *nasty*.

Tavia made a face and basically threw the bottle back into Wesley's hands.

"Many Gods," she said with a wince, at the same time as Wesley said, "Always so refined."

He poured himself a glass, smiling in a way that made it hard for Tavia to glare.

She took a seat opposite him and stared out at the ocean beyond the glass, endless and so impossibly blue.

They were racing through the waters, but when Tavia pulled down the window and took in a long breath of salted air, she felt peace and calm, and she could almost imagine that they were meandering along with nothing to do and nowhere yet to go. Just a couple of almost weary travelers seeking to find where the world ended.

Tavia didn't know how much time faded after that. The bottle passed between them, Wesley savoring each sip and she wincing as it burned at her throat, and soon the realms grew hazy and Tavia felt her bones relax. All the tension seeped from her and into the air, carrying away with the wind that bellowed outside the train.

Somewhere along the way, Tavia moved to sit beside Wesley, kicking her feet up on the chair opposite, and he had done the same, and now they were slouched parallel with their heads tilted back and the song of war too far in the distance to hear.

"One more?" Wesley asked.

He brought the bottle to Tavia's glass, but the train hitched over a wave and the Cloverye splashed onto his shoes.

"I forgot you could be a clumsy drunk," Tavia said.

Wesley scowled. "You forget that I'm your—"

"Underboss," Tavia said. "Yes, but you're also an idiot. Congratulations on multitasking so brilliantly."

The fact that Wesley seemed to take this as a compliment made Tavia shake her head.

"Give me that." She snatched the bottle back from him. "You're going to spill it again."

Wesley's frown was like a scar across his brows. "You're always saying something awful to me," he said. He tilted his chin up. "I'm awful to everyone except you. In case you hadn't noticed."

Tavia blinked.

The completely indignant look on his face caught her halfway between a laugh and the need to smack him.

"You don't get a gold star for treating people with basic respect, Wesley. That's how you're *supposed* to act."

Wesley gave her a childish sneer. "Because you're so pleasant to everyone."

Tavia snorted. "Should we delay the war so you can mourn properly for your ego?"

He straightened. "I can assure you, my ego is perfectly intact."

"Infallible," Tavia said with grunt. "Ever since we were kids. Do you remember that time when you first got to head the magic markets? You were the youngest busker ever to get a spot and that kid, Many Gods, what was his *name*?"

She shook her head, like it didn't matter. "He was one of the older buskers and he came to your show and tried to pick holes at your performance in front of the crowd. You just shook it off like rainwater and carried on. Like he wasn't even there. Like he wasn't worth considering."

"I thought we were in Ejm Voten, not memory lane," Wesley said.

Tavia rolled her eyes and chose to ignore him. "You poisoned the kid's rations so he was sick for two weeks."

"Actually," Wesley said, "*you* poisoned his rations."

"He called you and all of your friends phonies with trash magic," Tavia said. "*I* was your friend. That bastard brought me into it for no good reason. The least he deserved was a stomach bug."

Wesley touched a hand to his chest. "That's so sweet," he said.

Tavia took another sip of Cloverye.

"Do you think the Kingpin saw this coming?" she asked, looking out the train window with a sigh. "You of all people turning against him."

Wesley shook his head, which would have looked fiercely adamant if it hadn't thrown him a little off balance. Instead, he just looked endearing. Delicate, even, which was not a Wesley thing to be, and very much his age, which was also not a Wesley thing to be.

"It's awful, isn't it?" Wesley said. "He trusts me. The worst man in the realms, not even a man at all, really, and he's the closest thing I've ever had to family."

Sometimes you get to choose, Tavia thought.

"Will it be hard?" she asked. "When the time comes."

"To officially betray the man who gave me everything?"

Wesley made a sound that was not quite a laugh and not quite a sigh.

"No," he said.

He took another drink and Tavia didn't know whether this was to hide the lie, or drown in the bitter truth of it.

"The funny thing is that he won't see it as a betrayal. He'll be proud of me," Wesley said. "For coming so far."

"What about the girl?"

The Crafter child from his regret.

Tavia still couldn't fathom how so much time had passed without her knowing. Not that Wesley had befriended a Crafter, not that she could get inside his mind, and definitely not that her ghost still lingered there.

Tavia had been thinking about it nonstop and a thousand different questions whirled through her, but she was barely sure Wesley would answer one, and so she chose the most important, just in case.

"Do you hear her now?"

Wesley touched a hand to his wrist and, at first, Tavia thought he was going for his scars, absentmindedly pressing a hand to old injuries, hidden beyond the lines of his tattoos. Or searching, perhaps, for a piece of his skin not overtaken by Creije and the city lines. A small part of himself, untouched, unwritten.

Then she saw the crease in his eyebrows that followed as soon as his fingers touched skin and Tavia quickly realized that he'd actually been going for his cuff links, seeking to adjust the small pieces of metal, make them perfect, smudge-free and straight. Give himself some comfort in the chaos.

As it was, there was no comfort to find. Wesley's blazer was folded neatly onto the back of a nearby chair and his shirtsleeves were rolled up to the elbows, leaving his wrists bare and exposed. This was the haphazard Wesley, hair no longer clean-cut and his jawline rough with shadow, tattoos acting as a map of the city he had made whole, covering the length of his arms and back, reaching even for his throat until they nicked his jaw like a razor. His eyes were wild and deep brown, tie pulled gruffly loose. There was no order or comfort to find in this chaos.

Wesley bit the edge of his lip as his frown deepened and Tavia nearly came undone right there, watching as he untethered from the underboss and became the boy she knew.

"The dead can't talk," Wesley said. "She's nothing but an echo making sure I remember my place."

"Your place?"

"As the worst bastard in Creije."

His smirk was so hollow that Tavia took another gulp of Cloverye.

"Not that I'm one to turn down a drink," Wesley said, regaining himself somewhat. "But don't you think a reverie charm would be better in this situation?" His voice was raw, smile lazy and off-kilter. "We could fall into the stars and escape the world for a night."

Tavia bit the corner of her lip.

The last time they'd taken a charm together the curtain of friendship between them was featherlight, barely even there at all, ready to slip away and be replaced by something else if they dared. These days that curtain barely existed and so what was to stop them, with the feeling of infinity in their veins and the hopeless prospect of war on the horizon?

I could kiss you instead, Wesley had said, regret still fresh in his eyes. Close enough that Tavia could smell the salt and peppermint on his skin.

Wesley shuffled beside her now. His eyes were dewy with alcohol.

Dangerous. It felt so dangerous.

He moved closer and placed his hand on top of hers and Tavia's heart stuttered.

No matter how awful Wesley was, even when he was being the coldest bastard in Creije, he always *felt* warm.

He always felt a little like home.

After Wesley became underboss and left the busker dormitories, Tavia moved out as soon as she could, because all the fun and the memories they made seemed like cruel jokes after he'd left her behind. She wasn't part of his plans for realm domination and though she didn't want to be a career criminal like Wesley did, she hated that her friend didn't want her by his side.

The dormitories never felt like home after that.

It was strange then, that here, on this train, with magic on her belt loop and Wesley smiling like time was just an illusion they had created, endless oceans between them and the rest of the realms, Tavia felt at peace.

She felt at home.

And she knew why. She knew then that home could be anywhere, because it wasn't a place, but a feeling. It was made up of people, not bricks, and it was something you could create for yourself, just like family.

Sometimes you get to choose, Wesley had said.

He squeezed her hand.

"Tavia."

Her name, but not her name. More like a plea than anything else.

Tavia stood so abruptly that she nearly lost her balance.

She ripped her hand from Wesley's and the warmth evaporated from her fingers the moment their touch broke apart.

Tavia tried not to be nostalgic for it.

"I'm going to find Saxony," she said.

But she didn't move and her voice was too delicate and *why was she not moving?*

Wesley swallowed, and though he said nothing more, his eyes burned into her, screaming a thousand things.

Stay, they said. *Please stay*.

And that was the problem: Tavia wanted to.

Not just here, in this moment, but in Creije. So much of her wanted to run and be free, but an equal part of her, or perhaps even a larger part, wanted to stay. With Wesley and Saxony and the magic they could make together.

With every stilted breath Wesley took, Tavia's resolve wavered until she could almost feel herself inching closer to him, picture his hands tangled in her and every horrible, awful thing turning beautiful.

Tavia snatched the bottle from the space between them and damn near bolted for the door, ignoring the thump of her heart. She didn't look back to see if Wesley had moved. Didn't listen in case he tried to call for her.

She couldn't be the person he wanted her to be.

Wesley would pull her close and keep her there if she let him, in Creije and the clutches of the Crook. In a world that reminded her so much of the awful truth of her muma's death and of all the things she had done since.

Wesley would give her the world, even though Tavia hadn't earned it, and he'd give her power, even though she didn't want it. And among it all was the scariest thought: the fear that she might like it, might just grow to ignore all the bad things and the good people they happened to.

And so Tavia left Wesley and the wonderful, awful part of her that wanted so desperately to stay.

37

Karam

IT WAS MIDNIGHT WHEN Saxony brought a bottle of Cloverye, three glasses, and Tavia to the front carriage where Karam was trying to sleep. Karam eyed the bottle warily, because it was most definitely Wesley's, and Tavia even more so, because she took a glass and poured the first drink with far too much angst.

A full hour soon passed and the seasickness Karam had still not gotten used to was replaced with another kind of nausea.

Karam knocked her glass against Saxony's and tipped her head back.

The wind had quieted, and though Arjun was on hand every now and again to keep the seas in check, they were passing across the final stretch of Ejm Voten with little hassle. The phantoms had faded into the wind they were born from, and in a matter of days this whole thing would be over. One way or another.

Karam wasn't quite sure how she felt about dying.

She faced the possibility each day she stepped into the Crook's fighting ring, but this was different. Whatever happened, things were going to change, and either way they might not change in anyone's favor. Karam at least hoped to get a few good punches in before that.

"No more for you," Saxony said, pulling the bottle out of Tavia's hand.

The busker made a grab for it, but Saxony looked down at her admonishingly.

Tavia slumped against the headrest. "I don't get it," she said.

"You're about ready to keel over," Saxony said. "You're cut off."

"Not that," Tavia said. "Your regrets." Her head shot up and she pointed accusing fingers at Karam and Saxony. "You both got to see your families, but my muma was nowhere. All I got was that old bastard underboss."

Saxony brought her lips to the bottle. "I always thought the old underboss was a looker," she said. Tavia gave her a blank stare and so Saxony poured a drop of Cloverye into her glass, like a reward. "Sorry. Shitty joke."

The two of them clinked their glasses together and Tavia had to tip her head so far back to get the tiny amount of liquid inside that she damn near toppled over.

"Count yourself lucky," Karam said, placing a steadying arm on the busker's shoulder. "It was almost worse that I was able to see my pehta. It brought back every awful feeling."

She clutched her father's pendant, grateful that he was with her on this journey, even just in spirit. Karam would show him a legacy to be proud of, where their people helped protect Crafters and bring true peace to the realms.

"I'm sorry about your father," Tavia said.

"Do not be sorry. Be ready. When we get to the island, we will kill the Kingpin together."

Tavia held up her barren shot glass. "I'll drink to that." She knocked the empty glass against the bottle in Karam's hand and turned to Saxony. "Tell me killing him in the consort's mind was satisfying."

Saxony laughed. "Second time better be a charm."

Karam hoped so too.

The Kingpin drawing a breath beyond this battle was not an option, not after what he had done in Granka. He wouldn't be content to take revenge out on them if he survived. He'd go after their families, their cities, and their entire realm. There was no stopping a madman with an army and a cause.

"Do you want to know a secret?" Saxony asked.

"Only if it's dirty," Tavia said.

Karam clipped her on the back of the head.

"When this is all over and I get my sister back, I still won't be happy."

"There's just no pleasing some people," Tavia said.

Saxony nodded, like that was probably true. "I'll have to leave Creije to help my sister ascend to Liege, and for everything I hate about that place, I cherish something too."

She looked at Karam and Tavia in turn.

"Is this your way of saying you love us?" Tavia asked. "Because that's really corny."

Saxony scrunched up her nose. "Shut up," she said.

They laughed as the wind howled a little stronger outside, and Saxony conjured a flame in the palm of her hand to keep them warm. They gathered around her like a campfire, the Cloverye burning their lips as they forgot their glasses and passed the bottle between them.

Karam looked to Saxony, who she'd loved and lost and then loved again. She looked to Tavia, who she liked at least one out of every four times she saw her.

She hoped neither of them died.

Even if Karam had to do so in their place, she hoped they would make it out of this battle. For Saxony to return to Rishiya, and for Tavia to go wherever her heart took her, and for them both to be safe and free.

If nothing else was changed by this war, Karam at least wanted that.

"To killing our enemies first," she said, in a toast.

Tavia raised the bottle. "To the realms not ending."

Saxony grinned, wide and beautiful. She grinned in a way that made Karam feel weak in her knees and so strong in her heart.

"To family," Saxony said. "New and old. Blood and bond."

She took the bottle from Tavia and raised it above them all.

And then the train lurched violently left and the bottle of Cloverye flew from Saxony's hand and smashed on the floor.

The sky darkened and drummed.

The heavens opened in a downpour.

Tavia looked to Saxony with panic in her eyes, just as Wesley and Arjun's voices rushed into the carriage. Wesley grabbed the radio and they began screaming at buskers and Crafters alike. Barking orders at their army. Telling them to *turn* and *hold it off*.

The rain from an open window coated Karam's eyelashes.

Saxony's hand threaded into hers. She heard Tavia take in

a breath as loud as the wind, her eyes glued on something in the distance.

"Many Gods," Tavia said.

A maelstrom opened like the mouth of the sea, spreading and spreading with no end. It turned the inky-green waters of Ejm Voten a dark, lifeless gray.

The sea parted and Karam felt like she was seeing a path straight into the spiritlands.

Lightning shot from the sky like arms. Nine bolts of it held in a perpetual strike, feeding the growing chasm that pulled their train inward like it was nothing more than a toy tied to string.

"Reverse the train!" Arjun yelled.

Karam heard the rush of the crew running and rallying. She heard the Crafters scream spells into the air. Saw Arjun lift his hands to halt the weather and then—

"Stop," Wesley said.

His voice was level as he stared into the depths of the ocean.

"We are going to die," Arjun urged.

"No," Wesley said. "We're not."

"Your ego can't avert a natural disaster," Tavia said. "We need to haul ass back the way we came."

"This isn't natural. It's part of the plan."

"The plan is for the Kingpin to die!" Arjun yelled above the downpour. "Not us."

"I just said we weren't going to die."

"*Pelg.*" Arjun shook his head, disbelieving.

Karam couldn't help but agree. Wesley was acting like a madman.

Arjun snatched the radio from him. "I want every Crafter

to throw all the magic they have at that thing and for every busker to do whatever it takes to turn this train around."

Wesley looked like he was trying hard to restrain himself. "Any busker who so much as moves is going to be thrown overboard," he said. "As for the Crafters, go ahead and try your magic. I guarantee it won't do a thing."

"Wesley." The rain soaked Tavia's clothes, rolling down her cheeks like tears. "Tell me you have a plan."

"I always have a plan," he said. "Our final test."

"We already conquered it," Saxony said. "Falk is dead."

The train drew forward. The Crafters shouted spells and launched magic into the maelstrom, but it did nothing.

They did not stop.

They did not slow.

The vortex sucked in the sea like it was drinking it and their train sped forward, unrelenting.

There was nothingness inside that thing.

It would drag them to the bottom of the ocean.

"Wesley!" Tavia screamed.

He gritted his teeth. "You said you trusted me."

It was like an accusation.

"So trust me when I say I'm not letting you die," he said. "The phantoms told us to keep steady on our course if we wanted to see the Kingpin. They said the ultimate sacrifice would be needed and that we *all* had to be part of it. Killing Falk didn't finish a damn thing."

"*Death waits for you together*," Tavia said. Her voice was distant as she recalled the phantoms' words.

"You think they meant it literally?" Karam asked.

"They told us it was something we had to face as a team. After I shot Falk and they just let us go on our way, I knew we hadn't conquered anything. *This* is the last test. The ultimate sacrifice is us."

"You want us to kill ourselves, underboss?" Arjun was incredulous.

"We won't die," Wesley said again, a little exasperated at having to repeat himself.

The train reeled forward and they were all flung roughly onto the floor.

Saxony landed in a heap on top of Karam.

The train circled the maelstrom, spinning madly in its orbit. The force of it made them slide across the carriages.

Karam felt a pressure on her chest holding her to the floor, sucking the air from her lungs, and all the while they were spinning and spinning.

The rain sliced through the smashed windows and across her face.

She swallowed the taste of bile. She was going to throw up if she didn't die first.

"Are you sure that we should not turn around?" Karam yelled out to Wesley, wherever he was. "Are you sure that we will not die?"

There was a moment of silence as the train spun, and then Wesley's voice cut clear above the wind. "I'm sure that if I have to say it one more time, I'm just going to kill you all myself."

Good enough, Karam thought.

Wesley did not make a habit of being wrong and he did not make a habit of dying, so that was good enough for Karam.

Though nobody knew the Kingpin, if there was one person in the realms who might be able to understand how his twisted mind worked, then it was the underboss of Creije. Following him was their best bet. It had gotten them this far.

"If my Kin dies, I will drag you into the doomed spiritlands myself," Arjun said to Wesley.

"You won't need to. You'll be there right beside me."

The train swung forward again and suddenly Karam was looking into the gaping mouth of the sea. Into an impossible endlessness.

She placed her hand on either side of Saxony's cheeks and kissed her, one last time. Savoring her taste, her smile and her feel, just in case.

She wanted to say a thousand things, but the wind wailed and time was nearly up and everything that needed to be said was already known. Words could not do some things justice.

Karam braced herself.

And then they were swallowed whole.

Being inside a maelstrom was like dying, only it didn't end. The air choked Karam. The water choked Karam. Karam wasn't sure there was anything not choking her.

The train kept spinning and falling into an endless pit of black.

Karam was sure she should have been flung out the window and into the abyss by now, but she was pinned in place. The wind filled her lungs and the water washed it down, taking root in her stomach and then gurgling back up until she was breathing seawater.

She couldn't feel Saxony's hand in hers anymore, or anything but the pain of dying again and again.

And then the realms came rushing back.

The train crashed onto something solid and Karam's head flung backward onto the floor. Her entire body felt broken. Alive, but definitely broken.

She let out a groan.

It was bright out, but Karam couldn't see the sun. Only—

She rubbed her eyes.

There was no sky anymore, only the ocean floating above them, crashing like a thunderstorm overhead.

A sky made from Ejm Voten.

Karam jumped to her feet.

"Get up," she said, to nobody and everybody. "Get up right now."

Saxony stepped to her side. Karam wasn't sure if she was hurt, but she did not dare take her eyes off the sky to look. They had fallen through the ocean and now its storms floated around them, and then overhead like a cloud bank.

"That's impossible," Saxony said.

Karam could not have said it better herself.

38

Saxony

THEY WERE ON LAND.

They were alive and on *land*.

The sea raged around them like a cage, their train marooned in the eye of the storm with the moon shining above it like a beacon. It was like they were beneath a rip in the very fabric of the realms.

Or like they were in the perfect prison. Saxony almost wondered if they had broken in, or if they had actually been lulled into a trap.

The train was intact, miraculously, and beached on a large patch of sand. Ashwood's castle sprawled out from a rock face in metallic brickwork, floating atop the blackened nothingness like oil. Its steel towers reached for the growing darkness, while its pathways gradually dissolved to the water. Waves rocked, but never touched the walls, as though even the sea was scared to try its hand at an attack.

"If everyone is still alive, we go out as planned," Wesley said.

Tavia appeared beside him, rubbing her backside. "Because your plans have been working out so well."

She winced at the bruises that were sure to be covering her body.

Wesley pressed a hand to the radio again. "All of the Energycrafters on board will make this entire army invisible, then proceed in groups to plant the time charges around the castle."

Not including Saxony, there were nine other Energycrafters, which was more than enough to create an invisibility field to cover their numbers. They could spread out from all sides in an ambush, except the front door, where Saxony assumed she, Tavia, and Wesley would still enter.

"Karam will coordinate you," Wesley said. "When I give you the signal, I want you to rain time down on this island. Whatever happens, we end this tonight. The shadow moon is only hours away. We can't let Ashwood live long enough to see it."

The buskers and Crafters nodded, quickly filtering into groups, each with an Energycrafter to shield them from sight. Wesley's barrels of time, which he had *more or less* perfected over the last few days, were by their feet.

Before the Crafters made the army disappear into nothingness, Saxony hugged Karam goodbye. She promised that the next time they saw each other, she'd have Zekia in her hands and would finally introduce them. Karam told her that the next time they saw each other, she'd better have the Kingpin's head in her hands too.

Then Karam kissed her, short, but never sweet. She embraced Saxony all too quickly and then turned without a goodbye to exit the train. Saxony's stare lingered on her.

"Don't die," she called to Karam's back.

Karam didn't turn, but her voice was like knives in the night. "Make sure the Kingpin does."

<hr>

There was silence and not a guard in sight as they waited outside the drawbridge. Their train meandered behind them, pressed into the sand, where it had been thrown from the sky.

Karam and Arjun were long gone with their invisible army.

The flames of Saxony's magic licked her veins, ready to be let loose, but she held it in. Let the Kingpin think she was just another little Crafter out of her element.

When the time came, she'd burn him to cinders.

A bowl of flame atop the drawbridge sparked to life and a voice bellowed down to them. "Who has a death wish big enough to approach the Kingpin of Uskhanya's castle?"

Wesley sighed. "I guess my reputation doesn't stretch as far as I would have liked."

A bullet shot to the floor by their shoes.

Saxony jumped and Tavia swore, pointing her gun up to the guard tower.

"*Skeht!*" Tavia yelled.

Wesley didn't move. Saxony wasn't if sure he had even blinked.

"That was a warning shot," the guard said.

"Yes." Wesley nodded. "Thank you for explaining. Would you care to hear my warning?"

His gun was in his hand before Saxony had the time to take a breath. Wesley fired, just once, and a body fell down from the guard tower. A man, not much older than them, in a black guard's uniform with Ashwood's symbol imprinted on his chest. The bullet was lodged in the center of his brow.

"I don't give warnings," Wesley said.

He looked up to the empty guard tower, where the flame flickered unattended.

"Tell the Kingpin that the underboss of Creije has traveled a long way to find him," he called, to whoever might be listening. "And I think he's going to want to hear me out."

Wesley looked sideways to Saxony and smiled like the devil she suspected he was. There was a moment's pause and then the chains of the drawbridge shrieked and the great barrier began to lower.

A man and a woman greeted them, dressed in the same black uniform as the one Wesley had killed, with the Kingpin's crest like a brand over their hearts. *Crafters*. Saxony could smell it on them and when they smiled at her, catlike and fearless, she knew they could smell it on her, too.

"Wesley Thornton Walcott," the man said. He had a well-trimmed red beard, fox-brown eyes, and fair skin. He opened his arms in welcome. "My name is Gael. Please, come this way."

Wesley stepped forward, but the young woman held up her hand to stop him. "You leave your weapons here."

Her voice carried a familiar lilt.

Many Gods.

Saxony all but gasped. She almost hadn't recognized her. The thick braid that brushed against the sword at the woman's hip. The gold staves that covered both of her arms in the magic she had conquered. The tall, stiff stature of a warrior used to protecting her kind.

Asees.

She was alive, in the Kingpin's hold. And she didn't look like a prisoner.

"Asees," Saxony said.

She thought about the pained look on Arjun's face when the *delg* bat had spoken her last words. The guilt that took over Karam, thinking she could have prevented it all if she had stayed in Granka. If she had never met Wesley or Tavia. Or Saxony. A guilt Saxony knew was not Karam's to bear.

"You're alive. You—"

"Be quiet," Wesley said.

Saxony turned to him, about to tell him to go straight to the fire-gates, but Wesley was looking at Asees, guarded, his fingers twitching against his gun.

"That's not her," he said.

Asees narrowed her golden eyes and when she smiled, it was like her lips were being tugged upward by string. Saxony saw it now. Not just the mark peeking out from her collar, but the way Asees moved so rigidly and how her large, severe eyes didn't burn with fierceness and suspicion like they had back in Granka. Her stare was empty. Vacant. Glazed over in such a way that Saxony got a chill when Asees met her stare.

The magic—the very one they were trying to stop from spreading across the realms—had Asees under its power.

"Your weapons," Asees said.

"If you want them, you can pry them from my cold, dead hands," Wesley said.

Asees smiled again, the pleasant puppet. Saxony's throat tightened. If Karam were here, if Arjun were here, then Saxony knew what they would do. They would bring this island to its knees in an instant.

Grief and anger and wild, wild despair.

"That won't be necessary," Gael said.

His voice, at least, seemed to be his own, but that didn't make it any better. It only meant he was either brainwashed or a traitor by nature, and Saxony thought it better to be a puppet than a turncoat.

"The Kingpin wants you alive," Gael said. "This way."

He gestured once more and Wesley pulled a pair of mirrored glasses from his pocket, slipping them on.

Asees and Gael lead them through a large courtyard and into the main hall. Saxony's eyes scoured every inch of the place that might have held her sister captive for three years. She wanted to memorize the floors Zekia could have been dragged along and look out for any other Crafters. For the faces of any men and women who may have been the ones to bind Zekia and keep her here.

She wanted to remember that so she could know who to kill first.

The walls were brown-black like the floor, and gleaming enough for Saxony's shadow to seem like a reflection. The castle was quiet and the echoes of their respective footsteps became rhythmic among the silence. It was only when Tavia swore a few times as she took in the castle's interior that Saxony remembered she wasn't alone.

Wesley kept his focus on Asees and his hands on his gun. His eyes were obscured by his glasses, but Saxony had already seen the twitch in them back at the drawbridge.

They approached a room, barricaded with doors taller than mountains. The Crafters stepped forward, palms thrust out, and in unison they spoke. Half spell, half passphrase. Saxony didn't recognize the language—it sounded like a mishmash of every tongue in the four realms—but when they spoke it, the doors bellowed open.

The ceiling was made from glass, the sky calling down to them and giving a perfect view for the coming shadow moon. The floors were oil-slicked and great tusks of bone jutted from the ceilings and walls in decoration. Animal and human.

Dante Ashwood was seated in the center, on a throne of shadows. Six Crafters surrounded him.

Saxony could barely see his ghostly outline, if not for the pale, pale fingers that clasped the orb atop his cane, the magic illuminating the skin of his hand. His face was hidden in darkness, and his eyes, though Saxony could feel them on her, were nowhere to be seen.

She squeezed her hands to keep the flame at bay. He was the creature she had killed in a dream place. This time, she would do it for real.

From the shadows beside the Kingpin, a young girl stepped forward. She was dressed all in white, with black hair to her fingers and eyes like living embers. Unbound. Unafraid. Sitting alongside the Kingpin with a hunter's gaze.

"Sister," Zekia said.

Her voice had not changed. Her smile had not changed. Her neck was not marked.

"We've been expecting you."

39

Wesley

THE GHOST WHO LIVED in Wesley's mind was standing before him. Real and unchanged from the last time—the first time—he had seen her.

And she was alive.

Despite everything Wesley thought, everything Ashwood had said about absorbing her powers, she'd managed to survive, and now she was beside the Kingpin like she couldn't possibly belong anywhere else.

I need a left hand too, the Kingpin once said.

"Sister. We've been expecting you."

Her voice was still so composed beyond her years. It was not the voice of a captive, nor did it carry the smooth puppetry of Asees's.

This was her, the same girl Wesley knew, and she was very much in control. He didn't have to look at her neck to know it.

Saxony collapsed onto her knees. "Zekia."

The name was a cry.

Wesley flinched.

Saxony's sister. This whole time it was her.

Yes.

She smiled at him as her voice whispered in his head.

Not a ghost, like he'd thought. He wasn't crazy, like he'd thought.

All these years she had been whispering to him, spurring him to be awful. He wondered if Ashwood knew and if it had been part of some twisted plan.

"You've come a long way to find me," Ashwood said.

Wesley straightened, kept his chin high.

"You came a long way to make sure you weren't found," he said.

Ashwood leaned forward, his smile like a stain in the darkness. "But you were never one for following orders."

"And you've brought us a gift," Zekia said.

Saxony stayed on her knees, eyes filling with tears as Zekia approached her. She wore a ring that was a duplicate of the one Wesley had on his own thumb: the Kingpin's insignia, worn by all of his underbosses. Only Zekia was not an underboss and hers was not black. It was the same bright fire as her dancing eyes.

A mark of a loyal ally.

"I should have protected you," Saxony said. "I should have come sooner."

"Stand, sister. If you fall on your knees, you stay that way forever."

That didn't sound like the girl Wesley knew.

Time was such a bastard. It made fools of some and monsters of those they left behind.

"We thought you'd abandoned us," Saxony said. "I didn't realize you were taken until—"

"I wasn't taken," Zekia said. "I did leave."

Ashwood leaned back in his throne, arms sprawled over his shadows. "She offered her life so my boy might have his."

Hearing Ashwood talk in that twisted paternal way made Wesley recoil.

Zekia was the thing he regretted most. He had killed to be where he was, but betraying her seemed worse. It seemed worse because she had trusted him to be better.

Wesley's greatest talent was disappointing the people who trusted him.

All this time he thought her voice was punishment for that, her ghost haunting his thoughts to make sure he would never make the same mistake, but Zekia wasn't dead. She was haunting him from right here, as flesh and blood. Trying to coax him further into the darkness.

"She doesn't know who the underboss of Creije is," Saxony said.

Zekia looked straight at Wesley, lips twisting. "He wasn't the underboss of anything when I knew him."

"She's the girl from your regret," Tavia said, as though she had only just recognized her. "The Crafter you sacrificed to the Kingpin to become underboss."

Saxony turned on Wesley like a rabid creature, like if she wasn't so broken she might just rip him to pieces with her bare hands.

"I helped you," she seethed. "And all this time you traded her for a promotion?"

Wesley said nothing.

"It was the best of many futures," Zekia said.

Wesley was glad his sunglasses hid his expression. "You can't predict the future," he said, remembering her words. "There are too many possibilities."

"And I can see them all," Zekia said. "Hundreds of ways our fates were destined to entwine. One where the Kingpin found me and one where you turned me in." She paused and something like sadness flared across her eyes. "I didn't want to wait and see if that last one was true."

"You've lost your mind," Saxony said. "You've let him turn you into a monster."

"Such nonsense. I've made her into something glorious."

Ashwood snapped his fingers and, like a well-trained pet, Zekia blew into the palm of her hand. Images dropped from her skin like water.

Visions came to life of another Saxony, dressed in the same black uniform as Asees, with the Kingpin's insignia noosed around her thumb. Flame crawled along her arms, licking her neck and setting the ends of her hair alight in pure gold fire.

The conjured Saxony took a step toward Ashwood, who leaned forward to get a closer look at her. She let the flames die out as she approached, before falling to her knees and bowing before her king.

Intuitcrafter.

This was what Zekia did. Messed with people's heads and got inside their minds. It was how she'd gotten inside Wesley's all those years ago. How she stayed there, this whole time.

The vision of Saxony dispersed and the real Crafter spat on the floor by Ashwood's feet. "That'll never happen," she said.

"Your sister has foretold many futures. Do you want to know in how many of them you join me?"

"I want to know in how many of them I kill you."

Ashwood laughed. "And you, Wesley? My boy did not kill my consort and face his past just to present me a Crafter with a vendetta."

Wesley glanced at the clock that chimed above the Kingpin's throne, with a face of bone and hands of sinew. The shadow moon was coming, but he needed to bide time for Karam and the others to place the charges. For their army to get ready to strike.

Wesley pushes his sunglasses up his nose.

"So I was right," Wesley said. "The sacrifice we needed wasn't killing Falk. It was surrendering our own lives."

"It was theatrical, I'll admit," Ashwood said. "Though I am curious as to why your favorite spy was eliminated."

"He worked for you," Tavia said.

And when Ashwood only smiled, Wesley's stomach sank.

"If he did, I'd applaud the move, little busker. After all, traitors must be extinguished once they have outgrown their use. I taught Wesley that when he was just a boy."

"Falk sent *delg* bats to you," Tavia said. "He was the reason you attacked us in Granka."

Ashwood chuckled. "I attacked and you managed to survive? Why would I interrupt my own game like that?"

Silence followed and the air grew heavy around them all.

Something awful took over the moment, more awful than Zekia being on the Kingpin's side, or him being about to kill them all.

"It was me."

Saxony kept her eyes on the floor, staring straight through the earth.

"I made Falk send the bats," she said. "I told him they were for Wesley."

Tavia shook her head. "You wouldn't do that. You're on our side."

"I'm on Zekia's side," Saxony said.

"You're my friend!" Tavia screamed. "We said we were in this together. For your sister and my muma."

"You weren't at the train station back in Creije! I thought you'd gotten killed," Saxony said. Her eyes welled with furious tears. "And I already knew how to find the Kingpin, so I didn't need Wesley anymore. I sent a bat to the guards, tipping off our location, thinking I could slip out with Karam after it was over. I didn't know how many they'd send."

"You knew they would try to kill us," Wesley said, his voice as quiet as hers. He felt like if he raised it, then he might just explode. "You knew they would try to kill *me*. You hoped for it."

There was magic in him now and it swelled with every breath he took in anger.

"And Granka?" Tavia asked. "I was there then."

"That wasn't me," Saxony said, suddenly desperate, pushing herself to her feet and grabbing Tavia's hands in hers. "I swear it to the Many Gods. I was knocked out by my amja's magic. She took me to this place inside both of our minds to convince me to betray you. She was so afraid of losing me. But I told her no. I didn't realize what she had planned."

Tavia snatched her hands from Saxony's. "It was your Kin who attacked us?"

"Our allies," Saxony said. "I recognized the markings on them and I knew that my amja's concern for me had made her blind. After Karam got hurt, I didn't want my Kin near either of you. For the first time, I realized I couldn't trust them to do the right thing. Their fear made them reckless. So I had Falk send a bat telling them to back off. That I wouldn't let them know where we were heading and I would bring Zekia back myself."

"Arjun's Kin was attacked after that," Wesley said.

"I would never play any part in that!" Saxony said, but her voice held more guilt than anger.

Wesley knew liars well and Saxony was up there with the best of them.

"You didn't say anything," Tavia said. "Not even when we turned our backs on Falk."

Wesley shifted.

He had killed someone who was at least semi-innocent and he'd roped Tavia in on it. She'd put her faith in him, in his judgment, swallowing any morals she had, for nothing.

All for somebody else's games.

"I'm sorry for Falk," Saxony said. "But you have to believe that I wasn't responsible for Arjun's Kin. The bat was—"

"Ah yes." Ashwood leaned back in his chair. "Now I remember."

Zekia hummed. "Such a pretty creature. It sang to us quite sweetly."

"You intercepted it," Wesley said. "And then killed the Kin for helping us."

Zekia shook her head slowly, hypnotically, from side to side. "Not all of them."

She inclined her head to Asees. A weapon ready to attack them from behind.

"We saved some of the most delicious."

"I thought I had you on that last test," Ashwood said, almost excited. "After all, my Wesley would never sacrifice himself alongside crooks. Worthless lowlifes that they are. Yet here you stand."

Wesley swallowed.

Boredom. Curiosity. Just another game. All those lives ruined, the chaos they'd left in their wake for nothing.

Wesley never had the Kingpin on the ropes, even for a minute.

He was truly a puppet. A lapdog.

"I knew you would betray me one day," Ashwood said. "But a dog has to bite before you can put it down, Wesley."

Ashwood didn't sound annoyed, but impressed that Wesley was able to rise up against him. As though it showed initiative, rather than disloyalty.

His clever little prodigy.

"Is that what you're going to do?" Wesley asked. "Put me down?"

"I'm going to give you the realms, my boy. Betraying me was the only way for you to prove you were powerful enough to be my successor. You have shown me that you have what it takes to be just like me."

There was enough pride in his voice for Wesley to hate himself.

"Creije is the first of many cities we will conquer together,"

Ashwood said. "It has already begun, and one by one we will take Uskhanya from Schulze and pave the way for our new realm."

"By stealing people's minds, just like you stole my sister's," Saxony said.

"It isn't stealing," Zekia said, "if it's a gift."

"You're not an object to be passed around!"

Zekia tutted. "I meant the magic. A gift, from me to my Kingpin."

Saxony blanched and Wesley tried to reconcile the girl he knew with the one in front of him.

Zekia had created the elixir.

She'd used her specialty to make something powerful enough to take someone's mind, when she had once apologized for accidentally stumbling into his.

Just what had Wesley done, by leaving her behind?

"It isn't true," Saxony said. "You're lying!"

"Then how is your mind still your own?" Zekia asked. "How did you think you fought against the magic of the Loj?"

"Blood," Wesley said.

He was so stupid not to think of it.

My clever, clever boy.

"I felt it the moment you swallowed that elixir. A part of myself in you, sister. You even conquered the mark. Did you think it was because you were so strong and powerful?" Zekia asked, laughter circling from her lips. "It is because you are my blood and the elixir is my blood. That gives you a certain kind of immunity. Not what I planned, but you know better than anyone that a Crafter can't be enshrined by her own magic."

"My magic is your magic, my blood is your blood," Saxony said, looking at the floor with such awful sadness. "You were supposed to be our Liege, Zekia, and this is what you became instead."

"I was never supposed to be anything," Zekia said. "My futures are not my own. They belonged to our brother."

"Is the elixir permanent?" Wesley asked.

"The Loj cannot last forever," Zekia said. "Like all things, magic is temporary."

The shadows squirmed around the Kingpin. "That is why any who refuse to bow and instead cling to the past will be culled."

"You mean killed," Wesley said.

"I mean cleansed," Ashwood corrected. "Like the disease they are."

"Free will isn't a disease."

"Then how is it I've found the cure? How is it that Creije is already to falling to its knees?"

At the mention of his city, Wesley surged forward.

He didn't know how much madness Ashwood had brought down upon it in his absence, but just the idea, the thought that his home could be lost, stabbed at Wesley's heart.

He couldn't wait any longer. He could smell the fire on Saxony and see how Tavia's hands twitched by her sides as she tried not to go for the charm pouches clinched to her waist.

And Wesley. Even he could feel the new magic rising up in him, churning his insides.

He wasn't righteous. He wasn't a saint. But damn if he was going to let Ashwood destroy the minds of every single person in his realm. There was crooked and then there was just deranged.

Wesley cast one more glance to the clock. The shadow moon would be upon them any minute.

And then he paused.

A memory from Granka whirled through Wesley.

When midnight rings . . . Time will be carried in strange hands.

He could hear it singing to him all over again.

Not a hallucination, but his new Intuitcrafter magic, predicting this very moment. The orb had done the same for Tavia back in Creije.

"I'm going to destroy you," Wesley said.

He didn't reach for his gun. The Crafter magic was a well inside him, waiting to be opened. Wesley took another step toward the Kingpin.

Ashwood sniffed the air and his laugh was like crows in the night.

"Your magic is not borrowed," he said.

Wesley ripped off his glasses and looked directly into the darkness that hid Ashwood from him. And for the first time, the darkness could look back.

"I'm a vessel for the Grankan Kin of Crafters," Wesley said. "I carry their magic."

Ashwood leaned forward, regarding him with a serpent's smile. "Do you."

"They imbued me with their power."

"Did they."

He didn't look concerned.

He looked so, so proud.

Zekia shook her head and made another tutting sound. "Such lies," she said. "Such beautiful, dangerous lies.

I'll tear them out for you, one by one."

Until there's nothing left.

The six magic wielders beside the Kingpin glowered and when Wesley turned he saw that Tavia and Saxony were already facing the doors, facing Asees and Gael.

Wesley hoped they had enough magic between them to fight eight Crafters before the time charges went off, but Tavia didn't look worried—she palmed one of her charm pouches and hardened her glare, ready to fight.

"You can take your place now, Wesley," Ashwood said. "By my side, where you have always belonged. Let me be a father to you."

Such empty words.

Wesley had a father.

Even though he was probably dead, even though he might never have loved Wesley, even though Wesley had abandoned him and the rest of his family. He could forget their faces and their voices and the memories of the scars they'd given him, but never that they existed.

Never that they were his.

"I'm not your son," Wesley said. "And I'm not a traitor."

Because it was the Kingpin who had betrayed him with this madness and his greed. By destroying Ashwood, Wesley was protecting Uskhanya.

Ashwood stood. "Oh, but you are," he said. "And traitors must be punished."

He smiled, one last time, and then from his orb an army was birthed.

40

Tavia

WAR WAGED AT TAVIA'S footsteps.

Wraith-like incarnations of their army sprouted from the Kingpin's orb and took shape. They slaughtered one another by her feet, moving through the room like ghosts, howling with every blow.

Crafters and buskers and the Kingpin's people who looked to be a mix of both, stabbing and shooting and sending blasts of energy toward each other. There was blood and there was screaming and the skies wept down on them all. Rain like a torrent on the fighters and the bodies of those whose fight was over.

Tavia stumbled back and Wesley's hand locked into hers.

She didn't have time to question the feeling that rippled through her, or to savor it.

This was their army on the shores of the castle, dying at the Kingpin's hand, and Tavia didn't know if it was a vision of what was to come, or a reality of what had happened. She didn't know if their people were already dead, killed outside of these walls before they even knew the battle had begun.

Saxony held out a hand to touch the image of Karam. It went through her cheek. Karam raised a sword and brought it down upon a guard. Then another. And another. Until a Crafter with eyes as red as the fire-gates shot a beam of lightning her way.

It crushed against Karam's spine and sent her catapulting through the air. Through the battlefield. Through the walls of the room and out of sight.

"Karam!"

Saxony ran to the stone wall and pressed her hand against it, as though it might open and reveal her on the other side.

Wesley's grip tightened around Tavia's hand. He was shaking.

"I know what you're thinking, Wesley," Zekia said. "And you shouldn't."

"You're not in my head now, kid. You have no idea what I'm thinking."

"Then let's fix that."

Zekia launched herself into the air, nails like claws.

Quickly, Wesley shoved Tavia backward and Zekia landed on him like a jungle cat, the force of it sending them both across the room.

And then the Crafters attacked.

They threw magic like skipping stones. A shard of ice cut through the air and skimmed Tavia's cheek as she jumped out of the way.

Saxony returned the blow with a gust of fire that set one of them alight in an instant.

He barely had time to scream before he was ash.

"This will be fun," Asees said, with a horrible, unfamiliar smile on her lips.

Saxony conjured another flame in her hand, throwing it up and down. "I plan to enjoy it as well."

She heaved the flame at the same time that Tavia reached inside one of her charm pouches and threw the first marble she felt. There was no time to read it properly, so she had to go by gut and her gut was telling her to throw every single thing she had at these bastards.

One of the Crafters pounded his fists into the floor and it cracked. Tavia straddled a broken line and heaved another charm their way. It exploded above their heads and a great mass of stone crashed down onto one of them.

Two down.

Saxony lifted her shield, letting it envelop Tavia as the remaining Crafters circled.

They needed to send the signal to the others and let them know it was time to set those damn charges off.

Tavia whirled around. The Kingpin was watching, unmoved from his shadow throne. A spectator in his own war.

And Wesley. *Many Gods.* Zekia threw him across the room with little more than a flick of her wrist. But he was up in seconds, firing off bullets from one hand and orbs of energy from the other.

Tavia felt the ground shudder.

The Crafters were throwing charms at them, over and over, pounding against the shield Saxony had created.

Saxony stumbled back a few steps and screamed. From

her fingernails flame flew out like darts. The Crafters dove to avoid it.

"Go!" Saxony yelled. "Help Wesley!"

Tavia ignored her and pulled out another weapon charm, fingering it. Then she arched her shoulder and threw. The air above them gurgled and groaned. Lightning spat down on the Crafters, striking one in the heart.

He fell to the floor, lifeless.

But Tavia didn't have time to feel guilt or relief. There were still four remaining.

Asees grinned at her fallen comrade and then threw her hands toward the lightning, pushing water and wind until it quivered and dissolved.

She was a Spiritcrafter, just like Arjun.

Tavia cursed.

Her tricks were just that. *Tricks.* Against Crafters she felt like an amateur.

"I can handle this," Saxony said.

"You can't hold them off alone."

"Many Gods damn it, Tavia!" Saxony squeezed her fists so the force field thickened. "Go and make sure your fucking boyfriend doesn't kill my sister."

Tavia whirled to see Wesley diving toward Zekia with a knife in hand.

He sliced across her chest and Zekia lurched back. Wesley threw the blade and she lifted a hand to block it. The dagger stuck in her palm.

She pulled it out, slowly, as if she felt nothing, and sent it hurtling back to him.

It lodged in Wesley's knee.

Tavia cast one last look at Saxony, who was practically breathing fire. Her skin alight, eyes like coal. The more magic the Crafters threw, the higher her flame rose.

Then Tavia ran.

She ran across the throne room and toward Wesley, skidding so that her leg burned across the cracked floor. She reached for a charm, took her time to feel the weight of it. The shape. The way her soul curved around it.

Cutting charm.

Zekia approached Wesley. He pulled the knife from his leg and tried to stand.

Tavia crushed the charm in her hand. The shards scattered across her palm like glass and, with Saxony's little sister in her sights, Tavia blew on them like a wish.

They shot through the air. Ready to spike across Zekia's precious little face.

Only to stop inches from her.

The Kingpin stood.

Tavia blanched.

And then she was thrown across the room.

"Let my children fight among themselves," the Kingpin said.

He stepped down from his throne.

His footsteps were like drums. Pounding toward her.

One. Two. Three.

One. Two. Three.

Wesley yelled her name and Tavia saw him try to run to her, but Zekia threw him onto his back. He grunted in pain.

Even though she was a child, Zekia's magic was almighty.

No wonder she had been chosen to lead the Rishiyat Crafters.

One.

Two.

Three.

Tavia was pulled back to standing by the Kingpin's magic. Grabbed by her hair and pushed from under her feet. Squeezed at the neck, until she slid up the wall and was gasping and tearing at her throat to pry off his invisible hands.

She couldn't breathe. *Many Gods.* She couldn't breathe.

The room blurred and refocused. Wesley's screams echoed.

The Kingpin's shadowed outline loomed and Tavia could see it now—the blacks of his eyes against the blacks of his cheeks. The barely there tracing of a face beneath the darkness of a once-man.

"I know you, little busker."

She wanted to tell him to go to the fire-gates, but all she could do was gag.

The Kingpin was choking her. Not enough to kill her, but enough to keep her on the precipice of death. Relieving the tension every few seconds so Tavia could gulp in air and then pressing again, harder and harder, so he could squeeze it back out of her.

"I remember your mother well."

Death. His voice was death.

"You remind me so much of her. Poor, beautiful Coralina."

Tavia stilled.

A tear slipped from her eye.

She couldn't stand her muma's name in his awful mouth.

"She was one of my firsts," the Kingpin said. "Before Zekia

became my light, back when I thought all the Crafters in the realms were dead. I tried to forge my own magic. It was addictive, but not much else. It drove people mad with the cravings and then mad with my voice, but I couldn't control them like I can now. Oh, how I could whisper, though."

He leaned in closer to Tavia, voice slicking into her ear.

"Coralina hated the whispering."

The Kingpin loosened his grip on her neck, as though he wanted to bask in the grief of her response.

"You killed her," Tavia managed to say.

"Oh no," he said. "She killed herself. The only way to make the whispering stop. Poison, I think, though the details are a little vague. One pitiful human blurs into another."

"Murderer," Tavia spat.

And she actually did spit, right in his disgusting face.

The Kingpin didn't flinch. "You should be pleased, little busker, that Zekia was able to bring my vision of the Loj to life. Your mother was one of the few who helped me perfect my legacy. Her madness was a great lesson."

Tavia's chest shook with her sobs and she tried to catch her breath, but the Kingpin's magic was still so tight around her throat.

Her muma's face flashed through her mind.

Her muma's smile.

It's okay, ciolo. *It'll all be okay.*

What had this monster stolen from her?

"My magic crawled through her veins until she couldn't differentiate between her thoughts and mine. We trialed it on so many in the outskirts," the Kingpin said with near glee.

"Don't you see, little busker? Magic sickness is a myth. It was always me, my power, experimenting on one worthless street scum at a time, until I finally cracked it."

Tavia lowered a hand to her side.

He'd taken her childhood.

Her past and her future.

He'd ruined her.

Stolen the one person Tavia had and taken her off the streets under the guise of saving her. Convinced her to sell the very thing that had killed her muma to someone else.

And it wasn't just her family. He'd torn apart countless others. Even Wesley's.

Tavia gritted her teeth.

Dante Ashwood was just a man on a power trip and that didn't make him invincible. She could kill a man. She could kill him like he'd killed her muma.

"Feel that anger inside you and its thirst for darkness," the Kingpin said. "You have the potential to be just like me, little busker. To be just like my Wesley."

Tavia clasped a hand around her knife. Felt its hilt strong in her hand.

She looked up at Ashwood, her eyes darker than his could ever be.

"Wesley is nothing like you," she said.

And then she threw the knife into the Kingpin's heart.

41

Karam

THE CRYPT SMELLED OF death and decay.

The walls were damp with rotting flesh and it was dark enough that even Arjun's conjured light only illuminated a few steps ahead. The shadows seemed to recoil and then follow them.

Karam and Arjun walked slowly, their footsteps silent. They winced under the weight of the barrel, which was as heavy as all spirits, even with the both of them clutching it.

The charms rattled inside, eager to ignite.

Karam looked down to adjust her grip on the barrel and was once again surprised to see that her hands weren't there.

She sucked in a breath.

She was never going to get used to this invisibility field. She thought the Crafters would make them unseen to those on the outside, but she didn't realize they would slowly dissolve her skin and bone until she became air.

Karam hoped Wesley could stall for a little longer.

This was the last barrel left and Karam didn't want to be halfway through setting it down when the signal came. Even if her blood was coating the charms, she didn't like to take chances.

Especially on magic.

Especially on explosive magic.

Just a few more minutes, she thought.

"This place is endless," Arjun said in Wrenyi.

Karam nearly jumped at the sound of his voice so close.

She was *really* never going to get used to invisibility.

Arjun was right, though. The crypt seemed to go on forever. They'd spotted the hidden chamber behind a throng of skeleton trees and bushes with swords for thorns. Heavy chains secured the large steel gates and behind them was another door that even the lock picking she had learned from Wesley couldn't bypass.

It took a lot of Arjun's magic to burst through.

The crypt looked like it ran directly under the castle as an emergency escape. If they planted the last barrel here, then when the Kingpin or any of his people tried to run, they would be frozen in time, unable to use their magic to fight. Primed for the killing.

They kept walking and after a couple more minutes Karam breathed a sigh of gratitude when her hands reappeared at her sides. They were out of the parameters of the invisibility field.

Thank the spirits, she thought.

Karam watched her steps. There were nail marks in the floor. Blood dried into the cobbles like paint. She listened out for Wesley's signal. Or rather, Saxony's signal. The sound of her fire puncturing the air and hurtling toward the moon.

Nothing came.

Karam wasn't sure if that was good or bad.

Arjun hoisted the barrel up and Karam was relieved to be able to make out his face.

"How much farther do you think?" he asked.

Karam didn't know. For all she knew, they could walk for hours and not be where they needed to be. Or they could have gone past the best point already.

"I don't have blueprints," she said.

Arjun swiped the sweat from his brow and the light charm in his hand flickered, coating them in darkness for a moment.

The shadows lurched. A howl sounded.

Arjun brought his hand down.

The darkness shrunk back.

"What was that?" he asked.

Karam swallowed. Something shuffled in the shadows and a hungry growl caught her ear.

She placed the barrel down, slowly, and Arjun followed.

"Don't move," she said. "And don't let that light go out."

She pulled her knives from their hold, the steel shrieking as it was let free.

Arjun reached for his own blade and the light blinked.

The shadows wailed.

"I told you not to move!" Karam said again.

She knew that noise.

Spirits damn, she knew it all too well.

Arjun's eyes searched the darkness, the light charm steady in his hand. "What is it?"

"Conjure another light," Karam said.

~ 419 ~

Arjun opened his hand and a small orb appeared in his palm, dim, but enough to chase away the shadows.

Karam smiled in relief, but then a gust of wind blew through the cavern, carrying with it the stench of death.

The charm sputtered and blinked.

There were breaths in the darkness, each pant laden with magic, and in the dim glow where light melted to shadow, a clawed hand reached out.

The creature rose to stand, hunched back, talons as long as arms scraping over the floor. Its spine jutted out, body half-dispersed in smoke so the claws of its webbed feet were detached from the rest of its form. Spit stretched between the jaws that made up its face.

No eyes, for it lived in the darkness. Just a mouth. Just teeth.

Shadow demon.

A monster Karam had once seen rip apart nine fighters in a matter of seconds.

This wasn't an escape tunnel.

It was a cage.

And they had just opened the lock.

"Run!" Karam yelled.

But it was too late.

The shadows were everywhere, closing in on them.

Killing the light one blink at a time.

42

Karam

KARAM'S HEAD CRUNCHED AGAINST the cavern floor. The shadow demon hurled itself at her. It bit and clawed, drawing a long line from her temple down to her collarbone.

She yelled out to Arjun and he fumbled with the light charms in his hands, whispering spells Karam could barely hear over the creature's growls. And then, after it was about to kill her, Arjun finally thrust out his arm and a blast of light swept over the demon.

It burned through what little flesh the creature had and it flung onto its hind legs, letting out an ungodly screech.

"How do we kill it?" Arjun yelled.

Karam arched her blades above her head. "You don't kill a shadow demon. You just make it regret being alive in the first place."

"How do we—"

Karam charged toward the creature, knives cutting and

swiping through smoke and bone. Its blood sprayed across the walls, and it roared before clamping down its jaw and baring its teeth.

When it slammed into her a second time, Karam was ready. She grabbed the shadow demon, hands slipping through its smoky torso and fumbling until she latched onto the mounds of its spine.

She flipped the creature over her shoulder, bringing them both to their backs. Karam's hands wrapped around its neck and it gnawed at her arms, thrashing its claws to try to cut ribbons across her stomach.

Karam didn't loosen her hold.

"Now!" she screamed.

Arjun summoned another ball of light. Larger than the last and as scorching as Saxony's flame.

The creature cried out, writhing and thrashing as it tried to escape. But Karam's grip held firm and the smell of burning ripened the air. Within minutes the creature's cries ceased and its mangled body singed into the cavern floor.

Karam let go and the creature whimpered.

Arjun pulled her to her feet and she felt that familiar rush of adrenaline that came with being alive. Of knowing she'd won.

"*Hei reb*," Arjun said, slinging Karam's arm over his shoulder. "That was something."

"First time seeing a demon?"

"First time seeing you."

Karam leaned against him for balance and her breath slowly returned, but the joy was short-lived.

Out of the shadows, a slow growl echoed.

Karam and Arjun stumbled back, his grip tightening on her waist.

Then another rumble.

And another.

The light blinked in Arjun's hand as the demons' breath carried over to them.

Karam could just about make out their forms in the darkness. Could see teeth glimmer in the reflection of what little light they had left.

There must have been a dozen of them.

A dozen demons.

"Now what?" Arjun whispered.

"Try not to die," Karam said.

"That's your plan?"

He squeezed his hand and the light protruded a little farther, keeping the snarling demons at a distance.

"That's Plan B," Karam said.

"What's Plan A?"

"Run."

Karam pulled herself from Arjun's arms and sprinted for the cavern door with him hot on her trail. The creatures scurried after them. Arjun threw light charms as though they were knives, scattering the creatures that crawled along the walls and ceiling.

Their howls were hungry.

"Run faster!" Karam screamed over her shoulder.

"You try keeping these things off our backs and running at the same time!" Arjun yelled.

But his pace quickened and Karam smiled.

Karam spotted the door ahead and steeled herself, pressing her feet that much harder into the ground before throwing herself forward that much quicker.

Her shoulder rammed against the door and it lurched open, sending her careening out onto the other side.

Arjun followed, slamming the door shut behind him.

Karam forced herself to her feet and threw her weight against it alongside Arjun, keeping the creatures at bay.

Arjun screamed out a slew of words that sounded equal parts spell and swearing. Karam hoped it was magic to seal doors and make sure they could never be opened again. This seemed like a good enough guess, because the banging soon ceased and Arjun stepped away from the door and collapsed onto his knees. He sighed in relief.

Karam slid down the barricade and caught her breath.

In the distance, there were screams and thunderous rumblings.

The war was waging and they had missed its start.

"Nice moves," Karam said. "For a Crafter."

Arjun laughed into his hands before dragging them over his head and taking in another long exhale. "You too," he said. "For a runaway."

Karam got to her feet, shakier than she would have liked.

Arjun offered his arm, but Karam shook her head. Now wasn't the time to let herself give in to the pain of her injuries. It was the time to make sure their enemies were the ones who suffered.

The war was only a few feet away.

As soon as they rounded the corner, out of the burned

trees that hid the doorway and past the crumbling stone that shielded them, there was death.

Their army was bloodied and broken.

Screaming and lunging and dying, while the Kingpin's soldiers advanced endlessly. His armies tumbled from the drawbridge and seemed to spurt from the air itself. And magic. Magic hurtled through the wind.

They were wrong. *Spirits damn*, they were wrong. The Kingpin didn't have a few Crafters locked away; he had an entire legion, fighting like they would lay down their lives for his cause.

And they were winning.

"Arjun," Karam said. "Say the spell."

Her knives were primed.

"We haven't been given the signal," Arjun said.

Though he was gripping his fists, squeezing hard enough to draw blood.

Above, the skies roared with his anger and rain fell down on them all.

"Do it now," Karam said.

She ran forward, not waiting for his reply. Launching herself into battle.

Her wounds seared, but she tried her hardest not to stop. People were relying on her. Karam cut and sliced and threw herself at the Kingpin's soldiers. Knocking them down like pins.

She didn't know how long it took—seconds, or maybe minutes—but when Arjun said the words, Karam heard. Even from the other side of the battlefield, where she somehow found herself. She heard Arjun's voice through the wind and felt the ripple as time braced itself.

The barrels exploded.

Karam ducked, knees hard against the shore, fingers plugged into her ears as the island screamed. The ground shook. The wind hardened to rock.

Around them, the realms stopped.

Karam stood.

Their army was breathless and half-dead, but they were smiling.

She looked at the battlefield.

At their enemies, frozen in time.

43

Saxony

THE LAST OF THE CRAFTERS fell to ashes.

Saxony lowered her protection field.

Asees lay unconscious on the ground, the only Crafter left alive. She had Arjun and Karam to thank for that.

The tips of Saxony's fingernails were singed and jagged. Across the throne room Wesley was panting and favoring his left leg, but he was still very much alive, to Saxony's disdain.

She looked to Zekia and the blood that waterfalled from her sister's hand.

She looked so much like their mother. So much like *her*. And though they had always been different, Saxony had never felt it so much as she did now. Her sister, once the calm to Saxony's storm, was a monster.

She had aligned herself with the very man who destroyed their family.

Saxony was glad her father wasn't here to see it. He had already lost his son and his wife, and seeing Zekia this way would be like losing a daughter too. And Amja, after all she had gone through during the War of Ages, perhaps she would see Zekia as an enemy now, the way she did anyone who stood with Ashwood. Perhaps she would have attacked, the way she did in Granka.

Saxony clenched her fists.

She was going to kill Wesley for his role in this. He had no idea what—

Saxony stopped.

Wesley and Zekia weren't trying to kill each other anymore. *Why weren't they trying to kill each other?*

She followed their gazes across the room, to Tavia. Hands around her throat, crouched on the floor as she tried to catch her breath. And the Kingpin in front of her, a blur of twilight.

There was a knife where his heart should have been.

Tavia had killed the Kingpin.

The war was over and Saxony could take Zekia home, even by force, and everything would be—

Ashwood laughed.

He pulled the knife from his chest and it crumbled to embers.

"Little busker," he said. "I see you're still as stupid as the day you were plucked from the streets."

Tavia spat at his feet. "You didn't pluck me," she said. "You stole me, you stole my *mother*, and I'll find a way to steal you right back."

"I have become magic," the Kingpin said. "No weapon in the realms can kill me."

It sounded like an omen for their defeat, but Saxony had spent enough time spying on careful men to decipher truth from lies. Perhaps no weapon in the realms could kill him, as fraught with power as the Kingpin had become, but magic wasn't from the realms.

It was a gift from the Many Gods.

And Saxony had plenty of it to go around.

"Let's see you pull this from your chest," she said.

She summoned her flame into a spear. She'd pierce the same spot Tavia had. Only this time, the Kingpin would be ash.

The chandeliers shook. Saxony lost her footing. Her flame died.

Around them, the air thickened and thinned and then seemed to disappear entirely.

Time ruptured.

"The charges!" Tavia called out.

Zekia rushed to the Kingpin's side as his shadows began to splinter and Saxony caught a blink of his face before they swarmed once more. The magic was breaking through the darkness and threatening to expose the humanity buried underneath.

"Tavia, move!" Wesley yelled.

He threw out his hand and a beam of magic shot toward the Kingpin. Tavia lurched out of the way just as the beam struck Ashwood in the chest.

He careened across the room.

His shadows screamed.

Zekia screamed.

Wesley ran forward, but Zekia was in his path, magic pooling black around her fingertips.

Without thinking, Saxony pushed out with all her might, sending a wave of fire toward her sister. She prayed to the Many Gods that it would at least distract her.

The flames singed by Zekia's feet and she turned to Saxony with a spiteful gleam in her eyes.

Barely quick enough, Saxony raised her hands in a shield as Zekia charged, her energy rippling like bullets against Saxony's protection.

Behind her, the Kingpin sagged to the floor. Something like blood dripped from him. A black, viscous liquid that hissed like acid.

His shadows flashed and ruptured. He let out a guttural moan.

Time was unfolding inside of him.

"Zekia," he croaked.

Zekia turned just as Wesley grabbed one of his knives and hurled it into the air. Straight for Ashwood's weakened heart.

Time slowed.

The Kingpin reached out a bone-white hand and pulled at an invisible thread.

From across the room, Tavia soared toward him, like that very string was wrapped tight around her waist. Pulling her like a rag doll straight into the Kingpin's arms.

Into the path of the knife.

"Wesley!"

The blade stopped inches from Tavia's face.

Wesley's hands clenched to fists and the weapon stopped

midair. He shook with anger and the very world began to quake alongside him.

In all her years at the Crook, Saxony had never seen Wesley look like that. Irritated and perhaps a little psychotic, but never with such cold fury in his eyes.

"Get your hands off her," he said.

The Kingpin's grip on Tavia tightened. "Wesley," he said, hands primed around Tavia's throat like he might just snap her neck. "I am warning you."

"I think I'm warning you."

Ashwood growled. "I will not have this!"

Wesley smirked. His shirt was torn across the chest and he was bleeding and bruised, but still he smirked.

Above them, the sky grew to shadow.

Saxony looked up—they all looked up—and watched as the moon dragged across the stars and took the sun from the realms.

The shadow moon was like a light going out, only that light was what kept the monsters captive and now they were free.

Saxony's power swelled inside her and when she took in a breath, it was as though the air itself were made from fire and darkness.

She felt wonderful.

She felt awful.

She felt like she could do anything she wanted and nobody could think to stop her.

The moon slipped into place, and when a ring of fire from the sun surrounded it in a glowing halo, Saxony remembered that this was supposed to be a holy day of the Many Gods. But that light soon disappeared and then there was just dark.

Just shadow.

Just the underboss, with his eyes of night.

Wesley looked back to the Kingpin and his smile glowed in the gray of the world.

"You're going to regret touching her," he said.

Wesley rallied his magic, conjuring reality into his hands, letting it build and break between his fingertips.

Zekia let out a quiet laugh.

"There you are," she whispered.

Wesley's magic grew.

In his hands, images of the past and the future and the now merged together. Realities that were and could have been. Lives not yet lived and worlds not yet made.

They spread from Wesley's fingertips and swarmed around him in a squall.

When Saxony caught sight of his eyes, they were such a pure, unyielding black.

"Tavia," he said, his voice not entirely his own. "This is just another dead end."

Saxony didn't know what that was supposed to mean, but Tavia's eyes shone in recognition and her hand slipped into the charm pouch at her hip, so quick that Saxony nearly missed it.

Tavia squeezed a charm in her fist, closed her eyes, and then fell straight through the Kingpin.

Saxony blinked.

Tavia was nothingness, just for a moment. Passing through Ashwood with the shine of a wind charm on her newly translucent skin.

And then she ran.

As soon as Tavia was clear, Wesley's hands shot out.

The fragments of reality charged toward the Kingpin.

Ashwood thrust a hand out to create a barricade.

Wesley's visions crashed against it and the Kingpin slid across the floor, arms shaking as he struggled to hold the shield.

"No!" Zekia yelled.

She threw her magic toward Wesley in a powerful blast of energy, but it dissolved against his skin like water.

Wesley didn't even seem to notice.

Her magic was like nothing to him.

He snarled at the Kingpin and with each flinch of Wesley's jaw the visions struck harder. They whispered and screamed and pounded to be let in. To shred through the Kingpin and his barrier.

And then from Wesley's skin, staves appeared.

Saxony's legs nearly gave way.

The magical runes slid across Wesley's tattoos in thick lines. Up his arms and along his chest, finding respite against his heart. Saxony could see the lines of silver through the tears in his shirt. There were so, so many, but just two that made her heart stop.

One to see the possibilities of the world.

One to see into the minds of its people.

Intuitcrafter.

But it couldn't be.

Saxony thought back to the spell Asees had performed on Wesley.

Black. His blood was such a thick black.

She had known something wasn't right, but like an ignorant

child she waved it off, thinking it was only a discrepancy between her Kin's magic and theirs. But, *Many Gods*, even Asees looked confused.

Fools. They were fools. Saxony remembered Amja's stories and in each of them the blood of their allies turned a bright, vibrant green, like the color of the land the Many Gods had birthed.

Green meant growth and harmony, the vibrancy of a potential destiny.

But black blood . . .

Wesley had uttered a *spell* at the consort's headquarters, when the walls were threatening to close in and kill them all. That was why the magic had felt so powerful.

Her breath caught in a shudder.

The shadow moon stole the light from the realms, but not from Wesley. To him, it gave a gift: his magic was loose, finally. Awakened in its entirety.

Wesley was a true Crafter and he didn't even know it.

Asees's spell hadn't given him a thing. It only brought what was already there to the surface, and now the shadow moon was feeding it. Feeding Wesley's magic like the monster it was.

Wesley clenched his fists tighter and his power grew.

The Kingpin's barrier punctured.

"Stop!" Zekia yelled.

She threw herself forward and Wesley's assault of realities ceased.

"Move, kid."

His voice was throaty.

Zekia snarled. "I'm not a kid anymore."

She thrust out her arm and Wesley merely shifted to avoid her magic, barely a twitch.

"Go," Zekia urged the Kingpin.

She turned to his throne, whispering a guttural slew of spells.

Three more Crafters poured from it, summoned from smoke. One for each of them.

The throne was a damn portal. A rip in reality to ferry the Kingpin from danger.

Ashwood darted for the throne and Saxony screamed out in anger.

She threw her magic toward him like flaming bullets, but the Crafters formed a blockade and her sister was at the forefront and Saxony's fire died at their feet.

The Kingpin jumped into the smoke.

Tavia ran to Wesley and Saxony wondered if she had noticed how his eyes were still so void of color.

They backed away from the Crafters and Wesley held out a hand for Tavia, creating a blockade of their own.

Three against four, but Saxony's sister was one of the four and the Kingpin was gone and everything they'd done meant nothing if Ashwood lived.

Saxony found her sister only to lose her again and it was all Wesley's fault. She looked at him, clutching onto Tavia's hand like he knew what it meant to care about anyone other than himself.

Bastard.

He was just as bad as the Kingpins who traded in Crafters. He was the reason her sister had given herself to Ashwood.

They *knew* each other. Wesley had snaked into Zekia's mind and thrown her to his Kingpin like prized stock.

Ashwood might have escaped, but the underboss wouldn't.

Saxony would make sure of it.

There wasn't a chance in the fire-gates that she would let two snakes slither from her reach tonight.

Saxony would get her revenge—Zekia's revenge—one way or another. And if she couldn't have the Kingpin, then she'd settle for his lapdog.

"I'm going to kill you," she seethed.

"That's the spirit," Wesley said.

He stared at the Crafters, eyes narrowed like he was trying to think of a plan.

"Not them," Saxony said. "You."

Wesley dropped Tavia's hand. He looked over his shoulder.

Fire engulfed Saxony.

Charcoal flame, as dark and vengeful as she had ever felt. It was too strong. Too hot. Too much power from the shadow moon and she couldn't stop it even if she wanted to. She could smell it, her anger blackening the flames and scorching her skin, threatening to turn her into ash like the dead Crafters at her feet.

Wesley's face showed nothing. No emotion. No fear.

Saxony wondered if he was even human, or if magic had taken over his soul like it had the Kingpin's.

Wesley Thornton Walcott was a monster.

He *had* to be, because only death magic, the darkest of blood spells, could hide a Crafter's powers, and to use that would curse a Kin for eternity. It was why nobody had tried after the

War of Ages. Why they went into hiding and spent their lives as shadows, rather than kill to hide their power.

But someone had killed to hide Wesley's power.

Killed to quell whatever evil lived inside him.

And now it was awakened.

Saxony had to stop Wesley before it was too late.

44

Wesley

WESLEY WASN'T WEAK.

He didn't feel drained or weary from using that much magic. He felt strong, revitalized. Like it had been building inside him for years and releasing it just barely quelled the thirst.

It made him crave more.

The shadow moon was like a giant power source and with every second it held the sun at bay, he was charged, endlessly, by darkness.

Lava flowed from Saxony's hands and pooled around her feet, making the floor bubble beneath her, and all the while, Wesley's magic swarmed inside him, unafraid, begging to be let loose.

"Are you crazy?" Tavia screamed.

She made to step forward and talk some sense into Saxony, though Wesley could see they were beyond that.

He grabbed Tavia's arm, pulling her behind him.

Farther from Saxony, but closer to the other Crafters in the room currently set on killing them.

Wesley knew he had enemies left, right, and center, but this was bordering on ridiculous.

His magic swelled, dark and so, so thirsty.

It was like a switch had flipped inside him and he didn't know how to turn it off.

Not her, the magic said. *Everyone but her.*

Wesley was used to having voices in his head, Zekia made sure of that, but hearing his own power was different. He felt it in his bones.

Saxony practically growled. "There'll be nothing left for them to take when I'm through."

"Don't count your luck," Wesley said.

"Count your lives," she countered. Even her voice was fire now, croaking and spitting. "I reckon you're just about out."

She crouched low, ready to pounce, and Wesley squeezed his fists.

He had killed enough people in front of Tavia, and he vowed for each one to be the last, but when would people stop trying to kill him?

He could attempt decency, but it was never enough. The past wasn't the past. It defined him and screwed him over every time.

Tavia's back pressed against Wesley's as she faced off what remained of Ashwood's Crafters. He thought about that moment back on the train when he'd almost kissed her.

He wished now he would have just done it.

Saxony rose into the air like a phoenix, arms ablaze and ready to skewer through him. Wesley braced himself. Felt his magic brim beneath his skin and inside his heart, ready to explode the minute he took a breath. Ready to tear the world to pieces if he let it.

Don't let us, it said.

And then Saxony flew in the other direction.

Lurching across the room and cracking into the wall loud enough that Wesley nearly ran to her side, in what would have been piss-poor judgment.

Saxony's flames hissed, as though cold water had been thrown on them. Her skin reappeared and the only burning that remained was the floor she had melted to pools.

Zekia strode forward, glaring down at her sister.

She held a hand behind her, signaling to the other Crafters to stay back. Hold their ground, but not attack.

"That was very, very stupid," Zekia said. "You can't hurt him."

She waved a finger and Saxony was dragged to her feet.

"The plans you think you have for me, we have tenfold for him. You'd understand, if you knew."

Zekia gestured to Wesley and his jaw hardened.

He had just about enough of other people's plans for him. There were plenty of his own that he was far more set on, like taking Dante Ashwood's throne and shoving it where the sun didn't shine.

And with this new power inside of him, Wesley didn't think he'd ever be able to play lapdog again.

"Let's see if I can teach you a lesson about getting in my way," Zekia said.

She pressed a hand to her temple and the air rippled to Saxony in a tunnel, filled with images too quick for Wesley to make out. Memories or visions or hallucinations. Maybe a combination of the three. Magic so similar to the one he'd tried to use on the Kingpin.

The visions collided into Saxony.

Her nose ran with blood and it only took seconds for her screams to become whimpers.

Whatever Zekia was doing, it was going to kill her sister.

Don't let her do it.

Wesley knew it was stupid before he did it, and he knew for damn sure he'd think it was even more stupid afterward. But he wasn't one for vendettas and he wasn't one for losing, and whether he liked it or not, whether she liked it or not, Saxony was on Wesley's side.

Something in him couldn't let her die.

Something in him couldn't let Zekia become a murderer.

Wesley jumped in front of the beam and his mind splintered.

He fell to his knees.

The realms weren't solid anymore. They were made of nightmares that ran like water, and the air was screaming at him.

Wesley couldn't move.

Tavia was somewhere, yelling. Wesley saw blasts of magic erupt around him. She was fighting off the Crafters, but he couldn't focus on where, or move his head to search the room for her.

Zekia knelt in front of him and Wesley wanted to yell at her to get away. He wanted to move—to reach for his gun or his magic—but he was paralyzed.

The realms were disappearing and he was too.

Zekia's magic was poison in his mind.

"I suppose Saxony was wrong," Zekia said. "You still have some of those lives left."

Wesley found his voice. Or a voice that might have been his. It tasted odd in his mouth.

"Get away," he said. "You're not you."

Neither are you.

"Who would you like me to be, then?" Zekia asked.

Wesley wasn't sure what that meant, but then Zekia's fingers pressed to his temple and a shrill siren broke out in his mind.

Her face shifted.

Wesley recoiled.

The noise was too much and he could barely keep his eyes open, but he couldn't let Zekia out of his sight. Wesley couldn't take his eyes off her for a moment. He couldn't even—

Wesley blinked.

When he opened his eyes, Zekia was gone and someone new crouched in front of him.

He squinted.

Everything was so bright.

He blinked again and the person came into focus, eyes like midnight and a crooked half smile.

Tavia.

Wesley's busker. His friend, if she deigned to be that. His something else, if she lived long enough to kill him for thinking it.

Her smile was like sunlight.

She placed a hand on his cheek. "Wesley," she said.

Her voice was too level and smooth. But it was her. It had to be her.

"I need you to do something for me."

Wesley nodded. He'd do anything.

"I need you to run. Right now. *Run*."

And so he did.

Suddenly Wesley could stand. The room was a blur, but Tavia's face was clear, and though the air wailed in his ears, he could hear her voice through it all. Only her voice.

Whatever was happening, they had to escape. Wesley wasn't sure why they had come here in the first place. They needed to get back to Creije. It seemed odd he ever thought to leave.

What was so important about some island?

Tavia took Wesley's hand.

It was warmer and softer than he remembered. He couldn't feel her callouses or her scars, but she squeezed against his grip and pulled him across the floor and he followed.

They had to run.

They had to be safe from whatever was happening.

They needed to go home, together.

If they ran, things would be okay, and Wesley found that he didn't so much mind the thought of running. It had always bothered him before, but now he liked not having to stay and see things through. It felt good not to fight.

Shadows gathered like a storm in front of them and Tavia's grip on Wesley tightened.

Not shadows. A gateway. *An escape*.

Something nagged in Wesley's mind. Something he was forgetting. Something he was supposed to do.

In the distance, someone screamed his name.

Wesley looked to Tavia and she smiled and suddenly he forgot again.

Whatever the thing was, it couldn't have been important.

It didn't matter now.

It wasn't safe and they needed to run.

Tavia tugged Wesley forward.

Hand in hand, they jumped into the darkness.

45

Karam

KARAM TORE THROUGH THE castle like a tornado, with a handful of Grankan Crafters like magical shadows by her side.

For every neck she snapped and every knife she plunged into the hearts of one of the Kingpin's people, the Crafters brought lightning down as if it were raindrops, throwing blasts of energy that tore through bone.

They weren't pacifists anymore and they certainly weren't losing.

There was no saving the Kingpin's people, like they thought. Not all of them. Some had given up after the time charges, but so many—too many—were past that point. They didn't want to be rescued. They wanted to be with the Kingpin, in the new realm he sought to create.

Chaos raged outside the castle as Arjun and their army overthrew Ashwood's. Crafters on both sides fueled by the power the shadow moon brought. It was mania. And as Wesley's magical tech conquered, the seas began battering the island, no longer afraid of its might.

Karam didn't know what had happened, but something had shifted after the time charges and she hauled ass into the castle to find out what.

Maybe Ashwood was dead. Maybe her friends were. Maybe they weren't winning after all.

Karam ripped open the doors to the throne room.

At first there was nothing but the bright flashing of lights and a dull pulsing sound, but then Karam saw Tavia.

She saw *Asees*, hunched over a semiconscious Saxony, wincing as charm after charm laid assault to the barely solid protection field around them.

Crafters. Three of them trying to break down the walls Saxony was barely holding up.

Karam didn't have time to wonder just what in the spirits Asees was doing here and why the edges of her clothes were singed. She'd figure that out later.

Karam clutched her knives and prepared to unleash on the Crafters.

She charged forward in a battle cry, throwing a blade through the air that struck one of them straight between the eyes.

The Grankan Crafters followed, striking spell after spell.

"*Hei sukna*," Karam said.

Cover me.

One of the Crafters nodded and flung a protection shield her way, letting it follow her in a tunnel as Karam sprinted toward the Kingpin's once-prisoners.

Every spell and charm they fired at her ricocheted and sprung back to them.

The two remaining enemies darted backward and Karam held out a hand to signal her Crafters to stand down. Whatever the Kingpin's people had done to Saxony, Karam was going to make them pay.

She twisted her knives in either hand.

The first Crafter spun aside, but the blade grazed his shoulder and he swung back around to crack his elbow into the side of Karam's temple.

He was fast.

But she was faster.

She didn't need the protection shield.

She was going to make them bleed.

Karam slashed her blade across the chest of the male Crafter. Blood sprayed onto her cheek.

His female companion grabbed Karam's wrist as soon as she drew blood, twisting it so hard that Karam almost crumbled to her knees.

Instead, she pushed back. Pressing her wrist farther into the woman's grip and thrusting her body sideways. Her legs cartwheeled into the air and wrapped around the woman's neck.

She fell to the floor, Karam's thighs like a vice around her throat.

She twisted. Karam heard the crack—heard the man scream in grief—and then catapulted herself back up.

The man hissed and an orb of light burned in his hand.

"I'm going to burn you from the inside out," he spat. The orb grew brighter in his hands. "I'm going to liquefy every organ you have."

He roared and threw himself at Karam.

She grunted as the Crafter landed on top of her.

It was the second time today she'd let a mad creature bring her to the ground. Karam was hoping not to make a habit of it.

The Crafter brought his elbow to her chin and Karam's teeth shuddered. He raised his arm, the light in his hand bright enough to make her wince. Karam grabbed onto his neck with both hands and brought her forehead hard against his.

The Crafter rolled off her, clutching his face.

Karam had enough practice to know exactly the right angle to hit so her opponent's head would crack open like a coconut.

She stood over the man. The light was still inside his hand, shining like a beacon. She crushed it with her foot and heard the snap of bone as the light extinguished.

Saxony was still slumped on the floor in Tavia's arms. Karam walked toward them.

Alive or not, that Crafter was finished.

"He is yours," she said to the Grankans. "Take him prisoner or leave him to rot."

Karam crouched beside Saxony and stroked a curl from her face. Blood fell from her ears, disappearing beneath her collar. Her face looked ashen and the ends of her coiled hair were charred.

"You look awful," Saxony croaked.

Karam smirked. "I defeated a shadow demon. What is your excuse?"

"Her sister tried to kill her," Tavia said.

"Zekia?" Karam asked. "Where is she? She was not—"

Karam stopped short. Not daring to think it.

"Do not worry," Asees said. "She is alive. Unfortunately."

Karam's breath returned and her clenched muscles loosened somewhat.

"What are you doing here?" she asked. "Arjun was beside himself. Your bat said the Kin was attacked."

The moment Karam asked, she realized she already knew the answer.

"Ashwood took you," she said.

"More than that. He made her into one of his little minions," Tavia said. "Thanks to someone."

Karam had never seen Tavia look at Saxony the way she was now. It seemed akin to hatred, or something so similar.

"I was not a minion," Asees sneered. "He had me under strange magic. It was as though he could—"

"Control your thoughts," Tavia finished. "Yeah, we know."

Spirits damn, Arjun was not going to be happy when he found out.

"What happened to the Crafters loyal to the Kingpin?" Asees asked. "Did you kill them all?"

She winced when she said it, which was enough out of character that Karam felt a little hurt.

Kill all of the Kingpin's Crafters?

She was a warrior, not a murderer.

"After the time charges went off, we were able to get the upper hand," Karam said. "The elixir wore off almost instantly. I believe the charges disrupted the magic somehow. The Crafters who were enthralled came to their senses, but some had fallen prey to the Kingpin's twisted logic. Those who did not surrender fled to the far end of the island once the shadow moon came.

They were too outnumbered to fight. We did not chase them."

Karam hadn't seen the point. They weren't here to slaughter everyone. The Kingpin was the only person who needed to die. As for the others, they had only come to save those who wanted to be saved.

Karam looked around the room, noticing a sudden absence. "Where is Wesley?" she asked.

"He escaped," Tavia said. She kept her eyes on Saxony, blazing. "With Zekia."

Karam's eyes widened. "What?"

It didn't make sense for Wesley to flee, let alone with Saxony's sister. He had come to kill the Kingpin, just like the rest of them, and though his intentions weren't anywhere near as noble, they were set in stone.

Wesley was going to take Ashwood's place—he'd agreed it with Vice Doyen—and he would not just throw away those ambitions.

"Zekia was with the Kingpin," Tavia explained. "Willingly."

In Karam's arms, Saxony went rigid. She didn't speak.

Tavia gestured to an empty space on the upper ledge, where the bodies of the Kingpin's Crafters were sprawled.

"His throne was there," she said. "The Kingpin escaped after you set off the charges. The time weakened him, like it was separating him from his magic. Zekia and Wesley fled after and the gateway closed. As soon as they jumped through, the shadows disappeared." She looked to the floor and blinked. "They were just gone."

"You think that our leader is a traitor?" Karam asked.

Though she knew that Wesley was not a man to be trusted,

she couldn't quite believe he would just abandon them all in the midst of war.

Tavia opened her mouth to say something, but it was Saxony's voice that croaked through first.

"Zekia is an Intuitcrafter," she said. "She can get inside your head to control your thoughts. It's one of the reasons she was destined to be Liege. Intuitcrafters are the rarest of our kind. If they're good, they can use their gifts to have unrivaled empathy. Coupled with foresight, it makes for a wise Liege."

"And if the Crafter is bad?" Karam asked.

"Then hope whatever gods you believe in are on your side."

Tavia shook her head, like it didn't make sense. "Zekia was inside Wesley's mind before tonight. It was how they met. Are you saying she was controlling him, even then?"

Saxony shuffled upward to a sitting position, until her head rested against Karam's heart. "No," she said, wincing with the movement. "That wasn't control. It was shared consciousness."

"For the love of the Many Gods, speak Uskhanyan."

Saxony's breath stumbled and a tear slipped from her eye.

"Zekia used to get inside my head all the time when we were kids, because we shared a blood connection. If she was inside Wesley's, then it's because they share something too."

"Like what?" Tavia asked.

"A specialty," Saxony said. "Wesley has true magic. He's an Intuitcrafter too."

Tavia looked paler than usual. "That's not possible."

"I wish it wasn't," Saxony said. "But Wesley's blood was never supposed to be black and I've seen him use spells. And during the fight with Ashwood he—" She broke off, like she almost couldn't bear to say it. "He had staves," she said. "I saw them appear after the shadow moon."

Asees sucked in a breath. "Our spell did not make him into a vessel," she said, finally understanding. The regret in her voice was crisp. "We only roused power that was already his."

"How could Wesley not know?" Karam asked.

"It is a forbidden spell," Asees explained. "One that uses a blood sacrifice to suppress Crafter magic. There are not many Kins who would risk such a thing."

Saxony nodded. "Whatever Kin Wesley is from was willing to kill to hide him from the world. And if Wesley doesn't know, then they were willing to kill to make sure he never found out. They cursed themselves for it."

"But why?" Tavia asked.

Karam almost snorted. "Have you met Wesley?"

Tavia shot her a glare but didn't refute the sentiment.

With a sigh, they stood and heaved Saxony to her feet. Karam slung Saxony's arm over her shoulders and they made for the doors. But before they could pass through, Arjun ran into the room, breathless and bloody. He took in the sight of Asees and the absence of a dead Kingpin and confusion flashed across his warrior eyes.

"Asees." He rushed forward and for a moment Karam thought he might cry with joy.

He placed a hand on Asees's cheek, gentle and urgent, pressing his forehead to hers with a sigh of relief. Neither of them spoke, but Asees smiled, closed her eyes, and let her entire body relax.

"I am okay," she finally said in a whisper. "All is okay."

Arjun gulped down a breath and pulled back from her. "We need to leave right now."

"It's not like we were planning on staying," Tavia said.

"I mean *now*," Arjun pressed.

"What is it?" Asees asked.

Saxony coughed and her weight shifted a little heavier against Karam. "Yeah, what's the rush?"

"The seas are attacking the island. It looks ready to be swallowed," Arjun said. "Our Crafters are creating a field to stow the weather and protect the train, but they cannot hold it for long. So get moving, or by the spirits I will leave you behind."

But he was already heading toward Saxony, who could not walk unaided. He pulled her from Karam's grip and swept her up into his arms. Karam was grateful for it.

The castle began to groan.

"It is the Kingpin's magic," Asees said. "This island should not exist. Now that he has fled, it will go back to where it belongs."

"To the bottom of Ejm Voten," Karam said.

She stumbled as the great fortress swayed. From the ceiling, dust and stone fell like the first signs of rain.

They barely launched themselves from the room before it crashed to nothing.

The floor quivered beneath Karam's feet as they ran. The walls buckled around them and when they reached the great staircase, Karam threw herself from the balcony and rolled to a stand to soften the blow.

Arjun, Asees, and the other Crafter allies followed suit, their feet crashing against the floor. Fall broken by their magic.

Tavia winced when she landed and when they resumed running, Karam didn't fail to notice that she did so with a limp. Still, the busker didn't slow. Karam was half-impressed.

They sprinted ahead and the staircase fell to rubble in their wake.

From the windows, the sea burst through.

Saxony was right. Whatever magic had made this place was gone. Now Ejm Voten was taking the island back.

They jolted from the castle, across the drawbridge, and to the barely there shores where the train was stabbed into the sand.

The magic was palpable in the air. Protection fields and storm culling, and as they ran through the sand to board, Karam could taste the musk of the magic.

She flung herself into the train.

"Go!" Karam yelled, to nobody in particular.

The train rocked and churned, then lifted from the beach and lurched into the water. The engines screamed like banshees.

It was fast, faster than Karam remembered it being. The shadow moon had supercharged whatever magic the Crafters were using to move this great beast and she was grateful.

She just hoped that all of their people—and the people they had saved from the Kingpin—had made it aboard. Though, perhaps not those still intent on killing them.

The train fled from the island and Karam stared as wind and thunder ruptured the castle.

The water prepared to devour it. Waves like jaws ready to swallow any evidence the castle had ever existed.

Karam could hear screaming. She could see the lights of magic as whoever was left behind tried to stay alive.

Against their train, the sea roared. Above their heads, the storm followed. But the Crafters were keeping it at bay and Karam couldn't take her eyes off the island to worry.

The sea thrashed against itself. The screaming stopped. The castle fell to nothing.

46

Saxony

SAXONY DID NOT OPEN her eyes, even after she woke.

She didn't know how much time had passed since the Kingpin's island turned to dust. It could have been hours. It could have been days.

She didn't really care.

Zekia had tried to kill her.

Her *sister* had tried to kill her.

And not with blades and charms, but with their family's magic. Zekia had tried to drive her to insanity, flooding Saxony's head with visions of all the possible futures where she was the Kingpin's puppet. Images of Saxony killing innocents. Images of her killing Karam.

Saxony thought she would die with that being the final thing she saw. Instead, the Many Gods granted her mercy in the form of Wesley Thornton Walcott.

Saxony wasn't sure why he hadn't let Zekia kill her, when

just moments before she'd been ready to take him out. She didn't understand why Wesley would risk his life to save hers.

It didn't matter.

Wesley was gone and so was Zekia, and Saxony couldn't promise that she'd repay the blood debt Wesley had earned. She wasn't sure what she'd do when she saw him again. *If* she saw him again.

Saxony opened her eyes and found Karam sitting on a small wooden chair by her bedside. Her eyes were tired and bloodshot, as though she hadn't blinked, let alone slept.

When she saw Saxony was awake, her smile was cutthroat.

"Well-rested?" she asked. "You slept for days."

"Don't nag," Saxony said. "You never used to rise before noon."

She pushed herself upright and her bones creaked with the movement.

"Is Tavia very mad?" she asked.

"Yes," Karam said. "But she will get over it. Buskers have a quick recovery time."

"She thinks I betrayed her," Saxony said.

"You betrayed Wesley."

"I think that might be the same thing." Saxony took in a long, tired breath.

She had fences to mend and they'd be difficult. Tavia was stubborn and blinded when it came to Wesley. Any slight against him, no matter how much she tried to deny it, was a slight against her.

"At the very least, I have you by my side," Saxony said.

"I wasn't sure you'd want to talk once you found out what I'd done."

Karam's hard edges disappeared and though Saxony usually found them quite nice, she was grateful. Seeing Karam look at her with love in her eyes instead of hate was the greatest relief in the realms.

"If you are talking about the messenger bats, then somebody sentimental might tell you to stop blaming yourself," Karam said. "They might tell you that we have all wanted to kill Wesley at some point and that the Kingpin holds the blame for what happened to the Grankan Kin. You should not steal such a thing for yourself."

"It's a shame you're not sentimental," Saxony said. "That would've been real nice to hear."

Karam's grin strained. She looked at Saxony with a new seriousness. "I know what it is like to lose family," she said. "If you wanted to talk about Zekia."

"I haven't lost her," Saxony said. "When I get back to Rishiya, I'll tell my amja about everything that happened and she'll know just what to do. I can still save my sister."

"How about you tell me what happened first?" Karam asked.

So she did. Saxony told Karam about Zekia standing beside the Kingpin like a doting daughter and how she wore his insignia so diligently. How Zekia went to the Kingpin to help Wesley become underboss. She explained how Zekia had plans for Wesley and how she must have used her Intuitcrafter magic to trick him into escaping with her.

Saxony told Karam how her sister had tried to kill her.

To her credit, Saxony waited until after she finished to cry.

She sobbed against Karam's shoulder, and her beautiful warrior let her tears soak her collar in silence. When Saxony finished—when it seemed impossible for her to have any tears left—she gathered her breath and slumped against the headboard.

"What could have made Zekia turn like that?" Karam asked. "From what you have told me, she would not betray everything she believed for some pretty words."

"It wasn't just her," Saxony said. "You saw the other Crafters. Some wanted the future the Kingpin spoke of. They were *loyal* to him."

It made her sick to think it. The War of Ages was fought to grant Crafters freedom from exploitation. It killed countless people and destroyed cities. It didn't seem real that any Crafter who knew the stories would willingly join with a Kingpin.

"It could have been the elixir," Karam said. "Asees said that every time they gave it to her, it wore away a little bit of her spirit."

"Zekia was the one who created the elixir," Saxony said. "She wasn't under its influence. My blood connection to her is how I was able to overcome it back in Creije."

"Then the Kingpin brainwashed her," Karam said, like there couldn't have been another option. "Three years spent as his captive meant plenty of time to twist her mind."

Saxony wanted to believe that, but she couldn't quite convince herself. Karam hadn't seen the look in her sister's eyes. It was not that of a broken girl, but someone who did the breaking.

"It doesn't matter what happened," Saxony said. "I'll get

Zekia back. I won't lose another member of my family, I can promise you that."

"Whatever it takes," Karam said. She linked her hand in Saxony's, like a vow. "I am with you."

And Saxony knew that she meant it. That Karam would always be there.

They'd go to the ends of the realms, if that was what it took. When Saxony next saw her sister, she'd have Karam by her side and they'd save Zekia together.

They would bring her home and cut down whoever dared stand in their way.

47

Tavia

TAVIA DANGLED HER BARE feet over the side of the train.

Magic was still in the air, though they'd left the ruins of the Kingpin's castle at the bottom of Ejm Voten a week before its death somehow followed them.

The seas were calm, which was more than Tavia could say for herself or anyone else. Barely half of their army made it out alive and their new crew was made up of too many of the Kingpin's people for anyone to relax.

The time charges had turned the tide in their favor, but by the time Arjun had set them off, many were already dead. And though some of the Kingpin's Crafters were under the influence of the Loj, though some they saved, many more were killers through and through. With the exception of the sixty they took aboard the train—who still had everyone on edge—the rest were left to perish. Or perhaps escape, if they knew the way.

Just like Zekia and Wesley.

Wesley, who was a Crafter.

Not just a vessel, but a bona fide spell-slinging Crafter.

It didn't make a lick of sense. Except, the more Tavia thought about it, the more she found that it did. Wesley was the youngest underboss in the realms. He had more power than anyone she knew, and magic seemed to adapt and shape itself to him, like an old friend.

Even the orb that Tavia was sure had been a fraud had accurately predicted their time charges because Wesley had a hand in creating it. His Intuitcrafter magic seeping inside, connecting it to him, a thread of his power pulling tight.

Tavia sighed.

She needed to stop thinking about it.

Only, it wasn't so simple. She wanted to know what Zekia and the Kingpin were going to do with Wesley now that they had him. And what in the fire-gates they were going to do with Tavia and the army she was carrying aimlessly across the sea.

She wanted to know how Wesley's identity had been kept secret for so long. Spell or no spell, how did they not figure it out? Both of them were so busy trying to score points against each other that they couldn't even see what was right in front of them.

Tavia wondered if Wesley would have told her, if he knew. She wondered why his family did it. *Killed*, Saxony said, using blood magic to conceal Wesley from himself and the realms. Tavia wondered if they were still alive somewhere to ask.

She cursed herself.

She really could not stop thinking about it. But if she stopped thinking about Wesley, the only thing left to think about was her muma, and that was a punch to the heart that would not cease.

Her muma's life had meant little more than a rat's would to the Kingpin. She had simply been an experiment, a test for him to perfect his awful magic.

"Want a drink?"

Tavia turned from her thoughts to Karam.

She approached, a blade in one hand like she wasn't quite ready to believe they were out of the war zone, and a bottle of Wesley's alcohol in the other.

Karam had healed since the battle, but magic couldn't undo everything, and the scar running in a vertical slash from her head to her collarbone was faint, but visible. Tavia knew there was no more pain, the magic had seen to that, but she winced for Karam nonetheless.

"How's Saxony?" Tavia asked.

"Alive."

"Shame she wasn't unconscious for a little longer."

"You are not really angry at her," Karam said.

"Actually," Tavia corrected, "I really am."

Karam took a seat beside her, leaning back on her elbows. She placed the Cloverye bottle perilously between them.

The label was slightly torn. Wesley would've hated that.

"Any thoughts on when we might stop?" Karam asked. "Or where?"

"Since when did I become captain of a runaway train?"

"Since you are Wesley's best busker and Wesley is not here.

I think that makes you second in command. I doubt the buskers will follow anyone else."

"You're not interested in the job?"

Karam shrugged. "Maybe later."

Until then, it would fall on Tavia's shoulders, which was not a responsibility she was gunning for.

"Whether we're depleted or not, we can't let the Kingpin go through with his plans," Tavia said. "There's no way Ashwood will stop at Doyen of Uskhanya, and even if he did the amount of people he'd have to kill to secure his rule would be astronomical. It'd turn our home into a prison realm."

"Where does that leave us?" Karam asked. "The Kingpin was going to be hard to kill before we knew Saxony's sister was with him. And definitely before our underboss joined his ranks."

Tavia stiffened. "Wesley didn't join him."

Whatever happened back on the island, Zekia made him do it. Tavia couldn't afford to think otherwise and she definitely couldn't afford to doubt whether Wesley would come back.

It was not possible for that to be the last time they saw each other.

"The Kingpin ran when he found out we had time, which means there are forces that can hurt him, maybe even kill him," Tavia said. "If we can just figure out how, then I know we can win. All we need is Saxony's help."

"We had Saxony's help and it did not end well."

"That's not what I mean," Tavia said. "She can help us in a way she wasn't willing to before."

Saxony's problem was always Wesley, and as much as Tavia hated to admit it, he wasn't in the equation right now. If they were going to take on the Kingpin without him, then they needed the politicians Ashwood threatened to oppose. They needed the officials to officially step in and they needed as much magic as they could get.

Not just some rebels from Granka and Creijen buskers too afraid of Wesley to say no. They needed real fighters. People who had a stake in this battle, the same way Karam, Saxony, and Tavia did. They had to recruit people out for blood and revenge. Who weren't just following orders or trying to do the right thing, but who needed the Kingpin dead, whether it be for vengeance or power.

"Saxony has to take us to Rishiya," Tavia said. "We'll set up base there and gather her Kin. We'll gather every Kin hiding in Uskhanya. Just like the Grankans need to gather every Wrenyi Kin. We even assemble the Kins of Volo. We rally all three magic realms and find people who have a true vendetta against Ashwood. I was wrong before. We can't win with just good intentions. And after we have all that magic, we go straight to the Doyens. All four of them. We bring them into this war properly, rather than letting them watch from the sidelines like Schulze tried to. And we let them know that they better choose the right side."

There was no other option. No going back. With Wesley by Ashwood's side, even as a prisoner, the next move would be to take Creije completely. The Kingpin would sack the city and work his way through Uskhanya one piece at a time, until he got to Fenna Schulze.

They couldn't wait for that. They had to get to the Doyen first, send a bat to the Halls of Government in Yejlath and warn her of the dangers. They would offer her a true alliance in this fight.

"*Hei reb*." Karam let out a long breath. "Do you have anything positive to say?" There was an unlikely smile on her face. "We may not have won the war, but we won a good fight."

Tavia laughed. It was absurd to be smiling, but just that very thing seemed to lift a weight off her chest. Karam was right. There was a long way to go, but they had faced the Kingpin of Uskhanya and survived. They had him on the run. Whatever happened next, that was still a victory to be celebrated.

Karam sheathed her knife, finally, and twisted open the bottle of Cloverye.

"Drink up," Karam said. "You will need strength."

She handed the first taste to Tavia, who took it gratefully.

As the night went on and the stars faded into the black, they took turns having swigs, until the bottle was half-empty and the moon grew dim.

They had a destination and they had a plan, and that was enough for now. Once they reached Rishiya and found Saxony's Kin, a new battle would start, but until then, Tavia allowed herself to stop thinking and enjoy the fact that they were here.

They were alive.

And she planned to keep it that way.

48

Zekia

AT THE AGE OF SEVEN, Zekia Akintola discovered she was destined to be Liege of an entire Kin. At the age of thirteen, she became left hand to the Kingpin of an entire region.

She considered it an improvement.

Not that her amja would see it that way. Nor her dead mother and her magic-fearing father. Saxony definitely hadn't.

It didn't matter.

Zekia shouldn't care.

She *didn't* care.

She had a new family and a new purpose to go along with it. The Kingpin was going to pave the way for a place where Crafters weren't the hidden minority, but the feared leaders of a new world.

Zekia would help make that future a reality. It was one of the only futures that was clear to her anymore.

The shadow demon licked the blood from its claws and

turned to Zekia with its teeth bared. Behind the creature, her prisoner was slumped on the cold gray stone.

Zekia had healed him too many times to count.

She'd let the demon rip him apart a dozen times more than that.

Shadow demons were nothing but darkness. Forged from the evil left behind by cursed spells: those that stole a mind, those that stole a soul, and those that stole a heart. Shadow demons couldn't be killed because magic could never die, but they could be hurt. And anything that could be hurt could be controlled.

Zekia knew that better than anyone.

The demon howled a low, guttural sound and lowered its head. Zekia held out a hand and it prowled forward. When her skin touched the demon's, it whimpered and bowed, returning to all fours. Nuzzling under her touch.

Zekia stepped forward.

Wesley Thornton Walcott, the most dastardly of all underbosses, was bleeding again. The boy become a crook become a man. Just speaking his name these days struck as much of a chord with some people as speaking the Kingpin's.

And yet here he was.

Bound and blindfolded and caked in as much dirt as he was blood.

The lacerations on him were deeper this time.

Zekia was impressed that he was still conscious. Impressed and a little disappointed. It would do him well to take the opportunity to rest. He didn't have many chances for sleep.

Wesley was not pleading. They hadn't got to the begging part yet, but Zekia was sure they would. Everyone begged in the end. Even men like Wesley Thornton Walcott. Perhaps, especially those men.

Zekia placed her hands on either side of Wesley's temples, holding up his head as it dropped with his consciousness.

In and out, up and down.

Zekia stroked Wesley's cheek and even in his drowsed state, he flinched from her touch.

She kept her hand on his face.

He was very beautiful and Zekia very much wanted to keep him. As a brother, or maybe even as a pet. She wasn't too fussy with which, as long as he got to be hers.

"Come now," she said. "I need to see what's inside that pretty mind."

She let her magic surge, tapping into a connection with Wesley that could never be broken. She wondered what thoughts would be inside him now.

Wesley's jaw shuddered as he held in the screams.

Zekia smiled.

She would break him if it took her the rest of her life to do it. She'd break him so they could forge a new family and a new world, and if he resisted, then she would break him for the fun of it.

Zekia pressed harder, forcing herself into Wesley's mind.

She took the memories she didn't need and buried them somewhere deep, then replaced them with some of her own for good measure, real and imagined. Futures that wouldn't happen and ones that could someday come. She read every thought he had and saw every treasured memory he kept hidden away.

Wesley did not treasure much, but what he did, Zekia found. It took longer than usual and she bled for it, but once she was inside, there was no going back. It was when she ripped those memories from him that Wesley Thornton Walcott finally screamed.

The shadow demon cawed behind her.

The stars blinked.

Zekia plunged deeper.

To be continued . . .

Also by Alexandra Christo

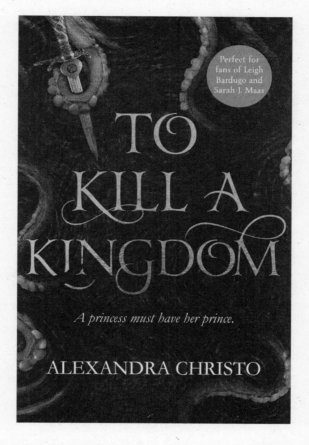

Turn the page to read an extract.

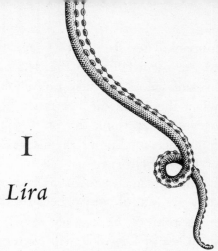

I

Lira

I HAVE A HEART for every year I've been alive.

There are seventeen hidden in the sand of my bedroom. Every so often, I claw through the shingle, just to check they're still there. Buried deep and bloody. I count each of them, so I can be sure none were stolen in the night. It's not such an odd fear to have. Hearts are power, and if there's one thing my kind craves more than the ocean, it's power.

I've heard things: tales of lost hearts and harpooned women stapled to the ocean bed as punishment for their treachery. Left to suffer until their blood becomes salt and they dissolve to sea foam. These are the women who take the human bounty of their kin. Mermaids more fish than flesh, with an upper body to match the decadent scales of their fins.

Unlike sirens, mermaids have stretched blue husks and limbs in place of hair, with a jawlessness that lets their mouths stretch to the size of small boats and swallow sharks whole. Their deep-blue flesh is dotted with fins that spread up their arms and spines. Fish and human both, with the beauty of neither.

They have the capacity to be deadly, like all monsters, but where sirens seduce and kill, mermaids remain fascinated by humans. They steal trinkets and follow ships in hopes that treasure will fall from the decks. Sometimes they save the lives of sailors and take nothing but charms in return. And when they steal the hearts we keep, it isn't for power. It's because they think that if they eat enough of them, they might become human themselves.

I hate mermaids.

My hair snakes down my back, as red as my left eye – and only my left, of course, because the right eye of every siren is the color of the sea they were born into. For me, that's the great sea of Diávolos, with waters of apple and sapphire. A selection of each so it manages to be neither. In that ocean lies the sea kingdom of Keto.

It's a well-known fact that sirens are beautiful, but the bloodline of Keto is royal and with that comes its own beauty. A magnificence forged in salt water and regality. We have eyelashes born from iceberg shavings and lips painted with the blood of sailors. It's a wonder we even need our song to steal hearts.

"Which will you take, cousin?" Kahlia asks in *Psáriin*.

She sits beside me on the rock and stares at the ship in the distance. Her scales are deep auburn and her blond hair barely reaches her breasts, which are covered by a braid of orange seaweed.

"You're ridiculous," I tell her. "You know which."

The ship ploughs idly along the calm waters of Adékaros, one of the many human kingdoms I've vowed to rid of a prince. It's smaller than most and made from scarlet wood that represents the colors of their country.

Humans enjoy flaunting their treasures for the world, but it only makes them targets for creatures like Kahlia and me, who can easily spot a royal ship. After all, it's the only one in the fleet with the painted wood and tiger flag. The only vessel on which the Adékarosin prince ever sails.

Easy prey for those in the mood to hunt.

The sun weighs on my back. Its heat presses against my neck and causes my hair to stick to my wet skin. I ache for the ice of the sea, so sharp with cold that it feels like glorious knives in the slits between my bones.

"It's a shame," says Kahlia. "When I was spying on him, it was like looking at an angel. He has such a pretty face."

"His heart will be prettier."

Kahlia breaks into a wild smile. "It's been an age since your last kill, Lira," she teases. "Are you sure you're not out of practice?"

"A year is hardly an age."

"It depends who's counting."

I sigh. "Then tell me who that is so I can kill them and be done with this conversation."

Kahlia's grin is ungodly. The kind reserved for moments when I am at my most dreadful, because that's the trait sirens are supposed to value most. Our awfulness is treasured. Friendship and kinship taught to be as foreign as land. Loyalty reserved only for the Sea Queen.

"You are a little heartless today, aren't you?"

"Never," I say. "There are seventeen under my bed."

Kahlia shakes the water from her hair. "So many princes you've tasted."

She says it as though it's something to be proud of, but that's because Kahlia is young and has taken only two hearts of her own. None of them royalty. That's my specialty, my territory. Some of Kahlia's reverence is for that. The wonder of whether the lips of a prince taste different from those of any other human. I can't say, for princes are all I've ever tasted.

Ever since our goddess, Keto, was killed by the humans, it's become custom to steal a heart each year, in the month of our birth. It's a celebration of the life Keto gave to us and a tribute of revenge for the life the humans took from her. When I was too young to hunt, my mother did it for me, as is tradition. And she always gave me princes. Some as young as I was. Others old and furrowed, or middle children who never had a chance at ruling. The king of Armonía, for instance, once had six sons, and for my first few birthdays, my mother brought me one each year.

When I was eventually old enough to venture out on my own, it hadn't occurred to me to forgo royalty and target sailors like the rest of my kind did, or even hunt the princes who would one day assume their thrones. I'm nothing if not a loyal follower of my mother's traditions.

"Did you bring your shell?" I ask.

Kahlia scoops her hair out of the way to show the orange seashell looped around her neck. A similar one just a few shades bloodier dangles from my own throat. It doesn't look like much, but it's the easiest way for us to communicate. If we hold them to our ears, we can hear the sound of the ocean and the song of the Keto underwater palace we call home. For Kahlia, it can act as a map to the sea of Diávolos if we're separated. We're a long way from our kingdom, and it took nearly a week to swim here. Since Kahlia is fourteen, she tends to stay close to the palace, but I was the one to decide that should change, and as the princess, my whims are as good as law.

"We won't get separated," Kahlia says.

Normally, I wouldn't mind if one of my cousins were stranded in a foreign ocean. As a whole, they're a tedious and predictable bunch, with little ambition or imagination.

Ever since my aunt died, they've become nothing more than adoring lackeys for my mother. Which is ridiculous, because the Sea Queen is not there to be adored. She's there to be feared.

"Remember to pick just one," I instruct. "Don't lose your focus."

Kahlia nods. "Which one?" she asks. "Or will it sing to me when I'm there?"

"We'll be the only ones singing," I say. "It'll enchant them all, but if you lay your focus on one, they'll fall in love with you so resolutely that even as they drown, they'll scream of nothing but your beauty."

"Normally the enchantment is broken when they start to die," Kahlia says.

"Because you focus on them all, and so, deep down, they know that none of them are your heart's desire. The trick is to want them as much as they want you."

"But they're disgusting," says Kahlia, though it doesn't sound like she believes it so much as she wants me to think that she does. "How can we be expected to desire them?"

"Because you're not just dealing with sailors now. You're dealing with royalty, and with royalty comes power. Power is *always* desirable."

"Royalty?" Kahlia gapes. "I thought . . ."

She trails off. What she thought was that princes were mine and I didn't share. That's not untrue, but where there are princes, there are kings and queens, and I've never had much use for either of those. Rulers are easily deposed. It's the princes who hold the allure. In their youth. In the allegiance of their people. In the promise of the leader they could one day become. They are the next generation of rulers, and by killing them, I kill the future. Just as my mother taught me.

I take Kahlia's hand. "You can have the queen. I've no interest in the past."

Kahlia's eyes are alight. The right holds the same sapphire of the Diávolos Sea I know well, but the left, a creamy yellow that barely stands out from the white, sparkles with a rare glee. If she steals a royal heart for her fifteenth, it'll be sure to earn her clemency from my mother's perpetual rage.

"And you'll take the prince," says Kahlia. "The one with the pretty face."

"His face makes no difference." I drop her hand. "It's his heart I'm after."

"So many hearts." Her voice is angelic. "You'll soon run out of room to bury them all."

I lick my lips. "Maybe," I say. "But a princess must have her prince."

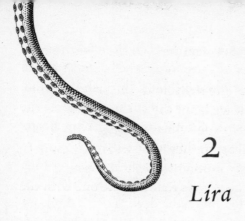

2

Lira

THE SHIP FEELS ROUGH under the spines of my fingers. The wood is splintered, paint cracking and peeling over the body. It cuts the water in a way that is too jagged. Like a blunt knife, pressing and tearing until it slices through. There is rot in places and the stench makes my nose wrinkle.

It is a poor prince's ship.

Not all royals are alike. Some are furnished in fine clothes, unbearably heavy jewels so large that they drown twice as fast. Others are sparsely dressed, with only one or two rings and bronze crowns painted gold. Not that it matters to me. A prince is a prince, after all.

Kahlia keeps to my side, and we swim with the ship while it tears through the sea. It's a steady speed and one we easily match. This is the agonizing wait, as humans become prey. Some time passes before the prince finally steps onto the deck and casts his eye at the ocean. He can't see us. We're far too close and swim far too fast. Through the ship's wake, Kahlia looks to me and her eyes beg the question. With a smile as good as any nod, I return my cousin's stare.

We emerge from the froth and part our lips.

We sing in perfect unison in the language of Midas, the

most common human tongue and one each siren knows well. Not that the words matter. It's the music that seduces them. Our voices echo into the sky and roll back through the wind. We sing as though there is an entire chorus of us, and as the haunting melody ricochets and climbs, it swirls into the hearts of the crew until finally the ship slows to a stop.

"Do you hear it, Mother?" asks the prince. His voice is high and dreamlike.

The queen stands next to him on the deck. "I don't think . . ."

Her voice falters as the melody strokes her into submission. It's a command, and every human has come to a stop, bodies frozen as their eyes search the seas. I set my focus on the prince and sing more softly. Within moments his eyes fall to mine.

"Gods," he says. "It's you."

He smiles and from his left eye slips a single tear.

I stop singing and my voice turns to a gentle hum.

"My love," the prince says, "I've found you at last."

He grips the ratlines and peers far over the edge, his chest flat against the wood, one hand reaching out to touch me. He's dressed in a beige shirt, the strings loose at his chest, sleeves torn and slightly moth-bitten. His crown is thin gold leaf that looks as though it could break if he moves too quickly. He looks desolate and poor.

But then there is his face.

Soft and round, with skin like varnished wood and eyes a penetrating shade darker. His hair swings and coils tightly on his head, a beautiful mess of loops and spirals. Kahlia was right; he's angelic. Magnificent, even. His heart will make a fine trophy.

"You are so beautiful," says the queen, staring down at Kahlia with reverence. "I'm unsure how I've ever considered another."

Kahlia's smile is primordial as she reaches out to the queen, beckoning her to the ocean.

I turn back to the prince, who is frantically stretching out his hand to me. "My love," he pleads. "Come aboard."

I shake my head and continue to hum. The wind groans with the lullaby of my voice.

"I'll come to you then!" he shouts, as though it was ever a choice.

With a gleeful smile, he flings himself into the ocean, and with the splash of his body comes a second, which I know to be the queen, throwing herself to my cousin's mercy. The sounds of their falls awaken something in the crew, and in an instant they are screaming.

They lean over the ship's edge, fifty of them clinging to ropes and wood, watching the spectacle below with horror. But none dare throw themselves overboard to save their sovereigns. I can smell their fear, mixed with the confusion that comes from the sudden absence of our song.

I meet the eyes of my prince and stroke his soft, angelic skin. Gently, with one hand on his cheek and another resting on the thin bones of his shoulder, I kiss him. And as my lips taste his, I pull him under.

The kiss breaks once we are far enough down. My song has long since ended, but the prince stays enamored. Even as the water fills his lungs and his mouth opens in a gasp, he keeps his eyes on me with a glorious look of infatuation.

As he drowns, he touches his fingers to his lips.

Beside me, Kahlia's queen thrashes. She clutches at her throat and bats my cousin away. Angrily, Kahlia clings to her ankle and keeps her deep below the surface, the queen's face a sneer as she tries to escape. It's futile. A siren's hold is a vice.

I stroke my dying prince. My birthday is not for two weeks.

This trip was a gift for Kahlia: to hold the heart of royalty in her hands and name it her fifteenth. It's not supposed to be for me to steal a heart a fortnight early, breaking our most sacred rule. Yet there's a prince dying slowly in front of me. Brown skin and lips blue with ocean. Hair flowing behind him like black seaweed. Something about his purity reminds me of my very first kill. The young boy who helped my mother turn me into the beast I am now.

Such a pretty face, I think.

I run a thumb over the poor prince's lip, savoring his peaceful expression. And then I let out a shriek like no other. The kind of noise that butchers bones and claws through skin. A noise to make my mother proud.

In one move, I plunge my fist into the prince's chest and pull out his heart.

ACKNOWLEDGEMENTS

So, HERE WE ARE, my second book! When did that happen? At least I didn't kill a bunch of people in this one. They might all die in the next one though. But, hey, your favourite will still live! Probably. Maybe. Who knows?

As always, thank you to my agent Emmanuelle Morgen, who is the best gift I could have asked for. Knowing you're in my corner is the greatest feeling and I am forever grateful to be on this journey with you. And Whitney, for always making sure my words spread across the world and reach as many readers as possible.

To all the folks at Macmillan/Feiwel & Friends who helped make this book a reality and worked with me through drafts and redrafts, who shouted about it from the rooftops. Anna, Morgan and Teresa, you guys are rockstars. Kaitlin and Starr, thank you for your awesome CE notes! To my UK folks at Bonnier/Hot Key Books, who are an absolute dream team. Fliss and Tina, I don't know how I got so lucky to have you guys, but your endless enthusiasm and cool event ideas and all the magic you sprinkle to make my books just that little extra . . . well, you're the coolest. Imogen, Carla, Ellen and Roisin, thank you guys for all your hard work too! I'm ridiculously happy to have such a great squad.

To Kimberly and Sanaa for your wonderful notes. And to everyone else behind the scenes who worked tirelessly and are forever part of the CROOKED crew.

Patrick, thank you for bringing Creije to life with that map. IT IS EVERYTHING I COULD HAVE WANTED.

To all the friends I have made in the publishing world, new and old: I'm so lucky. You guys bring the laughs, the support and the endless wisdom. Sasha Alsberg, Brigid Kemmerer, Sarah Glenn Marsh, Melinda Salisbury, Isabel Davis, Rebecca Kuang and Jacob York (who was the best Elian in *To Kill a Kingdom* and continues to be awesome in all things).

Thank you to my book-nerd pals Jas and Siiri. You guys never stop believing in me and even if we go for centuries without texting, you're there whenever I need you. I'm so lucky.

To Leanne and Becca for being the best friends a girl could ask for and teaching me that people really can finish each other's sentences and read each other's minds.

To my family, who are the best in the world. My parents, who raised me on so much love and laughter, who support me in all that I do, and who aren't just parents, but friends too. You guys taught me how to believe in myself, never give up and have the strength to get through anything. And, if I don't, you've got plenty of strength to lend me.

To my endless supply of aunts and uncles and cousins and second cousins and third cousins and everyone else I'm related to (wow, there's a lot of us!). You're always weird, sometimes wonderful, never more than a phone call away. I love you.

And to Nick, of course (because *psssst*, you're the favourite. And also because this is the only way your name is getting in one of my books).

And to my readers, always. You guys keep me going in the dark times. Your incredible passion for books is awe-inspiring. Thank you for the fan art. Thank you for coming out to see me at events. Thank you for championing stories that would otherwise only exist in my mind. Thank you for believing in me, the worlds I've made, and those I've yet to create.

Want to read
NEW BOOKS
before anyone else?

Like getting
FREE BOOKS?

Enjoy sharing your
OPINIONS?

Discover

Read. Love. Share.

Sign up today to win your first free book:
readersfirst.co.uk

HOT
KEY
BOOKS

Thank you for choosing a Hot Key book.

If you want to know more about our authors
and what we publish, you can find us online.

You can start at our website

www.hotkeybooks.com

And you can also find us on:

We hope to see you soon!